<u>Welcome to the WyattWove World</u>

Free Gifts/more info at **www.WyattWove.com**

Readers are using the following words to describe Wyatt's work: "Insightful, timely, funny, refreshing, suspenseful, unique, fascinating, inspiring, satisfying, beautiful, fantastic, unpredictable, endearing, exciting, overwhelmed, nail biting, great read, best book, plus:"

"Oh my! I am not a thriller genre enthusiast, but I enjoy Joel Rosenberg's novels. Like Joel's books, I couldn't put this one down." ~AR~

"Has…everything! Action, suspense, humor, and heart. The author… describes technical equipment as if the reader is looking right at it…The action scenes were like watching it on the big screen… For all the intrigue and gritty (but clean) cop lingo, I was pleasantly surprised when the author pulled out his 'sensitivity pen' for the love story hidden inside." ~Jen Jeffrey Billington, author of BREADCRUMBS-Finding True Love's Trail~

"It was great to find an action book without foul language and or sex! I love it and will seek more from this author!" ~Amazon Review~(AR)

"I like when a book does what movies cannot… Few seasoned writers know how to mix action, respite, and surprise to keep readers in an off-balanced crescendo of nerves. I was already thinking, OK, let's get our team out of there, when yet another surprise jumped at me." ~Don Bala, author, retired professor, John Brown University~

A fabulous storyteller, Kent Wyatt, spreads truth throughout the story while keeping you on the edge of your seat ! I'm hoping for more in this series!" ~AR~

"The action started within the first couple of pages and didn't stop until the end... I was immersed in the world Kent Wyatt created from the beginning. When I wasn't reading I was thinking about the characters and couldn't wait 'til I had free time so I could check in on them. The author's long involvement in law enforcement gave a depth to his prisoner interrogations and the process of catching the bad guys. His experience with criminals and firearms made those parts of the book realistic and intriguing. The author managed to make the book exciting while keeping the gratuitous violence out... The characters were likeable, interesting, and believable, and there were several interesting twists. Human nature at its best and worst was displayed." ~Evie Kalveleage, author of Locker Room Angels~

Entertains and blesses! This novel contains a who-done-it mystery, even a character with superhero like abilities, as well as a sweet love story. But, guys, don't let the romance scare you away. This book is action packed... a fun, engaging read with an enduring faith message." ~Robyn Hook, president, NWA chapter of American Christian Fiction Writers~

"I really enjoyed reading this series! I like Mr. Wyatt's sense of humor and the way he presents the truth of the Gospel." ~AR~

"This author creates very likable, unique characters and then gets them into situations you would never anticipate." ~AR~

"I was really excited to read this… and I was not disappointed! If you are looking for a good Christian read, I highly recommend… This… deals with a lot of realistic personal pain, but there is plenty of humor and hope to balance it out. (And some solid marriage advice, btw.) Oh, and for your information, the fight scenes are AWESOME… a very enjoyable and thought-provoking read, and I'm looking forward to reading more by this author." ~Camille Esther, author of Doctor and King~

"…well written with lots of action and advanced technology…similar to what has been going on in America the last few years. It really makes you think." ~AR~

"Kent has a very unique perspective and tells a compelling story with some very interesting characters. After just the first chapter I knew it was gonna be a page turner & finished it within a day…you won't be disappointed!" ~AR~

"I love it when I find a good read that you just don't want to put it down until the end. Reinforces faith and, through God, all things are possible." ~AR~

"…lots of action and intrigue. I am a Christian and I appreciate the fact that I could read this without worrying about filthy language." ~AR~

"I LOVED this..!! It kept me on my toes the whole time. I lost myself for hours without realizing it….I found myself praying for the characters! Lol." ~AR~

Not Immune
Special Heroes | Book Three

by

Kent Wyatt

Published by Gordian Books, a division of Winged Publications

Book Cover: Cover design by Kent, Rebekah, and Calista Wyatt.
Forest background Photo by
https://unsplash.com/@maritaextrabold
Photo of man in camo with rifle by
https://unsplash.com/@konyxyzx
Photo of SUV on rocky trail by
https://unsplash.com/@brice_cooper18
Photo of flying drone by https://unsplash.com/@misterdoulou
Image of woman in coat/jeans by
https://pixabay.com/users/nika_akin-13521770/
Image modification by Kent Wyatt
Author photo by Rebekah Wyatt.
Internal art: Section break image of drone by Kent Wyatt

Winged Publications
Surprise, AZ 85374

ISBN: 978-1-962168-98-4

Dedication

On Christmas Eve, Eve, God gave you as our gift. We are still getting to know you, loving each precious interaction with the newest member of our Wyatt clan. Your parents have given you a unique name—"Honor." It is a word fitting for a dedication. So it is with honor that we say that we are honored to have you in our presence—you, our grandson, Honor. Welcome.

To Laura Coen. Each book has been a tribute to you because you have placed your mark on them all. You selflessly give your time and editing talent at your own expense for little reward. You have made such a difference in these words. A thank you is inadequate, so we dedicate this volume to you, hoping this gesture will better convey our gratitude.

To those special heroes who live in the world of Divine uniqueness, a world of extreme challenges and unusual experiences. Thank you for sharing with us your extraordinary view of the landscape of this life.

Special Heroes

As part of our Special Heroes series, this book includes characters with special needs. We hope this series of novels will to be a tribute to the many people with special needs Rebekah and I have had the privilege to know. We appreciate your contribution to our world. How much we would miss without you.

This story particularly focuses on the characteristics of Schizoid Personality Disorder. I have tried to render the condition accurately based on my research. However, only those walking in that skin can truly know the challenges and the triumphs they experience. Any errors in portrayal of these fascinating people are due to my limited viewpoint, and I ask forgiveness.

While each syndrome has its own unique traits, people with special needs are as varied as the individuals that they are. We know from Psalm 139:13-14 that God guides the forming of every person. He makes no mistakes. Any fault is in our limited, flawed perspective and our arrogance to believe that any of us are anything more than vessels of clay waiting for the Master to fill us.

You can learn more about Schizoid Personality Disorder at the following link:

https://www.helpguide.org/articles/personality-disorders/schizoid-personality-disorder.htm

For further resources and information about the lives of people with special needs and their caregivers go to:

https://www.ellenstumbo.com/

https://embracingimperfect.com/

...So get rid of your old self,
which made you live as you used to...
Ephesians 4:22a **(GNB)**

Chapter 1

THE FORMER PLUM ISLAND ANIMAL DISEASE CENTER, PLUM ISLAND, NEW YORK

Landon Roshard knew everything had changed after what happened in a small town in Arkansas. The old man was hovering. He would arrive at any moment, and he wasn't going to like Roshard's proposal any more than Roshard liked being managed.

I've learned a lot from him. Roshard considered the history he had with his supervisor who was one of the founders of the organization. *Now he's in my way.* The old man kept saying he was going to retire but wouldn't set a date. *If he doesn't announce it soon, I might have to set his date for him.*

Roshard kept watch through the one-way glass of the hidden conference room. He had to peer around the overgrown vine that crawled along the peeling paint of the second-story window frame.

The team from the camouflage department had given the structure the appearance of an abandoned, neglected building. The DNA research being conducted in the three stories hidden beneath the surface was beyond top secret. If you were the wrong person, knowing about it could be unhealthy. Such was life in the organization that existed in the shadows between government and private enterprise. It was a dangerous world, both inside and out, and Roshard thrived on it.

Across the weed-infested lot, one of the old man's bodyguards, dressed as a maintenance worker, unlocked the gate in the ancient security fencing. Schmidt never used the tunnel. The underground golf cart route worked well to transport the researchers to and from the ferry docks without drawing attention. But Roshard suspected it made his boss claustrophobic. *Another weakness.*

A four-door pickup towed an enclosed maintenance trailer through the open gate, across the lot, and parked next to the building. Four men in matching coveralls got out, two on each side. In unison, they walked toward the back of the trailer.

From above, Roshard observed their little magic trick. Concealed between the trailer and the building, one of the men turned toward the structure. He lifted a hidden panel, gazed at the facial recognition and retinal scanner, and disappeared through the false wall that opened and then closed behind him.

When the men started unloading lawnmowers and weed eaters, there were four maintenance workers again. The one hidden in the back of the trailer seamlessly inserted himself into the work crew that began moving around the grounds.

Roshard walked to the conference table where Chidlow was seated. "He's here. Remember, act confident but not arrogant. You and I believe in this. We need to make a believer out of him." Adjusting his designer suit coat and tie, Roshard eyed the man's ball cap and T-shirt.

He took notice of the slogan on the front of the shirt for the first time. **I'm surfing for computer music, hoping to catch a WAV.** The shirt was probably a collector's item in Chidlow's circles. The old man wouldn't be impressed, but Roshard made allowances for excellence. He also demanded performance.

Across the room, the elevator hummed. Chidlow stood and adjusted his ball cap.

When the elevator door opened, an elderly gentleman dressed in maintenance coveralls stepped out. Roshard walked over and shook his hand. "Thanks for coming, Arlo."

Roshard noticed the stoop the old man had developed was bringing his six-foot frame closer to Roshard's five-nine. Was he paler? Roshard was used to seeing his own deep brown complexion and black hair in the mirror each day. The man's white skin and gray head were a stark contrast. *He's still looking strong, overall.*

Roshard led the man to the table. "Mr. Schmidt, this is Dayton Chidlow. He's in charge of the new AI computer division, and he has some intriguing information that might be the answer to our problems."

Schmidt showed a subdued smile to go with his handshake. "Mr. Roshard's told me a little about this. Your computer data suggests there's a mystery man who's been attacking us behind the scenes. Have you found him?" He waved for Roshard and Chidlow to join him in sitting.

Chidlow eased into his chair. "Designator U1586CM82. Yes, he is the most probable."

"Does Mr. Most Probable have a name?"

"Several, actually." Chidlow grabbed the bill of his hat and adjusted the head covering before picking up a paper in front of him.

He ran his finger down the sheet. "Mason, Demetrius, Shankleford, Welch, Clark, the list goes on. That's one of many reasons she thinks he's the brains behind these shadow attacks. That kind of personal concealment is consistent with the type of operations he runs."

Roshard glanced at Chidlow. *I wish he would quit referring to the computer as a she.*

Schmidt rested his chin on interlaced fingers. "Shadow attacks that none of our operations supervisors were aware of by a man that no one knew existed?" He eyed the computer expert.

Chidlow licked his lips and swallowed, looking at the table.

Roshard eased in to rescue him. "Dayton has made some amazing progress toward the organization's goal of taking advantage of recent technology." Turning back to Chidlow, Roshard tried to keep things upbeat. "It might help Mr. Schmidt to know a little about how the computer works."

Chidlow rallied. "This AI algorithm has been amassing data and training itself in all your operations. That's what separates AI from an ordinary computer. It has the ability to learn, teaching itself based on the information it analyzes."

Chidlow spoke like a proud parent. "We are into the 'deep learning' phase. AI is the ultimate intelligence. It's a way to separate the perfect mathematical reasoning of computers from the flawed programing of humans. You couldn't ask for a better ally in your goal of enhancing humanity…without…humanity knowing."

Chidlow grinned at Roshard and Schmidt like they were all in on a practical joke. When the expression wasn't returned, he went back to a more serious tone. "With that ability, it has reached an independent conclusion. Given the amount of talent and resources you're investing, the outcome of your campaigns should be far more successful than you're seeing. The rate of operation failure and loss of agents is abnormally high compared to those projected. The most probable answer is successful counter-operations—even if those operations are undetected."

Schmidt kept his gaze fixed on Chidlow. "Sounds very…theoretical."

Chidlow shuffled with the papers. "I have a list of anomalies the program has found in various projects and in the loss of key people. The computer is basing this solution on pattern recognition in a vast amount of data."

The old man held up his hand. "I don't have time for you to present data that, apparently, only an artificial intelligence can understand. But my gut's telling me your computer might be right."

Chidlow sat back, smiling, nodding.

Schmidt continued. "We're in a war, gentlemen. It has battles and counter-offensives, and it has spies. We need technology that can tell us things my gut can't. This world is rotting. It's contaminated, and if we don't purify it soon, there won't be anything left but rot."

Chidlow's face showed the realization that he relaxed too soon.

The old man took on a scornful expression. "Look at what happened in Arkansas—the top players had a feud and killed each other? That's convenient. We had to sacrifice some valuable personnel and resources to separate ourselves from the fallout. If we hadn't been so caught up on damage control and burying our connections with DNAble we might have been able to track down who did this to us. What we need are real people's names, faces, locations, so we can deal with the problem."

Roshard took advantage of the man's regurgitation

of the incident. "I agree. Becker and his team's disappearance, and several other events, already had me thinking that someone was interfering, but I had nothing to base my hunch on. Since the AI's coming to the same conclusion, I'm confident our computer might be right about the *who* behind those suspicions. We have detailed information, but I felt it important that you understood why we can trust this information."

Chidlow straightened with renewed confidence. "The theory of undetected counterattacks is just the premise she concluded as her starting point. Since then, she has been trying to identify the individual or individuals responsible. There's a man she's hitting on for numerous reasons, too many to list. I can tell you, one way she narrowed it down is that he is not on any of our agents' lists of threats." The man grinned. "Psyche doesn't have much faith in humans."

I told him not to go there. Roshard leaned forward with a quick grin. "Psyche is the pet name Mr. Chidlow has given his machine."

"I think she's more than a machine, sir." A new enthusiasm possessed Chidlow. "Psyche thinks. She just does it with electronic hardware instead of biological. She communicates with me beyond natural language generation and processing. I believe she's sentient. I would like to add some robotic interfaces to give her more options for interaction."

Roshard saw the look on Schmidt's face and intervened. "We appreciate that, Mr. Chidlow, but Mr. Schmidt is correct. This machine's ability to ID enemy agents that our men can't—that's what's valuable to us." He kept a calm smile.

Schmidt stared at Chidlow. "This isn't a science experiment. I was against this from the beginning, but our investors insisted. I gave Mr. Roshard the go-ahead to put it together because I know nothing about this AI stuff. But we expect an outcome from your computer equal to the investment the organization has put into it."

Chidlow stiffened. "We...I can provide the information, sir. I can't be responsible for how well it's implemented."

Roshard rose. "We'll handle the implementation, Mr. Chidlow." *This isn't working like I'd hoped.* "I think Mr. Schmidt will be impressed when I bring him up to speed on the new information you've developed."

Roshard gave a token glance at Schmidt as he motioned Chidlow toward the elevator. "Now that you've met our new talent, if you don't mind, I'll let Mr. Chidlow get back to crunching the data while you and I discuss the plans of how to use it."

Schmidt waved his hand in agreement as he worked his way up from the chair.

Ah. He is showing his age.

Roshard saw Chidlow out and joined Schmidt, who had moved to the window.

The older man smiled and patted Roshard's shoulder. "You really think this... *computer programmer*, has come up with something that a field full of our best operatives couldn't see?"

Roshard knew there was no advantage in appearing unsure. "I do. As you said, we both could feel it." He resisted the urge to bolster his position with unsolicited data.

"Smelling a rat's one thing. Pulling that rat out of his hole is another. How's this Psycho computer, or whatever he calls it, going to do that when it's down here in its own hole?"

"Through the internet. It's not stuck in this hole. Anywhere there's a computer, tablet, smart phone, camera, or scanner connected to the web, our computer can go. It receives a continuous stream of information. The AI evaluates the data to see how it fits with our man."

Schmidt looked doubtful. "You can't replace agents with blips on a screen."

Roshard was enthusiastic in his head shake. "No, you can't. In the end, bold men will deal with this. What we're doing is providing the information those men need to do it."

The old man glanced his way.

I scored a point with that one. Continue with that theme. "This computer processes vast amounts of information quickly through a process called data mining. It looks at a memo here, an event there, recordings, images and public records all over, grabbing them in real time as they're entered. Teams of agents would spend months doing what this machine does in seconds."

Roshard paused for impact, but launched in again before the old man could counter. "Then AI looks at that data in a way humans can't because they aren't inside each other's minds. It takes a unified brain to understand the big picture, but the information is too vast for a human brain to contain it. The computer does what *we* can't and then puts the information in the form we need to do the things *it* can't."

The old man was listening. Roshard switched back to specifics. "The computer has been generating an ever more detailed profile of this man. Before you wage war, it's wise to know your enemy. I'm getting to know our adversary better all the time. He's a man of compassion. He takes time to help others and never takes the credit. That's one way he remains so elusive. Many get impaled on the battlefield when they stop to do a victory dance. A man who doesn't lift himself up is hard to bring down."

The old man's eyebrows bent to meet each other as he gave Roshard a curious inspection. "Such philosophy from you is an interesting twist. Are you looking at making some life changes?"

Roshard gave the man a sideways grin. "I said I was getting to know the man, not that I was going to join him. I prefer the other path to invincibility. Take the high ground where no sword can touch you."

The man sniffed out a laugh. "If I wasn't too old to care, I might consider you a threat. That's the trouble with the high ground. Don't think it's not still dangerous at the top."

Roshard put his arm around the man. "We wouldn't be in this business if we didn't like risks. Don't worry. Until you're gone, you might have more to teach me.

Anyone who threatens you or the business is the one who should fear me."

Roshard dropped the carrot. "And I believe we've found the one threatening all of us. Since we last talked, the computer narrowed down his identity. He's a college professor in Oklahoma named Welch, living in an apartment just outside Oklahoma City."

"So you do know who he is?"

"It's not something we've been able to verify independently. He has no identifiable ties to the business. All we have is the computer implicating him. But I am inclined to trust it."

Schmidt returned to the table and dropped into a chair.

Roshard joined him. *Standing tired him out pretty quickly.*

"So why wait? Take him out. Even if there's a suspicion that he's responsible for the DNAble disaster, it would be worth it to make the hit and see if it solves our problems." Schmidt leaned back. "Does he have any political or family connections complicating it?"

"Doubtful. He's a ghost. This college identity doesn't track in the computer algorithm. It must be fictitious. Enough to stand up to an intelligence background check, but the computer sees deeper than that."

Roshard knew he needed to sell his answer to the rest of Schmidt's question. "We could make a hit on Welch, but it's not reasonable to believe this man's acting alone. The AI agrees. There's enough to suggest this professor is the leader of an organization."

Roshard placed his hands on the table as if laying out the facts. "DNAble was a well-established front for our operation. DNA science was the perfect cover. We were pulling in medical and ancestry customers from Arkansas, Oklahoma, Kansas, and Missouri. Our people were identifying and eliminating people with Jewish bloodlines and providing for Becker's research all at the same time. There were no signs anyone was on to us. With the experienced personnel we had and the fail safes in place, this shouldn't have happened. But the whole operation was exposed and we lost some highly productive individuals. The most concerning part is it happened in a way that made it appear our own people were to blame. That tells us it wasn't law enforcement or FBI. They'd be taking credit. We have to be dealing with an independent, highly organized team.

Roshard sat back. "They're like us. They're doing it for their own reasons—reasons they believe in. If we don't eliminate all the key members, they will continue to be a problem for us. Even more so if we take out their leader. That would make it personal."

Schmidt leaned his chin on his fingers again. "So we get this professor to lead us to the team. Then send a strike force and eliminate them all."

"He might lead us to them. But even if we find them, we need to consider that a tactical attack on U.S. soil is not in our best interest. We see the fallout in Gosnell with that type of body count. And it's unlikely their organization will go down easily. There's a better way to eliminate them. What I propose is like ant bait."

"Poison?"

Roshard prepared himself for Schmidt's reaction. "No, something more original. It's based on what Er Koch and Becker learned during their time in Wuhan, but without the drawbacks. Er Koch has developed a different type of virus."

The elder man straightened with a disturbed expression. "I may be getting old, but I remember giving the order to abandon that after the Chinese botched it so badly. We still don't know it wasn't intentional. It sounded good—a bug that would eliminate the inferior population. But it hasn't worked that way. There's no guarantee with this stuff. It has a mind of its own. Why am I now hearing it's still going on?" The man was almost yelling.

Roshard remained calm. "One of our organization's core values is still strategic population reduction. But because of your order we have abandoned the use of the broad application of virus technology toward that goal. However, as you may recall, I asked if we could continue to conduct targeted weapons research. And you agreed. That is what this is about."

Schmidt chewed on Roshard's explanation. "I did not envision the word targeted and virus falling into the same category."

Roshard kept his voice even. "You're right, the Chinese release was a tragedy. But this is a unique product and a different application. I've seen Er Koch's results in lab test scenarios. This truly is a surgical weapon. Each version of this virus is keyed to a specific person. The keyed virus is guaranteed to infect that individual and produce a cytokine storm response in twenty four to seventy two hours. In its initial phase, however, it's difficult for the virus to spread outside the host it's keyed to. If it does, it's fragile enough to be killed by normal immune systems. As the virus progresses, it morphs into the most contagious, fast acting, and deadly form seen. It exists like that for a short period and then self-destructs, becoming unable to replicate, and dies."

The elder's face remained troubled. "That's a nice theory, but a big risk to attack one man."

"Not just one man. Ant bait not only kills the ant that eats it, but before he dies he takes it back to the nest, and it wipes out the entire colony. Same idea here. We infect one agent, then pressure him so he knows his cover's blown. He'll retreat to his team's base of operations. He'll get sick, but it won't seem to be contagious. His comrades will make sure he can recuperate where he's safe."

Roshard motioned with his hand. "There, the virus will morph into its super contagious phase and begin killing everyone in that isolated area before they realize what's happening. When they are finally discovered and the authorities investigate, the virus will be dead, right along with our problem. It will be labeled as a unique deadly outbreak, and we will be rid of him and his team. Clean and untraceable."

The old man worked his mouth around in deliberation before turning to Roshard. "Work on finding this team with the idea of a tactical strike.

Meanwhile, I want to have a talk with Er Koch. I'll let you know about your virus idea." Schmidt gave Roshard a stern gaze. "And this time, my decision will be final. No loopholes. Like you said—until I'm gone."

Chapter 2

THE HOLLENBECK INSTITUTE FOR PEOPLE WITH SPECIAL NEEDS AND SPECIAL ABILITIES, LAKE GALLANT, OKLAHOMA

Ruben Welch shifted in the chair as he waited for the woman's appearance. He had chosen the sturdiest looking piece of furniture in the room. Still, the smallest adjustment of his bulk caused a creaking alarm that the chair's structural integrity was being challenged.

The extra weight on his middle was the least of his problems. It wasn't that he was obese. He was big— his hands, his feet, legs, chest, head, definitely his nose. Even his crop of unruly gray hair was big. Each large component came together in an awkward hulking package not meant for the elegant Victorian furniture the decorator had chosen for the Institute's sitting room.

At least when I was working out of safe houses or surveillance vans, my role afforded me the convenience of equipping it with a chair that accommodates this body.

Welch realized field work would be a less frequent event since he had become Director at the Institute. In the world of espionage, one had to be adaptable.

When the Sanders approached him, their proposal was an answer to prayer. Welch no longer felt comfortable working with groups he used to trust. Creating an organization independent of political or national interests was the ideal way to address the growing evil in the world. It could only be God that had miraculously provided the Sanders with a sudden fortune to invest at the same time Welch had met them.

To form such a group, they would need quality people with unique skills and gifts. He still felt his Creator had best suited him to work clandestinely designing elaborate operations to address specific wickedness, but for a while, he could also play recruiter.

You had better get used to these kinds of meetings. No, today was different. *She* was different.

She had been a part of his life for years. *Can one refer to someone you never met as a part of your life?* He couldn't recall when he'd first heard of her. The old spies had lots of stories.

She was the most successful bait for the Mossad honey traps. Welch had little respect for the tactic of using a woman's sex appeal to entice men into compromising positions. But she commanded a level of respect beyond her physical appearance. She was a prize talked about among the handlers—"Oh, you got her. That's perfect."

After he suggested her for a part in one of his operations, he noticed her code name often appeared as a role-player in his scripts. She had been instrumental in so many of his missions.

Still, they were strangers moving on parallel paths, never intersecting. Welch even avoided photographs or videos of the people the handlers cast to play his characters. It was easier in case anything went wrong.

When he heard she left the spy game to marry the Russian scientist they had liberated from Iran, he was happy for her. Then he learned of the horrible death of her husband and youngest son at the hands of Iranian assassins. *It's hard for anyone to leave this business.*

He could only imagine how it had devastated her. The attack moved Welch to intervene covertly on her behalf. It was his quiet tribute to her service and the price she'd paid.

Because of the danger, the woman had encouraged her older son, Joshua, to join the Mossad. She wanted him prepared to protect himself and his younger sister, Rahab. *God brought good from evil. Joshua will be a valuable leader on the Institute's team.*

When Welch asked Joshua's mother to join without an interview or references, he let Joshua believe it was based on Joshua's recommendation. That was far from accurate. Welch was fully aware of the lady's talent, having designed missions to take advantage of it in days long past. There were so many things connecting Welch with the family, so much he knew about this person he had never met. *Today our lines finally intersect.* What an interesting turn of Providence.

Who knew? This woman was not that much younger than him. Perhaps they could be friends the way he and Talisa Sanders were friends, without the age difference. Talisa seemed to appreciate the perspective of a man who wasn't distracted by her beauty.

Welch was not of a temperament to deny what was apparent. He was ugly. But rather than allowing it to hinder his self-esteem, he had made it a strength. He did not allow himself to indulge in fantasies that women could be attracted to his physical appearance. But it gave him no personal dissatisfaction. He was quite gratified by his situation.

The awareness of his lack of physical attractiveness served him well in his field. He wasted no time on vain attempts to improve his attractiveness or pursue romance. He had more time for intellectual endeavors, but more importantly, his contentment gave him immunity to walk through fire that might burn a more hopeful man.

No doubt the woman's legendary beauty brought constant harassment from men seeking her attention. Perhaps he could provide her camaraderie free from such a circumstance.

But Welch was getting ahead of himself. According to Joshua, his mother wanted to meet him. Meeting was the polite thing to do on her part and Welch's. He would welcome her to the Institute Team, and she would thank him for the opportunity. If a friendship developed, the companionship would be an interesting bonus. He would enjoy sharing thoughts with someone from his own generation who had been involved in the business of espionage back then.

There were noises in the hallway. *That must be her and Joshua.* He pushed himself out of the chair, causing it to engage every alarm system available to wood and fabric.

In the absence of information, the human brain creates details. Welch hadn't realized his mind constructed an image of the famous femme fatale in her older age until that image was upended when she walked into the room.

He was not prepared for the charmingly innocent face on the fifty-three-year-old woman. Framed with a full flow of beautiful dark hair, her olive skin and features would be the envy of a woman half her age. But hers was not the overt beauty of someone intending to be alluring. If she used cosmetics, Welch could not detect them.

Her nose had a unique shape—prominent yet captivatingly feminine. It gave her appearance a character all her own. Her soft green eyes seemed designed to pierce a man's soul and her perfect smile was like a physical force that lifted the spirits. No wonder she had been the downfall of so many of Israel's enemies. She had an irresistible countenance no one would suspect belonged to a professional beguiler.

Joshua escorted her across the room. "Dr. Welch, I would like you to meet my mother, Shifra Federov."

Before Welch could acknowledge the greeting, the woman beamed a smile that gave the impression he alone had inspired it. She used both her hands to take up one of his. "I already know you."

The voice was womanly yet pure, completely disarming. But Welch was most unprepared for the impact of the woman's manner—the way she leaned in holding him with her eyes, her brow furrowed in earnest, her head and shoulders moving with the statement.

He found himself speaking his thoughts. "I truly wish I could verify that statement, but you must be mistaken. I am sure I would not be the first to tell you that you are not a...person who could be easily forgotten."

"Good. I wouldn't want you to forget what I've been waiting a long time to tell you. Your friend, Bonnie Carruthers, in the New York CIA office, told me how you worked with them after my husband and son were killed. I am aware that your intelligence gathering made it possible for them to stop two other attacks on my family. Even though we have never met, I've known of your kindness and your character for a long time. Bless you. I owe you so much."

Welch had been unaware she knew. "Bonnie was quick to do her part. She has lost loved ones to this business as well. We have only given what your service deserved."

Shifra let her shoulders drop, lightly holding her

arms crossed at her waist. Her gaze touched him with admiration. "But I knew you even before that. I have seen your mind at work. I loved being a part of the operations you planned."

She leaned toward him, ready to tell a story. "I don't know if you remember, but I was the lost girl in operation 'Stopped Clock.' I also acted as the girl at the train station in operation 'Shake the Branches' and quite a few others." Shifra inhaled and breathed out the words. "I could always tell when you had planned my day."

Her brow furrowed, and she looked down into an unpleasant memory. "Any other time, it would be all about me using…myself to turn a man into an animal. I had to make him believe he could have me if he would betray himself and his loyalties. I always felt I lost a little piece of myself."

The lightness returned to her face. "But you designed masterpieces. I was one part of this intricate drama that all fit together. You let the true weaknesses of our target be his undoing. And they were so perfectly hidden. No political fallout. I felt like a theater actress with true depth to my character, but…I knew it was more important than that. Thank you. God used those times to help me regain the lost parts of myself."

Welch found himself appreciating the gaze Shifra fixed on him. Her eyes spoke of respect for his true essence. So intense was her expression, he had to glance down.

He fixated on her lovely fingers resting on his huge

hairy digits, and he felt the warmth of Shifra's elegant hands soaking into his oversized palm.

Oh, she is good at what she does. Welch removed his hand to break the spell. For a moment, he had allowed himself to believe the unbelievable. He hoped the woman realized she had no need to use her powers on him for the sake of gratefulness.

Welch gave a dip of his head in acknowledgement of her compliments. "It is my pleasure, Mrs. Federov, to know that it has been such a blessing. I am certain that each mission was better because of your participation. We both have benefited, so you owe me no gratitude that I do not also owe you."

Shifra beamed at him again. "You're like I imagined you would be. I feel as if I've known you for years. Please call me Shiffy."

Perhaps the mannerisms were natural to her, something she could not turn off. Welch needed to shift the conversation to break the power of the woman's attention. "How is your daughter, Rahab? I am sorry coming here has separated you. I know it will be difficult."

Shifra shook her head. "No, no. It is all right. Rahab has her own life that takes up most of her time. I don't see her much. As a mother, I worry, but her husband takes good care of her and has the money to keep her entertained. We talk on the phone frequently."

She smiled. "Nothing much will change except in Rahab's imagination. She is used to having everything. Even if she has no time for me, she wants me close. After I lost my husband and son, I confess I spoiled her. I pray the Lord will correct that in time."

Shifra focused her gratitude on Welch again. "When you promised to use the Institute's resources to keep an eye on her, it freed me to come here. I knew you would do everything you could to protect her, as you have already."

"It's my pleasure. All the intel says the threats are gone, but we'll never take that for granted." He had the urge to encircle Shifra with protective arms. *She's a colleague. Focus on that.*

"You'll never know what that means. A little distance might relieve some tension. It hasn't been easy keeping my past and Joshua's work a secret from my own daughter, but her nature isn't the type to be trusted with such information. She's been suspicious of this move. She views Oklahoma as the backwater ends of the earth. Your teaching offer on the OU stationery went a long way to convince her, but she still acts like I am in danger of being taken captive by the natives."

Welch laughed. *So far it's me whose been taken captive.*

The woman glanced at her son. "Joshua showed me the house you set up on the other side of the lake. It will be a perfect cover if she ever comes to visit. I'll text her the address and that might help her believe my story. But it's too much. Joshua also showed me the house you're providing me here on the Institute grounds. It's more than I could have asked."

"We are asking everyone who joins the Institute to devote their life to this calling. Much will be asked of you." Shifting topics hadn't worked. Welch turned to Joshua to free himself from the effect of Shifra's presence. "I assume the Sanders have provided everything your mother needs?"

Shifra reinserted herself to answer the question, forcing Welch to reengage her eyes. "Yes, they have. It is all too wonderful to believe. To live in such a place, to be part of all this, and be near Joshua and Amelia. And now to meet you. I feel like a princess in a fairytale."

A princess, Welch thought. *A fairy princess, timeless, radiant.*

That radiance was finding its way past every defense he had. Welch realized how large his own smile had become. He wrestled his face into neutrality.

He needed to reacquire control over his imagination before it controlled *him.* It was indeed a fairy tale. *But I am not the prince for whom she waits.*

Shifra was grateful and excited to meet the man behind the missions, but their exchange would soon become awkward if he could not contain how attracted he was to her.

His hope of friendship with the woman had evaporated. Too dangerous. She would perceive how he felt and would feel obligated to explain that she didn't feel the same way, and then she would be uncomfortable and avoid him. While he was no longer in danger of suffering the pain such things had caused him in the deep past, it was tension they didn't need at the Institute. He could not avoid interaction with Shifra, but he could limit contact. At least until her initial impact on him wore off.

He was disappointed to discover Shifra could produce such a weakness in him, but it had, and he needed to acknowledge that and deal with it. In planning his missions, he factored in such elements. He would have to treat this the same.

Again, he tried to escape into conversation with Joshua. "Have you told your mother about your mission to apprehend the DNAble fugitives?" *There. That might give me some adjustment time.* "I'm sure she will want to accompany you to France. She and Amelia would make an effective team in operations over there since they are both fluent in the language."

Shifra tipped her head at Welch with a disappointed expression. "Joshua tells me they have been busy helping design the Institute and haven't had a chance to have a honeymoon. It was my understanding before they started the hunt for these fugitives they were supposed to have that honeymoon opportunity. I think these young people deserve not to have a mother along. Three's a crowd."

Shifra's disappointment was like a wound to Welch. When she reengaged her smile toward him, it was like a healing salve. "If you find a role for me, I could go over later."

Joshua laughed. "It's not like we're going alone."

Shifra joined the laugh but shook her head. "I know Gabriel has to go. Having had an autistic child of my own, I know Amelia wouldn't feel comfortable leaving her brother behind. Ibbie will be a blessing, since Gabriel has attached to her so well. She can give you some alone time. And it's only natural that Marsha and Hevel should join you since you shared a double wedding." Shifra paused to laugh even harder. "Goodness. You already have the crowd. There's no room for me."

Welch's belly shook as he joined in. "Perhaps the rest of us should go and leave Joshua and Amelia here to be alone."

When the humor subsided a soft longing possessed Shifra's eyes. "Besides, I was hoping not to go on a mission right away. I'd like to see more of the planning side now. You could show me how you script the details of your operations. Who knows, I might have something to offer, having been involved carrying out your plans. I would enjoy comparing notes on those old missions. It has been a long time."

Sitting with her, talking of his work, that was the hope Welch had brought into the room with him. *It would be your undoing.* "I am afraid it will be some time before we have such an opening." Knowing the words he was about to say dropped an ache inside his heart. "And I work better alone."

Welch observed Shifra's face alter. He felt as if he had doused a warming fire in the heart of winter. *Compose yourself, old man. You're mistaking her thankfulness for attraction.* Welch's mind seemed unable to come up with a strategy to extract himself other than to turn toward Joshua once more. "Have you briefed your mother on what we know about the traffickers that supplied the girls for Becker's experiments? Perhaps she could play a role in bringing them to justice."

"Oh," Shifra sounded disappointed. "Of course. If I'm needed for something right now. I want to do my part in something that important."

Joshua gave Welch a knowing look. "Ruben, I think my mother was hoping the two of you could reminisce about the old days. Luke will be gone for several weeks. Why don't we put work aside for a little while? Amelia really wanted me to help her after I introduced you two. She also wanted me to invite you to dinner tonight. She's preparing a true French feast for the entire team. It'll give Eema a chance to get to know everyone better."

Welch saw his exit. "Now, that is an excellent idea. We can talk then, Mrs. Federov." *Where it will be safer.*

Shifra's face held restrained disappointment. "All right. I will look forward to that. But please call me Shiffy. It is the name my friends use."

"Very well…Shiffy. Please excuse me until tonight." Welch turned and hurried out the door.

Shifra felt the sting of Welch leaving so suddenly. "I didn't expect that from him."

Joshua faced her. "I'm sorry, Eema. I know you wanted to visit with him. He's not usually like that. He must be distracted with all that's going on."

"It's more than that. He wants to avoid me."

"Don't think that. He seemed quite ready to meet you. Our conversation must have made him realize how much there is to do."

Shifra sought out the pattern in the intricate floor tile. "It's not the first time. I shouldn't have taken his hand. I was too forward. When you look like this—." *That sounds so vain, but God, sometimes I wish you had made me...not so...* "This is not a conversation I should have with my son."

Joshua took her hand. "It's okay, Eema."

Shifra couldn't hold back. "The work I did gave me a reputation... You know I have to be careful...so many things get misconstrued."

She looked away again. "I know there were stories about me... People with dirty minds. Decent men don't want to touch me and indecent men...that's *all* they want to do." Shifra sighed. "But they both react that way for the same reason. They make assumptions about me because of the way I look." She closed her eyes. "The honey traps were dirty work. Maybe that does say something about me—since I was so good at them."

"Eema, that's not true." Joshua pulled her into a hug. "You loved the people of our country so much that you were willing to sacrifice to protect them. Someone has to do undercover work and not everyone can. I know playing those roles took a great toll on you. Knowing what it cost our family made me wonder if I should marry someone as gentle as Amelia, bringing her into the world of espionage. But God prepared her and Gabriel to be a part of this life. The same way He prepared *you* to do the work He called you for. The same way you poured your experience into me. God used all of it to bring us to this place."

She sighed and patted Joshua's arm that held her. "That's why I thought it would be different here. Different with him. I thought he would know I was just doing a job."

"I'm sure he understands that." Joshua's expression turned speculative. "He might feel a gentleman should wait until the second or third meeting before he talks privately with a lady. He comes from an older generation."

"I come from the same generation. We don't have time to waste."

Joshua smirked. "But you don't act your age."

Shifra half turned his direction and narrowed her eyes.

Joshua created distance and held his hands in front of his face. "It's a good thing." He grinned and shrugged. "Perhaps give him a little time."

"I just want him to give *me* a little time. Find out I'm not some harlot."

"He doesn't think that."

"Some days, I feel like I've wasted my life. You're right. The choices I made cost us so much. I want to feel like the sacrifice was worth it. When I was working on one of his missions, I felt like that. I just wanted to sit and talk with him, to feel that again."

Shifra examined the door through which Welch had left. "I really like him. It's strange. I don't care that we had never seen each other before today…I know more about him than most of the people I've met, his character, his goodness. He's done so much for our family."

Shifra faced Joshua. "I loved your father for who he was. Even with what he was forced to do, his mind was so removed from anything related to the intrigue. Being married to him made me feel like I had left the past behind. But I hadn't." Shifra scowled. "I relaxed too much."

"No one else could have done more. You're not to blame for what happened to Daddy and Caleb. If it wasn't for you, Rahab and I would have died that night too." Joshua gave her an extra squeeze.

He always knew how to reassure her.

"And Ruben knows all that. You'll see him at dinner."

"It wasn't fair of me to bring a man like your father into this life. I swore I would never do it again. But now…" She nodded to the door. "He's different."

Joshua bent his neck so he could grin at her. "What if you treated him like a mission?"

She huffed at the idea. "That would prove everything he thinks already."

"Don't write the mission like that. Write it like *he* would."

Chapter 3

A REMOTE LOCATION SOMEWHERE

A firearm was a beautiful thing, Peter Radley thought as he examined the disassembled semi-automatic handgun. The parts lay neatly on the piece of cleaning felt that he used to protect the kitchen table of the cabin he had rented for the week. He held the barrel of his pistol toward the light and examined it for any further debris. He loved the gleam of the pure metal and the milled grooves that added twist to the bullet as it traveled down the tube. A gun was complex but uncomplicated.

Two days of intense firearms practice should have cleared his head. But Radley still had Sarah on his mind. He must be in love with her. That was a complication. He rubbed the back of his neck, trying to get at the strange, tickling sensation.

He had no room in his life for love, especially the

kind that would never be returned. Not the least of the issues that made it impossible was her stance about guns.

"I don't like guns." She was there. Standing across the counter, arms folded, just as she had before.

The look on her face reached inside him again. He spoke aloud to the image. "I guess I can understand. You've seen the awful things I do with them. How did you ever stand being around me?"

"I saw the other qualities. The awful things you do aren't really you, Peter." The honesty in her eyes haunted Radley.

"At least I don't take the kinds of jobs I did before."

"Are you sure?"

"The old man knows I won't target good people. I want to do what's right."

Sarah's eyes drifted over the metal parts on the table. "But does *he*?"

Radley wanted to change the subject. "Why couldn't our lives have been different? So we could have—."

Her eyes met his again. "God knows why. He has a plan."

"You always say that."

His phone chirped in his earpiece, and Sarah vanished. With rapid precise movements, Radley began reassembling the gun. The device in his ear emitted the second double chirp as he slid the slide back on, slapped the magazine in, and chambered a round. The ringtone was assigned to only one person. He set the gun on the table and inhaled. Orienting his mind, he grabbed a pad and pen from the counter behind him. Settling himself into receiving mode, he touched the button on his earpiece. "Pro-Choice Feed Supply. Please verify your customer number."

"I'm a loyal old customer—number one, to be exact." There was authority in the statement even though the voice was weaker than the last time Radley spoke with the old man.

"It's been a while, sir. I hope everything's going well."

"I'm afraid we're going to have to take those steps we discussed last time."

Radley toyed with the pen as he considered the implications of the statement. "I'm sorry to hear that, sir. At least you're telling me in person instead of me having to self-activate because of some tragic news about you. So this is preemptive. That's better. Do we have time for it to be an accident, or does it need to be done quickly?"

"Roshard's gone too far this time. He's messing with the virus stuff again and we can't have that. I have great grandchildren to worry about. I can barely control him now. When I'm gone… I will not leave this organization with a leadership that might destroy the human race. The virus project hasn't been the surgical removal it was supposed to be, thinning the weak out of the herd. I had friends die." The old man fell silent.

"I know how he thinks, sir. He doesn't care as long as it's not him and he doesn't think it ever could be. He considers death as acceptable loss." Radley knew

Roshard. The man's indifferent attitude was like Radley's own lack of feelings. He would not have noticed until recently.

Radley was feeling different or, to be accurate, he was having different feelings. He felt more concern for the old man. "You need to be careful. He'll look at you in the same way."

"I can see it already." Some of the vigor returned to the old man's voice. "I treated him like a son. Now, he's become an enemy, and we need to make sure the loss is on *his* side. I'm limited here because he's been working on the board of directors behind my back. He's been making them believe DNAble was my fault. Since I was considering retirement already, some are hinting it's time."

"I'll head your way."

"Not today. First, I need you in Oklahoma City. There's a more immediate threat there. Roshard's people have possibly located an opposition player who's been running counteroffensives against us. I think Roshard is putting a virus into play against him, even after I gave orders not to. You've got to stop whoever is supposed to release this virus, so the bug doesn't wipe out half the city...or worse. That is priority number one. Then try and eliminate this agent and the team he manages. I know it's a lot. Get whatever help you need, but I want you to handle the virus issue personally. I want the job done right and kept quiet. Then come here and cut off the source."

"I understand. So you have people on the ground in Oklahoma City already?"

"Roshard does. They're tracking this new threat. He goes by the name Welch and poses as a professor at the college. You can see why we can't let him take a killer virus into a university environment. Those students will spread it everywhere. I'm sending you the info I have on this Welch and Roshard's operation in an email. You'll need to use my personal encryption key to access it."

"Okay. I'll get a flight there today. I'll use my own source for weapons and other resources. It's better his men don't know I'm involved."

"Agreed. I know you like to work alone, anyway."

"Will you keep me posted on intel from your side?"

"I'll pass along what I hear, but remember, there are probably things going on that I don't know about, and there might be others involved. He's telling me they're getting data from a computer with that AI stuff. My own sources are telling me Roshard's got an agent working on information from someone this professor is personally connected to, but that's all I know. Roshard is keeping his people quiet for the most part."

"Understood."

"That's everything I have for now. Be careful."

"*You* be careful, sir."

Radley tapped his earpiece to end the call. As he stared into his own thoughts, Sarah was there, watching him. Even having to endure her troubled face was worth it to Radley to have her near. "You don't approve, do you?"

Some of the tension eased out of her features. "God has a reason for it all."

Radley glanced at the counter between them before looking up at Sarah. "You always say that."

37

Chapter 4

THE HOLLENBECK INSTITUTE FOR PEOPLE WITH SPECIAL NEEDS AND SPECIAL ABILITIES, LAKE GALLANT, OKLAHOMA

Welch tried to focus on the words coming out of the pouty overbite under the tiny, round nose that held up oversized wire-rim glasses. It was hard to pay attention to the Institute's petite IT manager. His mind kept returning to Shifra. "I'm sorry, Gretchen. Could you repeat your question?"

Gretchen clacked on the computer keys, her red ponytail swishing back and forth between computer monitors. Her keystrokes were giving Shifra Federov access and clearance to the Institute's system. "Why did you post bail for me that day?"

"Because I believed God had something special planned for you."

The woman let her shoulders and head wobble as

she struck the keys. "I'll bet you say that to all the girls." Gretchen's hands stopped. She turned her horrified face toward him. "I didn't mean that how it sounded. I wasn't being flirty, I promise. It just sounded funny and I thought…sorry."

Welch gave enough of a smile to let her know he recognized her intent. *She's making a noble effort to leave her old life behind. Please help her, Lord. Perhaps she and Shifra could be friends and Shifra would be a good…but Shifra is old enough to be her mother.* The fact occurred to Welch because of the data they had just entered, not because of anything he perceived during his meeting with Shifra. It was hard to think of her as anywhere close to his sixty years.

Welch sometimes struggled to treat Gretchen as a work subordinate. She seemed more like a daughter. Even though he thought of Shifra as younger, it was equally difficult to imagine *her* as a daughter. The thought brought her smile to his mind and taunted him with his weakness. *Lord, I know you don't tease your children, so you must be trying to teach me something. Help me learn it quickly. I am unaccustomed to this type of tension.*

He forced his mind back to Gretchen's comment. "I do not say that to all the girls, but it's always true. God doesn't create things He doesn't have plans for. Of that I'm convinced. I've also observed that He loves to wade into the muddled chaos that our lives can become and turn them into triumphs if we let Him. That's what I discerned that day. God was ready to take the predicament you were in and produce a repentant heart and a reborn life."

Gretchen looked doubtful. "It took a long time for that to happen. I don't know where I would have been if you hadn't helped me all these years. What kept you from giving up on me?"

"A couple of things. Your counselor told me you showed an extraordinary aptitude for computer science. That is not something to be wasted. But it was mainly because God didn't abandon *me*. How could I do less?"

"But why me? There are a lot of people that would have given their lives to God sooner and would be better Christians."

"Even if that subjective assessment were true..." Welch lowered his head to give Gretchen his fatherly gaze. "...how many of them could have breached the special security features created by the professors of Oklahoma University's cybersecurity department..."

Gretchen pressed a smile between her lips and gave a slow side-to-side wag of her head.

"...to spend unauthorized time on the Schooner supercomputer..."

The IT manager assumed a guilty look of satisfaction.

"...so she could run her special program that processed football data to predict and defeat each rival's game strategy?" Welch folded his arms for his final verdict.

Her smile vanished. She knew where he was going.

"All in response to the promise of a date with OU's second-string quarterback when you delivered him said model."

Gretchen looked poutier than normal. "It was my in. I knew those guys could never figure out my program. All those hunks were going to need me right there with them before each game. Then Dufus had to go bragging and got us caught." Gretchen slouched, elbow on the chair arm, frown resting on her fist. "He stood me up for that date, too. I think the judge should have taken that into consideration."

Welch ran his hand through the yak's coat that grew on his head. "Considering his probation prohibited him from having contact with you, he might have considered you an expensive date."

Gretchen gave her typical head wobble. "Yeah, and he calls himself a man." She glanced at Welch's face. "I'm just kidding…kinda…I know, I should have done more considering myself, but it seemed harmless. I mean, why else would I tutor those boneheads?"

Welch appreciated the girl's honesty. "One of my motivations was to channel all that skill to a better purpose."

He wanted to return to the original flavor of the conversation. "But the actual answer to why you and not someone else is that I was listening to what God was telling me. You'll have to direct all further questions to Him." Welch smiled. "God specializes in seeing things in people that no one else does. And He's a Judge that takes all things into consideration."

Welch had been studying a Scripture that might apply. "The prophet Jeremiah spoke for God, talking about Israel—'For I will restore you to health, and I will heal you of your wounds, declares the Lord, Because *they have called you an outcast, saying, It is Zion. No one cares for her.'* I know what it's like to be on that side of things. Fortunately, when regenerating lives, God doesn't limit Himself to the easy cases."

Gretchen sat upright in the chair again. "I'm glad, but I hope all that computer training you got me into will be useful now that I'm part of the Institute. I owe you. I ought to work for free, but don't stop paying me, okay? And don't let that stop you from feeling like you need to give me a raise someday."

Welch chuckled. "I'm glad you're part of our family. And you do plenty of work around here. I'm already money ahead. If you feel any indebtedness, let it motivate you to keep your computer activities within Institute policy." The interaction had Welch curious. "I appreciate your gratitude, but what causes you to bring it up?"

"Something the chaplain said in devotions today about looking back and taking stock of what God has brought us out of and letting that guide where we're going. I really do want to be a better Christian, but I get so caught up in the other stuff, I forget. I know you watch me and probably wonder if I'll ever get it right."

Welch patted her shoulder. "Satan likes to whisper such things to all of us, trying to get us to compare ourselves to others, to puff us up or tear us down. Either will do nicely for him. Some days I wonder if I'll ever get it right." *Now is an excellent example, Lord. Help me get what you're trying to do here.* "I have to count on the Scripture's promise that the Lord is faithful to finish the good work He started in us."

43

Chapter 5

Welch hated being late, but he couldn't risk being trapped in an intimate, before-dinner conversation with Shif.... He considered the effect of using her nickname. It felt personal, but she must not view it that way. She appeared to be an informal soul. Perhaps she preferred for everyone to call her Shiffy. She wouldn't have insisted upon it if it had any intimate significance. The nickname did not pose the problem that being in her presence did. He would call her Shiffy as she asked - one battle he didn't have to fight.

Welch was used to letting himself in. Joshua's wife, Amelia, always insisted. When she gave a dinner invitation, her door was open an hour early and guests were free to come in and visit with each other in *le salon.*

Arriving a few minutes after the scheduled time, he made his way to where they would be eating. The large dining area and conversation room was the buffer between Amelia and Joshua's home and a sanctuary Amelia had designed as a common area of sorts for the Institute staff and guests to relax. The space included an indoor arboretum, along with lounging, gaming, and creative rooms tucked here and there around a winding, ambling art gallery. It was all surrounded by magnificent gardens.

"Dr. Welch, you're just in time." Amelia met him as he entered the large dining room. "We were about to start. I have your seat right over here." She directed him to a chair near the middle of the long table, which was filled with French cuisine delights. Around the table were a dozen people he had come to know well. The core of the Institute.

Amelia took the seat next to him. She had chosen the center seating style, in which the host and hostess sat opposite each other at the middle of the table. The guests were then arranged on each side of them according to their status. They had given him the seat of honor next to Amelia. Across the table, in the other honorable position next to Joshua, was Shifra.

Joshua had stood when Welch entered, and he now addressed the group. "As you all know, we are here to welcome my mother to our team." He grinned. "Apparently, Dr. Welch realized he needed to bring in a professional to keep me in line—someone with a proven track record."

Amelia pretended she was poising a pen to write. "Hold on, Eema. If you're revealing how to handle this son of yours, I'm taking notes."

On the other side of Amelia, Ibbie, who had come with Joshua from the Mossad to join the Institute, raised her voice over the laughter. "Good luck. I've been his partner for years, and I haven't figured it out."

Shifra put up her hand. "I want to let everyone know I'm not responsible for these two." She grinned at Joshua and Ibbie.

Ibbie returned the grin. "You're stuck with both of us. I've known you almost as long as I've known Joshua. I think we met when you spoke to our Mossad unit about how to aid in operating a honey trap. Here was this legend in the business, and she was my partner's eema."

Joshua nodded. "Ibbie's like part of the family." He paused. "The annoying little sister part."

Smirking, Ibbie flicked her hand in dismissal and Joshua got serious again. "When a man can be surrounded by his family and friends at both home and work, he is blessed indeed." He turned to Shifra. "Eema, your being here has completed my blessing. Welcome to the Institute and welcome home."

Everyone applauded.

Shifra grinned. "I'm glad you just call it the Institute. It will take me a while to get the name down."

Talisa spoke over the laughter. "It used to be longer. The more we have to say it, the shorter it gets."

Joshua waited for calm to return. "Eema, I know you met everyone except for Gretchen at our wedding in New York. I think this is the first time we have gathered as a group since Gretchen started working here. For her sake, I'm going to go around the room and tell a little about everyone."

He gestured. "To my right is Talisa Sanders. Her husband Luke is away on training right now, but you met him during interviews. The two of them are the financiers and founders of the Institute. Talisa legitimizes our cover with her dolphin therapy and other programs she has helped set up for people with special needs. As you know, parents send their kids here from all over the country as part of our camps and extended stay programs. The Institute appears to be an open book. We are so exposed, we're well concealed."

Joshua leaned forward and gestured around Talisa to her sister Janie. Long blond hair draped the girl's willowy form. "Beside her is her sister Janie, and across from her is Teddy."

Janie gave a shy smile more appropriate for a child. Teddy's perpetual grin fit perfectly with his stocky elf-like appearance. They both had the look of uncomplicated innocence.

Teddy waved at Shifra. "Me and Janie help Miss Tee." Teddy put his hand on his forehead and scrunched his face. "Only I keep forgetting she's Mrs. Tee now." The group joined him in his laugh which made his smile grow. "I could tell you all about it, but Mrs. Tee says I need to practice not talking so much at meals. I like to talk and Miss…Mrs. Tee said this was a night to honor you, so I shouldn't talk unless it is to say something nice about you. So I'll wait until there's something nice to say."

Talisa faced the tablecloth with a look of defeat and sighed.

Teddy looked even more pleased at the eruption of laughter.

Shifra raised her voice over the mirth. "I hope I don't make you wait too long." She gave him a big grin.

Teddy shook his head. "You won't, cause you have a pretty smile."

The collective agreement brought the calm Joshua needed to continue. "Teddy and Janie are valuable members of the team, helping Talisa with the therapy half of the campus. At times, God has shown them visions that allow them to help people."

Gesturing across the table, Joshua continued. "What you may not know about my wonderful wife, Amelia, is that besides being able to create this amazing food, she's gifted in languages. She also saved all of us with her quick thinking during the DNAble operation.

Amelia batted away the compliment with her hand. "Move on or this amazing food is going to dry out, sitting on the warmers." She spoke French to Shifra. "Je m'excuse." Then she translated for the non-French speakers. "I apologize." Again, she singled out Shifra with her gaze. "My brother Gabriel can't be with us tonight. As you know, autism makes gatherings like this difficult. He prefers to eat in his room. I know he will miss speaking French with you."

Shifra gave a gracious nod and smile. "It was the same with Caleb."

Welch marveled at Shifra's ability to shift her persona, chameleon like, to suit the person to whom she was talking. She made subtle adjustments to her accent, slang, expressions, and mannerisms, depending on the person she was addressing. She was Hebrew, French, New Yorker—whatever fit best with the conversation she was having. At first, Welch thought the changes might be because she spent half her life roleplaying. On further observation, he decided Shifra truly desired to make those around her feel comfortable.

Amelia motioned to Joshua. "I'm sorry. Continue with the introductions."

Joshua addressed his mother and gestured toward Welch. "As you mentioned earlier, you knew Dr. Welch from his work. In a way, Eema, you know him better than the rest of us. I'm sure you'll become fast friends with so much in common."

Shifra sent her pretty smile his way. "I hope so."

Moving his gaze to the right of Welch, Joshua gave Hevel an expression of camaraderie. "Hevel is a deadly opponent in a firefight or hand-to-hand." Joshua patted his side. "I have the scars to prove it. I'm glad the Lord let us both live through the DNAble mission because he's also a good friend."

Giving a head dip toward Gretchen, Joshua continued. "I'll save our second newest member for last and move over to Marsha, whom you know from the weddings. She has been on quite a few missions with Ibbie and me. We have had a lot of fun together and got into and out of a lot of scrapes together."

Marsha smirked. "That's on you and Ibbie. I was supposed to be eye candy. You know how that is, Shifra."

Welch felt himself stiffen at the comment. *Marsha is never one to tiptoe around a subject.*

Shifra gave a subdued smile and slight nod.

"But they always made me get my hands dirty to save them." Marsha exaggerated wiping her hands. "Don't expect that anymore. Since Eva packed some pounds on this body that she didn't take with her when she moved out," Marsha tickled at the baby in the carrier strapped to the chair beside her, "I've had to change my persona from sexy mistress to mistress of logistics."

Hevel crossed his arms and shook his head. "I keep telling her she looks just as good, but she won't believe me. I'm glad she's taking a safer role now, though. I don't want to lose her, and Eva needs her mama."

Marsha smooched a kiss in Hevel's direction. "You're the most dangerous thing I ever faced."

Joshua cleared his throat with a smirk and shifted to Gretchen. "I think most of you have met Gretchen. She's been filling the IT manager position for a few weeks now, but she has been here behind the scenes a lot longer. But, we have never had an opportunity to welcome her like she deserves. She comes to us last from the Texas Advanced Computing Center in Austin, where she was part of the Frontera Fellowship program. After that she was chosen to assist the planner of the next version of the Stampede supercomputer, which should be in operation next year. She has been working with Dr. Welch to assemble our own supercomputer program. Don't ask her to tell you about it because you won't understand anything she's saying."

Gretchen wobbled her head. "What? You don't speak petaflop?"

Joshua gave his own head shake. "I rest my case. Dr. Welch, will you pray for us?"

Welch bowed his head. "Dear Lord, we thank You for bringing us together for a unique purpose. Each day there seem to be more people plotting evil of every kind. Many of the forces involved are proving to be beyond the reach of law enforcement and governments. The ranks of these organizations we trusted in the past have been infiltrated by compromised individuals. They are no longer motivated by a Holy fear of You, oh God. Oaths mean so little."

Welch gave a moment for those around the table to consider the situation, then continued. "We have assembled as a group which is independent of manmade institutions. We dedicate our fight against this evil in the world to You and Your purposes. The human reasons are secondary to the spiritual causes. While we are people using physical tactics, you have told us that we are in a supernatural battle. We cannot fulfill our purpose without Your help. Please be with us. Bless this food tonight and help it make us strong, skilled, and wise to accomplish Your will on earth as it is in Heaven. Most of all, grow us together as a team to be a blessing to each other during the hard times as well as the good."

"Amen." Shifra said it ahead of the others and with force.

Amelia passed the food.

Marsha nudged Shifra with her elbow. "So Shifra, I understand you and I have similar skill sets. Apparently, you were quite the temptress when you were with the Mossad."

Shifra lowered her head. "Some of my assignments required me to entice men, yes. Those roles were not something I enjoyed."

Marsha smirked. "You probably like more of a challenge." Her husband, Hevel, hung his head and shook it.

Talisa looked around Joshua to speak to Shifra. "Did you ever get depressed doing that kind of work?"

With a sigh, Shifra gave a nod of agreement. "Sometimes. What woman wants to be thought of like that? But the men we were targeting were dangerous to Israel, and it was more important to stop them. Many people gave more than I did to protect our country. Fortunately, there were bright spots."

Shifra turned her attention to Welch. "When I met you today, I mentioned Operation Stopped Clock. Do you remember it?"

Welch nodded, thankful for the chance to change the tone of the conversation. He raised his voice for the sake of all around the table. "Shifra is referring to an operation in which we had to prevent a meeting between an ambassador and a courier. There was a narrow window for them to meet. If the ambassador was late by even just a little, the courier could not wait. We knew the ambassador would travel a certain route and always came early, so he wouldn't miss the meeting."

Welch gestured with his hands to emphasize the next part. "We had to prevent the meeting in such a way so that the ambassador would not suspect that he was late. That way, we could substitute our own courier. I had a group of clock makers create time pieces that looked exactly like his watch and the clock in his car. They manufactured the works to begin running at one quarter speed at a certain time. Then, when the operation was over, the instruments would gradually speed up until they caught up to the normal time. Operatives switched his watch and clock for our special versions before the ambassador left that day."

Welch motioned toward Shifra. "Shifra's job was to stop the ambassador, pretend to be lost, and ask him to drive her around looking for a certain address. She had to create conversations with the man, being charming and interesting for an hour, making the man think it was only fifteen minutes. All the rest of the team went ahead of them, adjusting any clocks they were going to encounter, to reenforce the idea that he had plenty of time. The theory was that when you're with a pretty girl, time seems to pass quickly."

Shifra jumped in with a comment. "It was like a science experiment. Could we really slow down the perception of time? It was so fun. But I really don't think it has to be a pretty girl. I think any time you're with someone you're interested in, you want to stay there forever. You are willing to believe that time might stand still for you." She looked at Welch for confirmation. "Don't you think, Doctor? Isn't that what our experiment showed?"

Shifra's relating the scenario to a science experiment captured Welch's thoughts. What an intriguing notion. The operation *was* like that. Welch enjoyed planning as much as he enjoyed his hobby of scientific research, but the comparison caused him to see the similarities. It endeared the mission to him even more. He thought of spending an hour with someone who had such ideas. "I'm sure you're correct."

Welch gazed for a moment at Shifra and thought of what it might have been like to be the ambassador, listening to Shifra for an hour. He could imagine time standing still. The sound of his name caused the clocks to run again. Welch realized Joshua was waiting for an answer. "I'm sorry?"

"I said, my mother told me she appreciated that your scripted instructions never called for her to dress seductively. She had dressed like a regular village girl for that scenario, and the ambassador seemed to be just as attentive. Is that what you intended?"

Welch was pleased. *She noticed my methods.* "I always believe you risk your target seeing through the ploy when a woman obviously puts her wares on display. Not every man is stupid in that regard. A woman who can hold an interesting conversation and make a man believe she is genuinely attracted to him, that is what stops the clock." Though he was answering Joshua's question, Welch could not help but glancing at Shifra with a smile. She had her gaze fixed on him.

Ibbie motioned toward Shifra with her fork.

"Besides bringing down a lot of men on the wrong side, I heard you captured the attention of some influential fellows who were on the *right* side. What made you choose Joshua's father over all your other suitors?"

Shifra gave a patient smile. "It was his mind." Her expression took a sad turn. "When people define you only by your physical appearance, you appreciate the value of thoughts. Besides that, Yuri was…a good man. I didn't see many in my line of work."

Amelia smiled across at her husband. "Joshua told me that your father wanted out even before you approached him."

Shifra affirmed it with a nod. "Yuri saw the lie of communism, and it had driven him to a hidden faith in God. He hated his work. His government was forcing him to give power to evil people. He wasn't a fighter, but he couldn't do it any longer. He determined that if God didn't free him somehow, he would kill himself to prevent them from benefiting any further from his knowledge."

Joshua regarded his mother with admiration. "But then my father had a dream about a beautiful woman coming to help him."

Shifra gave her son a grateful smile, then moved it over to Welch. "Did you know that when you were planning operation Mind Liberation, you were planning our romance?"

"A happy side benefit that God had planned."

Shifra held his eye. "I think the Lord made you a romantic, Dr. Welch. The character you created captured my Yuri's heart. He was kind enough not to be disappointed when I revealed who I really was. He was grateful for my help, but he fell in love with your creation."

It hurt to hear Shifra make such a comment. "I am sure it was what is inside you that attracted him. If there is any truth here, it is that perhaps I created opportunities for you to be who you really are. The times you were portrayed as a commodity were the deceit."

Shifra put her eyes on the tablecloth for a moment before looking up again. "You let me be who I wanted to be. Thank you."

Shifra's talk about being attracted to thoughts touched him. It made him think of his late wife Helen. *I like your thoughts,* she used to say.

Welch needed to change the subject. "We have the opportunity to do great things again. I believe God has called us together because a group like this has the potential to change the world. Each of you has been created with a unique set of talents. Thanks to Talisa's father's insight, the Lord has given the resources. Talent and resources are powerful weapons."

It was nearing 9:00 pm when Amelia announced she needed to get her brother Gabriel to bed and Joshua invited everyone to visit in the living room. The guests all expressed that it was time for them to go.

Welch moved to retrieve his coat, and caught himself looking for Shifra. She had moved to the living room. Slumped in an overstuffed chair, she looked troubled. She had been kind to everyone at the table, even after how the dinner conversation had begun. What was wrong with all the ladies this evening?

Welch found his feet leading him to stand beside her. "I want to tell you again how delighted we all are to have you here." *How do I apologize for this evening without making it worse?* "Forgive us if your past assignments have generated some questions that were less than tactful. I fear that everyone already feels comfortable with you, like you are family and they can thus ask you anything without offense. Everyone here has nothing but your best wishes at heart. I am certain of that."

"It's sweet of you to say that, Doctor…" Her face filled with a sunny grin. "May I call you Ruben?"

He was unable to refuse the request. "If you like."

"Would you be kind enough to sit and talk with me for a while?" She motioned toward the comfy chair beside her.

The prospect appealed to Welch. What other insights did she have on the past they shared—some other new way of looking at things? Things he could see better with her perspective. And he loved hearing her praise. Never had words meant more to him.

Shifra smiled her encouragement.

"Shiffy…" When Welch said it, he realized that he had been wrong. Using such a personal name did have an effect on him. He couldn't sit and have the conversation he wanted. It was breaking his heart *now*. What would happen if he lingered? "I…you are too kind."

Her eyes took on a troubled look. "I would really enjoy your company."

The words infused him, warmed him, terrified him. "Shiffy, I would love to sit and talk with you, but…"

"What's wrong?"

"You are kind to indulge me but I…you are such a woman that any man would count himself blessed at such an invitation…" Welch sighed and considered how to proceed.

"Any man but you? There is something you're not saying. Just tell me. Please be honest. I'll survive the pain better if you cut me quickly." Shifra laughed, but it had a nervous tinge to it.

Pain. "It is actually a cut to myself I am avoiding. You are correct. Honesty is best." Welch had to look away from the sweet face for a moment to plan his next statements.

When he looked back, Shifra was staring into her lap. He needed to be honest about his feelings. He prayed being candid about the situation would not cause future difficulties between them during their work. "The truth is this. You are an intriguing woman, and though I am not easily moved toward…" *Romance, affection. He needed a less intimate word.* "attraction…yet…I find that you have such an effect on me."

Shifra raised her head. She had a surprised expression and then seemed to be holding back a smile.

Welch didn't expect that. He thought he was immune to the pain caused by being laughed at, but…he needed to get this over with. "I am a pragmatic man. While I realize you could navigate a friendship between us with no danger to your…feelings, I fear I could not."

Shifra appeared to be struggling with the situation as well. "Feelings? You're saying you're attracted to me?"

I'm making it worse. He needed to end this and make his exit. "Don't be concerned that I have any imagination that you have feelings for me in the same way. I intend to keep our interactions very professional, so neither of us will be in an uncomfortable position. The reason I say this is so, in the future, you won't misinterpret my actions as anger or disappointment in your performance. I won't trouble you any more tonight, but I felt it best to get this out in the open. Thank you for listening. I will see myself out." Welch headed toward the door.

"Do you have to leave?" Shifra was up and following. "I think we should talk about this."

He wrestled himself into his coat and opened the door. He was afraid to look at her face again, but he didn't want to be rude. Turning, he saw deep concern that he wanted to relieve. "We will talk more another time. Don't think that I'm upset. I'm just tired and not communicating my best."

"Can you come by tomorrow?"

Welch didn't know how to answer. The concern in her eyes was heart piercing. *I think she genuinely cares about hurting me.* It made her more alluring. "It is a long drive from my apartment in Oklahoma City. I don't know if I will make it back tomorrow."

"Joshua and Amelia said you have an apartment here as well. It's late. Why make the drive tonight? Please stay."

It had been his original plan to grab some sleep before he went home. What if he stayed and came by and talked? What if she actually…? How easily she could upend his heart. So dangerous. Welch made the final turn to leave. "We'll see." He was out the door. If she asked again, he was done for.

Shifra pulled the curtain back and watched Welch walk away, again. She heard Amelia's quiet voice from the staircase behind her.

"Shifra? Is everything okay?"

"No. Not everything."

Amelia padded down the stairs and Shifra felt her hand on her shoulder. "What happened? Did we not do it right? Marsha, Ibbie, Talisa, they're all texting me, wanting to know how it's going."

"You were all great. Just like we scripted it. You gave me all the openings I needed to talk about who I am and who I'm not. Just like we thought, your rude questions caused him to feel bad for me, so he came to talk."

"What did you talk about?"

Shifra sighed. "I think I misread him. I don't think he's worried about my character. It's not about me not being good enough. I think he thinks *he's* not good enough. He came out and said he was attracted to me, but then said he was going to act professionally. It was hard to tell. He was so nervous, some of what he said was hard to follow. I don't think it was an act. I guess that's good news. But I couldn't get him to stay and talk. It seemed like he was going back to Oklahoma City tonight."

"When it's this late, he usually stays at his apartment here at the Institute and drives back early in the morning."

"I tried to get him to do that, but I think he's afraid of me now."

"None of this sounds like Dr. Welch. I'm trying to envision him nervous." Amelia giggled through a tightly pressed smile. "He must really be smitten." The statement came out as a laugh.

"Hmm." Shifra tried to share the amusement, but her own laugh was subdued. "You would think this would get easier with age. I think it's harder. It's been so long since I've tried to have a relationship. I feel like I'm back in high school." That brought a laugh, and Amelia joined her.

Amelia reined in her amusement. "So what's the next step in your plot, since the rest of us are leaving for Europe? The Sanders will be here, but Talisa doesn't have much of a poker face, so I doubt she would make a good solo coconspirator. Luke will be back eventually, but he would be *too* good at it. Who knows what mischief he would cause?"

"I think I need to stop plotting and start praying like I should have done in the first place. I'm sure God will come up with a masterful plan of His own. And if it doesn't include Ruben Welch, I shouldn't be chasing after something He doesn't want for me. I just had such high hopes."

Chapter 6

THE FORMER PLUM ISLAND ANIMAL DISEASE CENTER, PLUM ISLAND, NEW YORK

Roshard disliked the labs. They always made him feel like something was crawling on him. *I should have made him meet me in the conference room.* But Roshard had learned that every interruption only slowed the work of the man everyone knew as Er Koch—The Cook, in German. Popping into the lab for an update was more effective, and Roshard was all about results. Er Koch was slow at everything, and Roshard had no background to argue when the man told him that DNA science was not something that could be rushed. Er Koch had produced wonders when given enough time, so Roshard indulged him.

He tried to cut through the jargon of Er Koch's

specialty and sum up what the man was saying. "So this sample you need, will that have to be blood?"

Er Koch stopped one of his assistants with a hand on his shoulder. "I know they probably taught you to flick the sample like that in whatever school you came from, but here we use the vortexer. Shortcuts get poor results." Er Koch pointed the young man toward a machine on a counter.

Turning toward Roshard, Er Koch spoke like he was giving a lecture. "Any bodily fluid except urine and sweat. Tissue cells containing DNA can be found in those, but they break down quickly and bacteria can grow, which has its own DNA. Neither is a good source. Blood and saliva are the most practical to obtain. Blood would be more efficacious. Bring me blood—at least 3 milliliters."

"How much is that?"

Er Koch took a small syringe from a rack and handed it to Roshard. "Fill that."

Roshard voiced his concerns. "That much blood will be difficult without raising suspicions. How much saliva do you need?"

"Saliva needs to contain enough tissue cells. Sometimes it does, sometimes it doesn't. If you don't give me adequate samples, I can't promise anything." The man turned on Roshard. "You come here and ask me what I need, and I tell you. If you want to take your chances, bring me what you can get and I'll see what we can get out of it. Don't blame me if it's not enough." Er Koch ambled off, shaking his head.

Roshard liked the scientist's style but not his

disrespect. The day his mind started slipping, they'd use him to experiment on.

Chapter 7

VILLA FLORENTINE HOTEL, LYON, FRANCE

Doctor Welch is on the phone, sir."

"Put him through." Joshua sat up in the patio chair and glanced around to be sure no one was listening. The beeps told him the Institute operator was transferring the encrypted call to his cell.

The operator indicated the procedure was complete by saying, "Your call is connected now."

"What's going on, Ruben?"

"Nothing significant. How was your trip?"

"Tiring, especially with a little one. I'm glad we were all there to help Marsha with the baby. But we made it to the hotel in Lyon, so we're resting now. I think I'm the only one awake. You should see this view. They keep the cathedral lit up like it's on fire."

"I think I remember that."

"Okay, Ruben, when you say *nothing significant*, that means something. You sound like you're outdoors."

"Nothing I can't handle, but it is something I need to make you aware of. I'm just down the sidewalk from my house because I haven't swept it for bugs yet. Someone broke in. I have them on my hidden camera. They were masked and portrayed it as a burglary. There are some things missing, though, that suggest otherwise—a used drinking cup, my toothbrush."

"Sounds like they're after your DNA."

"That's what I was thinking. I must be on someone's radar, and they are looking to discover who I really am."

"That won't get them far. All your biometrics come back to your Professor Welch identity. Who do you think it is?"

"Someone who has a source that is telling them I might be something more than a college professor. The question is, who is the source, and what are they trying to link me to? My only trackable connection to the Institute is through Talisa's father and the native artifacts he donated to the college museum. The curator is a friend, and even after the story broke about the treasure Michael found, we have kept those donations labeled anonymous. It would be hard to trace it back, but we need to be on guard."

"You think the Institute might be under suspicion?"

Amelia came out of the French doors and onto the tiled patio, followed by Marsha carrying Eva. Amelia fixed Joshua with a questioning expression.

Covering the phone, he told them, "It's Ruben. Someone broke into his apartment, but he's okay."

Welch continued his course of thought. "It's unlikely, but caution is always best."

Both women stood waiting with concerned expressions.

"Absolutely. I feel bad that we're not there. We're not on the hunt yet. I think we should postpone this and fly home. "

Welch was already objecting before Joshua finished. "No. There's no need for anything like that. The better course of action is for me to respond like any civilian would. The most likely scenario is that they are waiting to see how I react. There's nothing you could do that wouldn't add to any suspicions someone has about me. Besides, by the time you returned, whatever is going to occur will have already transpired. Your pursuit of Becker's people is more important. I'll use our security if I feel in physical danger."

Ruben paused for a noisy truck to go by, then continued. "The camera showed my visitors wore gloves and probably didn't leave any evidence behind. I'll still use the new OCT forensic scanner our friends in India sold us. This latest version looks for fingerprints and other trace evidence. Since it's non-contact, I can capture images of any prints it finds and then call the police like any college professor would. They can come and throw their powder around, and I will not have inhibited them in any way."

Joshua felt uncomfortable being so far away, but he

understood what Ruben was saying. "All right, but call if anything new happens. As far as the Institute goes, if you call Jim, he'll brief his security team to be more alert to anything suspicious. Our perimeter's a little weak. He could put on some extra men so they can do more patrols."

"Hmm. That's good thinking, but we might confirm someone's suspicions if we look too heavily guarded. The motion alarms and hidden cameras around the perimeter are lower profile. Jim can have someone review the last several days' worth of video to see if we have any certain vehicles passing frequently. I'll talk to him about bringing on the extra guards, but skip the extra patrols. I think we should patrol less. Here's something I was going to suggest to you and haven't had a chance. Deer stands all around the perimeter. Put the extra guards in hunting gear and have them occupy the stands. We'll make hunting therapy another part of our service, but the slots will always be filled if anyone inquires."

"Eema was right. You do come up with masterpieces."

"God is good at giving me ideas. Your mother is too kind to me. She is an impressive lady. I can see where you get your winning ways."

"She still wants to sit down with you and swap old stories."

"I'm sure she will find more fruitful ways to spend her time. I should probably stick close to home over here if they're watching me. I don't want to slip up and lead them to the base."

Flimsy excuses. The doctor knew how to keep from being tailed. Maybe his mother was right. Joshua had to ask. "Are you trying to avoid her?"

Silence on the line. "Your mother is charming. Too charming for an old man. She would fit better with someone younger."

"She pointed out to me that you are from the same generation."

Welch again took time to answer. "Yes, but I was old in my youth and she is forever young. Our outlooks will be much different."

"Ruben, you're judging her by surface appearance and first impressions. You need to dig a little deeper."

The hesitation continued. "Let's give it a little time. I have a lot on my mind with this recent development."

Welch's behavior was unusual to Joshua. "Funny, that's what I told her. Give it a little time. You know what she said? She said that's all she wanted from *you*, a little time."

The other end of the line was quiet for several moments. When he spoke, Welch sounded melancholy. "We'll see." Not what Joshua was used to hearing from him.

They said their goodbyes and Welch hung up. After he gave the ladies a full update, Joshua dialed his mother. The phone rang several times before she answered. "Hello."

"How you doing, Eema?"

"I'm all right."

"You sound upset."

"Sorry, I was on the phone…with Rahab."

"How is she doing?"

"Oh, you know. Not handling the move well. She liked it when I was near, even if she didn't come over often. You know how she can be."

"We'll have to have her down to the mock house to help her feel a part of things."

"Not until I get settled a little more. I don't want to add any more stress on Dr. Welch right now. He might start regretting he invited me."

"He knows your worth. I fear what is standing in the way of your being friends is he thinks you might be dissatisfied with the relationship. He's not a man who suffers from self-esteem issues or false modesty. I'm sure he is trying to separate his own feelings and be practical about it."

"Did he say something to you, too?"

"Uh huh. Something about you needing someone younger."

"I don't know what I have to do…I take that back. I don't know what God is going to have to do. I've been praying He makes His will known to both of us."

"You know who you might talk to about him is Talisa. The two of them talk a lot. He helped Talisa when she was in a bad time. I'm sure she would love a chance to return the favor."

"I might do that."

"Well, I've got a good reason for you to get together. The reason I called is that there has been a new development concerning Dr. Welch. He just called me and said that someone broke into his apartment. He's fine, but it looks like it was someone in the business who is looking for intel on him, trying to get his DNA, that type of thing. It may be the group that backed Becker. Welch is going to call Jim, our security man, and have him make some changes around there. I thought you might want to get with Gretchen and see if there is any intelligence in cyber space. They may be onto Dr. Welch somehow."

"I wouldn't think he would have left himself open to anything like that."

"Perhaps it is just someone fishing and what they find will lay it to rest. But we need to prepare, just in case."

"Of course we do. What are the new measures?"

Joshua explained what he and Dr. Welch had discussed.

"Okay. I'll visit with Talisa and Gretchen. That will give me something to do. Keep me up to date on your situation. I'm not sure Dr. Welch will. I think I pushed too much and now he's reluctant to talk to me."

"I got the feeling it's more himself he didn't trust. I think he's quite impressed with you."

"Either way, it's the same result. I'm wandering around this gorgeous place with nothing to do but read. But I need to quit ruining your honeymoon. You guys have a good time before you have to get started on your roundup. And be careful."

"Don't worry. Amelia and I are having the honeymoon I promised her. Hevel and Ibbie, will be doing the groundwork right now. Gabriel will probably be with them much of the time. He always wants to be involved and Ibbie keeps finding creative ways to use his talent. Marsha will work with the European authorities to process the intel that they develop. When she can't do that by phone or email, we will watch the baby while she goes out. Amelia gets to practice being a mommy and supervise me being a daddy. We'll be so ready for our own kids when they come, there won't be any challenge left."

The chuckle from Shifra was not subdued.

"Just kidding." Joshua was glad he was able to get a laugh from his mother. "I still worry I'm going to strap my holster on Eva instead of a diaper."

"Well, considering her genetics and how cute she is now, that might be necessary when she's sixteen."

Joshua snickered. "Considering her mother, I'd be more worried about the boys." He turned to smirk at Marsha.

Marsha lifted her chin at him. "She'll be ready."

"I'm going to let you guys get back to honeymooning."

"Amelia and Marsha are right here. Let's pray together, Eema."

Chapter 8

THE HOLLENBECK INSTITUTE FOR PEOPLE WITH SPECIAL NEEDS AND SPECIAL ABILITIES, LAKE GALLANT, OKLAHOMA

Shifra marveled at how Talisa moved through the water. She melded with the dolphins that swam alongside her in the huge aquarium pool.

Teddy came from a side door. Janie bounced in with him, but stayed behind Teddy in a shy manner.

Teddy's T-shirt said, **I asked her**. Janie wore a matching color shirt, and when one of Teddy's movements gave Shifra a view of it, she read, **I said yes**.

The young man's smile was crowding the rest of his face. "Remember me, I'm Teddy. You like the dolphins?" His voice was loud and friendly.

"I like them a lot. Do you get to swim with them?"

The young man nodded, keeping the smile. "I swim with them and so does Janie." He laughed with excessive enthusiasm.

Janie took up the guffaw. "He almos dwown with 'em. I hadda pull him out."

Their laughter was a compelling force that Shifra had no choice but to join. "Oh, no. How did that happen?"

The girl had ventured to just behind Teddy's left shoulder. "He fo'gets to kick an sinks."

Turning, the man thrashed his head back and forth in objection while he pointed at Janie and cackled. "Uh uh. You was tickling me. It was your fault."

"Oo still fo'got to kick. Tha' part of the twaining. Oo can't let anything distwact you."

"Janie's teaching me how to swim. But she's better at drowning me."

The girl grabbed his sides. "No, I' not."

Teddy began to dodge around the poolside with the girl in pursuit.

"Hey, you two," Talisa's voice of authority intervened as she crawled out of the pool. "No roughhousing or running around in here. You'll crack your skulls, and I'll have to throw you in for fish food."

Janie gaped. "Oo said fiss, Tee. They not fiss."

Teddy pointed his finger at Talisa. "Oh, she got you Miss Tee, I mean Mrs. Tee. You called them what we're not supposed to call them."

Talisa smirked as she grabbed a towel off a poolside chair. "I wouldn't dirty up the aquarium. I'd throw you two in Lake Gallant and let the catfish have you."

Janie pointed at Teddy. "They 'pit him out."

Teddy wagged his head. "Uh uh. They'd spit *you* out."

Talisa ended the duel. "Knock it off, you two slackers. Go get some fish and feed the ones who do the real work around here."

"Okay. I 'ike feeding." Janie took off taking short, quick steps, her slender feet slapping on the concrete.

Teddy followed. "I'll carry the heavy buckets."

Shifra let her laugh subside. "Well, that was fun."

Toweling herself, Talisa rolled her eyes with a grin. "Yeah, the first few hours of it. Then I have to send them over to the indoor water park to let them torment the lifeguards. It's why we have to pay those kids so much. Forget that they're all trained to help people with special needs. It's really hazard pay. "

"I saw the shirts. Do they mean what it sounds like?"

"Oh, yeah. My nut of a husband got Teddy set on having those printed up. It constantly reminds me I have to plan a Valentine's wedding. And help Janie plan their house we're going to build next door to ours. You know when they say that God doesn't give us more than we can handle? I find He routinely gives *me* more than I can handle. He must like seeing me because I'm constantly coming to Him, begging for help."

"I can relate to that. But congratulations."

"Thanks. This *is* an answer to my prayers for Janie. We should all be so blessed as to have relationships as sweet and effortless as those two. But honestly I'll be a little lost when they move out. Even if they're next door, it won't be the same. They've taught me as much as I've taught them."

"I remember. My son, Caleb, left me too soon, but I grew so much during the I had him. You let me know when you need help or you just want to talk, but I don't know if I'll be able to keep up with you." Shifra tipped her head toward the aquarium. "I was watching you swim. Do you have some fish in your DNA?"

Talisa drew her eyebrows together. "No. They've been trying to teach that fish-to-humans thing for years, but it doesn't hold water."

"I didn't mean—."

"I know. I've been hanging around my husband too much."

Shifra smiled. "I fell for that one. I heard about your husband's legendary sense of humor."

Talisa motioned her head where Teddy and Janie had gone. "Between those two and him, why do you think I hang around with dolphins?" She grinned. "Luke's away at a four-week training course right now. He's all excited to be part of the team around here. He's only been gone a couple of days and I miss him already." She smirked. "I'm stuck wrangling this pack by myself. I figured Amelia sent you over to check and see if I was still alive. I'm in the water so much, I rarely carry a phone. You have to call the office if you're going to get me. It rings over the loudspeaker."

Shifra shook her head. "I just came by to visit if you had time."

"Sure. It'll be a couple of hours before we have another therapy session. We like to give the crew plenty of breaks. Don't we?" Talisa reached, and a dolphin wiggled up in the water to get a nose rub.

Janie and Teddy returned with five other little bodies clamoring around them. Behind them trailed a pair of older teen girls, trying to monitor the young ones. Talisa introduced the teens as part of their team of sitters who helped watch over the kids.

There was no mistaking Eve's children, as she had heard them called. Joshua had explained the mutation experiments the DNAble scientist, Becker, had used to alter the children's DNA. The little bodies were topped with heads that were like a large adult skull fused to a child's face. The cheeks narrowed down to tiny, pointed little chins. Their little ears pointed out as well. The thin, hooked noses were one of the most distinguishing features.

Talisa was acting as director again. "Now, be careful. Janie, make sure everyone gets equal time to feed someone. And remember, not too much. They need to appreciate their rewards during the next session." She motioned toward a table in a room with a glass window that looked out at the aquarium. "We can supervise from in there where we can talk."

In the room, Shifra took a chair. "So how is the children's mother, Eve? Joshua told me about the situation."

"Better than could be. She and the kids live in a home close to the medical center. We have teams of helpers around the clock. She still ends up in the ICU sometimes. It's been a battle to keep all her systems functioning while Dr. Malik's team tries to encourage her DNA to reconstruct itself. Her genetics were abnormal from birth because of Becker's tampering."

The unique circumstance was so foreign to Shifra, she said the only thing that came to mind. "I can only imagine how that has been for everyone."

Talisa brightened. "Dr. Malik always says God's blueprint is still there. Becker just tore some pieces out and spliced others in the wrong places. Malik's trying to reverse that. We keep praying. Every day she's still with us is a miracle. You know how people say we should count each day as a gift. Eve lives that out."

Shifra nodded. After a moment of silence, she felt it was appropriate to move on. "I also came because Joshua suggested I come down in person to tell you that someone broke into Ruben's apartment. Ruben is all right. It looks like someone was trying to get his DNA to find out who he is."

Talisa looked shocked. "They're after Dr. Welch. Wow." She took the chair beside Shifra. "I would never have seen that coming. He always seems so calmly untouchable. I didn't think anyone would ever suspect him of being a covert agent. I never would have the first time I met him. He was so good at playing the eccentric scientist when we first met."

Shifra moved her head in agreement. "I had the same feeling about him. He still seems in control of it all." Shifra explained the changes that were going to be implemented.

Talisa's face remained troubled. "So he thinks the

Institute might be in danger of being discovered?"

Shifra laid a calming hand on her arm. "Not really. But it's good to take precautions."

Talisa looked out at the activities around the pool. "Sorry, I guess I'm being selfish. This is what I love. I am so blessed. It doesn't seem real some days. Luke and I are trying to give back in whatever ways we can."

She faced Shifra. "I know God has his hand on all of it. We hope your team can make a difference. I experienced evil up close and personal, but I had no idea how much of it there is in the world until I started sitting in on some of the team briefings. When I heard everything your son and the others had discovered at DNAble, it was too much. I had to quit going. But I'm with you in spirit." Talisa pointed at the gaggle. "Look what God was up to through all that. He makes beautiful things out of the ugliness."

Shifra patted her hand. "Yes, he does. I think we can make a difference. We have good leadership. Joshua told me that even though none of you knew it at the time, Dr. Welch had designed the plan to take down DNAble. He is an incredible man. It is an honor to be working with him."

Talisa pointed at Shifra. "He said Joshua had to improvise a lot with what they discovered, so you have raised a remarkable son as well. It's why Dr. Welch wanted the whole team so badly. Everyone did an amazing job."

"It sounds like you and Dr. Welch talk a lot."

"He helped me through a dark time. We've been friends ever since." She gave a grin. "The conversations don't usually run real deep around our place."

Shifra nodded in silent understanding.

"Don't get me wrong. I wouldn't trade it, but I needed an outlet."

Shifra sighed. "I envy you. For years, I was part of the missions Dr. Welch created. I love how he thinks. I want to sit and talk with him, but I think I scared him off and don't know how to turn that around. Joshua suggested you might be able to help."

"My relationship with Ruben is an interesting one. God brought me to him when I was depressed and searching for all the wrong things. But his affections weren't anything I was after. I needed his ear and his advice. I think that's why he felt free to talk with me. I was safe."

"Safe from what?"

Talisa gazed upwards and searched for the words. "Romantic entanglements." She appeared ready to tell something unpleasant. "It was a high school thing. He got picked on a lot for his size and looks. You know how cruel kids are. But there was a pretty girl that convinced him she liked him because he was so smart. She strung him along while he helped her pass her classes. While he was working on her assignments, she was out with other guys. Ruben didn't go to parties or games, so she made no attempt to hide what she was doing, even bragged about it like she was clever. All the kids knew but him. When graduation was nearing, Ruben wanted to impress her, so he made a public declaration. She made her own, making it his fault for not realizing he wasn't in her league. You can imagine the impact that had."

"But later he was married. Didn't that heal the wound?"

"I don't know. Maybe scarred over is a better term than healed. It's not that he's still injured… He's a practical man. He's capable of great caring, but he's also capable of great self-control. I'm sure the incident stung, but instead of becoming depressed, he developed a life strategy. He decided the fault *was* his because he let beauty deceive him. He embraced the part of Proverbs 31 that says, 'Charm is deceitful, and beauty is vain: but a woman who fears the LORD, she shall be praised.'"

Shifra's mind was opened. "He became suspicious of beauty."

"More than that. He *spurns* beauty. Not the person. As long as there is no danger of an attraction forming, he feels safe to have a friendship. But when he went looking for a bride…he showed me a picture of her and…" Talisa looked as if she hated herself for even having the thoughts she had. "I'm sure she was a lovely woman inside. She must have been because it seemed like he loved her very much and they were happy. But…he definitely avoided any possibility of being deceived by beauty."

"So, I'm handicapped in this race by my face."

"Very eloquently said." Talisa gestured toward the rest of Shifra. "But I think it's more than just your face."

Shifra smirked. "Thanks, I guess."

Talisa chuckled. "That actually makes me realize that I'm still not getting it completely right. This is a paraphrase version of how he explained it to me. 'Since I know that you could not be attracted to me and since I am not attracted to your beauty, I think we can safely carry on a friendship.' I know that sounds like a putdown, but I'm sure what he was saying was, you're nice looking, but it doesn't affect me."

Talisa gestured with both hands to emphasize the next part. "And I have seen that he is, in reality, unmoved by beauty. Ruben and I used to discuss strategies of how to use my inheritance over lunch."

Talisa's face was a mixture of humor and disgust recalling the situation. "It got around that Ruben was going to come out wealthy as well. Some ladies in town decided he was their ticket to the life they deserved. They put everything into impressing him."

Shifra envisioned the lengths to which some of her sex might have gone to gain a part of the fortune. "Suddenly it became a contest and Welch was the prize."

"Exactly. It was embarrassing. He had to stop doing anything in the area. Which was better because he worried about people connecting him with the Institute, and he didn't want that. I circulated the story that he was representing the college in establishing the historical value of what my father discovered. And there was some truth to that. We did discuss it. I still had to put a few women in their place who kept asking me about him."

Talisa shook her head like she needed to get back to

the point. "But the reason I told you all that was during that time, I never saw Dr. Welch affected by beauty. And there were some well-equipped little actresses in that group. It didn't seem to be a struggle for him."

"And now here I come. One more woman trying to hook him."

"I don't think so. From what I saw at dinner the other night, I think you have a different problem."

Shifra was more than curious. "What's that?"

"I think you have penetrated his defenses. I think he finds you attractive. Dangerously attractive. He's at risk of falling, but he still has the idea that you could never be attracted to him in any lasting way. From what I know of him, he would approach a problem like that honestly and practically. He would avoid the danger."

"He said something like that, and after you've explained his reasoning, it makes more sense. So what can I do?"

Talisa examined her. "I have to ask, because I care for him. *Are* you attracted to him in a way that's going to last?"

Shifra gazed at the tabletop in thought. "The better I get to know him," she looked up, "more than ever. What a man."

"The only thing I can tell you is what I learned when Luke and I had our trouble. Unless the Lord builds the house, the laborers work in vain. God's going to have to do it."

"I had come to that conclusion, but I guess I started getting desperate again."

“You wanna pray?”
“Please.”

85

Chapter 9

THE FORMER PLUM ISLAND ANIMAL DISEASE CENTER, PLUM ISLAND, NEW YORK

Roshard walked into his office and closed the door. It had been a busy week. He was satisfied his bold move against the old man had been the right decision. Now he could concentrate on Welch without Schmidt looking over his shoulder. As long as his assault against Welch and his team went well, he was set up to take over the organization. There was no one above him as strong as the old man.

An added benefit was that everyone under him who suspected what he had done was well motivated. Er Koch had worked miracles. He had extracted Welch's DNA from root bulbs on hair the team obtained from Welch's bathroom trash. With that, Er Koch keyed his virus to the professor's genetic signature. It was the fastest he had seen the scientist do anything.

Roshard had his secure cell phone in his hand and dialed. He needed to make sure Er Koch's new creation was deployed correctly. He also wanted to back up his plan with some fail-safes.

The voice that answered was all business. "Go ahead."

"Did you get what I sent you?"

"Why do you ask me things you already know?"

Rico Kondo was unpredictable and defiant, but he was one of the best special contractors in the business. That was enough at the moment. Roshard tempered himself before he responded. "Because I want everything verified. Yes, the pilot said he handed it off to you. Now you have verified it. With something like this, I won't take chances."

"I heard the big boss is dead."

Roshard considered how he knew. The pilot.

The man interrupted the thought. "It wasn't the pilot. I have other sources…I also verify everything."

Roshard had ceased being unnerved by the man's ability to guess what he was thinking. Roshard tried to sound unmoved. "It was a sudden illness. His age was a problem."

"Not a problem for *you*."

"We are not releasing any information about his passing at this time. The organization doesn't need the publicity. I hope your source realizes that the leaking of secure information, no matter who it is to, is a serious violation. Even if you won't tell me, I will be launching an investigation and will deal harshly with any violators. Your compassion for your friend should inspire you not to encourage them in behavior that could have grave consequences."

"I didn't say it was a friend. It's a source, and my sources are loyal to me. You can't stop information from spreading. It's like a disease. You can't control it."

"I have ways of controlling the things that are important to our organization, and I will use them. Do you have information from any of the possible Welch connections the computer identified? How about the one you said you were developing? How long is this grooming going to take? We might be needing someone on the inside soon."

"I'm working with them the way it needs to be done. If that person knew they were betraying these people rather than protecting them, it would all be over. I'll call them later, when I know my source can be alone."

"You're still not going to tell me which one you're working with?

"No."

"I gave you the list."

"I find the less people know about what I'm doing the better. Keeps things more secure and it's extra insurance for me. It's a ruthless business. If you thought anyone could do it better, you'd be talking to them."

"Any information you get, I need to know right away. There are a lot of factors in play, and the outcome of one affects the others. Now about the package you were given. It contains a prepared device. I sent the installation instructions to your phone with the standard encryption."

"I have a better way of installing it. When your own people come down with sudden illnesses, it concerns me. Always remember, I'm a powerful asset but a dangerous liability. Even if I'm dead."

Roshard considered the threat. He doubted it was idle, considering the source. This was the reason the old man had sent out the directive to stop using Kondo. He couldn't be controlled. "The way you're planning had better work exactly as the prescribed method. We can't afford mistakes in any form. It could be dangerous to you, both professionally and physically."

The voice snapped back at Roshard. "Are you done?"

Roshard wouldn't waste more time. They understood each other. Kondo would do his job, or Roshard never would have chosen him. "Let me know the moment it's installed. I won't send the surveillance team in until you're clear. They can never know you were there."

"No one will know. After you sent me the profile on Professor Welch, I made it my business to know everything about him. He'll be wary since the break-in, but I'll make the installation while he's teaching at the college. That's the other reason my method is better. It's self-contained and I can install it on the exterior without making entry. It takes only a minute or two and doesn't require tools. I'll be done and gone before anyone has time to take notice."

Chapter 10

OKLAHOMA CITY, OKLAHOMA

Welch thanked the police dispatcher and ended the call. He glanced in his rearview mirror again. Okay, now the Chevy Tahoe was behind him. That made four cars tailing him, alternating following, running parallel, breaking off, and circling around to set up behind him again. Pretty typical. He suspected they had been on him since he left his apartment.

It was a standard and effective technique. But Welch was on to them. He began taking more turns, making it look natural, stopping at a shop here and there.

He purchased a hot tea at a fast food window to soothe the tickle that had developed in his throat. Making his turns look planned, he logged each vehicle that was following him in his memory. He made sure he knew as much about them as he could.

At the pharmacy drive-through, he grabbed a bottle of ibuprofen. It had been some time since he had been involved in the hands-on of espionage. He hadn't realized it would strain him so much. He was feeling the ache of the stress. Another sign that age had crept up on him. He could never keep up with Shiffy. She moved as if the years hadn't touched her.

The group tailing him was devoting a lot of resources to build a profile on him. He must have moved up on their threat scale. It was time for him to disappear.

He had prepared for such a time. Still, a sadness fell over him like a heavy blanket on a warm night. *Pity. I enjoyed being a college professor. Such bright young people. It was a pleasure to help guide them.* He had even been able to introduce some of them to Jesus. "Lord, please do not let my departure erode their faith. Hold them fast through the coming times."

He was about to tarnish the stellar reputation of Professor Ruben Welch, leaving his colleagues to cover for him at such a crucial time. It was the first day of finals week. *I guess it's finals for us all.* His leaving was going to cause a lot of problems, and a lot of speculation. But it couldn't be helped. The college would go on without him as life always does. It would adjust and his memory would fade much sooner than his ego would like to imagine.

Brief scenes from the life he had led for so long flitted through his mind. *It will be harder to do my research.* But in the business of subterfuge, a person shouldn't get too attached to his current identity. He had left behind a number over the years.

The Christian life was like that as well. Never get too attached to this world. It's only a temporary assignment. Someday he would leave all the facades behind and step into his true existence.

His thoughts shifted to wondering who might be after him. It had been a long time since he was on anyone's radar. Perhaps he had gotten a little too comfortable in his position at Oklahoma State.

Was it some enemy from his past that finally found him, or something more recent? *Probably the latter.* Powerful organizations such as the one connected with the DNAble lab wouldn't take such a hit without trying to find the person responsible. He had no illusions that he was immune to discovery, but he couldn't determine where he might have slipped up. He was always careful. The other possibility was even more unthinkable. Could someone he knew have betrayed him?

It was a question for later. What mattered now was an adversary had discovered where he lived. At least where he used to live. He wouldn't be going back. There was nothing there he couldn't leave behind. He had planned his exit from the first day he had taken on this latest persona.

As he drove, he called the Institute.

The electronic voice asked, "What extension, please?"

Welch spoke to his speech-to-text program. "Alphanumeric entry…" He gave the twelve digit code and then the code of the day, using identifiers specific to him, added and subtracted from the date.

A receptionist came online. "Good morning. How may I help you?"

Welch gave the designated question. "Is this the line to order fresh fish?"

The woman returned with the response. "It is, but our catch has been very poor lately. We only have snapper."

Welch took a moment to recall what response snapper required. "I have heard that it takes three of those to make a meal."

"Thank you, sir. To whom do you wish to speak?"

"Fifteen, please."

"I'll connect you now."

After a moment, Joshua came online. "Good evening from France, Ruben. Is everything okay?"

Welch made a turn and watched as the tail vehicle went straight in an effort to look like it hadn't been following him. The vehicle that had been behind that car turned after him instead. "There's a team tailing me. I'm going to abandon my residence. They probably picked me up there since they know it. I have all vehicles visually identified and tags on a couple. I don't think they're government, but they operate professionally, so it's doubtful the tags are registered to real people."

There was the sound of Joshua shifting in his seat. "I'm beginning to think we shouldn't have left. I hope this hasn't been a red herring. It seems conveniently timed."

"They still act like they're fishing. If their main mission today was to terminate me, they would have tried by now. They must be trying to learn more about me—find out who I'm with. If they know my home, it's certain they know my work as well. They are investing serious resources to follow me. That and the break-in indicate I am being fully targeted. They must consider me a threat and will keep pressing."

Welch paused. The decision he was about to voice came after careful consideration. Still, saying it out loud was making a proclamation of monumental proportions. "To allow that to continue might jeopardize the Institute. When they have reached the end of the information they can gain, I doubt they will consider it productive to walk away. At that point, they will move to termination. There is no value in postponing what I must do. I'm going to terminate Ruben Welch myself."

"That's a major step, Ruben, but I can't disagree with your assessment. What do you need?"

"Nothing. The situation does not afford me the luxury of a graceful exit. There will be no goodbyes. I'm proceeding to the storage unit. I wanted to let you know before I did it."

"There are people I can call. We've got friends in the feds that would help. Give me a little time to get a hold of someone."

"No. I need to make my move soon. If it starts to look like I'm stalling, it may cause them to escalate rather than give me a chance to escape or bring in reinforcements."

"You could go Christmas shopping at the mall and make the time passage look natural."

"I already bought your gift so you can quit hinting."

Joshua's comeback was quick. "Just one?"

Welch gave a quiet chuckle in his throat that started him coughing.

"You okay?" The amusement in Joshua's voice was obviously to mask real concern.

"Don't make an old man laugh like that. I've been out of the real game too long to laugh and elude at the same time."

Welch checked his mirror to see which vehicle was behind him after the last turn. "Despite your expanding Christmas list, I don't want to risk leaving my car anymore. Four vehicles with two agents in each are not good odds, and being on foot is not an advantage for my old body. You don't realize you're getting old until it hits you. I've provided a cushion for myself. I called the police about two people on foot having a disturbance around the storage business. A unit patrolling the area will put them on their best behavior while I make the switch."

"Why didn't you tell them it was your pursuers having the disturbance? If they stopped them, that would give you a better advantage."

"I don't want to risk the officer contacting them. They might connect it with me and do something desperate. No use some local getting hurt over this."

"Be careful and keep us posted."

"Okay. I'm going to concentrate on driving. Eat some French food for me so you can describe it to me since you took the best French cook with you." Welch disconnected.

Fifteen minutes more of driving and Welch turned into the entrance to the KeepSake self-storage units. The immediate tail continued past Welch. The secondary unit pulled into a laundromat right before it got to his position as if that was their destination. They parked where they could view him.

Welch entered the code on the entry keypad and the security gate opened. He drove in but lingered just inside until the gate was closed completely. A police car cruised by.

Driving to the back of the lot, Welch parked between two lines of storage units where he could not be seen from the street. Residential backyards and a wooded area surrounded the units. There was no way for the surveillance team to watch what he was about to do from their vehicles. Welch had planned it carefully.

The surveillance team wouldn't want to give themselves away if Welch was coming right back out, especially with the police in the area. To get eyes on him, they'd have to jump fences or run through woods. By the time they decided they needed to do that, he would be gone.

Welch unlocked one of the units, revealing a white pickup with ladders on a rack and placards on the side advertising *Louie's Overhead Door Service*. In a few minutes, he had his possessions out of the car and into the new vehicle.

Inside the storage unit, Welch pulled a set of white

coveralls from the truck and put them on over his clothes. Climbing into the cab, Welch pushed a button on an apparatus in the passenger seat. A small electric motor hummed as a life-size manikin inflated in the seat beside him. A realistic looking head rested on top of the inflatable body, which was also in worker's garb. "Hello, Louie. How has business been?" Welch completed the transformation by cramming the shag on his head into a cap like the one Louie wore.

Flipping a switch at Louie's hip, Welch activated his new partner's robotic head. Louie turned to engage Welch in conversation, faced front again, then looked out the window.

Welch fired up the truck and drove it out. He drove his own car into the unit and locked it inside. In a couple minutes, Louie was checking traffic as they left the storage facility and pulled onto the street, heading away from the laundromat.

They had to pass one of the surveillance teams, which was parked down the block. Welch turned toward the manikin. Louie's face was pleasant in an artificial sort of way. "I'll just keep looking at you, Louie, until we get past these gentlemen, so they don't see our faces. Two handsome fellows like us are hard to miss."

Welsh continued to address him. "I want to thank you for being here for me, my friend. I believe they think I am talking to you and you are listening. The whole affair begs the question, who is the biggest fool?" A chuckle brought another round of coughing. He did his best not to swerve and draw attention to the pickup.

Turning onto another street, Welch checked his mirror. No signs of anyone following. He would circle a few blocks just to be sure. He winced, putting his hand on his chest. "Louie, I think this is more than a tickle in my throat."

Radley watched Welch's pickup on the drone's monitor. Launching it when Welch went into the storage units was the perfect call. He got high above the units in time to zoom in the video and catch the last of Welch's vehicle switch.

The surveillance team's units had all lost contact. That was how Radley wanted it. While they tailed Welch, he had tailed them. Switching it up, always following the unit that was the farthest from Welch. He was playing the same game they were, only in reverse. They had occupied Welch's attention while he hung back where Welch wouldn't detect him. They had served his purpose, but now they would only be in the way. He was glad Welch had ditched them.

Welch was being cautious, driving a little way and then circling a block to look for anyone following him. Radley stayed out of sight two blocks away. Now, however, the pickup had sped up. He had to get moving before the drone was out of range. It had an image-lock on Welch's pickup. The drone would follow automatically, but he had to keep in range so he could watch the camera to see where the truck went and control the drone if needed.

It had been too long since he'd heard anything from the boss. The man wasn't answering his private line. He had called the company with a ruse that should have gotten him through to the old man, but he was informed the boss was out sick. *I should have gone to New York when we first talked.* The old man was a shrewd operator, but he was old and not as aware as he once was.

Now all Radley could do was complete the mission. Then he would go to the headquarters and find out what happened to the old man. He also needed to fulfill his last order concerning Roshard.

Sarah was in the seat beside him. He was surprised by her presence but didn't react. *If she comes from my imagination, how could I be surprised?* He wasn't schizophrenic, even though his disorder had a similar sounding name. Schizoid Personality Disorder didn't produce hallucinations.

Radley glanced at Sarah as he drove. *She's changing.* She had been coming to him for months, maybe over half a year. More frequently lately. How long had it been since he'd escaped…two years?

He tried to remember her before. To him, she was always pretty. Her soft brown curls rested on her shoulders. Her hair had been shorter. Athena hadn't wanted to mess with it when Sarah was a child. *She looks better, healthier.* Maybe it was how he wanted to see her.

She turned and looked at him with gentle, probing

blue eyes. "What are you going to do?" Her presence didn't feel like imagination. What if it was some kind of trap? *Am I exposing myself talking to her?* He didn't know how. He'd take the chance.

"I'm afraid the old man is dead. Someone should make it right."

She returned her gaze to the front. "Why so much death, Peter?"

Radley turned to stay parallel with the path Welch was taking. Sarah's question taunted him for an answer. "There's a lot of death in the world. I have a profession that puts me in its path."

Sarah shook her head. "We *choose* our paths."

He knew she would forgive him for his next statement. "I thought God always has a plan."

Sarah followed his eyes to the video feed from the drone. "It's like what you're doing." She pointed to the image of Welch's truck, which was a block over and just ahead of them. "When we are on the wrong path, God's always right there, moving alongside us, encouraging us to turn and come to Him. All we have to do is cross over. We're never stuck. We can always choose to change, start a new life at any moment."

He looked at Sarah. He wanted to reach out and touch her, but he knew he couldn't. "Some things you can't change."

It had been a long time since he had seen her smile. It came under eyes furrowed together in tender sorrow at the statement. "That's why Jesus died and rose. The past doesn't exist for those who have let Him take away the power it has over their future."

Had she said that before? Or did he only imagine that also? Could she forget the past? Forget what he had done to her?

He wanted to say something that mattered. "I'm sorry."

The regret on Sarah's face was visible. Was it too late? Of course it was. How could she—?

Sarah pointed at the screen and Radley realized the low battery signal was beeping. He sped up and got ahead of Welch. Stopping the Suburban in the first parking lot he came to, he launched the second drone. Once he had it locked on Welch, he brought the first one to his location. He jammed the charging cable into the drone's port, and took off again, speeding to close the distance Welch had gained.

Sarah was gone.

She was telling him he had a choice. He was supposed to keep Roshard from deploying the virus and take Welch out and then his team. How many people would be in the team? It was a lot of death. Maybe he should make the hit on the professor and leave. Let it end there. That would end the virus threat and fulfill his contract on Welch. The man who gave the order was probably dead, anyway.

Chapter 11

THE FORMER PLUM ISLAND ANIMAL DISEASE CENTER, PLUM ISLAND, NEW YORK

The team lost him, sir." The voice on the phone held apprehension.

Roshard remained calm. He knew the team supervisor giving the report would be moved by that more than an outburst. "You got too close. He must have seen you."

Roshard was satisfied. It had been two days since Kondo's installation of the release device. That was plenty of time for the climate control system in Welch's vehicle to circulate the virus. Welch was probably infected on the first day after it was installed. He could develop symptoms at any time. According to the surveillance team, Welch had no passengers in those two days, so they had no other complications.

Now Roshard needed to make his men believe how disappointed he was. "Tell me what happened. How did he lose you?"

"He went into a self-storage facility and didn't come out."

"Where is the car?"

"We don't know. The best guess is that it's locked in one of the storage units. The team thinks he might have had help that met him inside and smuggled him out in a handyman vehicle that left shortly after Welch went in. They are looking for that truck now."

It was perfect. The team had been ordered not to enter the vehicle if they came in contact with it. This was even better. Locked in a storage facility, the virus would die and not infect anyone else.

Roshard let the pain of failure reign in his subordinate for a few moments. He had expected Welch to escape. It was necessary for the plan to work. He might not retreat to his base if he thought he was being followed. It also verified they had the right person, a master of the business.

But Roshard wanted his men to feel the cost of failure weighing on them. "I am more than disappointed. You knew how much this meant. This man is responsible for countless losses to our organization. We needed to know who he represents, who else is working with him." Then he let silence be his bludgeon.

Now to exercise his magnanimous side. "I expected too much. I didn't think one man would be a problem for you. Let's use this as a wake-up call. You now know your weaknesses. Fix them. I am placing my faith in you one more time." He let the relief linger for a moment. "Go back to his apartment and see if you can get any leads. He might come back there."

"Sir, uh, do you really think he would have abandoned his car if he was coming back? It looks like he's bugging to me."

Roshard had to play along. "What do you suggest?"

"I'll put one man on the apartment, but I think the rest of us should be looking for this truck."

"And where will you look? We're talking about a major city and its suburbs. You have four cars. Do you plan to drive the streets and hope you see him? You couldn't even cover all the ways out of town. I appreciate your initiative, but I can't justify your presence there. You've convinced me about the apartment. I think you're correct. He won't be back. I have others following more promising leads. We found him once, we'll find him again. Especially now that we know what he looks like. Bring your men home. We'll do better next time."

"Yes, sir."

Roshard hung up and dialed the other number.

The phone connected. "Go ahead."

"It's me. Welch lost the surveillance team. He should head for his base. This would be a good time for you to find out the location from your source. Are you able to make contact?"

"Of course. But I can't push too much. She trusts me and I can't get her spooked."

Roshard paced as he talked. "I'm taking a risk. I

would like to be able to seal the place down so nobody leaves or enters. Like you said, diseases like to spread. We have created fail-safes to prevent that, but it would be better to know where Welch has gone."

"She'll help as long as she thinks she's doing it for the right reason. I've got an angle I've been grooming her for. I think it will work and she'll give us what we need."

"Good. Our first goal is to make sure he gets there and isn't mixing with the outside population. Then we can try to find the location. Even if it doesn't work, at least we'll have her. We can't risk her walking away from this with what she knows. Once it all comes out, she might put it together and talk to someone who could link everything to us."

"Maybe she'll have to get the virus, too." Kondo gave a mocking laugh. "There seem to be a great many variables you haven't accounted for."

Roshard tried to restrain his anger. "You can't do great things if you're not willing to take great risks. That's why I hired you. You're a troubleshooter. I expect you to handle all the problems that will invariably come up in a plan of this scope. You said you could work the woman. But you haven't given me much from her since the initial contact. You keep saying you'll be able to deliver this and, so far, you haven't."

The man's silence was something Roshard could never read. He knew pressing Kondo's pride in his work was usually effective. He hoped he hadn't pressed too hard. The woman was a loose end they couldn't leave.

"I'll do my part." Kondo's voice seethed with menace. "I told you from the beginning, getting her to cooperate wasn't a sure thing. But in the end, I'll make sure she won't be a problem anymore."

Chapter 12

NORMAN, OKLAHOMA

Welch moved out of the residential area and into some old businesses. He saw what he was looking for and took the side street. The long, round top, Quonset-style metal building suffered from some rusting. It would be more accurate to call the grounds mown rather than landscaped, and they included a section of overgrown trees at the back. The place looked empty at the moment. A poster board sitting in one of the front windows informed anyone going by slow enough that the building was home to the **Hand and Foot Martial Arts Studio.** Perfect. The normal hours for such a business would be later in the evening.

Welch pulled in the alley to the rear. A storage building next to the main structure hid him from the rear of the other businesses. On the other side of the alley was a vacant property full of trees to block the view from that direction. Down the alley was a parking lot with only a couple of empty vehicles. He was hidden.

He dialed the Institute and went through the protocol to be connected with Joshua in France.

"Ruben, we have been praying. Did everything go well?"

Welch glanced around. "With the Lord's help, I think Louie and I have pulled one over on our new friends. I'm getting ready to switch the truck over, but I wanted to let you know I was okay."

"Are you heading to the Institute? We'll rest better over here when we know you're safe. Eventually, the ones that tailed you will connect you with the pickup."

Welch took a breath and grimaced. "I'll do the best I can. Remember, we all have our jobs to do. It wouldn't be productive if you became so worried about me that you lost focus on catching Becker's group. They present a real danger to the world if they continue toward Becker's goals. I won't be calling anymore, so you can concentrate on that."

There was silence for a moment. "Ruben, I don't like you talking like that. Is everything okay there?"

"Don't worry. God has everything in His hands. Remember, we work in a business that requires sacrifices sometimes. I need to get moving and get this truck switched before I do get caught. Give my love to all."

"Be careful."

"I will. You do the same. Goodbye." Welch

disconnected. He probably shouldn't have said those things to Joshua. Now he would worry even more. But he didn't feel well, and he wasn't sure what that meant. At the least, it was going to make him more vulnerable.

Glancing around, he spoke to the dummy beside him as he flipped a switch at its base. "Sorry, my friend. This is your early retirement." The body on which Louie's head and shoulders sat deflated rapidly. Welch unbuckled the belt that held it and stowed the whole affair behind the seat. He took a blanket from the backseat and covered it.

Welch stripped off the coveralls and hat. He resisted the urge to run his fingers through his hair to return it to its wild state from where the hat had flattened it. He couldn't go back to his college persona. That life was over. He took a breath and shook his head at how labored it felt.

He stepped out of the truck and peeled the magnetic placards off the door. Louie's was going out of business. He unhooked the bungee cord holding the first ladder and pulled it from the rack. Another deep, hard breath. *I didn't think I was this out of shape.* He forced his large frame and his burden between the storage unit and the building and dropped the ladder. He panted for a moment. *Maybe I just need to hit the gym more often. After today, I guess I'll have plenty of time.* Something didn't feel right about the thought. Something in his soul.

As Welch headed to the other side of the truck, the world tilted for a moment, causing him to plop onto the rear bumper. He shook his head. His face felt flushed. Running his hand across his forehead, he realized he was sweating. A shiver went through him. What was his body up to? He'd never had a sickness like this. If he could make it to the Institute, he could rest…if he was going…but right now he had to finish his vehicle's makeover.

Up again, he took the ladder from the other side of the truck and hauled it to rest beside the first. He could feel a tightness developing in his chest. Pulling the light aluminum racks out of the mounting holes in the pickup felt unnaturally difficult. It was a struggle, but he got both racks resting beside the ladders.

Welch put his hand against the metal building, gasping. He tried to walk to the truck but had to stop, hands on his knees. The illness was progressing. He had been right not to promise Joshua he would call again. He had been hoping he was wrong.

Welch stood up and froze. A man was using the corner of the building as cover and pointing a gun with a silencer at him. He considered going for his own weapon in the belly band tucked in his waist.

The man shook his head. "I'd have to kill you if you tried."

Welch knew the look. He doubted he had a chance against the man on his best day. He panted, still not finding enough oxygen. But it wasn't the first time he had found himself in a situation he couldn't control. It was in God's hands.

He gazed into the man's eyes. "You have the advantage," Welch panted. "You see that you have found me helpless. Each moment, young man," he took a breath, "…we have a choice of what we do…" Breath in. Breath out. "…and thus we choose what we are and what we will be." Welch held his palm close to his heaving chest as if something precious was in it. "What are you choosing right now?" He eased his hand, which went up and down with each breath, toward the man until his arm was outstretched, empty palm up. "It is something…" Breath. "…we should never take lightly." Turning his hand over, Welch let the invisible opportunity fall to the ground. He lifted his hand, palm to the man and eased it back, bringing his other up as well until he stood with both hands in the air. Struggling to breathe, he smiled a gentle smile. "It's between you and God now…He brought us both to this point."

The man looked troubled. "You're sick."

"If you mean I'm twisted…I pray not. If you mean I'm…unwell…that is true." Welch couldn't hold his hands up any longer. The man said nothing as they dropped to his sides.

With a face full of consideration, the man examined him. "There's nothing I can do."

Welch took in the statement. "Well then, if you'll excuse me." He walked toward the truck.

The man stiffened at the movement, looking a little lost.

Welch half hoped he would shoot. It would be over quickly. He did not relish a slow death, drowning as he was, in the open air. But it was better he didn't die here, around people. He couldn't go to the Institute, he had begun to realize.

Something was happening to him that wasn't natural. *You're sick*, the man had said, but there seemed to be something more on his mind. This didn't feel like poison, but Welch was fighting for air. The symptoms pointed to a virus like Becker's group would make. That must be who found him. He couldn't take this back to the people he cared about…or to a hospital where it would spread.

The man wasn't shooting. Welch had to use the opportunity to take what was inside him out of the area. He would drive as far away from civilization as he could. Some place where the disease could die with him. His head felt squeezed, like things were closing in. How long was a body contagious after—? He opened the pickup door, taking hold of the frame of the cab. He pulled to get himself inside. The world narrowed down to a blurry view of his foot trying to get a hold on the step to climb in. It slipped off and his body swung out as he tried to keep the grip with his hand. His fingers came loose as night fell over his mind.

Chapter 13

THE HOLLENBECK INSTITUTE FOR PEOPLE WITH SPECIAL NEEDS AND SPECIAL ABILITIES, LAKE GALLANT, OKLAHOMA

A strange sensation went through Shifra. She watched Talisa cut through the water while two dolphins leaped above her and then crisscrossed under her to make another leap. Even as Shifra watched the wondrous scene, a heaviness descended on her. The sensation seemed deeper rooted than the shock of Joshua's latest news. Ruben leaving behind his college professor cover was life altering. But she got the feeling something worse than that had happened.

She wished she could call Ruben, but how would he take that? If people were on to him, she didn't want to compromise his position.

Gretchen sat across from her, clicking at her laptop,

as she had been doing ever since Shifra had told her the news. She envied the IT manager's ability to lose herself in searching through data.

Shifra stood, needing to move. She walked along the edge of the aquarium watching Talisa return by holding onto a dolphin's dorsal.

Behind her, Gretchen's phone chirped. "Hello."

Shifra glanced back, feeling uneasy at every new sound.

"Okay. Hold on a minute." Gretchen spotted Shifra watching her. "It's a technical problem. I've got to run over to the office."

Shifra gave her a smile and a nod.

Gretchen left the building, laptop tucked under one arm and phone in the other hand. Shifra stepped into the conference room. Through the window, she saw Gretchen was on the phone again as she made her way down the sidewalk.

Moving a chair around a corner, out of sight of the aquarium, Shifra sat to pray. "Father, please. Help me know I am doing the right thing."

She needed to talk to Ruben, to know he was all right. Was all this her fault? The notion had been nagging at her. Now she had an awful feeling about Ruben. Whether he liked it or not, she needed to talk to him. Taking her phone out of her pocket, she turned it over just as it rang.

It was the special ring she had set up. How many times did this make? She didn't need this pressure, but she knew she had to answer it.

Shifra took the phone out and prepared herself.

"Hello…Yes. Me too…Yes, I've thought about it. I'm not sure yet…Look, it's too soon. I just got here…No. I can't. No. I don't think that's a good idea either."

"There you are." Talisa's face was peeking around the corner, toweling herself off.

Shifra gave a jerk of surprise.

Talisa saw she was on the phone, "Oh, excuse me," and disappeared around the corner again.

Shifra gushed into the phone. "Listen, I have to go." She stood up, phone at her side. She snatched it back to her mouth. "Love you."

Shifra returned to the main part of the conference room.

Talisa turned from the window where she had been watching the kids gathered around the pool. "Everything okay?"

The woman obviously noticed the tension in Shifra's manner. What should she tell her? Shifra tried to sound unaffected. "My daughter, Rahab. She's been calling me frequently since I left. Now she wants me to come back to New York to see her because she can't live without me. I haven't even been here a week. I don't need the extra things to worry about with everything going on. Joshua just told me Ruben's going to have to abandon his professor cover."

Talisa looked shocked. "Is it because of the break-in?"

"Partially." Shifra started to sit but was too anxious. "Now a team of people were tailing him. He thinks it's time for Ruben Welch to disappear. That will be a big change for him. I remember having to leave places and people behind. It was always hard because you never get to say goodbye and have to leave them wondering what happened."

The women stood in silence, considering the significance of the situation.

Talisa gave a look-on-the-bright-side shrug. "But hey, it sounds like he's coming to the Institute to stay for a while." She gave Shifra a nudge and a grin. "He'll have nowhere to run."

Chapter 14

NORMAN, OKLAHOMA

Radley whipped Welch's truck into the parking lot, which was about fifty feet from the metal building where he first encountered the big man. He sucked in a breath, hoping the N95 was enough as he turned the truck into a stall. He shoved it in park and stowed the keys above the visor.

Before he got out where people could see him, he checked the gun he had taken off the man. It was loaded and ready. He tucked it in the cargo pocket of his pant leg on the opposite side from his own gun.

Once outside the truck, he stripped off the mask and the protective gloves. Crumpling the mask into a tight ball in his palm, he pulled the glove over it inside out. He transferred the wad into his other hand and pulled the other glove over it in the same manner. He slammed the truck door and pulled on the handle.

Good, all locked up.

As he walked back to his Suburban, he detoured to a trash dumpster. Finding a small clean trash bag, he opened it and put the gloves inside with the other trash. He shoved it under one arm. He would deposit it in some dumpster far removed from the truck. He couldn't leave anything that might connect him with the vehicle.

Heading to his car, he took out a bottle of hand sanitizer and poured it on. Working it around, he made sure it got between his fingers and under his nails.

Sarah was walking next to him. "Why did you do that?"

"So no one will get into it until the sun has a chance to cook away the virus."

"You know what I mean. You don't seem to be following orders."

"Did you want me to?"

"I never said that."

No. Radley knew she never wanted him to do the things he had been trained for. It was the only life he knew. The only life he needed…until lately. "The man who gave the orders is probably dead."

Radley noticed how much shorter Sarah was than him. She had a strong body, yet womanly, scarred here and there from what she went through as a child and teen. Not unlike his own.

Radley thought of a happier subject. "It's coming up on our birthdays in a few weeks."

Sarah nodded. "I'll be twenty-three, so that makes you twenty-five."

"More or less."

Sarah regarded him with sadness. "I'm sorry you don't know your real birthday."

He shrugged. "I like using yours. I remember that party you gave me when you were ten."

Sarah gave her first real smile in so long. "When you were twelve."

"Yeah. More or less." He had known her for so long, yet knew her so little. It was as if his eyes had been opened…too late.

"Peter, you didn't really answer me. Why did you take that man to the hospital?"

"I don't know."

Sarah glanced at him, concern and hope seemed to mingle on her face. "I think you're changing. I think you did what you knew was right. What kind of man is this Welch? Did you talk with him?"

Radley was surprised by the question. She should know what he knew. That part of his mind must shut down when he had to make a hit. "He talked about the same thing you did—about choices."

"God is speaking to you, Peter. It's time for you to choose Him. You shouldn't wait any longer." Sarah looked at the sky for a moment before speaking again. "We may not have much time left."

Radley glanced her way. *If she's in your mind, you control what time you have.* "What if the virus spreads?"

"We're responsible for our choices, but that doesn't mean everything depends on us. We have to trust God and not fear. That's the part I'm trying to do better, too."

Radley considered the idea of Sarah trying to do better. "I'm sorry for taking your time."

Radley was back at his vehicle and crawled inside.

Sarah was beside him. "You're not taking my time. I like being with you."

Radley put the key in the ignition but didn't turn it. "No, I mean the time you would have had."

She looked at him, confused. Even when she seemed to finally realize what he was saying she took a moment to answer. "There's always hope. God is working it all for our good if you listen to Him and let Him guide things."

"I remember that verse. You showed it to me when I asked you why God would allow what happened. I'm sure you know I've been reading the Bible."

"Uh, huh. That's why I know God is using all of this to reach you."

"I still remember when I found out. How little I felt. I knew what I had done and just felt numb. How can you be so okay with it?" Radley felt warmth in his eyes. If she was in his mind, responding the way his imagination willed, what did that say about him? "If God used that to get to me…it's not right." He put his hands on the steering wheel and pressed his face into them to hide from what was happening. The memory hadn't caused such an ache before. Something was coming alive in him, something that made his whole life difficult.

"Peter, with God, it's not a matter of what's right. He defines that." Sarah's voice sounded close. Inside him. "It's a matter of what it takes. He didn't find a way around sin and death. He made a way through them."

Radley could almost feel the warmth of a hand on his shoulder, but he knew it wasn't there. He wanted to hug her, to show her how much he loved her and wished he could make things different. He turned, a slight, uncertain movement toward…She wasn't there.

With God, it's not a matter of what's right. She had never said that to him before. Could he have come up with it in his own mind? It wasn't something he would think.

Radley started the lonely vehicle, leaving behind the alley and everything in it. His interactions with Sarah seemed different. Did it mean things were getting worse? Was he losing his mind?

It's a matter of what it takes. Was he hearing someone else now?

Chapter 15

NORMAN REGIONAL HOSPITAL, NORMAN, OKLAHOMA

D r. Welch, you need to stop talking and let the BiPap machine do its work." Vicki gave the large man her best stern nurse eyes over her N95 mask. It was a look reserved for her difficult patients. Since the big man had come fully awake, the only thing on his mind was making a phone call. "I'll let you borrow our phone and take your mask off for one call. That's all. If there's no answer, you've got to go back on the mask. This really is endangering your life."

The man's heavy chest heaved, and his muffled voice came as gasps through the mask that covered his mouth and nose. "This is important. Someone will…answer this line…thank you…for the phone." Under his breath, she heard him say, "Please,

Lord…help me. Help them."

Vicki could tell the man was struggling with something besides the illness. It sounded so strange—a man in a pickup dropping him off, then driving away before they could get any information.

Right now, though, her main concern was the struggle inside the man's chest and the flashing, beeping pulse-ox alarm telling her his breathing wasn't enough to keep his blood adequately oxygenated. She reached up and silenced the alarm again.

It was the worst case of COVID they had seen for a while. It had diminished his lung capacity, and the BiPap machine was maximizing the effectiveness of each precious breath. She believed Welch when he said it had come on him suddenly. They said the man who dropped him off told them to be careful. He had something very contagious and deadly. It was debilitating Welch at an alarming rate since the ER tech brought him up. Now Vicki didn't think he would be able to make it across the room without collapsing from lack of oxygen. She looked at how much the man, who had given his name as Welch, filled the bed. Whoever brought him in, unconscious, must be quite a man.

Welch lifted the mask onto his forehead and with his hand, requested the phone. Vicki was reconsidering. She dialed up the seriousness of her expression. "Whatever call you want to make isn't worth your life."

Welch raised one shaggy eyebrow. "I'm afraid it is."

Something in the man's gasping tone made Vicki believe he was serious. "Put the mask on and let me dial. You can take it off when I get hold of someone."

The man looked like he was determined to argue, but his body wasn't as willing as his spirit. His breathing increased and after a moment, he pulled the mask back on.

Vicki still needed him to relax and rest. She reengaged him from her new position of influence. "If I help you make this call, will you promise to lie still and try to get some sleep so your body will stop fighting the BiPap?"

The large head turned so the man could examine Vicki around the straps that smashed the mask to his face. He nodded, scribbled a number on a page of a notepad he held, tore it off, and handed it to her.

Her protective gloves didn't make it easy for Vicki to dial on the phone.

The call connected and an electronic voice said, "What extension, please?"

Vicki switched to the phone's keypad. "What extension?"

The man responded by holding out his hand for the phone.

Vicki gave him another stern look as she relinquished the handset. "Okay, but then you give the phone back and I do the talking."

The man panted as he nodded. Vicki estimated his breathing rate at over forty times a minute. If she didn't find a way to get him to rest and stop breathing over the machine, they were going to have to tube him.

Welch held the phone up so he could see around the mask. With one of his huge hands, the man shielded the phone from her view as he typed in a string of numbers. He started to move the phone to his ear, but Vicki thrust out her hand.

Welch held the phone at bay. "They won't talk to you…unless I okay it."

Vicki kept her hand outstretched. "You promised."

Welch pointed to the paper that had the number on it. They traded.

Vicki waited for someone to come on the line.

"Good afternoon. How may I help you?"

"Hello. My name is Vicki Anderson and I am a nurse at Norman Regional Hospital. I'm trying to help one of my patients make a phone call that he seems to think is more important than breathing. He's very sick and shouldn't be talking, so I agreed to pass on a message for him."

"What extension were you trying to reach?"

"I don't know what number he typed in. He's right here beside me."

"Very good, Ms. Anderson, but before I can discuss anything with you, I will have to verify that person is there, and it is okay for us to talk. Is it possible he could get on the line for a moment just to answer a brief question?"

"It's very hard for him to breathe. We have placed him on a machine that helps, but he should be resting and certainly not trying to speak."

"It will only take a minute, Ms. Anderson, I assure you."

Welch was holding out his hand, waiting.

"All right. He seems determined. But only for a second." Vicki handed over the phone.

The big man hooked his thumb under the mask at the chin and strained the elastic straps, sliding it up to rest on his forehead. Worry lines showed under the mask as he took a gasp of air to speak. "Is this the line…to order fresh fish?"

Vicki reached for the phone. "Mr. Welch, I didn't give you that phone to order…"

Welch blocked her hand and leaned away as he tried to listen. Turning toward Vicki, he examined her like her presence concerned him. His countenance shifted, as if he had made a reluctant decision. He turned his head away and breathed a raspy whisper into the phone. "I think it is because…there are a lot of…Pelicans…in the delta this year." Another gasp for air. "That's now been compromised…will need reset."

Vicki was flabbergasted as she watched his belly swell even bigger to take in air. She didn't know what kind of game they were playing, but she didn't have time for it.

Welch spoke again. "Give me whoever is available locally."

Vicki felt a little better when Welch pulled the mask down while he waited.

Soon it was up again. "Shiffy, is that you?" Welch gave a heaving breath that turned to a smile at whatever was said on the other end. "The…" He glanced at Vicki out of the corner of his eye. "I lost my phone…Yes…She's a nurse." There was another smile.

The woman in Vicki told her he was talking to his love. The conversation was having a profound effect on the man.

"I'm so glad…it's you, Shiffy. There are things…I need to tell you."

At the man's glance, Vicki moved away and busied herself with folding the extra blankets that had come up with the man from the ER and had been tossed aside in a chair.

It was impossible to talk quietly over the BiPap machine, but the man seemed to forget Vicki was there. "I am so sorry I was not more available to you. I wish we could have had more time together." Welch's voice strengthened as he spoke. "Please, let me speak. I may not have much time." He sucked in a breath and seemed to swallow down a cough. "Meeting you has been…such a highlight to me. I am sorry…I did not demonstrate that better. You deserve all the best in this life and…I fear I did not give you what I could of that."

The person obviously interrupted. The man's face was strained as he listened.

When he responded, his voice was broken, but Vicki felt it wasn't related to his illness. "I wish that was possible but…Shiffy…I cannot leave here on my own, but every minute I am here…I am endangering these people."

Vicki marveled at the man's concern for the staff. She wanted to assure him, but she was reluctant to interrupt.

"You read the file on Becker. You know what he tried to do…This is like that. We need to protect these people…yes that must happen, and soon." Welch coughed, then regained control. His weezing was growing louder, faster.

Vicki hated to cut the conversation off. Welch had such an earnest expression. "No." His voice was concerned. "You must not. I can't come there. You must let me go. Send someone who is well protected and can take me away from people. Please let someone else. I could not bear for you…Shiffy…you do not understand…You…If anything happened to…" The man sputtered out the last statement. He dropped the hand that held the phone in his lap as a coughing fit seized him.

The monitor beside Welch's bed began to alarm. His oxygen saturation had dropped into the low 80s and was still going down. "Mr. Welch, you will have to give me the phone back. You need to get back on the machine *right now*."

Welch's face said he agreed. He handed the phone back to her and pulled the mask over his face again, sucking rapidly at the oxygen.

Vicki realized how long she had allowed the man to talk. She couldn't believe he had lasted as long as he did. But it was not the first time she had witnessed the power of the human heart. She took the phone and spoke to the person on the other end. "This is the nurse again. Mr. Welch can't talk anymore."

The woman's voice held concern. "Is he all right?"

Vicki placed her hand on Welch's shoulder. "Mr.

Welch, do you mind if I talk to this woman about your medical condition?"

Welch shook his head and gave a go-ahead-gesture with his hand.

"He is very sick. He has COVID pneumonia, causing his lungs to be diminished. He is having a hard time getting his breath, and it is causing him to breathe too rapidly. We have him on what we call a BiPap machine that regulates his breathing and pushes more oxygen into his lungs. If he would relax," Vicki leaned toward Welch so he would hear her, "and not fight the machine, it would help a lot."

She got the raised eyebrow for her trouble, but then Welch reached, squeezed her gloved hand and nodded.

"All right, Vicki," the woman on the phone took on a more business-like tone, "does Mr. Welch have any more to pass on to me?" The woman's breathing and footfalls said she was hurrying to get somewhere.

Welch's coughing had subsided. Vicki pointed to the notepad Welch had in his lap. "I don't want you to talk, but she wants to know if there is anything else you want to pass on?"

Welch scribbled for a minute, then tore out the piece of paper and handed it to her.

Vicki read, "Don't remember being brought here. Only man I met today showed me his calling card, and I wasn't interested in what he was selling. Don't let him in the door. He engages in high-pressure sales tactics. Keep an eye out for my phone and my calling card. They are missing." Vicki patted Welch while she talked to the woman. "Mr. Welch is obviously concerned about everyone else's welfare, but right now, I want him to concentrate on his own and get better."

"Tell Mr. Welch not to worry. We'll be on guard against anyone like that, and we'll watch for his items." There was the sound of a door opening as the woman continued on her quest, her shoes clicking on the floor.

Vicki relayed the message and took another page that Welch had finished.

Again, Vicki read the message. "Please let someone else come. Not you." Vicki realized the problem with what she was reading. "I'm sorry, Mr. Welch, but this is a COVID unit, and you are not allowed visitors. You wouldn't want other people getting this, would you?"

Panting, the man gave a frustrated grimace. He quickly scribbled on the notepad and handed her the sheet. Vicki read it to herself without speaking. Not seeing any problem with the message, she relayed it to the woman. "Definitely don't want anyone else catching this. Isolation from everyone is a must. Improvise."

"Tell him I understand." The woman went silent, waiting for Vicki to pass on the message.

"She says she understands. Now will you rest?"

Welch nodded.

Vicki was pleased when she saw Welch close his eyes. She turned her attention back to the phone. "Okay, Mr. Welch is going to rest now." Vicki left the room to continue the conversation. "I'm sorry about the no visitor policy."

The woman Welch had called Shiffy didn't speak right away. The sounds of walking had ceased. There were muffled voices, like a hand covered the phone. Then she responded, "Thank you, Vicki. I so appreciate what you're doing for Mr. Welch. He's my co-worker, and also a good friend."

Vicki decided to say something the woman needed to hear. "I could tell he cares for you. Even though he could barely breathe, he lit up when he heard it was your voice." Vicki waited several moments before the woman responded.

"Thank you for saying that." The woman's voice faltered. "Please do all you can to help him. I don't want to lose him."

"Should I put you down as his emergency contact? We didn't have one for him. The man who brought him in didn't stay long enough for us to get any information."

"Absolutely. Let me give you another number that will be easier to reach me. The number you called is a work number that no one should be calling so please don't put that down."

"I don't have it anymore. Mr. Welch took it back."

"I should have known. He is always so good at thinking about little things like that. Just out of curiosity, is this an in-house hospital phone or a cell phone?"

"It's a hospital cordless phone."

"Those are handy for things like this, aren't they?" Again, it sounded like the woman covered the phone. Someone was typing on a keyboard in the background.

"Yes…" There was a series of tones in Vicki's ear. "I'm sorry. I think the line is having trouble." The sounds ended.

"It's probably on my end. Our phones have been having problems all day. But back to Mr. Welch. Honestly, Vicki, how bad is he? Is he in danger?"

"That's a hard question to answer. His condition improved on the BiPap. He was unconscious when he came in and his oxygen sat. was in the fifties. So he's better, but a lot of it depends on how well he responds to the BiPap machine through the night. If he doesn't improve soon, they will have to intubate him."

"When would they consider doing something like that?"

"The doctor will come in the morning and evaluate how he's doing. Right now, the BiPap is keeping him stable. If he is having as much trouble breathing as he is now, they may intubate tomorrow morning."

"I see. He can refuse that, can't he?"

Oh no, another one of those. "He can, unless his oxygen saturation gets so low that he gets hypoxic and passes out again. Then he wouldn't be able to make decisions. But it's not in his best interest to refuse medical care. The doctors base their treatments on the best practices sent down from the CDC. Better to let them do their jobs."

"I'm sure you're probably right. Will you be taking care of him all night, Vicki?"

"No, it's almost the end of my shift. But I'll be back in the morning."

"Well, let's just hope something positive happens

before then. I'll be praying."

"All right then. I will let you go because I need to give report to the oncoming shift."

The woman expressed more thanks, said goodbye, and hung up. There was something odd about the whole situation, but it was not something Vicki had time to worry about tonight. She had one last round of meds to pass before the night shift showed up.

Welch woke to the click of the latch on the door to his room. Someone had entered and was on the other side of the privacy curtain that was pulled between him and the entrance. Too stealthy for a nurse. Even struggling to breathe, he had noted his surroundings. His isolation room was near what must be a staff entrance, the greatest distance from the nurse's station. They had magnetic card locks, easy to get around with the right equipment. Wait for the nurses to be busy in other rooms and you're in unnoticed.

The mask was blocking his view of the clock, and he didn't dare move. Surely, he'd only dozed for a minute. No one could have gotten here that quickly from the Institute.

He remembered the man with the gun. His weapon had a silencer. The way he approached, the look on his face. The man had been sent to kill him. God had intervened, and he was still alive. Maybe someone was here to correct what went wrong with the first hit.

If the intruder had meant to shoot him, he would be dead already. Even a silencer might be heard in a quiet ICU. They must be opting for something silent and more intimate. He could still have a chance if the assassin got close enough.

He contemplated what he had considered in the alley—whether it was better to die. But God had not allowed that. It was a miracle, and he was not one to argue with miracles. There must be something more happening in the Heavenlies.

The fact that someone wanted him dead was half his motivation to live. The other half was Shiffy. She might be coming to get him, despite what he told her. If they killed him, they might wait outside and kill her, too. In any scenario he could imagine, the assassin would not be satisfied with him alone. The man with the gun could have let him live as bait. With the Lord's help, and all Welch had in him, he wouldn't let the killer get Shifra.

Welch eased his hand toward his leg. He was slitting his eyes so he would appear asleep and still have a partial view.

A dark figure slipped around the end of the curtain.

Welch wrapped his hand around the handle of the pair of scissors he'd lifted from Vicki when he had asked her to adjust his mask earlier. He eased them to the edge of the blanket, still concealed but ready for quick deployment.

There was the rustling of plastic. Using a bag to suffocate him would work well if they thought he was still unconscious. It would look natural, considering his body was making a significant effort toward that outcome on its own. But the person he was seeing would be smarter than to try that, considering their size difference.

The mask was going to make it difficult, but he wouldn't last long without it. He needed the attacker closer. The scissors were blunt tipped, so only good for slicing. The neck would be his best move. He knew that was a risk if they meant to stab him or they had an auto injector full of a poison to stop his heart.

He had finally gotten in sync with the horrid contraption that was forcing oxygen into him. His body had the urge to take in extra air to prepare for the assault, but he resisted. He didn't want to give away that he was aware of the other presence in the room. Would his heart rate on the monitor betray him? Fortunately, it was already running high.

He could just make out a female frame carrying trash bags. Not the normal hour for cleaning up.

Inching the scissors into position, he waited for the person to get closer.

The woman stopped a safe distance away and whispered. "You're not going to need that, Ahuvi."

Welch knew the Jewish endearment from the times he had worked in Israel. It was like honey pouring over him. "Shiffy." Her name meant more to him than the breath it took to say it. "I should not be so happy you're here. I did not want to expose you."

The mask Shifra wore looked like a regular N95, but it covered a face that was definitely not Shifra's beautiful features. She was wearing another mask under it that was flawless in its creation of a less-than-flawless face. "Quiet now. You just breathe. I have a few things to set up." Under her scrubs and protective gown, Shifra was wearing something that made her womanly figure look heavy and dumpy.

From the trash bag that she carried, her gloved hands pulled out a more compact and streamlined version of the mask Welch wore. Its hose was attached to an egg-carton-sized canister. She laid it on the bed beside him and pulled the blanket over it. "We'll need this later. It will get you to the parking lot. I've got something better in the van."

Welch looked toward the door. "Who's with you?"

"I couldn't think of anyone to bring that wouldn't just be in the way." She cleared items off the bedside table. "You just have me. Aren't I enough?" Her smile shone in the dark, the only thing that might give away her disguise.

"More than."

The woman continued smiling as she set one of the trash bags she carried on the table.

Welch grabbed his next breath. "The Institute number…is on the phone I used."

"Not anymore." The woman pulled down the sides of the trash bag, revealing an electronic instrument. "I ran to the IT department and got Gretchen to erase the caller ID remotely while I still had the nurse on the line."

"Smart. I should have known you'd handle it."

Shifra pushed a button, and a single red light on the side of the box indicated it was on. "It's been a while since I pulled a hospital extraction. Good thing the Institute has all the latest idiot-proof equipment. Gretchen walked me through it. It's much easier than it used to be. With God on our side, we might pull it off."

Holding her cell phone toward the monitor screen, Shifra glanced at the box on the table. A small screen on the side of the box lit up. A representation of the vitals appeared on the screen, right down to the normal fluctuations. After a moment, the woman seemed satisfied and pressed a button to lock the numbers in.

Turning her phone to the display on the BiPap machine, she locked that in as well. "The AI will set up the portable and the full size unit in the van outside. It will be all ready for you when we get to the parking lot."

Shifra took hold of the cable that was hooked to the blood pressure cuff around Welch's arm. "The monitor says it's set to measure every hour, and we have about twenty minutes to go." She unhooked the cable from the cuff and attached it to the box instead. "The instrument will fake a pressure by making minor changes from the last measurement."

Next, she picked up the cable that measured the oxygen in his blood. Timing it for a quick movement, she jerked the cable loose and jammed it into the matching receptacle on the box. The waveform and numbers faltered on the screen for only a moment, nothing to cause an alarm.

The heart rhythm monitor caused a longer break. In whispered tones, Shifra assured him they would just think one of the patches on his chest was a little loose. Not worth waking the patient for that unless it stayed off.

Shifra examined the display, and once satisfied, she pressed another button, and the screen went dark. She reached into the other bag and took out a mannequin head that resembled his wild hair. She blew in the large trash bag like a balloon, holding it up to Welch's girth for comparison. When it was expanded to an ample size, she tied it. Smiling, she patted Welch's tummy and then the bag. "There's my man. This will fill in for you under the blanket while I wheel you to the parking lot."

Welch used several puffs to say, "I flattered myself…that it would take…a little more…to replace me. At least…he's a handsome fellow."

The comment was worth the effort because it earned him another smile. Shifra ruffled his hair that poked between the mask straps. "Nothing could replace you." She slid the bag under the bed and put the machine and the fake head beneath the blanket next to him. "There now. Nothing better happen to you while you're unhooked." She put her hand on the side of his mask-clad face. "You stay here and rest. I've got to give the girls a little something to do and then I'll be back. Try not to slit any throats while I'm gone."

Vicki yawned as she got off the elevator. The night

had been too short and now she was back at it again. She was running behind and had to forgo her morning coffee stop, so she wasn't ready for this day.

When she carded herself into the ICU, two police officers were leaning against the nurse's station counter. Cheryl, the night charge, addressed them when she saw Vicki. "Here she is. She can tell you about when the guy was admitted."

"Ms. Anderson." An officer came off the counter to greet her.

Vicki read the tension in the faces of the staff. Cheryl came toward her, and Vicki passed the officer to confer with her co-worker first. "What's going on?"

"That guy in room two, Welch, he's gone."

"Oh no. He could barely breathe. Who let him sign out?" Vicki glanced at the cops. "He's not dead…is he?"

Cheryl was shaking her head. "No, I mean he's gone, disappeared. No one knows what happened to him."

Vicki tried to process the statement. "What?"

"It's like that freaky religious movie about the rapture, when all the Christians disappear."

"All the patients are gone?"

"No." Cheryl rolled her eyes. "Just that Welch guy."

"Where'd he go?"

"That's what I'm telling you. We don't know. We were sitting here, and his monitor went dead."

"Like he tore everything off?"

Cheryl wagged her head. "It wasn't like when

someone starts pulling stuff off. Everything stopped at the same time. All the alarms went off at once, like he vanished. There was even a housekeeper in the room when it happened. She went in to empty the trash and was coming out with the bag when we went running in to check on him. All the cables were laying on the bed and he was gone. The housekeeper said no one was in the room when she went in. So we all took off looking for him. I mean, there was no way he could've got out of the unit without us seeing him, but he was gone. Now we can't find the housekeeper either. I just want to get out of this place. It's like the body snatchers or something."

"Which housekeeper? Why was she taking out the trash at that hour?"

"I don't know. It was an older lady I've never seen before. You know how hard it is to keep help. They have new people in here all the time. It wasn't something we were worrying about when we were trying to find a missing patient."

Vicki let the story roll over in her mind. "The guy couldn't even breathe. He would have collapsed in the hallway."

"I know, but we have looked everywhere. That's why the house supervisor called the police—this guy disappears and we had someone who might have been impersonating a doctor."

"What do you mean?"

"It was crazy," Cheryl sighed out the statement in frustration. "The whole night was crazy."

Vicki stared at Cheryl, waiting for her to explain.

"Some doctor from corporate came in and sent us downstairs to the lobby to get COVID swabbed for some surprise health audit. She told us she had a special team coming up to cover for us. They were finishing up in one of the other units. She took a quick report and told us to go ahead and go down because the team would be there in a minute."

Vicki was trying to understand it all. "They had a team come and replace you in the middle of the night?"

"Well, that's what she said. You know how since COVID, they're always doing some wacky new thing. Her corporate ID looked official, and she badged her way into the ICU like she knew what she was doing. She said it wouldn't take long, but everybody had to do it. It was because of some new federal regulation, and the hospital would be forced to discipline anyone who didn't comply. She was talking about how everyone was just trying to get through it. How she wanted to hurry so her team could get home to bed. She was really convincing. We only had five patients, and since she was a doctor, it seemed like it was okay. But when we got all the way down there, there's a sign on the table saying the testing would have to be rescheduled and to return to our stations. So we turned around and came back up. The corporate doctor was gone and there was no team in here. We called around and no one else knew anything about it."

Vicki tried to put it together. "So no one was watching the patients? Do you think that's when the guy in two got out?"

"No. We peeked in on everyone. They were all

asleep in their beds and everyone's vitals were stable. We weren't gone very long. It was almost an hour later when the guy disappeared."

Vicki shook her head. "That wouldn't matter, anyway. He couldn't get far without the BiPap."

Cheryl plopped into her chair. She turned a tired, defeated expression toward Vicki. "So this patient's missing. The housekeeper, the corporate doctor, they're all gone. When I leave here today, I don't know if *I'm* coming back."

Chapter 16

THE HOLLENBECK INSTITUTE FOR PEOPLE WITH SPECIAL NEEDS AND SPECIAL ABILITIES, LAKE GALLANT, OKLAHOMA

Shifra held a nervous hand to her lips as the Hollenbeck Institute doctors evaluated the condition of their newest patient. Doctor Daanish Malik, the supervisor of the team, gave her a confident smile through the sealed glass that separated them.

The doctor walked the sophisticated suit he wore to the wall opposite the observation area. The back of his suit was attached to a docking station by high-tech plastic that expanded like an accordion bellows as the suit was moved away from the wall. The device allowed the doctors to get to the patient's bedside without entering the environment of the room.

Turning, Malik backed the accordion like attachment into its docking area and crawled out of the suit. He left the staff area and in a few moments joined Shifra in the observation room. "He'll be all right in a few days. He should be honored. I think they created this little strain just for him, to take him down quickly."

Shifra hoped her face conveyed her gratitude. "Thank you for not letting that happen." In her heart, she worried how anyone had gotten close enough to Ruben Welch to pull this off.

The doctor looked at his patient. "Since COVID, my team and I have been doing some creating of our own. This virus is worse than COVID but it's similar enough that the DNA therapy we developed worked to stop the cytokine response. The swelling in his lungs is subsiding. The antivirals and immunotherapy will help his body kill off the virus just like God created it to do, now that it's not fighting itself. Whatever you did to bypass the red tape involved in transferring him here got him to us in time. It saved his life."

Shifra warmed at the sight of the large frame, now resting comfortably. *Thank you, Lord, for protecting Ruben.* "The Institute can't afford to lose him."

Turning back, she saw the doctor smiling. She shrugged. "Even if there had been time, we couldn't have asked that hospital to transfer him to a research medical facility that doesn't exist. This building is the Institute's clinic and rehab center as far as the public knows."

The doctor shifted to a grin. "Anonymity beats malpractice insurance any day."

She returned the grin with a grateful smile. "Bless

you for what you're doing. It's a much more dangerous game than when I was in it before. People are playing with things they really don't understand." Shifra shook her head. Human arrogance. "It's so easy for these kinds of weapons to spill out to people who never signed up for it."

The doctor's countenance took on sternness. "There's a lot of snakes tangled around each other in this whole mess."

"I heard you mention this is worse than the COVID virus."

"There are similarities. It shows up on a basic test like COVID. But this is a much more sophisticated little gem."

"Can you share this treatment regimen with the world?"

The man nodded. "We'll share it where we can without bringing scrutiny on the Institute. It would jeopardize some of our more delicate operations if we became world celebrities." He let his grin widen again. "And our work would get a lot more complicated. New regulations would follow. You can't go around solving world problems unchecked by politics and corporate greed. Someone spent a lot of money and took a lot of risks to craft a bug this effective just to have us kill it with our DNA fly swatter."

"I hope Joshua and the others can catch up with Becker's group. They're the best suspects in this. If you can get Dr. Welch back in the fight, it will help." She gave an admiring glance toward the bed.

The doctor squeezed her shoulder. "We'll do our

part, but he will need some special nursing care when he gets through this. I think I know who he'll be looking for. He's been saying a certain name in his sleep."

Shifra squinched her face. "Some guys talk too much. Must be the drugs you're giving him. But I'll be here."

Shifra watched Gretchen Fordham's delicate white fingers fly over the keyboard. "Thanks for helping me get that caller ID erased on such short notice. We couldn't afford to leave the Institute's phone number at that hospital."

Gretchen's oversized glasses were reflected in the three large, curved computer monitors as she glanced from screen to screen. "Whaddya think? We're cyberspies. We wouldn't be worth much around here if we weren't available for pop-up emergencies. That's why we work shifts."

Shifra watched the back-and-forth swish of the small red ponytail. The Institute's lead computer expert looked to be about thirty. "Yeah, but I see you in here most of the time."

"The manager has to set the example. That's why my apartment is part of the IT wing. Not that I want the others working as much as I do. Someone needs to have a life, so the rest of us will have family pictures to pretend to be interested in." Gretchen produced output almost as fast as her supercomputer. "But since I'm in here most of the time, by someone else's necessity or my desire, I might as well give the others the night off. It's one of the perks I created—surprise time off. They love it. Don't tell Dr. Welch, but I'd work here for free just to have access to this beautiful darling." She made a sweeping gesture toward the rows of black computer cabinets behind a transparent wall.

Gretchen's hands continued to work as she talked. She clicked on an icon, and the warning "Encrypted File" displayed. She worked with incredible speed. The warning vanished and Shifra barely saw the announcement flash that the decryption was complete before a data table came up and Gretchen's cursor was zipping down the columns. She highlighted an access code labeled **Dr. Welch's phone** and threw it on another screen, where a map came up and zoomed in.

Gretchen pointed at a set of crosshairs on the satellite view. "It's no longer transmitting. For that to happen, the phone would have to be destroyed. Even if he was using some type of GPS blocker, our phones use redundant signals not affected by blockers. Also, there is a small battery hidden in the circuit board that sends a simple satellite location signal even if the main battery is removed. I'm not getting a signal from it, so someone destroyed the circuit board. Here is its last location."

Shifra squinted to see the screen. "Looks like a parking lot. What's this building?"

Zooming out, Gretchen read the words

superimposed on the roof. "Nancy O'Brian Center for the Performing Arts."

Shifra added the name of the street that had come into view. "Timberwolves Trail."

Gretchen pulled the view out even farther. "Looks like part of the Norman North High School complex. I'm guessing they are the Norman North Timberwolves. Shall we go to a game? I love football."

Shifra narrowed her eyes. "I thought you didn't get out."

"I'm in here whenever I'm home, but I bust out of this place sometimes and check out the local." Gretchen gestured with her hand as if the word *local* encompassed all of life in the area. "I love college sports. The Sooners are my mains." Gretchen rocked a scowl back and forth. "At least some of them."

Shifra pointed. "There's where the phone went. It's a reservoir. Whoever took it, pulled into this parking lot, probably tried to get into the phone without success, disabled it, and pitched it in the water."

"Let's see what he gave us in the process." Gretchen talked as she typed. "Or it could be a she. Spying is an equal opportunity employer, as we are living proof."

"Ruben said a man showed him his calling card. So, we've got a man with a gun on him at some point. Best guess would be he took the phone and gun after Ruben passed out."

Gretchen kept typing but sent Shifra a quick glance. "Ruben?"

Shifra grinned. "I mean Dr. Welch."

Gretchen wiggled her shoulders back and forth.

"Hey, you go, girl. Dr. Welch is cool. He treats me like gold. But I'm not sure he's into younger women. I tried flirting a little with him. I mean, I'm not getting any younger and I intimidate most guys that have a brain. But he just acts like he's my dad or something."

Shifra patted her on the shoulder. "I'm almost his age, but I'll take that as a compliment."

Gretchen peered over her shoulder and looked Shifra up and down. She turned back to the keyboard. "Whatever you're using, I gotta get me some."

Shifra gave her a squeeze around her shoulders. "No wonder he treats you like gold."

A video of a man's face appeared on the center monitor with the title **Front Camera**. Beside it was a view labeled **Back Camera,** showing the black hood of a vehicle through the windshield with an asphalt lot and trees beyond.

Gretchen's voice went into training mode. "The phone is keyed to the owner's biometrics. When it sees a strange face looking into it, the phone begins sending out video from both the phone's front and back cameras to a server. So this is our bad guy." Gretchen's hands stopped for a second. "Hmm. Not what I expected. He looks too normal for a killer. I wouldn't look twice at him in the mall."

Shifra leaned toward the screen. The face was not bad looking, but not a standout either. His eyes scowled at the screen as his fingers worked the phone. Shifra's trained eye could see the lean muscles moving under his shirt. There was hidden strength there. But the man had worked hard to look average. After a few minutes, he put the phone in the center cup holder.

Gretchen was back to clicking rapid fire. The image of the man opened in another program on the left screen and a series of intersecting lines appeared on the man's face.

The current image from the seat came up on the right screen and parts of the image of the interior of the car began being highlighted, one after another, with measurement lines. In a few moments, the label **2021 Chevrolet Suburban** appeared across the screen.

Shifra was hearing something…like a faint voice.

Gretchen tapped again and the right screen image was replaced by images of various angles of the vehicle in question.

The woman's fingers moved too fast for Shifra to follow, and the printer on the stand beside the workstation spit out prints of the dark SUV.

Shifra leaned in. "Hold on. Who do I hear talking?"

The printer finished. Gretchen raised her finger and made an exaggerated point at the center screen. "He's talking. I had the sound low. She machine gunned the volume key.

The man's voice came through clearly. "I'm not frustrated. I just don't know what to do since I didn't make the hit." The man paused and turned toward the passenger side. "Change isn't always good." Another pause. "No, you haven't. You can't change. You'll always be like I remember you. That's all you can be."

Shifra raised her hand like she was trying to listen. "He's talking to someone, but I'm not hearing the other person."

Gretchen was already rewinding the video. "He must be on a Bluetooth. He has one in his ear."

They ran the video again. The phone was at an angle in the cup holder that showed part of the man's head.

When they got past the part they had heard already, Gretchen stopped it. They both stared at the screen.

Shifra pointed. "He's turning his head toward the passenger side like someone's there."

Gretchen ran it again and tweaked at the settings. "There's no one else speaking. I'm getting nothing."

Shifra pointed again. "Look at him. He's looking at someone."

Gretchen scrutinized the screen. "He must be doing that out of habit. You know, visualizing the person he's talking to on the phone."

Shifra shrugged. "I guess someone might do that. Let's listen to the whole thing."

The video picked up where they left off. The man spoke, pausing after each comment as if listening to a response.

"You are saying things to me you never said before. —— *Maybe* it's a problem. Maybe it means I'm delusional. —— I thought it was my imagination going to the next level, remembering you in a new way. But maybe it's something else. —— It's like we're really talking. —— Of course. If it was possible. But it's not. You're not...here. —— I don't know. Myself maybe. Who else could I be talking to when there's no one else here? —— If He's listening, He's not helping. —— If He has a plan like you're always saying, why would He do this to you? —— If He loves me that much, He wouldn't have done this. —— Because I…needed you. And we both deserved to get out of there. —— If that's true then I want nothing to do with Him. What happens to me is my own fault. It shouldn't have anything to do with you. —— Maybe it's okay with you, but it's not with me. —— Don't leave. I'm listening. —— I don't care. It's not right. You're more important than me. —— Please don't keep saying that. I need you to stay —— I'll try to talk to Him —— I don't know. Tomorrow maybe. —— Don't look at me like that —— I don't mean to. I just want to talk to *you*. Not Him. —— It's not that easy. I can't talk to Him like that. —— Soon. Stay with me 'til I'm ready. Okay? —— No. Stay. Don't go. —— Why does it have to be soon? —— Please, don't leave. Please, don't…Sarah? Please, come back…You're here. You're in my mind. You're always here." The man broke down, sobbing.

Shifra was torn between terror and tears herself. "Turn it off."

Gretchen shot a finger out to the pause key and snatched it back. "I don't think he's on Bluetooth."

Shifra stared at the screen. "He's wrestling."

Beside her, Gretchen's face was fixed on the frozen image of the man. "Yeah, but with what? Is his car haunted?"

Shifra shook her head. "That's not the kind of ghost he's wrestling with. We need to pray for that man."

"Wow. I never thought of that."

Shifra put her hand on the woman's shoulder. "God's doing something. It looks like this man was supposed to kill Ruben and he rescued him instead. God must be doing something in his life. I think there's a chance for him to be saved, too."

"Who do you think Sarah is?"

"Hard to tell. It sounds like it might be a real person from his past. Maybe a wife, girlfriend, sister, someone he lost. Someone who tried to tell him about Jesus but he didn't listen, maybe. Or maybe they were both believers and something happened to her and he blames God. Maybe the reason he went bad. I don't know, but I think God is using her memory, or hallucination, or something to reach him."

Gretchen gave a shiver. "Or maybe the devil's talking to him. Sounds eerie to me. Don't be too quick to throw out that ghost idea. Didn't Solomon raise a ghost from the dead or something in the Bible?"

Gretchen looked serious. Shifra considered how to temper her comment. "Well…you're close. There's a passage that's similar to that description and there are some names that start with S in the story."

Gretchen wiggled her head and shoulders in triumph. "I thought so."

Shifra patted her back. "God sent Samuel, which is…pretty close to Soloman, back from the dead to confront Saul when he went to a witch who lived at Endor."

"Oh. Maybe I need to go to a few more of Dr. Welch's Bible studies."

Shifra squeezed her shoulder. "We'll both go. We can cheer like we're at a football game and see the look on the doctor's face."

Gretchen's smile was reflected on the monitor. "But there was a witch in the story, so that's pretty close."

Shifra nodded as she considered the connection. "Definitely cut from the same sheet."

Gretchen sent her a half turn smirk of understanding. "I'm still not giving up on the ghost idea. I watch this show called Modern Hauntings, and there is some pretty convincing stuff on there."

"The world is full of convincing stuff."

Gretchen regarded her through her screen. "Convinced is not really the vibe I'm getting here. You don't believe in ghosts?"

Shifra smiled. "Most people recognize that there is more to life than what is obvious to our senses. If God chooses to raise the dead, He can do that. But besides God and Satan, the Bible only talks about a couple of supernatural things that are running around on the earth—demons and angels. And both of those stay hidden most of the time. The demons get more mileage out of deception than making appearances. As for the angels…God plays things low key and usually keeps things hidden for His own reasons."

"So, do you think this guy is talking to a demon or an angel?"

Shifra shrugged. "The Bible does talk a lot about demons possessing people, and I'm sure this guy has a lot of them running around in his life. But God specializes in making good happen out of evil. Something bad happened to this man. Whatever it was hit him hard, and he's struggling. I don't know what Sarah is, but it sounds like she's telling him he needs to talk to God, and that's true."

Gretchen shook herself. "Okay. Well pray for me, too, 'cause I'm a little freaked out. Maybe there isn't any story. Couldn't he just be crazy? A nice, everyday, ordinary crazy?"

Shifra sighed. "Gretchen, he's an assassin. I don't think you're going to get ordinary here." The word assassin grabbed at Shifra—the shadowy figure, years ago, in their family apartment in New York. "I dealt with a lot of messed up people during the missions I worked. Some I worked against, some I worked with. In this business, ordinary takes on a whole new meaning."

Faces came up in Shifra's memory. Faces she loved, covered in blood. She focused on Gretchen to try to clear them away. "One thing I can tell you is the devil is always trying to freak us out or fool us. And demons are a whole lot smarter than humans. That's why there are so many convincing things in the world. If we don't stay close to the Lord, we'll get fooled. No matter what hap…" It was all there—the blood, trying to find Caleb's pulse, pushing on his chest…Shifra turned away.

"Hey. You okay?"

Shifra straightened herself, drawing in a deep breath. "Even if it looks like we're losing everything now, in the end, He wins, and we want to be right there with Him when He does."

Gretchen stood and put her arms around Shifra. "I'm sorry. I forget everyone here has seen way more bad stuff than I have. Sorry, I brought up memories like that."

Shifa squeezed the girl. "It's not you. It's what we're talking about. Demons, are always around us, whispering things in our minds, bringing up the past. I have to give it to God. He's knows why it happened. This is where our faith in Him matters the most."

"I'm new to this." Gretchen's voice was muted against Shifra's shoulder. "Things could get tougher around here, couldn't they?"

Shifra gave a shrug and a nod together.

Drawing back, Gretchen looked in Shifra's eyes. "I'm up for that prayer."

Shifra took Gretchen's hand. "Lord, help us. Help this man. Help us listen to You and no other voice— human or spirit. We don't know what's going on, but You do. Something is messing with this man's mind, but I can hear your voice in there trying to reach him." Shifra looked to Heaven, but all she could see were tears. "Thank you for not leaving us alone. You're always trying to reach us no matter what kind of mess we're in the middle of. We let our minds get so full it's hard to hear You sometimes. Heal whatever's happened to him." She bowed her head and squeezed her eyes to keep from dripping on the floor. "Help me not forget what you've done for me." She let God's spirit wash over her again. It was a continuous process—being healed, a painful process.

Gretchen sniffed in preparation to speak. "God, I don't know You like I should. But I want to. Don't let me be fooled by…something else. If You can help this guy, please do that too…before he hurts any of us, okay?"

They hugged for a moment. Gretchen pulled away, looking at her screens. "Check this out." Sitting, she scooted her chair closer and pointed.

The program displayed several images of the same man walking through an airport, entering a hotel, and a face shot looking intently at something. The label, **Unknown individual flagged as a person of interest by Department of Homeland Security - Do not inform subject of this notice** was displayed along with a phone number to contact.

Shifra pointed at the screen. "Can you tell why they want him?"

Gretchen shook her head. "You would have to contact an agent to get that information. If he was on the terrorist watch list, they would come out and say that. He must be involved in suspicious activity. It's pretty rare that we can't find an identity for him with all the facial recognition databases available now. The DHS is probably trying to figure him out, too. He's a spook of some kind. Foreign intelligence or underground crime."

"Will they know we did a search on him?"

"No. But Oklahoma City PD Officer 73 will have some explaining to do."

Shifra shoved the girl's shoulder. "That's rotten. Why are you accessing federal databases in some innocent cop's name? What did he ever do to you?"

"Gave me a ticket."

"How terrible of him. It would be different if that was his job or something. Did you deserve it?"

Gretchen twisted up her face. "Okay, I'll put some impressive stats on his monthly record to make up for it."

"One good crime deserves another, I guess. How about just paying the fine and leaving the officer out of this?"

Gretchen gave Shifra a side of the eye evaluation. "You and Dr. Welch really should get together. That's what he would have told me. You do realize this is what cyber hackers do, don't you?"

"I know we can't share what we do with the police, but they aren't our enemies, either."

"Don't worry. If the DHS checks, it will know it's bogus because his terminal can't access that kind of info in the way I did it. We're trying to keep the Institute's activities concealed. The sides are getting blurred."

"Point taken. I'm starting over, so I guess I'm new at this, too."

"But since you jabbed my conscience, I'll start randomizing my logins among the other officers— probably less obvious that way." Gretchen gave Shifra a quick glance. "And I'll pay the ticket." She typed with a gleeful expression. "Out of my expense account."

Shifra chuckled and indicated the picture at the hotel. "Where's this?"

Gretchen pulled up the details. "The Skirvin Hilton. Oh, wow. See, I told you. The Skirvin was on Modern Hauntings. They say the ghost of a maid walks the halls and appears in guests' rooms. It's because she had an affair with the owner back in the early nineteen hundreds and to protect his reputation, he locked her away in an upper room until she jumped to her death with her illegitimate child in her arms."

Shifra tipped her gaze toward Gretchen. "You might want to watch something else."

"A lot of strange things pop up while I'm doing research. You can get kind of hooked on it."

Shifra gave the woman a concerned smile. "Can you print the man's picture from the hotel for me? He's the only spook I'm looking for."

In a moment, the printer hummed, and Shifra took the printed photo as it came out. She pointed at the computer again. "Where does this face image come from?"

"That's the Alamo rental kiosk at the Oklahoma City airport."

"Any chance of finding out who paid for that rental car and the hotel room?"

Gretchen slid her chair over to a separate monitor and keyboard. When she hit a key, a blue and black screen came on. "Give me a little while. I'll poke around in the net's dark alleys. There are always passwords for sale."

"How much does something like that cost the Institute?"

Gretchen's look said she was disappointed at the question. "I don't pay those slime real money. When it comes to this jungle, I'm the predator, not the prey."

Shaking her head, Shifra gave Gretchen a pat on the back. "I'm going to check on Dr. Welch."

Gretchen smirked. "Don't you mean Ruben?"

Shifra inhaled with a shoulder lift and a look of contentment. "Yeah, I think I do."

Shifra jerked awake in the recliner in the observation room. There was coughing and an alarm coming over the speaker feeding the sounds from Ruben's room. Her ears had heard the sounds many times during her vigil over the last two days. But her heart was still in tune with the suffering of the man on the other side.

She hurried to the sealed glass window as the doctors pushed into their accordion suits. They shuffled to Ruben's bed.

During her vigil, She had watched with concern and fascination as robotic equipment did everything from turning the patient to inserting needles for new intravenous lines. Still, the faces looking through the clear face shields of the protective suits were showing the strain of their work.

Shifra waited as they conducted their examination. They conferred with each other and gave instructions to the nurse technicians operating the equipment. She didn't want to interrupt them and cause any chance of error, but she was impatient for the latest prognosis.

In time, Dr. Malik entered the observation room. He gave a troubling sigh. "The virus is morphing rapidly. We have had to re-trigger Dr. Welch's cytokine shutdown several times. It's a wily bug. It's changing and re-initiating the process."

The doctor walked to the window and looked at Welch. "It's become the most aggressive strain I've ever seen. It's weird, though. Before yesterday, it didn't seem to want to spread. It seemed happy to remain in Welch's body and not grow much."

Malik faced Shifra with a frown. "But it was enough. It was as if Welch's system was already prepared to have an overzealous immune response. Like I said before, whoever made this found a way to tune the virus genetically to Welch's system. His little germ fighters see this strain as public enemy number one and start sending out the big guns right away in an all-or-nothing fight. A fight that wasn't really necessary until yesterday afternoon."

The words landed on Shifra like a weight. She turned her frown toward the window. "It's getting worse?"

"It's growing rapidly now, like a switch was flipped. Now it *is* the number one enemy. We are praying we are stopping it before it causes organ damage. If he had not been here, he would never have made it through the night."

"Can you keep doing that, triggering him? Is it hurting him?"

"The disease is as new as the treatment. We are dealing with a highly advanced bioweapon. The designer knows how we fight disease and has designed this strain to take advantage of that. The only plus is that the creators didn't account for our ability to apply the DNA switch on portions of the immune response. But we can't completely reprogram Welch's body, so the process restarts every time the virus spreads. There's a lot we don't know. So far, he is responding, and each treatment reverses his body's response. We're also managing his fever to keep it at an effective but safe level."

Malik gestured toward Welch. "We need his system to kill the disease. We're just trying to keep his body from killing itself in the process. That is a lot of what we do in medicine. Now this thing is expanding so rapidly that I'm wishing we had let his immune response go a little longer at the beginning. See if it could have killed it while it was more fragile."

"Is there anything more you need?"

"We're quietly bringing in specialists in a number of medical disciplines. The Sanders are providing for everything."

"Can I see him? I was exposed early on and I'm fine."

The doctor shook his head. "The virus has changed. It's super contagious now, worse than we've seen before. As you see, we are taking extraordinary precautions to protect our staff. If you hadn't got him out of that hospital…It could have taken out the whole place and moved on from there."

Shifra thought about the staff she had interacted with there. "Do we need to warn them?"

"We have. We called pretending to be the CDC. But until yesterday, the virus was not much of a threat to anyone except Mr. Welch. Like I said, I think it was designed for his DNA. Now it's a different bug. It is the ultimate contagion, and normal precautions wouldn't have been enough. If Mr. Welch hadn't realized that it was a bioweapon and warned you, this virus could have devastated that hospital. We might not have been as prepared as we needed to be, either. If we hadn't treated Welch like a bio attack victim from the beginning, this bug could have wiped out everyone at the Institute."

"Maybe that is what they wanted. Thank God, Ruben realized what was happening. It's just like him to be willing to sacrifice himself. The only reason he called was because he thought the staff at the hospital were in danger and he couldn't get out on his own."

Malik turned to look at his patient. "He's a smart man. If he had waited any longer, this could have decimated the country. Look at the resources it is taking to treat one man." With a sweep of his hand, Malik indicated the machines and people surrounding Welch.

Shifra gave her own gentle smile in Welch's direction. "And no one but us will ever know what he did."

Chapter 17

R adley was ready to make his assault on the Institute. Alone, driving back to his camp, his mind churned with thoughts. It had been days since he had spoken with Sarah. For all he knew, she was gone forever.

She's in your imagination. You control this. Or did he? *Was* he in control anymore? Had he ever been?

Whether his bleak childhood or genetics or both produced his disorder, there had never been normal in his life. But there had been consistency, and he needed to find that again.

Radley pulled off the roadway. Stepping out of the vehicle, he moved the logs and brush he had used to conceal the entrance to the forgotten road. Once he had the SUV past the blockade, he put it back again.

So many hidden things.

When he took the man to the hospital, he had not intended to go back. But sitting in his vehicle the day

Sarah left him, he didn't know what else to do. Staking out the man had been an effective way to get his mission, and his life, back on track.

He had been unsure of what he would find when he followed the woman from the hospital with his drone. The name of the organization surprised him—an institute for people with special needs.

Radley considered the concept as he climbed back in the cab and pushed the rented Suburban up the rugged abandoned trail toward the base camp he had been working out of the last few days. *What is this Institute really?* He hadn't learned that much.

He couldn't see past the main gate, so he had followed the people that left the facility. There were adults and kids with various disabilities. Most had caretakers. A few were on their own. At their homes, they unloaded gear for all types of activities, water, equestrian, sports.

After tonight, they'll have to find somewhere else to go. Why did that trouble him? It wouldn't have before. *I wonder if a place like this could have helped when I was a kid?*

Those thoughts won't get the job done.

He had spent several days surveilling the grounds, getting to know the place. He posed as a hiker photographing the woods around the property, taking recon pictures from a distance, staying out of view of the facility's security cameras. But he had discovered little about the people inside.

Why do you care? You have the information you need to overcome their defenses. Radley reflected on how lonely he felt the last few days. In the past, he had been able to do his recon work like a machine—hiding, watching, collecting data, planning the target's destruction—never truly considering the humans involved.

Would the feelings go away again? Did he want to go back to the way he was before? He knew the thoughts were because of Sarah.

There's one thing you can do to bring her back. Radley considered it. He didn't think he could do that, even for Sarah.

How could he trust in God? No one had ever been watching out for him. Not when his parents sold him to Nelson and Athena Corbondo. Not through Nelson's experiments. Not when Athena and her group made him into something they could market as a powerful person's final solution.

Don't think about it. It would only lead to the violent daydreams. The ones Sarah had taught him to replace with the scenarios in which he was kind and caring and people loved him. Like Sarah loved him. Like Sarah...*had* loved him.

Get your mind back.

The old man knew Radley wouldn't kill innocent people anymore, just other rival criminals. The way Welch threw off the surveillance team tailing him in Oklahoma city...he had to be in the business. But it couldn't be only him. *There has to be more to this Institute.* It must be a front.

He wouldn't risk a fly over, but from a distance, his drone showed that the facility was huge. The buildings were all impressive in size and architecture and the amount of land the security fencing circled was unbelievable. He wasn't sure how much acreage was involved because of the way the fencing ambled around the lake and through the woods.

The money it must have taken to build the place would be over the top if not for the cover story of the founders discovering a huge treasure. The story itself was too much to believe, but it was well grounded in the community and had received national media attention, so no one questioned it.

He wasn't sure how they had pulled that off. No wonder no one in the business had identified the group as a player in the game. It was so out in the open and yet so clandestine. *Welch created the perfect cover.*

Radley saw the big man again in his mind, holding the choice out before him. Encouraging him not to miss his opportunity. And Radley had taken it. He let Welch live. He thought Sarah would be pleased. But she wanted more from him. Doing good wasn't enough. It had to be all about Jesus. How could he be thinking about basing his life on what some imaginary person expected of him?

The real Sarah was gone. She was the only human he had ever known who tried to have his best interests in mind all the time. When she began to appear to him—It must have been his mind's defense mechanism.

He wanted her back, but she wasn't coming back. He didn't deserve her. *Stop it. Sarah wouldn't let you get away with that if she were here. You can't go back to the depression.*

But he couldn't keep the past from shoving its way into his thoughts.

When he faked his own death to escape from the Corbondos, he thought he could be free. No one was supposed to die in the lab explosion. The body he planted in his place was already dead, an inconsequential opponent he had to dispatch. He was a spook like Radley. No DNA or fingerprints on file. But he was exactly what Radley had been waiting for—a corpse that matched his physical description.

Staging the scene in Nelson's laboratory was Radley's way of making sure no one else could be tormented there. He placed the body so it would be burned to the point the Corbondos would mistake it for him. That's how he had left things, and he had run until he thought the nightmare was behind him.

The old man had paid the Corbondos for Radley's services in the past. One time, he secretly slipped Radley a card. It said, **In case you ever want a job**. Calling the number on the card seemed like his only option. At least he was working on his own terms. He could retreat after each job and hide from the world.

That was his life until he got brave enough to check the newspapers from that day. He learned local authorities had identified the unknown body in the lab as a homeless man the Corbondos employed and people in the area knew only as Peter. Athena Corbondo was still being sought for questioning in the matter. But the rest of the story was embodied in the headline that would be forever burned in his memory—**DNA Used to Identify Reclusive Scientist and Daughter Killed in Lab Explosion.**

At first he felt numbness. Killing was how he lived, but this was different. Then the feelings came, a gradual ache, then internal pain he had never felt before.

When the depression was unbearable, Sarah had come to him. She helped him through it.

He didn't understand all the psychological reasons for her visits, but he was sure there were plenty. Especially in a mind that had experienced all the things he had been through. But he still needed her, and now she was gone.

Without Sarah, he didn't think he could fight the darkness.

Radley sniffed a laugh that was half cry. He'd never had a sense of irony before, but there it was. That's exactly what Sarah had been telling him all along. He couldn't fight the darkness alone.

But Radley *was* alone. Now he didn't even have the old man. The boss had always been good at sniffing out internal enemies. *I guess he was right again, but the old lion got too weak.*

If Radley didn't get himself together, someone would get him too. He could daydream about Sarah all day long, but if he didn't get a hold of himself, he'd make a mistake. They would catch him and lock him up.

Nelson might be dead, but Athena was the one he feared most. She and her group would never give up if they knew he was alive.

If the authorities caught him, it would make no difference where he was incarcerated. Athena would find a way to reach him. It wouldn't matter how strong he was, how skilled he was. She would just send more, and he would have nowhere to run. He had tried running before, but she always seemed to know where he was, what he was thinking. She had created what he was.

The only thing he knew was to go back to the plan. What choice did he have but to get his life back to the way it was before Sarah appeared? *You always have a choice.* Radley shook his head. *No, I don't. She's gone. And it's all my fault.*

He fixated on his headlights illuminating the rutted trail. His mind flooded with thoughts of choices and God. He chose to ignore them.

When he reached the campsite, he got out and made a visual sweep of the area. The wireless camera he had hidden in the tree was still there. The only trips he'd gotten from it and the other cameras he placed around the area were from wildlife.

He didn't expect any humans in the area. The first day, he had trekked a good distance in both directions and done a drone survey. There was no reason for anyone to be around.

Opening the back hatch, he rolled up his sleeping bag and tossed it to the front of the spacious cargo bed. Making a long reach, he pulled one of the plastic storage cases to the rear and unlatched it.

Radley began to prep for his attack. Opening packages of plastic explosives, he stuffed the white putty into his backpack. He needed to access and mold the material quickly once he was inside the Institute property. Next, he stored the remote detonators in the outside pockets of the pack to keep them separate.

He filled the rest of the interior with duct tape, wire, various fasteners, and other supplies he might need for a major assault on a facility. To the outside of the pack, Radley fastened a cordless tool that would snip the fence wire and a chest harness filled with multiple rifle magazines. Last, he folded the stock on his rifle, reducing it to a compact form, and secured it to the pack.

Reaching forward again, Radley pulled out the high security container. Inside were some of his most prized possessions. Entering the combination, he unlocked the case.

Stripping off his outer shirt, he took from the case a suit, which included attached hands, feet, and headpiece. It was all made of thick, rugged, dark material. He stretched it over his body, rolling the excess of the headpiece on his forehead like a stocking cap. Radley looked like a jogger in a full-body workout suit. The legs of the suit had pockets with flaps. Radley had installed a holster on the right side that he put his handgun in and extra magazines in the other side.

There were three other pieces made of the same material. One was about the size of an individual blanket. Radley called it a cloak. The other two were half that size. He checked them to make sure all the powerful magnetic fasteners were working. By connecting them in different ways, they could be configured as a jacket, overcoat, poncho, or cape. The cape fastened to the shoulders of the suit, so it could cover anything carried on his back.

Rolling the large, and one of the small pieces, Radley attached them to the top of the pack like a bedroll. The other small one he used to go over the pack like a rain cover, concealing the items under it.

Radley paused. He had not deployed the suit and fabric in some time. For the first time, he was struck by what possessing them meant. The feeling had never occurred to him before. To his knowledge, he was the only one in the world who had anything like it.

He didn't use them often. If anyone knew what he had, every government in the world would be after him. Especially his own, since they were the ones who contracted him to wipe out the Chinese high-tech lab where he found them. All the U.S. knew was that the lab was near completion on a project that would endanger national security and upset the balance of power. It was expedient for them to use someone anonymous and expendable, like Radley. He had accomplished his mission, destroying the facility along with the people and data used to create what was inside. Those who sent him had to take Radley's word that he was also unable to determine what the lab was working on. The government officials wouldn't be happy that he hadn't shared with them what he found.

For this operation, however, he was prepared to deploy the technology. Something told him that Welch would have designed a facility not easy to breach. He would be making use of his magic tonight.

Throwing on the pack with the concealed items, Radley looked like he was going camping. He hiked far enough to be out of range of the GPS blocker he had in the vehicle to prevent the rental company from tracking him. Pulling out an unregistered handheld GPS, he looked at the logs he had made earlier. The Institute property was about a mile away through the woods. One last gear check and Radley headed out.

Chapter 18

Shifra gave Gretchen an update when she returned. "*Dr. Welch* is about the same." She emphasized his name to head off any comments from Gretchen.

The other woman swiveled to face Shifra. "Our mystery man told the hotel his name was John Martin and paid in cash for room 1002. Here is where it gets fun. He rented a black 2021 Chevy Suburban from Alamo. I tried to initiate the company's GPS tracker, but it's not responding." Gretchen waited with a mischievous grin.

Shifra knew she had to give the girl something to draw out whatever information she was holding onto. "There's not much there we didn't already know. Your image matching software already gave us the vehicle."

"Well, a confirmation is better than nothing." Gretchen's attempt at an innocent face wasn't going to win her the Super Spy Oscar.

Shifra decided to show the young woman that she could talk the talk from her years in New York. "Oh, come on. Don't go to the grave with this."

Gretchen cracked up, leaning back in her chair. "Okay, okay." She held her palm toward Shifra until she was in control again. "The rental was paid with a credit card to an animal feed company out of Chicago. I figured that had to be a front, so I dug deeper and found an interesting customer of that company with a name you might find interesting."

Shifra realized Gretchen's pause was her cue to inquire. "What are you, a game show host? Give over with the goods."

Shifra's response caused another chuckle, but Gretchen kept it under control. "The Plum Island Animal Disease Center, which happens to be just off the tip of Long Island, not far from your old haunts in New York City. Doesn't that sound interesting? From what I understand, the DNAble headquarters was supposed to be in New York."

"New York is a big place."

"Yeah, but how many places have *disease* as part of their name? Sounds to me like the perfect place to be making viruses. I did some research and there is a lot of connection between Plum Island and bio-weapons research. Maybe it's all conspiracy theories. Maybe not."

"Is it a private island?"

"No. It's government. Most recently, they have been moving the animal disease operation to Kansas, where the Department of Agriculture is running it.

Before that, it was under the Department of Homeland Security. Maybe someone in one of those agencies has gone to the dark side."

"That would be scary. Give me the number to that hotel where our man checked in. I'm going to see if he's still there."

When Shifra connected with the hotel, she put on her official voice. "I would like to leave a message for John Martin in room 1002."

"I'm sorry. He's already checked out." The clerk sounded regretful. "He left yesterday."

"Oh, no. Well, thanks anyway." Shifra hung up the phone and pointed toward the dark web computer. "See if he's turned in his rental car."

Gretchen's hands attacked the keys as she moved through several screens. She grabbed passwords she had on electronic sticky notes, copying and pasting them into boxes on the deep web screen to gain access to the Alamo site. "No. It shows it's still in use. He has three days left on his rental." She read further. "There's also a note in here that he might need to extend, depending on how his work was going." Gretchen swiveled her chair to face Shifra. "That was written on the day Dr. Welch went into the hospital."

Sitting back in the chair, Shifra hung her head. "I have been away from this for too long. That must be why this guy took Rub...Dr. Welch to the hospital. He was using him as bait. I was so concerned about getting Dr. Welch back here to be treated, I probably led this man right to the Institute. I have already become a liability."

Gretchen scooted to Shifra and took her hand. "Not true. Dr. Welch knew this could happen to any of us. After they broke into his apartment, he beefed up security. We'll be ready if he comes here."

Radley closed in on the location he had determined was his best point of entry. The fence stretched farther until it was out of sight. A lot of land for a therapy center. The hike around the property had been a good workout to get him ready. It was time to make his move.

He used a hill for cover as he advanced to where he could inspect the property. As Radley worked his way up to the top of the ridge, he came up behind a good-sized tree.

A well-financed organization should have thermal fusion cameras with the latest terrain recognition software. They would pick out a normal person like a poppy in a daisy patch.

Both the suit and cloak would block his thermal signature. Radley had heard of thermal image blocking technology, but it was not widely available, so that was one advantage. But to slip past an advanced image software package, he needed to be invisible.

Radley took a self-drilling spike from the backpack. Reaching as high as he could, he pushed the spike against the tree, engaging the quiet device to drill itself into the trunk. Taking his cloak loose from his shoulders, he unfurled the fabric until it reached higher than his head. He fastened a corner of the cloak to the spike.

Radley pulled the ski-mask-like headpiece over his face until only his eyes were showing through two holes. Above them was a visor, so all he had to do was bend his neck forward and his eyes were also covered by the camouflage. That limited his view to what was right in front of him, but covering his eyes wasn't necessary in most circumstances. He fastened another corner of the cloak to his shoulder.

Pulling back an extra flap of fabric that covered the control unit fastened to his wrist, Radley set the suit to **Full Surface Touch Reproduction**.

Touching his thumb to the top of his pinky, Radley engaged the suit and placed his hand on the tree. The scanner built into the fabric on the top of his head interacted with the tiny sensors, layers of synthetic chromophores, and ferrofluids comprising the suit and cloak.

Radley's research had determined the technology was based on the color and texture-changing skin of cephalopods such as the octopus. The fabric of both suit and cloak rippled. Color and texture blossomed on the surface to assume the appearance of tree bark. Even close up, it was hard to distinguish it from the tree it rested against.

The material was like a flexible computer monitor, displaying the image of the bark. Metallic nanoparticles in the ferrofluids reacted to miniaturized electromagnets to produce texture. The sensors melded image and texture to produce a three-dimensional effect, fooling the eye. It was like the artists who drew holes on the sidewalk that look genuine enough to fall into. Radley and everything covered by the material had become part of the tree.

Radley detached the thermal fusion scope from his rifle. Under the cloak, he eased out from the tree, taking it slow, so the expansion of the tree trunk wouldn't draw attention. He pushed his scope between the tree and the fabric. It would appear as nothing more than a knothole. Radley examined the tall metal fencing about forty yards below.

Let's see what surprises they have set up for me. There was another deer stand. According to the website, the Institute did some kind of hunting therapy.

The scope picked up a heat signature inside. He adjusted the image. There was the outline of a man and a hotspot where a tent heater was warming the inside of the stand. *If he's a hunter, he should be packing up. It's illegal to hunt deer at night.*

The human image was stationed in front of a laptop. The light from the screen blazed with the scope's enhancement. *What are you watching?*

Radley panned the scope over the terrain. He had his own software, which outlined an anomaly in a tree. Zooming in, the light enhancement revealed a camera mounted high up on the trunk. *There you are. I knew they wouldn't disappoint me.* Radley was able to identify more cameras as he panned the area. From the angle of their aim, he estimated that anything coming within twelve feet of the fence would set off an alert to the sentry, who would be able to see everything going on.

The sentry would be only part of the perimeter network. Taking him out would risk being detected. He had to get past the man without engaging him. They needed to feel confident in their security while he worked his way to the main people inside. Radley allowed himself to be absorbed into the tree once again. Behind the cover, he reset the fabric to **Full Surface Ambient Reproduction** and began assembling his next magic trick.

Shifra made her way back to the observation room. She had been away from Ruben too long. When she entered, she saw that he was on his side, facing her, eyes closed. She walked to the window and watched him pull in the air from the mask.

Ruben's eyelids lifted, straining to open fully.

Shifra drew her hand to her mouth and blinked back tears.

He gazed at her for a moment, then smiled and nodded.

She took her hand from her lips and placed it on the glass between them.

After a second, one of the massive hands reached out to her. The fist closed as if grasping something and drew back to his chest as his eyes clenched tight above the mask. The hand then dropped weakly onto the bed.

The lids opened halfway. His eyes fixed on her until they eased shut again.

The door opened, and Dr. Malik entered.

Shifra turned, anxious to hear the doctor's assessment.

Malik smiled. "I think he's out of the contagious stage. We took some blood for another test that will tell us if the virus is still present in his body to know for sure. The virus suddenly weakened and died off. There was no reason for it. It appears he's recovering with no organ damage."

Shifra was crying again. "Praise the Lord."

Malik nodded. "Amen."

Radley inched forward, holding the cloak in front of him, stretched on a frame to produce a flat surface. It was more effective than the suit alone because it produced a more stable image.

The technology in the cloak shifted almost instantaneously, micro adjusting as he advanced. Still, he didn't want to risk the camera on the tree detecting any sudden change in the terrain.

Pain was developing in his arm muscles. The frame he had assembled to spread the cloak out was lightweight, but he had been holding it for a long time. Radley ignored the discomfort. It was odd. In the past, he barely noticed such pain.

The blank non-camo side of the fabric faced him.

All indicators said the device was working, but not seeing the front of the cloak was unnerving. He could only trust that the landscape behind him was still being mimicked on the other side, rendering him invisible. If there was any glitch in the software, he would never know it until he was surrounded by armed security officers. The sensation was not overpowering, but it was also something new to him. Whatever was happening inside him was not productive.

There's the fence. Radley moved close enough to slip two thin hooks over the chain link so the framed cloak would hang on its own. He took a moment to work the kinks out of his sore muscles. Then he peeked around the cloak enough to aim the main detector on his head at the tree cameras that would be viewing him. Using the controller, he programmed the camera angles into the image generating software.

Like standing in front of a movie projector, Radley saw the surrounding scene replicated on his body from head to foot and gloved hands. It had been hard getting used to working with his hands while moving images were displayed on them. Over time, his mind had adjusted to a more touch and feel approach.

Taking off his pack, he took out the other pieces of fabric and activated them. Setting his pack on the ground, he draped one piece over it. Fabric and pack vanished into the landscape. He laid the other piece on the ground, and it disappeared. Staring at the place he laid the fabric, he could see a slight difference that allowed him to detect the edge. If he looked away and turned back, he had to feel for it before he was able to distinguish the edge again. The effect was incredible. Radley was counting on his suit working as well as the cloak, because he was about to unveil himself.

He inched the framed cloak upward. Again, he felt apprehension, wondering if the image on his legs would render them invisible to the camera once the cloak was removed. *Forget it and get the job done.* With concentration, Radley was able to mute the emotion and recapture his flat temperament.

When the bottom of the cloak was about three feet from the ground, Radley hooked it on the fence again. He added two more fasteners to the bottom to keep it in place in case there was a stray breeze. The forecast had predicted a calm night. He was counting on that, but there was no sense in overlooking a precaution that was easy to take. Pulling the visor over his eyes, he crouched to reach the material he had placed on the ground.

Radley made a slow turn to face his back toward the cameras, concealing his hand movements. Might as well give the technology the best advantage.

He left the image display on the fabric he held but disabled the texturing. This allowed him to roll it small enough to fit through one of the holes in the chain link. Taking two more fasteners from the pack, he clenched them between his teeth.

Making a gentle pivot, Radley eased forward and fed the material through the chain link. Even rolled, the sensors were blending it with the surroundings.

The farther he pushed the roll, the more it drooped toward the ground. He knew there would be some distortion. He hoped it would only appear like a smudge on the camera or an insect flying in front of it.

Unfurling the rolled material when he was on the opposite side of the fence was a tedious process. Radley had to reach his fingers through the holes in the chain link and move the corner of the fabric from hole to hole. After several minutes of inching it up and across, Radley had the material stretched to cover the lower three feet of the other side of the fence.

The sensors on the fabric would add the chain link it was resting against to the image on the opposite side. Since he was concealed again, Radley raised his visor and hastened his movements. Accessing the controller, he locked the image of the fence into the fabric he had just installed. Now he could cut the fence and the image on the other side would still display the intact chain-link.

Radley had to look twice to find his backpack so he could get the fence cutters. He soon had the bottom of the fence cut away from the concrete footer that attached it to the ground. A few more minutes and the sides were cut high enough that he could bend it up, creating a hole big enough to crawl through. Pulling his visor down, he stood.

Unhooking the frame from the fence, Radley lowered the cloak to the ground until it vanished, becoming the leaves and sticks that covered that area. Pulling the cloak toward him, he disassembled the frame until he and it were hidden behind the lower hanging material. He tried not to move his head because the angle of the camera was probably high enough to see that much of him over the lower material. His suit would have to keep him hidden.

From his backpack, he took out the duct tape and a piece of PVC pipe he had cut in half. He placed the PVC pipe over the jagged part of the chain link that was left in the concrete where he cut it. Using the duct tape, he secured it to the concrete. He couldn't risk tearing the suit. He turned the third fabric off and stowed it and the frame pieces in the pack. Wrapping the cloak around his pack, he eased it through the hole in the fence and out of his way.

Lying on his back, Radley inched through the hole, sliding across the PVC and duct tape and under the hanging fabric. The image should be micro-adjusting to keep the fence looking intact as best it could. If he eased through the hole, the camera shouldn't detect the fine errors.

Half-way through, he was able to see the intact fence displayed on the fabric and on his own legs. The view was distorted at the bottom. Radley continued. It should be displaying correctly from the camera's viewpoint.

Radley heard the sound of a breeze through the trees. *Oh, no.*

The bottom of the fabric lifted. The software accommodated, but it would be difficult to maintain the correct perspective if it went horizontal. The wind was increasing. Radley risked picking up the pace. He pulled his legs through and put his feet on each corner of the fabric, pushing it back down. One corner escaped and flipped up. Radley clenched his teeth and swept his leg around to capture it again higher up. Shoving both corners against the fence, he saw the image of the uncut chain link once again.

Radley struggled to get his breathing under control to limit the rise and fall of his suit. *Did the camera detect all that?* He heard the sound of boots on the leaves. They were coming. He needed to dive back through the fence and—.

No, it was just the breeze blowing the leaves. Why was he feeling such anxiety? He needed to get his cool back.

The breeze subsided. Radley took a breath. He pulled the cloak and backpack to him. Keeping the cloak between him and the cameras, he fastened it to the fence, allowing it to drape over him, the pack, and the hole. Under its cover, he stowed the other fabric.

Bending the part of the fence he had cut back to its original position, he wrapped gray duct tape to cover each place he had cut the wire. It should stand all but the closest inspection. Soon he was walking away, pack on his back, hidden under his cloak. Once he was past the camera, he raised his visor. It occurred to him that the sentry probably blamed any distortion on the breeze that he had been so worried about. *You need to get hold of yourself.*

Past the perimeter, the cameras should thin out even more. They had put so much into guarding their boundaries, they would have confidence that no one could get inside unnoticed. That confidence was going to be their undoing.

Chapter 19

Shifra's emotions were swinging in both directions as she watched over Ruben. He was recovering. For that, she was grateful. But her thoughts kept shifting to the Mystery man, which produced anxiety. *Did he follow me from the hospital? I hate just waiting for the guy to do something.*

The man had confronted Ruben even after he switched vehicles at the storage units. Ruben had thought he lost the rest of the surveillance team. Did that mean this man was acting alone or had the exit plan failed completely? Was the whole group still after them. And who or what was Sarah? Perhaps Gretchen was right, and he had lost his mind. That might mean he was a rogue operative.

What did they know about the man? She was certain his name wasn't John Martin and he might be driving a black Suburban. He had managed to keep his identity secret even with the DHS searching for him. He had also caught Ruben off guard when he was vulnerable. Was this man the one who infected Ruben with the virus? If so, why would he take him to the hospital? So many pieces with so few answers. They could easily underestimate the man.

Perhaps they should let Homeland Security know the man might be in Gilead County, Oklahoma. The feds might be able to help. But that would risk revealing the Institute. It was unnerving having the strange man out there, knowing he was probably ordered to take down their team. How many others that they had not identified were working with him? Having Joshua and the rest around would be helpful. It was important that they stay on the trail of Becker's group, but…so much was at stake on so many fronts.

Shifra turned off the intercom to Ruben's room so she wouldn't disturb him and pulled out her phone. She wanted to call Joshua, but it was still too early in France. She needed to wait a few more hours. He needed rest to be sharp if he was going to track down the people that might be trying to continue Becker's nightmare vision for humanity.

She looked at the time again. Rahab would still be up. Staying up late and sleeping in was her habit. Feeling the need to hear her daughter's voice, Shifra stepped into the hallway. The desire filled her to tell her *Tasil* she loved her…just in case.

Dialing, Shifra thought of the English translation of *Tasil,* the pet name she used for Rahab. It meant *Dove.* She was the wide-eyed innocent dove—the only one of what was left of her family who wouldn't be concerned about all these things. But what her daughter didn't know could hurt her. Had it been wrong to leave her?

She had felt it was time to let her daughter stand on her own. She hoped what she was doing was the right thing. Now she wasn't sure. She had hoped Ruben would be someone she could talk with about such hard things, but everything seemed to be against them in that regard.

Maybe she had left her little *Tasil* on a false errand. *Lord, I need to know Your will. If I'm wrong, turn me around quickly.*

She knew the important choices of Rahab's life were her own, and only God knew the right way for her to go. The most important thing was for her to learn to follow God's leading. *Bring her to You, Lord.*

The phone rang until the voice mail took over. Shifra left a message expressing her love. The girl frustrated her. Always out late. Shifra would have to try both children again in the morning.

Radley low crawled under the bushes. He kept the suit off to conserve power since there was natural cover.

His recon of the core complex had identified many of the buildings. He'd found the main rehabilitation facility. It was dark but had continuous water filtration pumps operating. That must be where the famed dolphin therapies took place. The humans had vacated it for the night, so it was of no concern to him. Same with the indoor sports park.

There were several private residences on the grounds. Once he finished his recon, he would go to them first, rigging explosives on likely bedroom walls in ways that would bring the buildings down, making them burn. The chance of Welch being in any of them was slim. He would blow them and the security building first to thin out the opposition force he would face.

He pushed forward through the underbrush. Bringing the detached scope to his eye, he examined the building below that blazed with light.

The structure appeared to be a medical building. There were lights burning throughout it. In his scope, he saw the ambulance in the rear.

The virus infection would land Welch there, in an ICU somewhere. If the disease had progressed, those close to Welch, the major members of the team, might be there, as well. It was the building where Radley would make his major attack.

Welch should be dead from the virus, but the man was full of surprises. Other team members might be suffering from various phases of the disease. They would be like shooting fish in a barrel.

Radley would lure anyone who survived his initial explosions to the medical building with gunshots. Smoke bombs would funnel them to the entrance he chose, where he would have two claymore mines to catch the team in a crossfire explosion of shrapnel. Then he would blow the entrance ceiling, blocking the exit. Any survivors should be easy to pick off.

If there were any security left on the perimeter, he would get as many as he could on his way out. If he missed some, they wouldn't be a threat once the leadership was gone. The organization would be eliminated like the big boss wanted. Even if the old man wasn't alive to see it, Radley would have accomplished the mission.

He was glad he got half of the money up front. It was more than he needed to survive. The rest of the money would have been a testimony to his skill, nothing else. He needed little to exist. His home was minimalistic, his own vehicle, utilitarian. The money would allow him to go underground for a while, where he could be alone with his thoughts. Maybe they would produce Sarah again.

Radley felt sick at the idea of her being nothing but a conjuring of his imagination. His fantasy world had always been vivid. He preferred it to real life with…real people.

But Sarah was real. The idea of living in his imaginary world now felt empty. Sarah had loved him even though she had known everything about the real him. Now she wanted to work with God to save him. Thought he was *worth* saving.

She's gone. He clenched his fists and drove them into his forehead. *Why?* He wanted to scream it, but his fear stopped him. He envisioned being caught, taken alive, locked up, trapped, surrounded by people that would be talking, staring, and trying to interact with him. The shiver that went through him took him by surprise.

The images of Sarah he was experiencing couldn't be real. He needed to forget about her, forget her name, forget everything. He didn't need this kind of pain. She was gone. Just like his parents. They left him with someone they didn't even know. Someone who——.

Forget it. No names. No faces. Just forget.

Radley took a long breath and held it. He needed to center his thoughts, get his edge back. He would breathe when he had his body and emotions under control and not before.

His thoughts were on the big man named Welch. He hoped the virus hadn't killed him. The more he considered the possibility, the more he believed Welch was alive. The man was smart and resourceful. So were his colleagues. If he still lived, Radley would have to kill him. He would also kill the others. Killing was his job. He no longer had Sarah to consider.

The desire to breathe came, but Radley rejected it. He imagined Welch, his face, his large frame.

A painful need for oxygen crept up his throat and tried to force his mouth open. Radley ignored it, scoffed at it. His lungs burned, trying to force him into action.

He would not let Welch influence him. He pushed the big man down, squeezed him until he was smaller in his mind. The man was compressed to almost nothing when he noticed the smile still on Welch's face.

A convulsion struck Radley's chest. Something large was behind Welch, bright and glorious.

Another heave from inside forced a strange sound from Radley's lips. He clenched them tighter. In his mind, the brilliance moved past Welch and came forward, dancing before Radley's eyes, seeming to reach out and touch him right in the heart.

Air spewed out of his mouth and he inhaled fresh oxygen, pulled in before he could stop it. He shuddered to his core as it went into his lungs. Gasping, Radley's chest heaved like Welch's had done that day.

The dark woods had a crisp freshness. Cricket song dawned on Radley's senses. The unseasonably mild temperature brought them out. There was a purity about the sound and smell combination. It was healing.

He could go on, avoiding cameras and laying explosives. It was the plan he had made…the choice. He took in a long breath and held it. Or he could walk away. The option felt new, unavailable before. He could change his mind, his plan, his… He exhaled.

Looking up, he saw a few faint stars peeking through the autumn leaves. They were muted by the compound lights, which illuminated paths and parking lots and transformed the trees into silhouettes.

Radley had the desire to run, to escape, just like he had from the Corbondos. But this was different. Instead of coldly calculating a way to hide from his tormentors, he felt like there might finally be a chance for him to live.

More feelings. Could he trust any of them? They hadn't been a part of his life. He hadn't needed them.

That had been his choice. To stay hidden and not to let people in his life. He would come out of his hole when forced by necessity. The hits he completed gave him money so he could hide away again.

He lived in the world of his imagination, where people did what he wanted. He was the one in power. Growing up under the Corbondos' control, it had been his only escape. In the real world, fear dominated his life. He had determined to leave it behind when he was free, but he never really had. He was never really free.

Welch's image was in his mind, smiling. There had been no fear in those eyes. Radley realized Welch wasn't afraid of him that day, even though Radley had been sent to kill him and was pointing a gun at him. Welch had left the decision in his hands. Radley had been in complete control of the situation. But he had not been in control of Welch.

What had moved him to let Welch live? To take him to the ER? He had thought he had done it for Sarah. Had something else moved him, overriding the plan he had constructed in his imagination?

Radley loaded the idea into his thinking. He let his thoughts fire a few practice rounds, keeping his mind on target, holding his pondering in a tightly controlled group.

Then his sights shifted. His imagination took him to what could have been, had he only— The crosshairs were on Radley now. Every round was hitting home, penetrating the surface, ripping through his memories, doing lethal damage to the façade he had created.

Radley had always been able to escape into his own head, where it was safe. His strength was his imagination. Now it was a weakness, producing thoughts that had him questioning everything about his life.

It was spilling over into the real world. Normally he could plan, recon, create tactical advantage, deploy superior technology—until he was in control. Now control eluded him.

There was no question Welch had control. Even more so in his weakness. When there was no hope left, he had hope. It gave the big man a power outside of his circumstances.

Was that what Sarah had, giving her the power to reach beyond the grave like some kind of guardian angel? Or…had God taken control of Radley that day?

Stop it. Radley shook his head. What good was there in such philosophizing? He had a mission. That was the bottom line, and it was time he got back on task. He needed to return to the plan. That made it easier to do what he had to do.

First, he had to get to the medical building. He needed to make a closer inspection so he could plot every detail. There were other buildings surrounding the complex that he could use as cover on his approach. That would limit the amount of time he was out in the open. Get moving.

Chapter 20

Ruben watched Shiffy as she dozed in the chair on the other side of the observation window. He had a fuzzy recollection of the phone ringing in the nurses' station and the nurse in a whispered conversation. He couldn't concentrate on it. Exhaustion blunted his normal curiosity, leaving him to focus on what was most important.

With a start, Shiffy came awake and saw him looking at her. Sitting up, she attempted to straighten her clothes and untangle her hair. She gave up, dropped her hands in her lap and shrugged her shoulders, eyes squinched in a grin that made him want to reach through the glass and hug her. Walking to the window, she spoke into the intercom. "How long have I been asleep?"

"Not long enough. I was enjoying watching you."

"I must look a mess." She wiped the sides of her mouth. "I was drooling."

"I doubt there is anything that could dim your glow. It was good to see you getting rest. You have been wearing yourself out. Go home and get some sleep."

"I couldn't sleep until I know you're okay." Shifra examined him. "You look and sound better. The doctor said he might be able to clear you. He should be getting the test back soon to see if you're still contagious. How do you feel?"

"Better is an apt description. I feel like I have my wind back. I'm out of danger, just tired now. Go home and sleep. There are doctors and nurses abounding."

She gave a narrow-eyed grin and shook her head at him. "That's not the reason I'm here, Ahuvi."

The name lifted Welch from his exhaustion. In Hebrew, Ahuvi meant *My Beloved*. Could that be possible? Was that what she hoped would happen or was she attempting to use her charm as a medicinal effect?

A young woman might misunderstand the cruelty of such an action, giving a smile or even a kiss out of kindness with no real intention toward the person. An immature girl might not realize that the strength of the gesture lay in the hope attached to it. There had to be a dream of full commitment. Heartache was defined by the pain of being the only one who had that dream.

But Shiffy was near his age, mature, even if her face and form did not betray it. She knew the power of the feminine. She had practiced the art to its full impact. Surely, she would not practice it on him, even out of good intention.

She had come for him at substantial risk to herself.

She had stayed through the hours of his suffering. Watched over him as if he was truly someone special to her. Her words, her gaze, all spoke of something beyond kindness or pity.

The thought scared him, to even imagine that a woman so rare could be in pursuit of his heart. She could have it at any time. He was powerless to resist, if it was possible for her to love him. He also realized it would kill him if the love was not real.

Welch gazed into the spellbinding brown eyes. All he could do was shake his head in despair of the right words. "Shiffy."

Shifra pressed her forehead to the barrier between them. "Yes, dear?" The words escaped her mouth in a breathy entreaty that left its imprint on the glass, fleeting yet meaningful.

Welch felt his lip quiver. "Why would you…? I am an ugly old man… I don't know if I…if you…?" Words were Welch's faithful servants. How could they be failing him now?

Shiffy's face turned gloomy. "Are you saying you cannot love me?"

"Look at me, Shiffy. I am saying that my love, even at its best, may not be what you deserve."

"Is that what you believe?" Her gaze pierced him. "Close your eyes."

Welch wrinkled his forehead at the request.

Her smile implored. "Please."

He could do nothing but indulge her.

In the darkness behind his lids, her voice came. "If tomorrow something happened that made me crippled and disfigured, could you love me?"

The question had an immediate answer in his mind, but he did not voice it. Instead, he marveled at the epiphany Shifra produced in him.

He thought he was immune to the trap of beauty, but beauty could cut both ways. His efforts not to be trapped by physical appearance had caused him to focus on it. He had feared what his eyes could see and ignored what his spirit could sense. Shifra was so much more. His sight had blinded him, and she had known how to reach past it. No wonder he loved her. He marveled at the feeling for a moment. She had found a way inside him. He felt himself smiling broadly.

Shifra responded to the smile. "If you could love me regardless of my appearance, why would you think my love was dependent on something so shallow?"

Welch dropped his head, his eyes closed now in shame.

"Besides, what you apparently see in the mirror is not what I see."

Before he could respond, she spoke again. "Now, are you going to answer my question?"

A sob escaped Welch. He squeezed his eyes and wept. What a fool he was. Even in his admiration of Shifra, he had underestimated her. She was more than he could have dreamed. He couldn't imagine such a blessing at this time in his life. Eyes still closed, he nodded with no reservations. "Yes, I could, I do—"

The door burst open across the room, halting his words and bringing his eyes open.

Gretchen stood in the doorway, laptop case hanging

from a strap that crossed her chest and hung on the opposite shoulder. Her eyes swept the room, then she hurried toward Shifra. She gave a weak smile toward Welch.

Her whispers were too quiet for Welch to hear, but he could see her hands were shaking. "What's going on?"

Shifra put on a smile. "Nothing. There is some intel that Gretchen needs help with. You rest and I'll be back." She followed Gretchen out of the room.

Once they were in the hallway, Shifra felt free to find out more of the situation. "So, the fence has been cut?"

Gretchen's nod was more of a head vibration. "Toward the back of the property." She blurted the sentence like it was one long word. "Jim thinks someone might be on the grounds."

"Do they have any idea when it happened?"

Gretchen had to stop biting her bottom lip to answer. "They know exactly when it happened. The guard says he last checked that part earlier in the evening but it had already been cut by that time. He just didn't notice it. Whoever cut the wire put it back and concealed it well. Jim said they only found it because an owl got caught in the barbed wire that topped the fence. The flapping set off the alarm. It was right above where the fence was cut. While they were getting the owl loose, they pushed against the fence and ripped the duct tape that was concealing the cuts. What're the odds of that?"

The comment moved Shifra's spirit. "Probably zero without Divine intervention."

Gretchen did her little head wobble. "Well, yeah. I guess so." She turned up her intensity. "But get this. All the alarms go off immediately from nothing but a flapping owl. But someone takes the time to cut a hole big enough for a full-size human to crawl through, and then pushes the wire back, and tapes up each cut, and there's not a peep. They have no idea how someone could have done it."

Gretchen widened her eyes and leaned forward with her hands out, fingers spread wide. "But here's the spooky part. You know why they have the exact time it happened? They checked the video. They found where the fence is intact and then a little later, just because they know what to look for, they can tell it's been cut."

Gretchen was quivering with excitement. "And in between, right where the fence is cut, all they see are these weird camera distortions." The computer genius looked like she might burst. "I'm telling you, it's the next episode of Modern Hauntings right here at the Institute."

Shifra reached out and took Gretchen's hands, hoping to slow her down. "What's Jim going to do?"

"He's got the guards going house to house to make sure everyone is okay. People are supposed to fortify in place while the guards search. After they came to my place, the guards brought me here so I could tell you without upsetting Dr. Welch."

Shifra let Gretchen have her hands back and tried not to smirk. "That's thoughtful, but I don't think we fooled him." Deceiving Ruben felt wrong. "He's recovered a lot. I don't want to keep this from him."

"Sorry. I was a little excited. I've never been in the middle of anything like this before. I thought he should know. Then I thought if I tell him," Gretchen rocked her head back and forth as she weighed each side, "he might feel like he needs to get up and supervise, and hinder his recovery. Then again, maybe we need him to supervise. So I thought I'd let you make that call."

Gretchen had her hands out and was bouncing at the knees. "But if you decide to tell him, can I tell him…? Because I know the story and…I want to tell it."

Ruben might be ready for the story, but Shifra wasn't sure he was ready for his IT manager. "I'll let things stabilize a little, then *I'll* tell him." Shifra was conscious of Gretchen's disappointment. "We just have to wait and see. What were you doing before this happened?"

The young woman scanned upward in search of the answer, then jerked her gaze back to Shifra. "I don't know. Hacking something, I guess, but I can't remember now. There are two security guards outside waiting to drive me back home, but, ummm," Gretchen did a little dance with her fists clenched. "I don't want to go home." She cast a hopeful eye on Shifra. "What are *you* gonna do?"

Shifra walked past Gretchen and headed down the

hall. "I'm going to access the building's weapons room and arm myself. Have you had any firearms training?"

Gretchen hurried to follow. "No. Nobody's been that crazy. I'll, like, hold the bullets for you or something." After a moment of thought she added, "But if you really need them, you better keep them yourself because I can't guarantee I won't run."

Welch gazed at the empty observation room. He knew that *nothing* was not an accurate description of whatever news Gretchen had brought. His mind ran through the possibilities. The strongest candidate was that there was a threat in the area.

Shifra's reaction was too calm for some type of personal tragedy for her or him. Gretchen's manner was too tense to be dismissed. If it was not a threat, Shifra would have put his mind at ease immediately. Instead, she told an unconvincing lie.

She was trying to protect him. That meant she might be putting herself in harm's way to do it. He couldn't lose her. Not now. Never had any club, knife, or bullet panicked him more.

He threw his legs off the bed and rose. The room spun. Staggering forward, he grabbed the tray table to right himself, but didn't linger. His body was wobbly and sent him sideways. Through the glass enclosure he saw the nurse, wide-eyed, rising from her station. He was able to steady himself and make it to where he could lean against the glass. He remembered the door latch could only be opened from the control center.

The nurse was moving toward one of the accordion suits. She yelled. Her voice was muffled by the airtight seal to his room. "Mr. Welch, you should not be up, and you know we can't unlock the door. It would endanger everyone. Please."

Welch knew why he was locked in. He couldn't expose others to the virus. His desperation grew. Hands against the glass, he yelled to the woman. "Please, could you tell me what's going on? Am I right to believe there is a threat to the facility?"

The woman had one leg in the bio suit and gave him an exasperated expression. "Some kind of threat, yes. They have told us to lock the outside doors and keep away from windows. I don't know any more. There's nothing you can do, so please go back to bed."

"Would you go find Shifra for me? She just left. Tell her I need to talk to her right away. Please. It is extremely important."

The woman was half in the suit and was gawking at him. Her darting eyes betrayed her mental struggle between giving in to his request or using the suit to get him back to bed.

Welch pointed to the computer. "Check and see if the lab posted my test yet. That's how you checked before. Please look."

"Mr. Welch, please go back to bed." The woman's face showed her understanding. "I'll check, but there are security guards handling the situation. There's nothing you can do."

"I am worried that Shifra has gone to do something that might endanger her. If you go find her and have her come back, so I know she's all right, I'll go back to bed. Otherwise, as your supervisor, I am demanding you check my test results. If they are negative for the virus, I want you to open the decontamination chamber and allow me to clean up and leave." Welch pointed to the door leading into the chamber. He hated rudeness, but he was desperate.

The woman turned and headed toward the exit. He could see the side of her jaw moving as she told herself what she thought of Ruben Welch at the moment.

Shifra scanned her badge and her face to enter the vault. Her gaze darted over the weapons while Gretchen watched. *If there's a possibility of an assault on the Institute I don't want to be out gunned.* She grabbed an assault rifle, loaded up a thirty-round magazine, and slapped it in the weapon, which she slung across her back.

Gretchen held up her hand. "I'm, like, having a moment. You're really going with that? This is majorly serious if you need a gun that big. I don't know if I'm ready for this action."

Shifra's cell phone rang. Pulling it out of her pocket, she examined the screen. It was Rahab. "Tasil, where have you been? I tried to call you."

"Eema, just listen. I'm sick and I need your help.

Come home."

"I can't…What do you…where are you?"

"I'm at your house, here in Oklahoma. I came to visit you. But, I'm sick. You need to come home."

"Why are you sick? I mean, when did you…? What are you doing here?"

"I came to see you. You're so far away and you won't tell me what you're doing and everything is weird with you, so I came to see you, but you're not here. I got real sick on the plane. I just need to go inside and lie down, but it's all locked up. Come hoooome."

"I…why didn't you tell me…? Okay. I'm…at a friend's house. I'll be there as soon as I can. How did you get from the airport? Are you in a car?"

"Yes, I rented a car. Don't ask questions, Eema. Please, I'm sick."

"I'm coming, Tasil. Lie down on your seat until I get there." Shifra clicked the phone shut. "That girl. Of all the times to do this."

"That was your daughter?" Gretchen's face said the world was spinning too fast for her.

"Yes. The one that is supposed to be in New York. She doesn't know anything about—" Shifra unslung the rifle. "I can't go over with this or she'll know…I…I'm not teaching French like I told her."

"Why didn't you tell your daughter?"

"She can't keep a secret to save her life." Shifra popped the magazine out of the rifle and tossed it on a shelf. *I'll unload that later.* She set the rifle in a rack. "I hate to say it about my own…she's a bit self-consumed. She was little when she lost her father and brother. Joshua and I spoiled her.”

Shifra grabbed a handgun and clip on holster. “She married a rich older man who pampers her, and the life…suits her.” *I can leave this in my car while I’m over there.* “She wouldn’t be able to fit this into her world.”

Tearing into a box of ammo, Shifra loaded a magazine while she talked. “And her knowing would be dangerous to the Institute. I thought…that was going to work fine, but now…this.”

Shifra grabbed two more magazines and shoveled bullets into them. “I guess I’ve been a little guarded lately. She’s wanting to know all about my new life, like any daughter would…I thought it would be easier to hide all this from her. I didn’t think she’d be that interested. I’d go visit her. Maybe once a year, she’d come down here.” Shifra gazed at Gretchen. “Never expected this.”

Gretchen was nodding, trying to take it all in. “Okay. This is drama overload. What are you going to do?”

Shifra shoved the extra mags into her jeans pocket. “She said she’s sick, so I need to…” The word sick hit Shifra. *Oh, no. Could they have?*

The nurse came around the corner. “There you are.” She sighed with relief. “Dr. Welch thinks you’re going to do something dangerous and won’t get back in bed unless you come back to his room.”

Shifra turned to Gretchen. “I’m going to…let you explain all this to Dr. Welch, and I’m going to go and check on my sick little girl.” *Please let it be motion sickness, Lord.* "Feed her some chicken soup or something. I'll call and let you know, but I'll have to pretend you're someone else."

"Rahab called Shifra?" Welch was trying to process all the information Gretchen had spewed on him. He was sorting the data, separating ghost story from security breach and unexpected company.

The implications of it all took away some of the relief Welch felt since Dr. Malik had cleared him. He breathed heavily, trying to recover from scrubbing to decontaminate himself so he could leave the biohazard wing. He was thankful to be in a new gown and in an open room, but he couldn't rest. This news brought a need for action. "Did she elaborate on her sickness?"

Gretchen shook her head like he wasn't listening.

Surely Shiffy didn't go through this with me without coming to realize what kind of weapons our enemy could wield. "How long has she been gone?"

"She left not long after I came and got her." Gretchen shifted back and forth on her feet. "To the house on the other side of the lake." She looked like she had explained that when she spilled out the story the first time.

"She came to Oklahoma without warning? That is unfortunate timing. Why did Shifra go alone? We could have sent one of the guards to pose as her date. That could have been the explanation for where she had been, and it would have been safer."

"You'd let her go out with another man?"

Welch couldn't tell if she was joking or not. "Of course, to assure she was protected."

"You should have seen her slapping bullets in guns and throwing them across her back. She looked like she knew what she was doing. I'm a little worried about *us,* though. Do you think there is still someone on the grounds?"

"The procedure is to give an all-clear announcement when the threat has been resolved." Welch was still envisioning Gretchen's last narrative. "Shifra didn't go with a gun slung across her back, did she?"

"No. She put that back and got a smaller one. But she was packing in the bullets. Do you think there might be more than one person out there?"

Welch's expression said he was considering the question. "If I were planning a raid on a facility this size, I would send a team. If the fence was cut earlier, whoever did it could be anywhere. It will take some time to search the area. Unless a team was deep in the woods, we should have contacted them by now."

He looked at the clock on the wall. "A team would have attacked sooner. They would have moved while they still had the element of surprise, hitting us fast, eliminating threats as they encountered them. Once we were alerted, they would have either pressed forward, using explosives and suppression fire to cover their advance, or pulled out."

Welch had to pause to get a good breath. "Since we

have had no contacts, I suspect we are talking about a lone sniper or assassin with a definite target. He also might have pulled out or he could be well concealed and waiting for the right opportunity."

Gretchen was chewing her lower lip. "If you're trying to reassure me, I could have done without that last part. I'm probably going to need a stress day tomorrow. I'm not sleeping tonight."

"Has a canine been deployed?"

Gretchen spread her hands out and gave him a look of disbelief. "I really don't know, Dr. Welch."

Welch reached out and squeezed her hand. "As you said, you're not able to sleep. You need something to do. You can go to my apartment with the security guards and bring me back some clothes. Since I haven't succeeded at dying, I think it's time I rejoin the living."

Chapter 21

I *didn't think I was ever getting out of there.* Shifra knew the front gate guards were only doing their job. Trying to protect her. She won them over by telling them, "I'm a trained agent, so leaving a complex that might be under attack will make me safer, not less safe."

She kept reminding her eyes to focus on the dark asphalt of Lakeside Drive. Because of the hour, the road was empty, so she pushed the limit. *Gretchen would be shocked…or proud. Who knows? Why am I thinking about these things now? I'm coming, Baby Girl.*

Ruben said he loved you. At least he was going to…I think. And she was leaving him. What if it was an attack? What if something happened to him while she was gone? She left him when he needed her, had asked for her. *I could turn around.*

Rahab didn't sound that sick. It seemed like one of

her *I need my mommy* times. As much as she wished she would act more mature, at the moment she hoped that was all it was. Perhaps she and Benton had another fight. The man put up with a lot to have a young, beautiful wife.

Rahab's situation depressed Shifra if she pondered it for long. She had to give that to God as well. *Maybe I'll get her raised before I'm dead.* But her faith for that had taken a beating. God was going to have to perform a miracle.

Would Ruben ever feel that way about her? Their ages weren't as far apart. Still, she prayed she would never rely on her looks and forget to fulfill the more important parts of a marr—Now she was getting ahead of things. There was still so much that would have to happen before…not the least of which might be them all getting through this night.

First, she needed to focus on what to do with Rahab. It must be a regular illness. She was just paranoid because of her and Malik's conversations about the virus. Over the phone, Rahab had not sounded like Ruben. She would get Rahab tucked in and be back soon. Her daughter would whine and fuss, but she couldn't keep catering to every moment of weakness the girl had.

Am I missing a crucial moment in Ruben's and my relationship? Will he forgive me for abandoning him? Of course he would. Ruben was a wise man. His practical mind would see the sense in it…But had he finally given up some of his rigid practicality to love her? *Were you doing something here I missed, God?*

Her tires rumbled on the edge of the asphalt. Her hands tensed, but she remembered not to jerk the wheel, easing back onto the road. *Keep your mind on what you're doing.* One thing at a time. She would trust her mothering instinct and find out what Rahab needed, do what she could for her, and get back to help Ruben. *Oh, no.* What would she tell Rahab when she had to leave—that she had a boyfriend she needed to get back to? She hated lying to her daughter, but maybe it wasn't a lie. *Give me wisdom here, Lord.*

It had taken Radley longer than he planned to move down the hill to the complex of structures surrounding the medical building. He had seen more security than he expected. Perhaps it was an odd shift change, and they were coming and going.

He had hidden in the woods, waiting for an opening to get to the first building. Finally, he had to use the suit to make the run across the road, where he hunkered in a dark inset, red brick on both sides of him.

Radley glanced around the corner of the building. It was clear. He used the suit's fingertip activation to go to instant camouflage and left cover. Moving along the side of the structure, his suit shifted with the brick pattern next to him. If anyone was scrutinizing, they might get the impression of a slight lump moving across the face of the building like a high-speed gopher burrowing just under the surface.

Radley left the building behind. He was grass, concrete, shrubs, asphalt, a light pole, and the dark woods behind, as he melded with his ever-changing background. He had a little farther until he could shut off the suit again.

A door opened in the building across the street. Radley dropped next to a retaining wall and became stone and mortar.

A couple of guards came out. They scanned the roadway and buildings, taking their time to cross the street, flashing their lights in dark corners. Taking the sloping sidewalk, they passed above where Radley pressed against the wall. Still probing the nooks with flashlight beams, they were oblivious to his presence as they went to the building he just left. Unlocking the door, they went inside.

Radley was up again and hustled to get behind the next structure. Hidden for a minute, he shut off the camouflage.

Shifra prepped herself as she drove up the drive to her fake home. It was only the third time Shifra had been to the property. Joshua had helped arrange it the way that suited her, and she kept enough clothes and personal affects in it to seem like she lived there. She had been living in her house on the base and *that* was still new to her. This was strictly a cover for Rahab.

Demonstrating familiarity with the home was going to be a problem. She would have to play it off as still getting used to the place and working a lot. It had been some years since her undercover days. This was feeling similar, only now the person she was fooling would be her daughter. She hadn't considered how that would work. It was going to be complicated and uncomfortable. Fortunately, Rahab enjoyed talking about herself.

A red Ford Mustang was on the concrete in front of the garage. That would be Rahab. She loved something flashy. Shifra didn't see any threats, so she took her handgun out of the console and stowed it under the seat with the ammo.

When she pulled in behind the Mustang, the driver's door opened. Getting out, Shifra peered into the car as she approached.

Rahab had the seat laid back and was groaning. "What took you so long?"

Shifra examined her daughter. Her breathing was fine, and her color was good. She displayed none of Ruben's symptoms. "If you had told me you were coming, I would have picked you up and this wouldn't have happened. Don't worry about it now. I'm here. Let's get you inside. How are you feeling?"

"Terrible. You'll have to help me. I can hardly walk. I'm so weak and dizzy." Rahab put her arm out.

Shifra bent down and pulled the arm around her neck and lifted her daughter out of the car. "How did you get in such terrible shape? Did you get some bad food on the flight?"

Rahab made a whimpering sound. "I don't know. Don't ask me questions."

"All right. Let's get you in the house." Shifra suspected Rahab was being more dramatic than seriously ill. Her daughter leaned on her, and they staggered toward the front door. Shifra's cell phone started ringing, but she couldn't answer it. It stopped by the time they were at the entry of the home.

Shifra leaned Rahab against the entryway wall. She was thankful Joshua had insisted on putting the key on Shifra's key ring right after he had it made. She fumbled a little, but soon managed the lock. She pulled her daughter over the threshold and started to close the door.

Rahab staggered forward, pulling Shifra.. "Leave it. Just get me to the couch."

They made their way to the long sofa, and Shifra lowered Rahab onto the cushions.

There was a noise of heavy boots at the entryway. Shifra whirled. Armed men came through the open door. Her chest jerked, expecting to take a bullet. When the men poured in without shooting, she found her voice. "What are you..." The faces were purposeful, intent. They knew what they were doing. Her complaints were going to mean nothing to them.

Six men with assault weapons fanned out into the room. Two covered her while the others hustled by.

For a fleeting moment, she regretted leaving her gun in the car. Then she realized it was best. She wouldn't have survived had she gone for a weapon. Her heart was pounding, but she wasn't dead. Without taking her eyes off the men, she tried to position herself between them and Rahab.

A man with a spiky blond haircut came from the entrance, pointing a silenced pistol at her. He spoke to the ones who covered her with their rifles. "I've got her."

The two men joined the others that Shifra could hear searching the rest of the house, banging doors open and yelling, "Clear," as they went.

She had to start thinking. They must have been watching the house. How had they discovered it was connected to the Institute? Now Rahab was in the middle of the danger. She didn't see the mystery man in the group. Was he somewhere outside?

The man with the blond spike was examining her.

She glared at him. "What do you want?"

Rahab spoke from behind her. "It's okay, Eema. They won't hurt you. They just want to make sure that none of those people you've been with are here. We came to help you. You and Joshua don't know what you're mixed up in."

Shifra jerked her gaze to Rahab, who rose, looking healthy. "Rahab…" She breathed out her daughter's name as the crushing realization fell together in Shifra's mind. "What have you done?"

Chapter 22

Radley was being forced to use the camo more than anticipated. Maintaining images over his entire body, along with the cloak to cover the backpack, took massive amounts of battery power.

He was moving at the back of a building without camo, trying to use it sparingly. Two more guards were on the sidewalk in the trees behind the building. One of the men snapped his gaze toward Radley, just as he became part of the window behind him.

The second man must have seen his partner's reaction. "See something?"

Radley had ducked his head to let the visor cover his eyes. The image of the men, muted in shadow, was on his chest just as it would be on the window.

The first man had squared off to look directly at him. "I thought so, for a second, over in front of that window."

The second man smacked his partner's arm and

pointed dead at Radley.

The muscles in Radley's arm tensed as he prepared to go for his gun.

The man chuckled. "You're seeing our reflection in the glass."

The other man shook his head. "Come on."

The men moved on, the second ribbing the first for being jumpy.

Radley waited until they were out of sight to move. He was further amazed at the suit's technology. The rear sensors had read the reflectivity of the surface and translated it to a simulated reflection of what the front scanner was seeing.

He was glad it was night, which made it more difficult to see three dimensions, otherwise he might not have fooled such intense scrutiny. But Radley knew that people often saw what their minds thought they were supposed to see. That peculiarity of the human brain was what made the magician's art possible.

Ah, it feels so much better to be clothed. Welch stepped out of the bathroom where he had been changing.

Dr. Malik stood outside the door of his room. "This is against your doctor's advice. You are not ready to be out of bed."

"With full respect and agreement, I accept your

diagnosis." Welch smiled at the man to soften his statement. "But the situation warrants that I disregard it. I'm sorry, Doctor. We have a breach in security and the only other senior agent has left the grounds under suspicious circumstances."

Welch turned to Gretchen. "Have you gotten hold of Shifra yet?"

"She didn't answer."

"That concerns me. Rahab arriving unexpectedly at this time is odd. Such thoughtless behavior is not necessarily inconsistent with Rahab's character, but the timing…and her saying she was sick?"

"Shifra said she was going to feed her some chicken soup."

"Shifra could be busy caring for her. But we can't take it for granted." Welch took a weary breath and sat on his bed.

Malik must have realized how tired he was. "That shot I gave you will take effect soon. It's a little something we developed to give the body a boost to heal. A side effect will be decreased pain and increased energy. You'll feel better, but don't abuse it. As soon as you can, get to bed and rest. Not only were you knocking on death's door, but it almost let you in. Don't do what you don't have to do."

"Thank you, Doctor. I'm grateful." He turned to Jim, the head of security, who stood waiting. "What is our progress in the search for our intruder?"

"The canine is on the way. I should have thought of it earlier."

"No. It's my fault. I knew we didn't want guard

dogs roaming the grounds with all the various guests we have, but I should have a canine patrol unit on staff. We will from now on."

Jim shrugged. "Hindsight. I'm not sure our man's still around, anyway. The anomalies that occurred with the perimeter cameras didn't last long. We're hoping it was only time enough to let one man get through. A lone man has to know he is way outgunned with all the guards on alert. He probably bugged out."

Welch considered the idea. "Getting out might be harder than getting in if that is the case. How is your search going?"

"We have notified everyone staying on campus and made sure all the buildings are secure. None of the alarms tripped, so we don't believe he could hide anywhere inside. If he is still on site, he must be hiding in the woods somewhere. We checked around all the buildings as we went. We're beginning a grid search with thermal night vision in the forested areas, but as you know, that takes in a lot of acreage."

"Pull your men back. We can use a drone to search that area. There's nothing at the ranges and training sites we have in the woods that we need to worry about. Tighten patrol around the complex. There's been too much foot traffic with your men searching. The canine will have too many scents to sort out for a track. Normal procedure is to set up a perimeter around the area where the dog is going to track and keep people out. We'll work on those operating procedures when we have a canine on staff."

Welch fell silent to complete the mental construct

of his new strategy. He envisioned each component in front of him and moved his finger as he confirmed it.

Then he looked up and gave Jim the results. "Keep a tight perimeter around the complex. Inside that area, have the dog and handler join the patrol in a slow roving fashion. But find a place away from any areas where we have residents and guests, and leave a believable gap in coverage. Set up a hidden stationary team with thermal and night vision to concentrate on that area so nothing can get through without their notice. Let's drive him where we want him. If he tries to slip through, we'll spot him, and everyone can converge to catch him. If he doesn't try before morning, we'll assume he must have gotten into the woods earlier and fled." Welch smiled at Jim. "I'll let you work on that. Keep me informed about how it's going."

Jim hurried out of the room.

Welch turned to Gretchen. "Keep trying to get Shifra. If she doesn't answer soon, we need to go check on her."

Rahab spoke to Shifra as if she was lecturing a child. "I've come to rescue you, but you may not understand yet. I can't believe you've gotten yourself into this, Eema, but I've come to get you out. You'll thank me later."

Shifra couldn't respond. It wouldn't help to voice

what was going through her mind. *Stupid girl.* She had done some foolish things before but this— Shifra put on her mental brakes. *How can you think that way about your own daughter?* Their relationship was as much her own fault as it was Rahab's.

The other men returned and stationed themselves around the room. A short one with a mustache addressed the man with the handgun. "It's good."

Spike was apparently the leader. He motioned toward Shifra. "Search her."

Mustache slung his weapon and came toward her. When she tensed, Spike cautioned her. "Easy." He cocked his head toward Rahab. "Think of her."

Shifra allowed the man to paw her. She had to stop thinking of what her daughter had done and figure out how to deal with the consequences. Shifra knew these type of men. They wouldn't hesitate to kill them. Thoughts of watching her little girl die clouded her thinking. *Please, Lord, not that. Not another child.*

Mustache seemed satisfied she was unarmed. Taking a nylon bag from his cargo pocket, he eased her cell phone from her pocket so that it went directly into the bag.

Shifra watched him. *It must be a faraday bag that will block all signals. He didn't let the phone's camera's get any view, so Gretchen won't have any video to analyze.* Shifra wondered what the others would do if they couldn't get ahold of her. The thought caused a hope to flash through her mind. Then she realized, *They might be walking into a trap.*

Mustache handed the bag to Spike, and the leader

put it in his pocket.

Spike came forward, still pointing his weapon at her. "Let's get right to business. You are part of an organization run by a man named Welch. I need you to tell me where their base is right now."

Shifra couldn't help stiffening at the words.

Rahab kept her superior tone. "They're not going to hurt you, mother. They're worried because these people you're with are militia members. I know you didn't know. Just cooperate and they promised they won't charge you with anything."

Shifa wanted to cry over the girl's naivety. "Rahab, please. This isn't what you think."

Spike examined Shifra, and his eyes narrowed. "Let's make this easier." He turned the gun on Rahab and raised his eyebrows as if waiting for a response.

Rahab huffed. "Oh, stop that." She advanced on the man as she spoke. "She's not going to believe that."

The man's hand shot out as Rahab reached to move the gun away. There was the smack and thud of the blow connecting, and Rahab went backward. She crashed over the end table and sent the lamp flying.

Shifra's mother instinct propelled her forward, but the man shoved the gun toward her daughter. "Don't."

Shifra stopped herself. "Please. She doesn't understand."

The stun wore off Rahab, and she began screaming. "What are you doing? That hurt!" She sat on the floor in disbelief. Blood seeped between her fingers where she held her mouth.

The horror of the situation bit into Shifra's stomach.

She was going to have to do something. Rahab's life and the lives of anyone coming to check on them were at stake.

The man moved close to Rahab, but kept his eyes on Shifra. "What I'm doing is making sure your mother does believe that I have no problem hurting you to get the information I need. Since I don't need to be dealing with your stupidity at this point, I think honesty is the best policy."

The word *stupidity* jabbed at Shifra. *I'm the stupid one, not her.*

Spike leaned closer Rabab. "I've been lying to you. You have no idea what's going on and I'm not going to waste time trying to explain it. Here is all you need to know. Now that you've helped us get your mother, the only thing you're good for is to make sure she does what we want. So keep quiet and do everything I tell you. If your mother cooperates, you and her can go. If she doesn't, well, that's where your usefulness come in, and I'm sure it's going to hurt her just as much as it hurts you. You might not think that though, since you'll be the one experiencing the pain." Spike gave Rahab a rough pat on the cheek, smiling at the girl's wince of pain, and straightened, staring, again, at Shifra.

Rahab's eyes darted around as she processed what he said and the reality sunk in. "Please, Eema. Do what he wants."

Spike continued his glare "Good advice, *Eema*. Or shall we move to the next step?"

At Spike's words, Rehab sunk to the floor, her

hands covering her head.

Spike leaned toward the girl again. "Give me your phone."

Rahab snatched the phone from her pocket and handed it to him. Her eyes displayed that she comprehended the situation well enough to be scared out of her wits.

"Now you stay right there while I see how much your Eema really loves you."

"It's okay, Tasil. Just pray." It was the best comfort Shifra could give her little girl. God could get them through this. She had to hold on to that.

She directed her gaze at Spike. "She may not understand this, but I do. I know what will happen if I tell you anything without some type of guarantee. But I promise you, if you hurt her, there will be nothing you can do that will make me tell you anything."

The man evaluated her then leaned his head toward her daughter without breaking eye contact. "You hear that, *Tasil*. Eema is going to make me have to hurt you."

Rahab pulled herself into a ball and screamed, "Eema, please."

Shifra glared at him. She had to show determination despite the terror inside her. *You have to be as hard as they are.* "If you do that, I'll know for sure you'll kill us when you get what you want. It will prove I don't dare tell you anything. My daughter is my only priority. I will help you if I know there is a way out for her. Otherwise, you'll fail at what you came here to do."

Spike maintained his own hard expression. "I don't fail." He glanced at Mustache. "Stand behind her and watch everything her fingers do." He handed Rahab's phone to Shifra. "You're going to send a text for us." The man aimed his gun at Rahab again. "If we're going to learn to trust each other, we'll have to start with little gestures of good faith. You first."

Chapter 23

A flashlight panned across the open area to Radley's right. It was coming from the front of the building. Radley was out of its view, so it was no threat at the moment, but he kept ready to go into camo mode in an instant.

He had doubled back and played ring-around-the-rosie with guards so many times it took forever to move a short distance.

So many guards. It couldn't be normal. Something had alerted them. It was forcing him to use the camouflage more frequently and for longer durations. The homes further up the hill were lit up. They must have done a house-to-house search. Everyone would be on the alert.

The situation was altering rapidly, and he was still running through options without finding a suitable alternative plan. He was feeling like he did when he had first confronted Welch.

Even with all the advantages, surprise, superior technology, a good tactical plan, he was feeling out of control. He had made it inside, but now everything had changed. It was more than what he could see. It was a feeling inside. Someone else was calling the shots. Moving him into position for something.

"Dr. Welch, I got a text from Shifra's daughter Rahab." Gretchen was reading the message. "It's Shifra. Her phone got broken, so she's using Rahab's. She's okay, but can't talk." Gretchen was finger typing a response.

A feeling of dread dropped into Welch's middle. "Don't answer it." His command was abrupt and stern.

Gretchen nearly dropped the phone. "Good grief. Why not?"

"Because we don't know it's her." He should have been thinking more about Shifra. He had become caught up in the hunt for the man on the grounds.

Gretchen examined him like she didn't know if he was serious. "It says it's from Rahab Lauder. I remember her full name from entering Shifra's info in the database."

"We still don't know if Shifra's sending it willingly." The feeling that something was wrong increased. From the way Shifra described her daughter, Rahab was not the type of person to come here. She would whine until her mother came to *her*.

Gretchen's phone vibrated, and she glanced at it. "She says she'll call in a bit."

Gretchen removed her laptop from its case and sat in a chair with the computer on her lap. "I'll see if I get a signal from Shifra's phone. Even if it's broken, I should get a signal and I might even be able to activate the cameras or audio, depending on what happened to it."

"Be careful they don't know you're doing it."

"They won't." Gretchen used the keyboard and touchscreen to zip through the programs. It wasn't long before she announced, "No signal, even from the backup transmitter." Gretchen's brow had deep furrows. "It would take more than the average phone mishap to cause that."

Welch didn't want it to be real, but he had to plan accordingly. He dialed Jim. "Jim, change of plans. We received a suspicious text from Shifra. She went to meet her daughter at the mock house on the other side of the lake. With everything that's going on, the whole situation has me concerned. We're waiting for a call back. I wanted to give you advance warning, so you and your men can prepare what you might need for a hostage rescue operation over there."

"Hostage rescue?"

"Just a precaution. Let's pray I'm wrong and this will only be a drill, but I need you to be ready. Can you call Talisa and have her on standby in case she needs to take you over on one of the boats?"

There was a moment of silence. "I'm not trying to back out on this, but these guys are security." There was a reluctance in Jim's voice. "They're good, but they don't have any experience with that kind of operation. You sure you want us to try to handle this?"

Welch wished Joshua and the team were available. *If someone has Shifra, you need to be a leader more than ever.* He needed to convey confidence in the men if they were going to have confidence in themselves. "There's no one in a better position. Even if there was some local agency I could trust, there isn't time. I know this might be outside their experience, but they're good men. They've had the training. I have confidence in you and them. I'll call you when we know more."

Gretchen's face showed her shock. "You really think something bad happened to her? Maybe it's no big deal. You want me to call her?"

"Not yet. I don't want to force the situation until we're ready to respond, but yes, I am concerned. With everything that's happened, we have to look at anything unusual in that way. Two weeks ago, this might not have meant as much, but we are in a different scenario now."

Gretchen's phone vibrated, and she glanced at the screen. "She wants to know where you are."

Welch faced off with the phone in Gretchen's hand. "*Someone* does, anyway."

Mustache announced the text message response to

Spike. "All it says is, he's right here. That doesn't help us any."

Shifra lowered the phone. She put all her skills into altering her face to fit a certain character. *I'm about to perform the act of my life. Help me, Jesus.* She pulled out her hardened, abused mistress persona and dusted it off. "I've shown my good faith. And it could cost me big time, later. Now please stop pointing your gun at my daughter. I know you're serious without that. An accident could ruin all your chances of finding Welch."

Spike sneered and didn't move.

Shifra firmed her features to show resolve but not contempt. "Look. There is no point in us going on if you're not going to work with me. Killing us now or later means the same. You need to show *your* good faith."

Lowering the weapon slowly to his side, the man eased his sneer. "Okay. There's mine. Now, I want you to tell me where Welch is at."

"I told you, I need some surety that my daughter will be safe."

The sneer returned. "I'm not playing this game with you." He pointed the gun at Shifra's leg.

She spilled out her offer. "I can make it easy for you to take Welch down. Give you more than you even counted on. He'll kill me and her if I give him up and you fail, so I'll give you what you need to make this work." The man hadn't pulled the trigger. He was hooked, but she had to keep going. "I know how you can get Welch, but if either of us can't walk, it will hinder the idea I have. I just have to make sure I can get my daughter out of this alive, or I won't help you."

"If you keep playing with me, it might come down to whether you die fast or incredibly slow."

"If it comes down to that, you get nothing. I get tortured by Welch most days anyway and if you torture my daughter, I'll make sure you fail. It'd be risky for you to gamble on that. At the very least it would cost you time that you don't have. I know when you're through with us, you won't have the luxury of taking too long. I've worked around enough of you guys to know the mission takes precedence over any personal satisfaction. If it comes to that, you'll have to get rid of us quickly."

"Don't push me, woman."

"I'm not trying to. If you can get us free from Welch, it will be a blessing. I just want my daughter to live. You said it, she doesn't know anything. You can let her go and she'd be no threat. I have a proposal to make that could get us both what we want."

Shifra noticed Rahab's sobbing had subsided. She was listening, but Shifra had no choice but to discuss the gruesome details in front of her. *Please, Lord, let her keep quiet and not give my act away.* "You and I, and your friend there," Shifra indicated Mustache, "we'll take two vehicles, Rahab's Mustang and one of yours. You can tie her up and leave her in the Mustang in a parking lot in town where she won't be found until morning. We leave her there and come back, and I will give you everything you need to take Welch down. You can do whatever to me after that. At least I'll know she has a chance."

The man's expression said he didn't like it, but he was still listening.

Shifra tried to read his face as she talked. "If I don't fulfill my part, I know you can kill me and go back and get Rahab. Once you're involved in the operation, you'll need every man. I don't think she'll be worth your time. I'll take that chance."

"We already don't have time for this." The man acted perturbed but there was the hint of something else in his expression. It was what Shifra was hoping to win—an inkling of respect.

"It will take longer without it, if it's possible at all. I know Welch and his whole operation. I can get you in and tell you how to take him down quick and easy. I've thought about this a lot. There's nothing I'd like better than to see him taken down. You've invested a lot of time and resources getting to this point. You might as well make them pay off. The sooner we get Rahab out to the picture, the sooner you can move on. I can't help you any more until that happens. It's too risky for her. If you've got a counteroffer, I'll listen, but I don't see anything else working."

Spike was thinking. He scowled and shook his head. "I don't like driving into town. Too risky for us. Doing things in parking lots after hours is a good way to get cops checking on you. They patrol parking lots at night. They also might find her too soon."

The man evaluated her as if seeing her in a new way. "You might even be counting on that. Here's my counter proposal. We tie her up in the car, like you said, and we drive her down the road and park the Mustang on a side road where no one will check on her until morning. Then you set us up to take Welch and the rest of his team down. Like you said, she won't be worth our time to come back for." He cast a look of contempt at Rahab. "I'll be glad to be rid of her."

Shifra considered the idea. "Okay, but who knows when someone would stop on a back road, so you let me send an email about where she's at to the library or something. Someone who won't get it until tomorrow morning."

The man nodded. "I'll send the email, so I can be sure where it's going. I'll let you watch me press send."

"Deal. Now I need to make this call or he's going to know something is going on. I normally wouldn't leave him hanging like this. He's made sure I know better."

The man moved closer to Rahab as a warning. "Go ahead. I'm listening carefully."

"I won't give you away. I gotta make this work now. If you don't kill him, he's for sure gonna kill *me* if he finds out I helped you."

Spike scrutinized her. "Call him, but be very careful what you say."

Shifra gave a tired look of downtrodden resignation. "I have to do that all the time, anyway."

Welch saw Gretchen getting his attention by pointing at her phone as she spoke into the device. "Finally. We were…" Welch could tell someone on the other end cut her off. "Okay, but—." Gretchen scowled at the electronic in her hand. "All right. Here he is." She thrust the phone at him.

Welch started to say, "Shiff—."

But Shifra's voice cut him off as well. "Listen, baby, I know you're mad, but just listen for a minute."

She called me baby?

It was Shifra, but not like he had heard her speak before. "I'm really sorry for not getting back to you sooner, but it's been a mess over here. Rahab is really sick. Blowing chunks and a fever and everything. I haven't even been able to get her to bed. She's laying here on the living room floor 'cause she's too weak to get up. I don't know what she's got, but it's nasty. I know I got what's coming to me, but please let me take care of her for a bit. I've been exposed now, so you probably don't want me back right now, anyway. I'll make it up to you when I'm through. I promise, baby."

Baby again. She's letting me know it's for someone else's benefit. Welch went into an analysis of what she had said already. *Know you're mad, got what's coming to me, make it up to you.* Realization came to Welch. *Shifra's using the ploy from Operation Kind Stranger.* It was a mission he designed. She was sending the message that he had a part to play. Now, if he could remember what it was.

Whatever Shifra had said to Gretchen had made sure that Gretchen didn't have an opportunity to talk, even at the risk of hurting her feelings. Shifra wouldn't do that unless much was at stake. He had to think quickly. Shifra's life depended on it.

I know you're mad. It was his cue. He remembered his part, and it didn't involve being a nice guy. He was the mob boss, but he'd have to adapt the character.

Okay, old boy, get this right. He was a college professor living a double life. Intelligent but a tyrant. Shifra was scared of him because he beat her when she didn't please him. He was cruel, selfish, and thoughtless. *That ought to cover it.*

Welch took a breath. "I don't care what that little brat you raised has." He yelled into the phone so anyone listening nearby on the other end would hear it.

Gretchen jumped backward and stared.

"She's none of my concern, but you are, so you better get your butt back home as soon as…" Welch paused like he just realized something. "So now you've been exposed? Is that what you're saying? You better not be bringing home that crud of hers. Throw her in bed and don't touch her. Scrub up afterwards. You get me sick and you'll wish you hadn't. And you better believe you're going to make it up to me, double."

Shifra broke in. "Okay, baby. I know. I will, I promise."

Welch listened for further clues. *I hope I didn't overact.*

"But I might not get home tonight. I want to make sure I ain't gonna be sick for you. I'll get her in bed and then I'll call you. Let you know how things are going. I'll talk to you later, baby. Goodnight." She hung up the phone.

Wise choice. Get off quickly so I don't say something I shouldn't.

Shifra saw Spike probing her with his eyes as he held out his hand for the phone. "You didn't let him talk much."

As Shifra handed him the phone, she dropped her head and shook it as if disappointed he didn't trust her. She was considering her response. "I know how he works. If I let him keep talking, he just gets madder. Better to let him cool off. If he kept hearing himself rant, he'd come up with something like wanting me to come home and sleep in the basement 'til I'm not sick anymore. He wants to show he's the big man. But if I talk my way out of the conversation, he'll start thinking about it. If I'm gone, he can have one of his other bimbos over. It's all about him thinking he's in charge. If he thought I was defying him, he'd be over here to take care of it."

The man shoved the phone in his pocket, the corner of his mouth turned up a little. Shifra knew he liked the idea of Welch coming to him. She needed to pull the rug out from under his feet. Wiggle his confidence a little, enough to make him need her. "Maybe that sounds like what you want, but it's not. He's just a figurehead. He's the one they push out in front and puff him up. That way, if anything happens, they'll have someone to sacrifice."

There it was. *Now he's listening.* "I've watched them do it. It's like one of those lizards that snaps his tail off while the important part gets away. And then you've exposed yourself. You'll lose a lot of your advantage."

Now came the hard part, getting past her innocent face to show him something dark lurking beneath. Shifra intensified her stare into the man. It had to be hard, resolved, desperate. "Welch isn't the first one they've sent me to report on. And all I get is abuse from one after the other of these idiots. Now my daughter's been made a part of it. I didn't take the risks to get her out of this life just to let her be pulled back in again."

Okay, mix in the right amount of feminine victim with hopefulness glimmering underneath. Work on all that arrogance I see in him. Just like Ruben would write it. "Getting Rahab out is my first priority. But now you're here…" Shifra made an expression to show she was evaluating him. She let it shift to show her own respect. "You're smarter than most. I think I'd be willing to gamble on you."

She adjusted her countenance to let the helpless little girl peek from behind the hard façade. "I've been around this long enough to know people. Maybe I can help you get to the ones at the top. I wouldn't risk it with anyone else, but you might be good enough to take them all down. If I could help you do that, I might be completely free and wouldn't have to run for my life when this is over. If we do it right, we might both get what we want."

Chapter 24

Radley pushed himself back against the wall as the security vehicle came to an abrupt stop thirty feet away. *They must have spotted me.* He didn't lower his eyes. He needed to see, to react. If he ran, would they shoot at something they couldn't really see? The driver threw open his door and headed Radley's direction. *I waited too long.*

The passenger called out. "What are you doing?"

The driver made a half turn toward his partner. "I think I left my flashlight on the counter when we searched in here."

They don't know I'm here. This is going to be close. Radley tried to flatten himself more, but something was poking his back. Dropping his gaze, he saw a doorknob. He was in front of the door...he *was* the door. The ferrofluid texturing effect caused the image of the doorknob to protrude from his suit just enough to be a target for the man's hand as he neared.

From under the visor, Radley saw the guard's feet approaching, his legs coming into view. Radley eased his fingers under the flap of material that covered his pistol. As he prepared to pull it open, he mentally rehearsed putting a shot in the closest man's head and then several in the man in the truck.

"No, I grabbed it for you. I forgot to tell you. It's right here in the truck. Come on. We're going to be the last ones there."

The guard stopped less than six feet away. With a huff, he turned around.

When Radley heard the vehicle door slam, he raised his view. Watching the SUV disappear around the corner, he moved his hand away from the flap and let out a breath. Relief washed through him.

Radley groped at the sensation. *What am I feeling?* He wasn't afraid. He had complete confidence that he could have drawn his gun and shot both men before they had time to react. The emotion firmed in his thoughts. He understood what it was, but the confusion was still there. *I'm glad I didn't have to kill them.*

Radley put the feeling away and went back to assessing his situation. The guards had thinned out. That was the third time he had seen a team hurrying to their vehicle and speeding away. Something new was happening. It didn't make him comfortable, but at least it took some of the pressure off.

Coming out of camo, he moved to the corner of the structure he was behind. Across a landscaped area was the medical complex. He had reached it.

Everything seemed to implode inside him. *Why am*

I here?

He no longer had the desire to continue with the mission. He had too many questions. Radley had always imagined he played an elite role in protecting the country. He allowed himself to believe the old man was giving him assignments to take out dirty players in the game.

But his conversations with Sarah and his encounter with Welch had changed him. He wasn't sure what side he was on. Or what side he should be on. Maybe he had believed what was convenient…about a lot of things.

He never cared to spend much time considering the morality of what he did in his occupation. He wanted to do the job and go underground until the next one. But…if there was something bigger than all of this…something or someone with grander plans that somehow included Radley…someone that Sarah would call God…

He needed to get away from this complex, get home, and think it all through.

He was the only one who knew where Welch's group had their base. He would keep it to himself and see what kind of shake-up there had been inside the old man's organization. He had agreed to eliminate Roshard if anything happened to the old man. But he didn't know where that fit with all the new questions he had. *First things first.* He had to get out.

He lifted the arm flap and checked the meter on the controller. The battery was critically low. He didn't dare trust the suit anymore, never knowing when it might fail. Radley tossed the headpiece off, so it lay like a hood on his pack. He had run out of magic.

I need an exit strategy. He no longer wanted to hurt anyone, but leaving the Institute without eliminating security team members was going to be a challenge without the suit.

Using bushes as concealment, Radley got to where he had a view of the front of the medical building. Two security guards stood near their SUV. The vehicle would get him out quickly if he could get the guards to leave it unattended. What would get them away from it? A plan formed in his mind. With how things were going in the world, there was one thing in which every security force would receive regular training. It was a rapid, standard response. He could use that training to manipulate them.

Welch motioned for Gretchen to follow him as he dialed his phone. When Jim answered, Welch spoke clear but fast. "Shifra called. She's okay for now, but she is under duress. They had her call so we would think she was okay, but during that conversation, she was able to secretly let me know she was being held. I'm still extracting what information I can from what she said."

Welch heard Jim suck in a breath. He knew he was asking a lot of the man in a short time. "Leave enough men to make sure everyone here will be safe. Prep the rest for a rescue from an unknown number of hostage takers, which we must assume are heavily armed. Have them readied as fast as you can. If my fears are correct, Shifra might be bargaining for her life right now." Saying it was like punching himself in the stomach.

"If that's what's happening, we'll do everything we can to get her out."

"I know you will." Welch came to the armory door. He was winded from the walk. He grabbed a couple of deep breaths. Malik was right. The shot was helping, but he needed more recovery time. Speaking to Jim, he turned his gaze to Gretchen as he swiped his card. "Have a man grab the recon drones and come get Gretchen to run them."

Gretchen turned her wide eyes to Welch and mouthed the word, "Me?"

Welch nodded and turned back to the facial recognition scanner. Opening the door, he continued talking to Jim as he armed himself. "It's got a fifty-minute max runtime, so it's best if she launches it from the boat when you get close. She should be able to get you some good intel images by the time you land. I'm going to take the two guards you left at the medical complex and use their Expedition to drive to the house. We want to be ready in case they try to leave by vehicle. Call me when you're on the move. We'll keep in touch with cell headsets so we can coordinate the operation. I'll talk to you again when you're in the boat."

Gretchen was talking the moment he was off the

phone. "Dr. Welch, are you sure about me going?"

"Can anyone operate that drone better?" He handed her the rifle he had loaded while he donned a ballistic vest and filled it with equipment.

Gretchen held the weapon in front of her with stiff, outstretched arms and worked her lips like she was trying to keep something in her mouth. "No." The word came out like she had confessed to a crime. "It's like a video game. I'm the best. But what do I do when we get there?"

"You will stay in the boat with Talisa. I'll have her land the boat down the bank from the house, and the men will approach on foot through the trees. Without that drone footage, we don't know what they might be walking into. It has thermal imaging that's going to be crucial to pick out enemies in the dark woods around the house."

Gretchen looked a little pale but was nodding. "Like a video game."

Welch paused to get his wind back. He took the gun from Gretchen and put his hand on her shoulder. "Similar. In some ways, it will be easier. All you have to do is send the signal to my phone and I will direct the team." That seemed to relax her a little. He gave her shoulder a gentle squeeze. "But prepare yourself to see brutal things. Pray. Concentrate on what you have to do to save Shifra. God will get us through it."

Gretchen was quiet.

Welch analyzed what Shifra said as he locked up the armory. *What was she trying to tell us?* He desperately tried to glean what he could from the conversation. *She's right here on the floor of the living room.* Welch headed to the front exit.

Gretchen trailed behind him. "So, do you think it's the same guy that took you to the hospital? The one that stole your phone?"

"I don't think so. Right now, I'm concerned about deciphering what Shifra might have been trying to tell us in our conversation." While he walked, Welch went through what he was coming up with. "She said a lot about Rahab being sick and having something nasty, and her wanting to take care of her. I think she is letting us know Rahab is in danger. Whoever has them must have hurt Rahab or is threatening her. That would make sense. Shifra wants us to know that she is worried about the danger to Rahab."

"God, please don't let her get hurt." Gretchen's voice trembled with emotion as she poured the plea into the air.

"And the part about her being on the living room floor and not being able to get her to bed. Why would she go into that unless it was to let us know they're still at the house?" Welch had to stop for a minute and lean against the wall. He got his breath and was off again. He needed to get to Shifra. Once he could get in the truck and sit down, things would be better. "She said she was exposed, and I probably don't want her back…that she'd make it up to me." What was Shifra going through? *Keep your mind on your reasoning.* "She knows she's a liability if she brings them here. That must be what this is about. Whoever it is must be threatening to hurt Rahab if Shifra doesn't give up the

Institute's location." *Torn between us and her daughter. Lord, keep me focused on what I need to do to help her.* "She ended by saying she's going to try to get Rahab to bed and she would call later. That must be her way of telling us she has a plan to get Rahab out of danger. She'll also be trying to stall, hoping to be rescued."

Gretchen appeared perplexed. "But if the guy cut the fence and got in, he already knows where we are."

Welch raised his eyebrows at her. "You may have answered your own question. We must have two different attackers. One side seems to have targeted me and the other side has targeted Shifra. It would be remarkable for two groups to have found us simultaneously, so there must be some connection we're not seeing."

Welch stopped at the front exit. "Wait here until the men come and get you."

Welch stepped out to where the two guards stood near one of the Institute's Ford Expeditions parked at the front entrance. "If you're ready, we need to get going."

An explosion shook the concrete beneath his feet.

Shifra's heart was ripped open by Rahab's pleas.

"Don't leave me, Eema, please don't." Rahab lay on the seat of the Mustang, which Mustache had laid down so she couldn't be seen. They had bound her hands behind her, then fastened her neck to the metal base of the headrest so she couldn't sit up or use her teeth to untie herself. Her feet were tied to the base of the seat. All condescension had left her daughter. What was left was desperate pleading. "I heard what you said. You're going to leave me."

"We have to, Tasil. Just until morning. Someone will come to get you." Shifra tried not to think about her baby being like that until morning, but at least she would be alive and away from the men. It would give Shifra time to come up with some way out of this horror or for Ruben to rescue them. If that didn't happen, the men might vent their anger on her, but hopefully, they wouldn't bother going back for Rahab.

"It will be all right, Tasil."

Rahab sobbed. All the acting was gone. Actual tears covered her cheeks.

Spike sat in the large SUV beside them, waiting for her to get in with him. "Let's go."

Shifra was fighting a battle between keeping the men satisfied and comforting her daughter. "Just give me a second. She's scared."

Spike took an exasperated breath.

Shifra knew he was losing patience. *Lord, help me.* Shifra turned to the man. "Let me ride in the back seat and talk to her on the way."

Mustache leaned down to make eye contact with Spike through the open door. "I don't want her behind me while I'm driving."

Shifra kept engaging Spike. "I'm not going to do anything. What sense would that make? I'm trying to keep her alive, not get us killed in a wreck. And you'll be behind us, so it wouldn't gain anything." Shifra put everything into the face that had won over so many men. "Please. I'll work hard to get you what you want. I know this might be the last time we're together. Let me be with her as long as I can."

Spike's eyes lost a bit of the hardness. "Let her go. She's not stupid enough to try anything."

Mustache huffed as Shifra threw her leg over Rahab and crawled in the back before Spike changed his mind. She stretched back and grabbed the door handle, sending a smile to Spike. "Thank you."

Shifra pulled the door closed, then plopped into the seat behind Mustache. The man had left his rifle and ballistic vest behind, making him look thinner. "Thank you. I won't bother you. All I want is to be with my daughter." Shifra wanted to connect with the man. She guessed he didn't have any children that claimed him. "You'd want to be with your mother as long as you could in the end."

The man glared at her in the rearview mirror. "I haven't seen that hag in years, and I don't ever want to see her again."

Looking into the eyes in the mirror, Shifra said the only thing she knew. "I'm sorry."

Chapter 25

The security guards moved to the edge of the building, assault rifles ready. But they were smart enough not to go running toward an explosion. One of them yelled at him. "Dr. Welch, you better go back inside."

A volley of semi-auto gunfire came from the rear of the building, only muffled, like it was contained inside somewhere.

Welch was also prepared, weapon up, searching. He knew he was weak, but he was at least one more gun in the fight. There was more shooting.

Gretchen came out the door, screaming. "There's shooting inside."

"Are you sure it's inside?"

An interior door burst open and two nurses dashed into the waiting room. They saw Welch and the others through the large glass windows and rushed toward them. Once outside, the nurses were yelling together, overlapping each other's voice, saying someone was inside, shooting.

The security guards were there. Trying to ask where the shooter was. More people came pouring into the waiting room.

Welch grabbed one of the women and pulled her away from the other. "Where's the shooter?"

"Somewhere toward the back. We heard shooting back there, and we just ran." She hadn't seen the shooter, didn't know how many. Yes, there were more medical employees inside. Couldn't say if anyone was hurt.

The guards headed into the waiting room. "Dr. Welch, get these people out of here and cover the entrance. We'll try to stop the shooter." They hurried through the door from where the others had just fled. They were doing the right thing—find the active shooter and neutralize him. *God be with them.*

Welch took Gretchen's arm to get her attention. He pointed across the street. "See that building over there? It's probably locked, but get everyone behind it. Get a good count of people and keep count. Don't lose any."

Welch held the door while the employees hurried through it.

"Don't move." A voice came out of the darkness.

Gretchen appeared frozen in place with her eyes on the corner of the building.

Welch let go of the door and brought his rifle up, but all he saw was a gun barrel pointing at Gretchen from around the corner.

Just a sliver of a man's head peered around the

bricks, but the eye was on Welch. "Drop your gun. All I want is the vehicle and you to drive. Put the rifle down and crawl into the driver's seat. Hurry. I don't have much time. You with the gun. I'm talking to you. I let you go once. I'll do it again. All I want is to get out of here. Don't make me hurt someone."

It must be the man that took him to the hospital. Welch saw Gretchen with hands up, eyes closed, lips moving. The others were all fixed in position on the lawn, whimpering. The man could have killed them all if that was what he meant to do. Welch knew the guards would be inside, going from room to room, searching for the shooter. It would take some time.

But Welch was sure this was the shooter. The man had blown the back door to the building, and gone inside, firing rounds to get everyone running. Then he came back outside and ran to the front. He knew the guards would go in, hunting an active shooter, and he would have his chance to escape. Welch was the only thing in his way.

"I can't wait much longer. I'm going to have to shoot someone to prove I mean it."

He was getting desperate. "Okay." Welch laid the gun on the ground.

"Handgun too."

Welch drew the sidearm and put it beside the rifle.

"In the driver's seat, with your hands up where I can see them. Hurry."

Welch hustled to the driver's side and crawled in. *I need to get him away from the others.*

The man came out. Welch recognized him from the

alley that day.

He hustled to Gretchen and pushed her ahead of him, having her open the passenger side rear door.

Welch yelled, "Gretchen, tell Jim I said go after Shifra. I'll take care of myself."

It startled the man, drawing a curious glare toward Welch. He jumped in. As he pulled the door, Welch yelled again. "Shifra first."

The door slammed, and the man yelled, "Go, go!"

Welch started the Expedition and sent it flying down the road with Gretchen and the other potential victims safely behind them.

Shifra held Rahab as best she could with the restraints. She whispered in her ear. "Tasil, listen to me. This could be the last time we're together until Heaven."

Rahab sobbed. "No Eema. Don't leave me." She called out to Mustache. "Please don't hurt my Eema."

"Shhh. Quiet. That's not going to help. Just listen to me. We don't have much time." Shifra stroked her hair. "In this life, we were going to have to lose each other someday. This may be my time. It doesn't matter when. Maybe this is what had to happen for you to get serious about God."

"I don't want to be serious about Him if He lets them hurt you."

"Listen to me. This is not God's fault. This man has

his choice to make. So do the others. It will be their choice, not God's."

Mustache glanced her way. "You're wasting your time trying to play games with me."

Shifra kept her voice calm. "Then it won't hurt you if I tell my daughter the truth. I'm not trying to change your mind. I just want my daughter to live better than I have. Let me talk to her. You don't have to listen."

Shifra ignored the man and continued to talk to Rahab. She had to break out of the hard character she was playing, but Rahab's soul was more important. "You have your choices too, Tasil. You don't have to be against God to lose Him. All you have to do is forget about Him. I love you, but you've been caught up in your own life so much, you've forgotten Him."

Rahab stopped sobbing. She was listening, sniffing now and then.

"Listen to what I'm telling you. Don't hang onto this life so much. If you keep hold of God, it won't matter how or when it ends. That's the thing I want you to remember when I'm gone."

Rahab squeezed her eyes shut. "I'm sorry, Eema. I love you."

"If you love me, Tasil, then love the Lord and I will see you again. Don't ever forget what I'm telling you. No matter what happens. Even if He doesn't answer our prayers tonight, you hang on to Him."

Rahab curled up as tight as she could with the way she was tied. "Please, God. Please, God."

Shifra prayed silently, holding her daughter as they drove.

Chapter 26

Welch glanced in the back seat.

The man had drawn his handgun once the SUV was in motion and propped his rifle against the seat. "Call them and tell them to open the front gate, and don't stop us. I don't want to hurt anyone. I'll let you go once I know it's safe."

Welch pulled out his phone and did as he was told. The guards at the entrance looked confused as Welch waved at them, but didn't stop.

The man gestured with the pistol. "Keep straight on this road. There's a driveway about a mile up. You can let me off there and head back."

"Thanks for taking me to the hospital that day."

The man regarded him. "I did it for a friend."

That struck a note with Welch. He had an impulse so strong he couldn't disregard it. They were coming to the turnoff that would take them to the other side of the lake. "Funny you should mention that. I have a similar incentive." Welch applied a sudden brake and turned.

The man grabbed the seat in front to catch himself. "Where are you going?"

"To help a friend. You might remember the woman who got me out of the hospital. I think you might have followed us to our base."

The man aimed the handgun at Welch. "Turn around. I don't have time. I need to get home."

Welch ignored the gun. "She needs my help. I don't know if she has that long. It might be how you felt about your friend. I need to help her. She's been kidnapped, her and her daughter. The kidnappers may torture them to find out where the base is. They might be doing that now. I can't bear to think about it. We have to get there." Welch could see the gun and the face in the rearview mirror.

"Turn around." The muscles in the man's hand tightened, his eyebrows came together, and he spoke through clenched teeth. "Turn around right n—." The head jerked toward the seat behind Welch. The tenseness left the man. "Sarah?"

Sarah's gentle smile was encouraging. "You need to go with him."

Radley didn't want to hear that. "Can't we just go home?"

"He's trying to help someone who needs it."

"How do you know? Are you from my mind, or not?"

"God wants to reach you, Radley. He's going to great lengths."

Radley was puzzled. "So, He sent you?"

"He speaks through many things—donkeys, angels."

"Why did you leave me?"

"Just because you don't see me or hear me doesn't mean I left you. That's something you need to know about God as well. You still haven't talked to Him."

"Why can't I just talk to *you*?"

"Help this man, and we'll talk more."

"Sarah?"

She was gone again.

Welch kept his eye on the mirror, worried by what he was hearing. *What is this man struggling with, Lord? What would you have me do?* He got the impression to start with something simple. "Are you okay?"

The man lifted his head as if in a daze. "I'm supposed to help you. What do you need me to do?"

All right, Lord. Your miracles come in strange ways. Here we go. "My name's Welch. Is there something I can call you?"

The man seemed deep in thought. Welch's question sat like an unfilled hole in the conversation.

"Let me connect with my group." Welch steered with one hand as he pulled his ear bud case from his pocket. Inserting a bud in his ear, he touched a button and spoke to his phone. "Call Jim in security."

It was answered on the second ring. "This is Jim. Is this you, Dr. Welch?"

"Yes. I assume Gretchen told you what happened."

"Yes, sir. Are you all right? My men at the front gate said you had them open it so you could leave the base."

"I'm well. This will sound strange, but this man has agreed to help us. We're on our way to the mock house. How soon before you head across?"

"Gretchen just pulled up. We'll be leaving as soon as we get her aboard."

"Good. When you get close enough to launch the drone, call me and we'll coordinate off what she's seeing. You'll want to put in down-shore about a hundred yards with the wind blowing toward you. No lights. We can't let them know we're coming."

"Understand that, sir. Weapons are all silenced, radios hands-free in the ear."

Welch fell into coordination mode. "Do you have anything for me?"

"You're sure you're all right...with your situation'?"

Welch considered the alternatives. He was headed to help Shifra. That was all he could worry about. "This is the best scenario at the moment. When Gretchen gets her bird in the air, we'll switch to an open channel between the three of us, and you can relay to your men."

"Copy that, sir."

The man took off his backpack and set it on the seat behind Welch. Crawling over the center console, he plopped onto the passenger seat. "My name's Radley."

Chapter 27

The asphalt was well maintained, but Shifra couldn't see any house lights or driveways. *Please let someone find her soon. Tonight, if possible.* It was late enough that the last car of the night had probably traveled down this stretch of road.

Shifra tucked one of the blankets she brought around her weeping daughter. *It's supposed to be decent tonight, but I don't want her to get cold before morning.* She hugged Rahab one last time as her daughter wept.

When Shifra stepped back, Mustache grabbed another blanket and threw it over Rahab, covering her completely.

Shifra glared at him. "It's not that cold…"

Mustache silenced her with a hand in her face. "We don't want anyone driving by and realizing she's in here until we're ready for her to be found."

It was a battle Shifra decided not to fight. Rahab

wasn't going to suffocate under one blanket. The sight reminded Shifra of how she would find Rahab after one of her nightmares as a child—huddled under her blanket, weeping piteously. Closing the door and leaving her little girl took all the emotional strength she had…and more.

Walking back to the Suburban, she forced her mind to shift to what she was going to do now. She had promised to deliver. She needed to concentrate on what that delivery was going to look like, or her efforts on Rahab's behalf might be in vain. She had to create something to keep the men busy for as long as she could, so Rahab would be the last thing on their minds.

Mustering composure to appear confident and ready, she climbed in the passenger seat. With a smile, she addressed Spike. "Let's head back to the house. I think there are some maps there I can use to show you what I have in mind." *And on the trip maybe I can figure out what that is.*

Welch tapped the button on his Bluetooth earpiece. "This is Welch."

"It's Gretchen, Doctor. The drone is in the air."

"Good. Bring Jim into this call." In a few moments, the three of them were connected on an open line.

Welch needed to take charge of the operation. "Gretchen, keep the drone high. In whisper mode, it's supposed to be undetectable at three hundred feet. Can you zoom in on the house as you approach?"

"Okay. Zooming. Wow. That brings it right in. There are some lights on in the house. I'm streaming the video now."

"Jim, tell me what you see." Welch concentrated on the road as he flew down the highway that would take them to the other side of the lake.

"I count three people through the windows in the house. Two are moving in the driveway. All those have long guns. Can you switch on the thermal fusion view?"

Welch could hear Gretchen's movements, making the adjustments. "How's that?"

The whisper of Jim's counting went on until he stopped, as if he wasn't finished. "I'm seeing a lot of enemies in the trees guarding the house—a full squad of players, at least. I think they planned on hitting the base tonight."

Welch groaned. "You're going to be outnumbered at least three to one." He grimaced at the ache forming inside. Saving Shifra and Rahab was a long shot. Without a miracle, the best he could hope for was to force the enemy to end their pain and his along with it. "I do not feel comfortable having you go any farther with this. I will have this gentleman wait for me down the road and I will go in alone. I feel the Lord will be with me. It is a mission better suited to a one-man stealth attempt. I would ask the rest of you to return and prepare to defend the base. Jim, drop Gretchen someplace safe. She can use the drone as my eyes and use its laser as a distraction as I move in. She'll report my success or failure, so you will know what to expect."

There was silence on the line. Jim broke it. "I need to mute while I inform the men."

In less than a minute, Jim was back on. "Dr. Welch." Jim's voice sounded serious. "I'm afraid there's been a mutiny on the boat. Every man aboard is refusing to carry out your last order. My recommendation is we go ahead with your original plan because no one here is going to leave Ms. Federov with whoever has her. No discussion…sir."

Welch felt proud to associate with such men. "You'll get none from me." Welch's voice grew softer as he spoke. "All I have to give you is my gratitude."

Chapter 28

Shifra had been thinking as she watched the roadside. Ruben would put it all together, everything she hid in their conversation. He would be on his way. But putting an operation together would take time. "Pull over at the top of this hill."

Spike smirked toward her. "You should have thought of that before we left the house, sweety."

She needed to stall. It was all she could do. If she tried anything else…she wasn't big enough to take them both out with only force and skill, even without the guns. If one of them was left to go back for Rahab…

She gave him a mischievous smile. "No, really. That's why I brought you this way. I'll show you the top end of Welch's compound."

Now she had his attention.

"I'll lay it out on the map when we get back, so you can see the big picture, but right now, I wanted to show you this."

If Ruben came, what was he walking into? *How many more men does this guy have?* Right now, there were only the two of them. She'd probably never have this opportunity again.

She needed something more to entice Spike. "It will be the best way for your men to come in from the top when the time comes. You need to know it."

Ruben must be coming, or all this is for nothing. God had always come through for her, but often not in the way she expected. *Father, help me know if I need to do something else. Don't let me miss an opening, but keep me from making a mistake.*

Spike eased the SUV to the side of the road and turned it off. "Get her out. Let's take a look." He swiveled in the seat and stared. "You're full of surprises. You must really hate this guy." The glare he gave was penetrating. "Remind me to never leave you mad. You're not someone to just walk away from."

Shifra gave him a smile. "That's Welch's problem. You've already been nicer to me than he has, and you threatened to kill us. What does that tell you about him? I'm the one that can't just walk away. You're my best chance at getting away from these people without leaving someone behind to come after me."

Mustache jerked open her door. "Get out."

Shifra made casual glances around to examine their stopping place. It was even better than it had looked from inside the vehicle. The roadside dropped away into darkness. The tops of trees in front of Shifra told her they were attached to the earth a long way down the steep embankment. She could jump, roll down the hill and be out of their reach…but then they would go after Rahab.

Spike came around the front, his gun in the holster on his side. In the dark, she couldn't tell if the keys were in his pocket. He had come around quickly. They could still be in the ignition.

She couldn't stall out here forever. What was going to happen when they returned to the house? If Ruben had a team assault the house to free her, Spike would kill her as the last thing he did. No question. How would Ruben react? Blame himself? *I don't want him to live the way I've had to.*

She wrinkled her brow. "I think this is it." Turning, she went around Mustache, starting toward the rear of the vehicle.

Mustache grabbed her arm. She lifted her other hand. "Where am I going to go? You still have my daughter. Let me figure this out. Make sure we're in the right place. It's been some time since I've been up here."

"Let her look. We want to be right." Spike's voice came from behind her. Closer than he had been. He was following.

Mustache released, and Shifra headed to the back, staring into the canyon with her guard following. She rounded the rear bumper and headed toward the opposite side. At the driver's side corner, she stopped. She had to get this little dance just right.

Mustache almost ran into her. He was just behind to her left side.

She pointed across the road, mumbling. "Those trees." Turning again, she displayed her puzzled expression and walked by Mustache.

Spike was at the other corner of the bumper near the edge. She headed his direction as if to look in the canyon again. He moved back around the corner to give her the view.

No, not like that.

Mustache was behind her again. Closer, but still too far.

Again, she turned and was face to face with his mustache. A cute scrunch of her cheeks. The one that made her look like a playful little girl. Did one side of his mustache lift in the start of a grin? Good. Relax. She looked over his shoulder. "No. Those are the ones."

Turning again, she saw Spike had come back around the corner. She stopped so he wouldn't move, finger in the air like an idea was balanced on the tip. Mustache stopped at her back. Another turn to look at the trees. Stop. Spin back. She lost her balance on the spin and stumbled forward.

Mustache's left hand reached for her out of instinct, his gun held loosely in the other.

Shifra brought her momentum into a spin, left hand striking the side of Mustache's gun, right hand driving into the wrist, forcing it to twist into his middle. She jammed her right thumb inside the guard, forcing his own finger hard against the trigger. She felt Mustache's other hand grab her hair. The gun thundered, discharging into the man's chest.

Shifra headed for Spike as Mustache dropped.

Spike's wide eyes moved from Mustache on the ground to Shifra coming at him. He backpedaled, hand pulling his gun from its holster.

Shifra rammed him, both palms into his chest, shoving at the same time. The man's feet made a desperate, stumbling connection down the steep hillside. The gun went off as he went over backward. The shot was muffled by the ringing she already had in her ears.

Shifra's leg locked hard as she pulled up before she went over herself.

Spike landed on his back down the embankment. His leg momentum propelled him into a backward somersault as his shadowy form disappeared into the darkness. Underbrush snapped and curses echoed across the gulley.

Shifra spun, attention back on Mustache. She ignored the charley horse in her leg that her lunge for Spike had produced. She rushed to stand over where Mustache had collapsed forward in a heap. The brilliant expanse of stars overhead revealed the dark stain of an exit wound on the back of his shirt. The stain was not expanding. There was no longer a beating heart to drive the blood.

The image came of holding her son, unable to bring him back, the blood. Shifra blinked away the memory.

From the canyon behind her, Spike yelled, calling her filthy names as he grunted and scrambled, trying to work his way back up.

She scooped up the gun beside the body. A sharp

pain grabbed onto her upper left leg and began clawing its way to her hip. She stumbled and went down.

Rolling onto her back, her hand went to the offending area. The blood her fingers touched told her Spike's wild shot before he went backward hadn't been so wild. The adrenaline had backed off enough, her leg realized it had been hit. The sting-inducing touch told her exactly where the bullet had gone into her thigh. *Spike's coming. I'm easy prey.*

She grabbed the bumper of the Suburban and dragged herself back to a standing position. An electric-like shock came when she put weight on her leg. It didn't feel broken. Just pain from torn muscle.

She examined the weapon in her hand. A Glock. She could tell it even in the dark, forty caliber, sixteen rounds fully loaded. She glanced at Mustache's body. *Minus one.*

The climbing sounds were getting closer. She couldn't fight, couldn't run. If Spike got to level ground, what would she do?

Hobbling toward the edge of the road, she zeroed in on the sounds below. She made a hasty lean out from the cover of the edge and fired. Pow! Pow! Pow! Jerking back to safety from any return fire, she listened through the ringing in her ears. For a second, there was nothing. Then she heard renewed scrambling that sounded like it was receding.

Why did you do that? You should have let him get closer so you wouldn't miss. She was letting fear drive her, doing all the wrong things. She couldn't waste another round on a blind shot. Spike wasn't wasting any.

As fast as her leg would let her, she limped to the driver's door, jerked it open and reached inside. No keys. *Why, Lord? I have to get to Rahab before they do. Spike's probably on the phone already.* She reached for her own phone but stopped. It had gone down the mountain in Spike's pocket.

The Suburban had too much modern security to hot-wire with no tools and no time. She wasn't driving out like she had hoped. Spike might be back at any time. She should check for things to defend herself.

Mustering the fortitude, she crawled inside. In the back seat was a rifle and a ballistic vest with six thirty-round magazines. *If only I had this when he was climbing up.*

She fought the desperation that had her considering taking the rifle and blazing round after round into the gulley, hoping for a lucky hit.

It wouldn't solve the problem. He was sure to have help on the way. What would Spike do? Take the easy route, down to the bottom, and follow the gulley to the road. Would he wait for his men at the bottom of the hill or come up after her on his own?

It didn't matter. What mattered was Rahab. *I'll go down after him. Make him call off his men. If I can find him in the dark before he shoots me while I'm hobbling along the...*

Why had she taken those useless shots? Why hadn't she stuck to her original plan and taken them back to the house? They were going to go after Rahab and she was helpless to do anything. Her eyes blurred again.

Please, Lord. Help me.

Think straight. She put on the vest and grabbed a first aid kit she saw under the seat. What to do next? She opened the hood. Standing a good distance back, she fired several rounds into the battery. Then she checked what electronics she could without the key to be sure the vehicle was dead. If Spike came back, he wouldn't be using the SUV to get to Rahab. Now what?

If she stayed with the Suburban, she was an easy target. No more collecting gear. She needed to get to the trees on the other side of the road where she could hide, maneuver, think. *Hurry.*

Was trying to trek across country to Rahab better than waiting here and doing nothing? She glanced around, trying to determine how to get there.

A muted ringtone came from behind the SUV. *Mustache's phone! Of course he had one.* The fear was making it hard to think. She hustled to the body, searched pockets, and had the phone in her hand as the ringing stopped. The screen identified the caller as **Boss**. They probably didn't use real names on operation phones. *Must be Spike checking if Mustache is alive.* He heard the rifle shots and was hoping.

She needed to get hidden before she used the phone. She pushed it into the back pocket of her jeans. The phone stuck out a little. Good. I can get it quickly if I need it.

In another pocket, she found the keys to Rahab's red Mustang. She would need them if she was able to make it to Rahab. She crammed them deep in her front pocket.

What if the phone hadn't rung before she fled into the trees? *Thank you, Lord. That call Spike meant for evil, You meant for good.*

Chapter 29

Welch made quick glances, watching Radley work with the Expedition's entertainment features. Welch's phone screen appeared mirrored on the monitor built into the vehicle's dash. The human heat signatures were shifting. The dots close to the house were moving to several of the vehicles. Those further out were moving closer to the residence, closing their perimeter.

"Dr. Welch, are you watching the screen?" Gretchen must have noticed the same thing.

"I see it. Something has changed. Zoom in. I need to know if they're putting our ladies in one of those SUVs. Mr. Radley, can you determine that for me?"

The image of the vehicles grew until they were the only thing in the view.

A pop-up box showed a call from an unknown number. *Of all times to get a telemarketer.* "Cancel that. We need to see the screen."

Radley strained to evaluate each figure that was piling into the rigs. "Men with long guns is all I see."

Welch reconsidered their tactics. "Jim, how long before you make your landing?"

"We're ready to do it now. Talisa brought us in to a private dock that is a long way from any house. We're going to deploy onto that."

"Hold where you are." Welch let Jim relay the message to Talisa then continued. "If they're moving the hostages, our plan is obsolete." Welch had to prepare them for the other possibility. "If they all move out, it might mean they know where the base is. In which case you will need to get back as fast as you can to be ready to defend it."

A knot twisted in Welch's stomach. He didn't dare voice what else that would mean. If they had forced Shifra to tell them, she and Rahab would no longer be of any use. They wouldn't be taking any hostages to slow them down or leaving anyone to identify them. The line grew horribly quiet. The others must have reasoned it out as well.

In his heart, Welch begged God. *Please…no.* If all the vehicles left, he and Radley would have to go in…to be sure the hostages were…to be sure there was nothing to be done. Of all the things he had been through in his career…*Shiffy…* he didn't know if he could emotionally survive it.

A text message popped up, getting in the way of him watching who was getting in the vehicles. Anger rose in him like he hadn't felt for a long time. He used the steering wheel controls to cancel the box, but it left an after-image floating in his vision—the first part of the message—**This is Shiffy.**

Welch yelled into the phone. "Gretchen keep watching. I may have…" Welch shifted to pleading with Radley. "Bring back that text." *She called herself Shiffy. Let it be her, God.*

Radley tapped, swiped, tapped some more and began reading **This is Shiffy. I have escaped and am using a stolen phone. Rahab's life depends on you calling me back right now.**

Hope leaped in him. He poured out words to those on the phone. "Shifra has escaped and is texting me. Rabab's still in danger, so keep watching for her. I'm calling Shifra."

"What…Where is Sh—"

Welch cut Gretchen off. "Call that number back." His return call was answered immediately, and Radley put it into the group call so everyone could hear.

"Ruben, thank God." Shifra's whispering voice came over the vehicle's speaker.

"Are you all right?"

"I don't have time to tell you everything. I escaped, but they'll go after Rahab. Please, you have to get to her first. They'll do something awful to her to get back at me."

"Where are you?"

"I'm okay for now. I'm hiding and well-armed. Promise me you'll go for Rahab first. She's about a quarter mile off South 4565 Road on Slurry Lane. She's bound, lying down in the seat of a red Mustang with a blanket over her. She's helpless. You've got to hurry."

Radley entered the location in the GPS.

"Yes. We're on our way, but stay on the line with me. I want to know you're okay."

"I'm here. How long will it take you to get there?"

Welch eyed the GPS. "Ten minutes."

"Doctor," Gretchen sounded like she had been looking for an opening in the conversation, "two SUVs left. Four men in each. There are four SUVs still at the house. They look like they are staged, waiting for something."

"Oh, no. Please, God." Shifra's voice faltered with emotion. "I missed the leader. He's still alive out here, and I'm sure he's called the others."

"We're going to drive as fast as we can. We have a drone up and Gretchen has eyes on the house. But you're not there anymore, correct?"

"No. I'm on the same road, but I'm several miles away from Rahab."

"Closer to the house?" Welch was trying to create a mental image, but it was not an area he had traveled.

"Yes. What road are you on?"

"Lakeside Drive."

"If they're leaving the house now, they'll be ahead of you. They'll get to Rahab before you do."

Welch didn't like how desperate Shifra was sounding. "We'll be there before they have time to do anything."

Shifra kept talking like he hadn't spoken. "They'll come this way. On the map program, it looks like a long way around for them to go the other direction.

The leader is still here. They will also want to pick him up. I'm going to try to stop them here so you can catch up."

"Shiffy, don't do that. You've got a lot of firepower coming your way. Stay hidden and let them pass. You're the higher-value target. If you draw attention to yourself, they'll concentrate everything on you, knowing they can get Rahab later." *Oh, Welch, that was the wrong thing to say.* But it was too late to pull back the words.

"Exactly." Shifra's tone said her determination was fixed. "I don't have a headset, so I need to shut this phone off."

"Shiffy, no."

"Sorry, the noise might give me away. I love you, Ruben."

"Shiffy, listen to me." Welch heard the sound on the line change. "Shiffy?" She was gone.

Welch needed to strategize. "Jim, do you think you can move out and try to capture or neutralize the men that are left?"

"We'll deploy now."

"Try to take the entrance to the drive to prevent any more vehicles from getting out. Gretchen, how many enemies are there?"

"I counted thirty-two heat dots for the other side."

Jim needed an advantage. "We'll need to use the dazzler."

"Oh, I love those things." Gretchen sounded excited. "Thank you. I need something to do. The stuff with the guns and all isn't me, but this is. I can play this game…even if I'm scared." There was the sound of Gretchen moving things. "The dazzler will cut into my fifty-minute flight time, but I've got a second fully-charged drone and extra batteries."

Welch felt hope at the enthusiasm in Gretchen's voice. "I appreciate your willingness. But if any of the other side head your direction, make sure you get on the boat with Talisa and the two of you get out of rifle range."

The noise on the phone signaled Gretchen had shifted. "Talisa is giving a thumbs up to that. Right now, I'll stay on the dock. It's more stable than the boat. But I've got a thirty-mile transmission range. I can still help if we need to hit the water."

"Good. Don't hesitate if you need to retreat. May the Lord protect you both, and thank you. Pray that we can get to Shifra in time. We're not that far away, but it's hard to get any speed on these winding roads."

As Welch sent up his own prayer, an idea came into his head.

Chapter 30

There it was again. Branches snapping. Shifra wasn't imagining things, but it was still far enough from where she hid to be indistinct. She was twenty yards or so south of where the Suburban sat. Estimating the sound, she decided it was coming from the trees farther down the road north of the Suburban. She was glad she had thought to disable the vehicle so it would do him no good if he got to it.

She wasn't in a good position seated on the log, but she had to get the pressure off her leg. The muscle around her thigh had settled into a deep ache, a better feeling than if she moved. Likewise, the bloodstain on the bandage she had wrapped around the wound had stopped spreading once she sat still.

The large tree she hid behind gave coverage between her and the road. She was glad it was a dark night, but she had to expect the enemy to have night vision. She would be better concealed lying on the ground, but she didn't think she could get up again when the vehicles came.

Another snap. She tried to zero in on it. It was too far away to see anything moving in the dark trees. She hoped her opponents wouldn't be able to see her either, but she wasn't going to risk moving any more than she had to.

Not being the outdoorsy type, she couldn't be sure it wasn't an animal. It was more likely Spike. He was the type to come after her personally.

She wanted to fire a volley of rounds in that area to be safe, but giving away her position was a bad idea. If he was hiding somewhere else, he could spot her muzzle flash and pick her off. She had to stay alive. She was the only thing standing between them and Rahab.

Another sound came echoing up the gulley—engines. Still a distance away but they were coming.

When the first vehicle topped the hill, it would see the Suburban. She hoped it would slow down and check. If Spike was there, they would stop to pick him up.

Walk through what you're going to do so you won't make a mistake. She would take out the driver of the first vehicle so it would block the path of the second. Then take out the radiator so it would never get them to Rahab. Next, work on any other vehicles in the same manner. Keep them pinned down until Ruben arrived behind to finish them.

The engines were getting louder. She eased off the log and made a move toward the tree. Her leg had stiffened and wasn't cooperating. The engine sound grew closer. She tried to force her leg forward. A spasm went through it, and it locked. Trying to hop on one leg, she stumbled forward and hit a smaller tree to keep herself from falling. The sound of the smack of her rifle against the bark made her cringe as much as the pain.

The vehicles were close. She half hopped, sliding the bad leg until her shoulder was against the large tree. Rotating with her shoulder against the trunk, she leaned around, exposing as little of herself as possible, and aimed her rifle at the road.

By the sound, the vehicles could be showing up any...The lead SUV topped the hill. A second vehicle came behind it. A figure came walking out of the trees. Spike must be confident she had fled the area.

Shifra resisted the urge to target the man. She took aim and opened up on the driver's side windshield. The vehicle lurched forward and veered, colliding with the parked SUV.

Spike ran for the trees. The second vehicle's backup lights came on. The driver was probably ducking, planning to use the backup camera. Shifra poured rounds into the radiator of the rig. Steam drifted up behind the glow of the headlights.

Someone was returning fire. She felt the air part near her head and she was spattered with bark. Rolling behind the tree, she felt rounds pounding it. It had to be the men from the first vehicle. The firing slowed. But rounds hit the tree every second or so. It was cover fire.

Other men would be moving out wide to flank her. Probably in the trees across the road where she wouldn't see them until they could get a shot. With their night vision, she wouldn't last long.

With her back against the tree, Shifra imagined men watching her through a night scope, putting the crosshairs on her. Any minute, a round would take her out. She had to do something just to stop the horror in her head.

She pulled the magazine from her rifle and shoved it down the front of her vest. It still had a few rounds she couldn't afford to waste. Grabbing a fresh magazine from her vest, she slammed it in the gun. Shifting the rifle in her hands, she stuck it out blindly around the tree, keeping herself as unexposed as she could, and squeezed the trigger. Back and forth, she moved her barrel, hoping some bullets would find the men who were providing the cover fire.

A man's voice cried, "I'm hit, I'm hit."

Taking advantage of the opening, she peeked out long enough to send the remaining rounds in her gun into the front of the lead vehicle. She heard the whistle of escaping steam. They might pull it loose from the other Suburban it had hit, but it wouldn't go far.

Behind the tree again, she felt bark on the other side being impacted by a renewed volley. Grabbing another magazine as she let the empty one drop, Shifra loaded the new one in the rifle and smacked her palm on the bolt release, chambering a round. She had done it. Both vehicles were disabled. They would not be going after Rahab in them.

Rounds clipped off leaves and branches around her. She was going to die before Ruben reached her. She knew it. The killing shot would come any second. They had to be in position by now. Swiveling her rifle again, she blazed the rounds into the trees across the road. Again, she reloaded swiftly when her rounds were gone. There was no use saving them for a special occasion. She might as well keep firing until they killed her. Maybe she would get another lucky hit.

Would Ruben be the one that found her body? She hoped they wouldn't hit her in the head. She didn't want him to see a bloody mess instead of her face. Would it haunt him like the images of her son and husband had done to her for so long? Soon she'd see Caleb again. What would he be like without his disability? *Help Ruben think of that, Lord. Don't let him blame himself like I've done.*

She took a breath and prepared to send her attackers what might be her last round of resistance. One of them had to have her in his sights by now.

Zing! A dark shape whistled through the air with a buzzing hum. It tilted and came to a stop, hovering above the roadway. A piercing light appeared like a bright line from the object to a place in the trees across the road. A silhouette ducked. The light sparkled on the bark where the man was hiding.

The dark shaped rotated in the air, shifting the bright line toward the men behind the Suburbans. Dancing starbursts reflected from where the line of light connected with the vehicles' reflective surfaces. It was a drone with a blinding laser. Shifra had seen them before. The light was so bright it could dazzle the eyes from yards away and render a person blind for a few moments.

The object zipped upwards as the men behind the first Suburban began to fire at it. The drone dived and bathed the men in laser light, moving too fast to present a target. It must be on her side.

Shifra took the advantage. With the men blinded, she moved to a different tree and took her time to aim. She sent two rounds at a man near the back of the lead Suburban who was too dazzled to realize he had strayed from behind cover. He dropped.

The laser light was on the trees across from her again. Shifra sent bullets to the area it lit up near the base of a trunk. The man tried rolling away, but only revealed himself more. Shifra fired into him until he lay still.

She searched the skies. The drone was gone.

Across the road, the trees lit up again. The aerial vehicle had zipped through the foliage, no doubt using its own night vision to navigate in the dark, and come up right behind a man's hiding spot. He made the mistake of turning toward the light. Shaking his head, he tried to move and ran into the tree. The shock caused him to step backwards where Shifra put two rounds in him.

The men behind the Suburban fired wildly, trying to bring down the flying attacker. It was in front of them, then behind them, never staying in one place for long. Their efforts to target the drone only made them vulnerable to the blinding laser. They retreated.

The disabled SUVs blocked her view. Shifra caught glimpses of the men stumbling down the road, hands over their eyes, looking at their own feet for fear of being blinded again. The brief openings she got were not enough to score hits, but she sent rounds in their direction to keep them moving.

The drone came zipping back to the woods across the road. Shifra heard the hum of the rotors as it hovered in the woods, laser fixing on a spot in the leafy undergrowth behind a tree. It must be seeing someone else there. It was the place where Spike had run back into the woods when the firefight started. He might have been smart enough to hunker down with his face toward the ground.

Someone was there, waiting. Waiting for what?

The humming grew faint, and the laser went out. The drone sank into the brush and stopped, lying at an angle in the branches of some scrub. Shifra stared at it for a moment before she realized what was wrong. *The battery ran out.*

At the realization, she brought up her rifle. She fired two rounds on one side of the tree, then two rounds on the other. *Got to keep him pinned down.*

Spike's voice bellowed from behind the tree. "The drone's down. Get back here."

A voice responded from down the road. "On our way."

Shifra cranked off some more rounds at the tree, then started her own retreat. *I can't stay here and let them surround me again.* Half dragging her wounded leg, she hurried to a tree farther down the hill. Her leg must be swelling. It wouldn't bend, and every movement was more painful.

From her new position, she couldn't see Spike's hiding place. Maybe she could discourage him from coming after her, anyway. She fired another volley.

The slope of the hillside was increasing the farther from the road she traveled. She clenched her teeth and stepped out into the dark to gain some more distance. Dirt and leaves slid under foot and carried the rest of her with it. Landing hard on her seat, she kept sliding down the suddenly steep embankment.

Like a rush of water, she cascaded feet first on her back down the slope, weaving around trees and rocks. Her body followed a path that actual water must have deepened each time it rained. It deposited her at the bottom of the ravine, scraped, battered, and overwhelmed by the pain in her leg.

She was behind a rock that blocked her from anyone looking from above. Feeling no compulsion to move at the moment, she tried to grasp a mental handle on the throbbing. For the first time, perhaps in her life, she felt her age—with a lot of years added.

"As much as I want to kill you right now, I'm not coming after you," Spike's voice echoed from high on the hillside. "I can hear a vehicle coming and we're going to commandeer it. I've got the rest of my men headed this way as well. We're going to drive to where we left your daughter and kill her, slowly. That is all you have accomplished. So I really don't care if you lay there and die or end up in the hands of your Mr. Welch. You'll live whatever life you have left knowing you're the reason your daughter's dead. When she's suffering, I'll make sure she knows she has you to thank. I wanted to leave you with that to think about." Above her, the man crunched through the underbrush as he hurried back to the road.

A vehicle's coming? It must be Ruben. Shifra rolled onto the bad leg, disregarding the wave of pain, grabbing for the rear pocket where she'd put Mustache's phone. Ruben would be charging to rescue her and drive right into an ambush and never reach Rahab. *If I can call him, he can turn around and go a different direction and still reach her first.* The pocket was empty. She gasped. The phone had been sticking out. *It must have caught on something.* She ran her hand over the ground, frantic, searching. Nothing.

Rolling onto the opposite hip, she patted all around on the other side of her. No phone. Using her uninjured leg and arms, she pushed herself further up the hillside. She rubbed her hand raw, sweeping over the rough ground, grabbing at any rectangular rock, then casting it aside in horrified disappointment. Higher and higher. *It has to be here.* Her leg slipped and she slid back to the bottom. *No. Please.*

She was lying on a lump. Rolling again, she felt the middle of her back. The earlier slide down had wedged debris under the ballistic vest she wore. She tried sitting up, bending the good leg and forcing against the board-like stiffness of the other. Shifra plopped on her back. *I can't even do a sit-up?*

She snatched at the Velcro straps on the vest, pulling them free. Rolling off of it, she pawed the vest—only pebbles, leaves and sticks.

She grabbed handfuls of the forest trash and squeezed. A sob seeped out between her clenched teeth. Through tears, she looked up the hillside. The phone could have come out the moment she hit the ground or it might be only a little further above her. How could she find it in the dark?

"No!" Shifra cast away the junk she held. She grasped the large rock beside her, clenching her teeth as she forced her body up. She could not be the reason Rahab died. Or Ruben. The ache at the thought of the possibility generated pain that eclipsed anything coming from the bullet in her leg.

She grabbed the rifle, rotated the safety to the **On** position and jammed the butt of the gun into the ground. Driving upward, she got her good leg under her and pushed on the rifle. Up. Up. She forced the wounded leg to join in the support, sending firebrands to its core. A whimper came from her mouth. She ground her teeth and forced the sound into a growl, deep and guttural as the pain, commanding her leg to straighten.

She was upright, leaning against the rock. Panting, she turned herself and examined the dark expanse of hillside stretching above her like Mount Everest.

A dark voice came into her head. *It's your fault again*—images of Rahab being tortured were developing in her thoughts.

You're wasting time listening to him. Yes, she was. The thought was like a hand reaching down for her. Her Savior knew when the fight was too much. He knew it better than she did. He was there with her, regardless of how things appeared.

What if Spike's waiting, luring you up there? That was the other voice, and she wasn't going to listen. She didn't care. She couldn't live with the current situation, so she might as well die trying to change it.

Chapter 31

At the speed Welch was traveling, he had to monitor the road. But he risked glances in the rearview mirror.

Radley, now wearing a harness that covered his chest with magazine pouches, rummaged through the items in the back of the Expedition. "You have excellent equipment."

Welch eyed the pile of ballistic vests the man made on top of a bulletproof shield.

Moving forward again, Radley grabbed a vest and slapped it against the windshield in front of the passenger seat. He found a large roll of black tape and secured the vest in place. "I need you to stay alive long enough to be a convincing distraction."

In a few minutes, Radley had three of the vests covering the windshield except what was right in front of Welch. Pulling down the passenger sun visor, he taped it in place to reinforce what he had done. He was armoring the vehicle against gunfire.

Bringing the ballistic shield over the seats, Welch saw that Radley also had a large knife in his hand. The man turned the shield on its side and shoved it into place against the vests. Sliding it to the edge of the open area that was left for Welch to watch the road, he held the shield in place with one hand.

Radley was leaning over the center console toward Welch. With a sudden move, he jerked the knife upward. Welch's breath faltered as the blade poised above him. With a powerful strike, Radley embedded the knife in the dashboard close to the shield.

He pulled the sun visor down to hold the shield in place and taped it. Sliding it back and forth, Radley addressed Welch. "Sorry about the damage. I don't know how long this tape will hold against rifle fire. The knife will reinforce it."

Welch nodded. "Thanks for thinking of me. I assume you'll be taking out the enemy while I draw their attention?"

Radley was looking at the map app on the phone. He glanced up as if something Welch said made him pause. "Yeah. Now that I know who the enemy is."

As if coming back to the situation, Radley leaned close to Welch so he could see out the window. "Stop here."

Radley grabbed the last vest and shoved it past Welch, positioning it to cover the corner of the windshield to Welch's left, and part of the driver's side window. He taped it in place and slid the shield to overlap the vest he had just placed.

Radley pointed at the narrow viewing window in the shield that was positioned right in front of Welch. "This ballistic glass is the only forward visibility you'll have. Since it's not meant to be used sideways, your view will be even narrower. But you'll be driving slow. Once they hit the windshield a few times, it will be so shattered you won't be able to see ahead, anyway. Keep yourself that same distance from the side of the road and you'll be fine.

Radley brought another assault rifle from the rear and chambered a round, so it was ready to fire. He reached across Welch again and pulled the handle, opening the door a crack. The cab light came on and Radley shut it off while he moved the gun over Welch's head. He shoved the barrel out of the crack and above the vest. "Keep the gun high and aim low. Since we don't know where your agent is, we don't want to risk hitting her."

Welch had been sending up continuous silent prayer for Shifra. Since the drone died, he was scared to call her. She might be hiding and he didn't want to give away her position. Little could be gained by a call, and the loss could be unbearable. She would call if she was safe. The thought did nothing to relieve his anxiety. Welch took hold of the gun with his left hand.

Radley slapped a piece of tape on the door so it wouldn't open further, then sat back in his seat. "I'm getting out here. I'll be moving fast through the trees on this side." He tipped his thumb toward the passenger door. "I'll stay down the hill enough that I'll be out of sight in case they have night vision or thermal. The suit I'm wearing blocks most of my heat signature, but I'll come up low behind some cover to keep it minimal. With you to draw their attention, they shouldn't see me. Give me a few minutes to get a head start and don't drive over 5 miles-per-hour. I'll be trying to keep it quiet, so I won't be running full out." He motioned ahead. "When you come over that rise, they'll get their first glimpse of you. They'll want you close before they shoot. You'll have to shoot first to get them to return fire. Start shooting right after you crest the hill. Once they start shooting back, I'll use the exchange to cover my shots and take them out one at a time. You've got thirty rounds, so shoot slow, but not too slow. With luck, they will focus on you, thinking you're making the hits, and not realize I'm there until it's too late."

Welch was impressed. "Good tactics. Even if it makes me a target. Just make sure you protect Shifra if something happens to me."

Radley stared at the dash. "That's the woman that got you out of the hospital?"

"Yes."

"She's special to you?"

"Exceptionally special."

"I'll do what I can. I know what it's like to lose someone like that."

"Do you pray?"

The man glanced at Welch, but turned away again. "I don't think I can."

Welch didn't have time to probe. "I'm going to pray. Father, we need Your help. Please keep Shifra safe until we can reach her. Guard my friend and me as we do what we can and what we must. Make us strong, keen sighted, and quick. If You can keep our enemies alive during this, please do. If they can live to know you, we ask for that, but do not let evil rule the day. In the name of the only One who truly saves— Jesus." Welch clasped the man's shoulder. "Go with God."

Radley nodded his head, just enough for Welch to notice. He turned Welch's direction again, but his gaze landed short of eye contact. "Okay." The man turned, and in a moment, Welch was facing an empty seat.

He put the SUV in gear and eased it forward.

Radley slung his rifle onto his back. He flipped up the flap that covered his gun in the leg holster, fastening it in the open position for a quick draw. Loping through the trees, he allowed his excellent night vision to take effect. Gradually, he picked up the pace until he was at an easy sprint that still allowed him to avoid branches. Up the hill, he could hear the engine noise of the SUV idling forward. It would help cover the sound of his advance.

"Please be careful. I don't want to lose you."

Radley slowed as he snatched glances right and left. "Sarah?"

"Just my voice…for a minute only…so I don't distract you. I just wanted you to know what you mean to me."

Radley was distracted. "What I mean to you?"

"Yes. I didn't want you to think I don't care. God has to be first in my life…but you are second. Please call on God and ask Him to help you. It's time, Peter. I think you're not sure you will live through this, and I don't think you care if you die. I can see the depression in you. Please don't think like that. I need you to let God help you stay alive. I have something to tell you when it's over. When you have let God rescue you…from everything. It can't be about me…the reason you seek God…but if you can and He helps you survive…it might be about us. Trust me."

His mind had snapped. It was what Radley had feared. He rubbed his neck to the point he could feel the friction heat. He was hearing the words he longed to hear…from a dead woman that he was having a romance with in his head.

"Don't let the depression win." Sarah's voice was desperate. "I believe you need to do this, but I need you to live through it. Don't give up, Peter. Hold on to hope. With God, there is always hope. Just believe me, okay?"

"Believe you? You're in my head. You're not real…not anymore. I told you not to go in the lab. Why did you? Were you trying to—?" Radley shook his head. "You died in the explosion."

"We both did. Yet here we are." Sarah's voice was almost a whisper. "Sometimes you can't believe in things you see and you have to believe in things you can't."

Radley wanted it to stop. "I know what happened. I set the explosives. I killed you."

"I know." The gentleness returned to Sarah's voice. "You wanted out, but they would never let you out. You had to make it look like you were dead. You never meant for me to be in the lab. That's what I know."

Pow! A gunshot echoed through the canyons.

Radley hadn't realized he had his head down and was leaning with his hand against a tree until the shot made him jerk upright. Welch had closed the distance. Return shots cracked from the enemy. Another shot from Welch.

Sarah spoke what was obvious. "You've got to go. He needs you. But you have to let God in. He can help you and I can't wait much longer. Please, Peter."

Radley turned his attention to the strategy, which was well in play without him. He heard the blasts of the rounds being fired at Welch, heard them pinging off the metal of the Expedition and smacking into the windshield.

The windshield had already shattered. Welch could no longer see anything through the slit in the ballistic shield. He used the glow of his headlights to keep the Expedition the same distance from the side of the road as Radley had directed. The smack and thud of rounds hitting the vests and shield were interspaced with metallic hits on the vehicle. His fear had him waiting for the bullet he would never hear. *Please, Lord, protect me. Help me find Shiffy and save Rahab.*

"Dr. Welch?" The voice in his earpiece sounded worried.

"I'm busy, Gretchen. Talk fast."

"I'm bringing in the first drone to change batteries before it crashes. I used a lot of juice with the dazzler. It was tough switching between drones, here and there, but your idea worked. Jim and the security force have the kidnappers pinned down. They have the advantage now. But two vehicles got away. I followed them as far as I could, but I had to get the drone back before it died. I'm not sure where they went. They might be headed your direction or they might go the long way around to get to Rahab. I will be back in the air as soon as I can. I have the advantage of being able to fly in a straight line, but I still don't know if I'll catch up in time. You might have company before I get there."

Welch considered the best use of the drone. "We'll handle this. Check first for any vehicle going the other way to Rahab and see if you can stop it with the dazzler. Make your first burst count. Time it on a curve or something and see if you can wreck them."

Chapter 32

Radley hurried to the fight, but he couldn't put Sarah's words out of his head. He made a quick glance at the starlight coming through the trees and spoke in his mind as he ran. *I know I deserve it. I deserve to relive it. To feel how much I loved her now that it's too late, but please take it away. I know I'm a killer, but I didn't mean for it to happen to her. Could you forgive me for all of it, like she says?*

The idea took hold in Radley. Welch seemed like he knew God was real. That belief made a difference in Welch and in his life. Radley wanted that. He was ready to believe what he couldn't see.

If You've been speaking to me through her, then I'm ready to listen—just You and me. I need to know what's real. Please forgive me. Jesus, if You're the only one who saves, save me. I'm all Yours from now on. I can't keep going like this. Radley experienced a new feeling. It was difficult to define. He decided that he felt like God was with him, right there in the middle of the gunshots.

He estimated where the shots were coming from and scrambled up the hill. A man with a rifle hop-skipped down the slope. He skidded to a stop when he saw Radley. In the moment of shock, the man hesitated when Radley did not. The pistol was out of the holster on Radley's leg and already on target when the man decided he should raise his rifle. Radley made two headshots, and the man dropped before he could pull the trigger.

After a brief scan for more enemies, Radley re-holstered the pistol and unslung his rifle. The man he shot must have intended to flank the SUV and engage Welch from the side, just as Radley was doing to them.

Radley approached the crest of the ridge, easing up through some brush beside a large stump. Through his fusion scope, he searched the trees on the opposite side of the road. As he feared, there was another man moving through the trees, trying to target Welch from the other side.

Radley pulled the trigger and the boom and the ching of his rifle's recoil spring were still ringing in his ear when the enemy fighter fell in the dark trees. Doing a sweep of the area with his naked eye, he saw no sign that his engagement was detected. It was to Radley's advantage that the Ozark terrain caused the shots to echo, making it difficult to discern where they were coming from.

Through his scope, he picked out other targets. Three men were using SUVs for cover. He started with the one farthest back behind the others and dropped him. The other two were too busy firing at Welch in front of them to notice the man fall behind them. Radley took out the next one with the same result.

Then the other fighter turned, perhaps realizing the ones behind him had stopped firing. He ran to his cohort and Radley's next bullet laid him right on top of his comrade.

Radley tallied five. The only gunfire was coming from Welch. Switching between the various views of his night vision and thermal, Radley scanned for the sixth man. Where was he? He wasn't in front of him. Maybe he had—.

Behind him, a rifle boomed. Radley rolled, bringing his own weapon to face the sound. It wasn't shooting at him. Shot after shot flashed from a barrel protruding from behind a tree. To his right, someone doubled over. The rifle barrel that was aimed in Radley's direction drove into the dirt.

Another round from Welch smacked the asphalt on the road above them.

A female voice spoke from behind the tree. "I don't know who you are. You're shooting at them, so you must be on our side. But until I find out, put your rifle down and spread your hands out to your sides."

The next round from Welch made Radley tense, hoping the woman didn't mistake it as an attack.

He laid his gun down and stepped away from it. "I'm Radley. I came with Welch. You must be the one he cares for. Yes, I'm on your side." Radley hoped it was enough to convince her.

The woman used her cover well. "Go roll him over."

Radley went to the man. When he got close, the woman spotlighted them with the light on the rifle. Radley put himself in a position of advantage in case the man was still alive. He rolled the body over, and stepped back.

Keeping her gun pointed between Radley and the man on the ground, she made her way to the downed man. Stopping about ten feet away, she shifted the gun to point directly at the body. "Spike. I thought it was him." Shifra said it as if there was significance in the fact. "Is he dead?"

"Yes. You made good hits."

"Did I?" Her tone was hard. She held the rifle low so the glow from the light made her expression visible. Her face seemed to soften. "He's in your hands now, Lord." Her voice was almost a whisper. "That's enough."

She spun away. "Where is Ruben…Dr. Welch?"

"In the vehicle. He is the one firing blind."

Another round from Welch.

"Can you call him and give him the all clear?"

"I will if you promise not to shoot me when I reach for my phone."

"Deal. Tell him we need to hurry and get to my daughter."

The drone was silhouetted against the rising moon. "Come on, come on." Gretchen urged the dark shape back to her as if her voice could add battery power to the UAV. It was sinking toward the lake's surface despite her efforts to keep it aloft. The moonlight reflecting on the water showed that the craft was moving faster toward the shimmering lake than it was toward the dock. "It's not going to make it."

Talisa stood in the boat, watching the struggle. "Is it waterproof?"

"Maybe. I doubt it floats, though. A dead submarine isn't going to do us much good either."

Gretchen flinched at the sound of a large splash. A glance around showed that Talisa was no longer on the boat. "No way."

After a moment, the moon's wavering reflection was pierced by a sleek head popping out of the water right in the drone's path. The aerial vehicle was almost in the drink when a hand broke the surface under it and lifted it from its liquid fate. Keeping the drone as far from the water as possible, Talisa scissor-kicked her legs, propelling herself and her catch to the dock.

Gretchen grabbed the drone, and Talisa rolled onto the wooden surface.

"Wasn't that cold?" Gretchen shook droplets of water from the drone as she gazed at her soaking, shivering partner.

Talisa shook violently as she got to her feet. "Uh huhhhh." The response ended with a chatter of teeth as Talisa slap-footed her way to the boat and crawled aboard. Despite her shaking limbs, she soon had herself wrapped in a large blanket she pulled out of a storage compartment.

Gretchen had no more time to marvel at the bundled figure on the boat seat. She replaced the dead battery with quick precision. Launching the UAV straight up, she waited until it was well above the trees and then fired it forward like an arrow. On the laptop beside her, she had her satellite map view adjusted to the same green tint that was displayed on the drone's screen in night vision. Trying to identify the terrain by matching what she saw on each screen, she followed the roads the vehicle would have to travel to get to Rahab.

Chapter 33

Shifra clenched her teeth in pain. "Don't pay attention to my groaning. Get me up there."

She had an arm over each man's shoulder while they each had an arm around her back. They clasped their other arms together, making a seat for her to sit on. "Did Gretchen say how long ago these other vehicles left?" She glanced over at Welch's flushed, sweat-drenched face. "Never mind. You can tell me when we're driving."

A vehicle roared by on the road above. The tires of an SUV skirted the edge of the roadway to get around the other Suburbans she had disabled. Only their enemy would be making a move like that.

"Stop them!" Shifra motioned her head toward the SUV as she jumped out of the men's arms, sending pain like a needle through her leg.

Radley flipped his rifle from the slung position to his shoulder as quick as a switchblade. The vehicle had traveled too far down the road for the tires to be in sight, so Radley riddled the back of the SUV with bullets. Coming from their low angle down the bank, any rounds that penetrated probably exited uselessly through the Suburban's roof.

There was the screech of metal on metal as the SUV made it past the roadblock she had tried to create and became a fading engine sound. The two vehicles that left the house must have split up to fulfill their commander's last order. Now this one didn't have far to go to get to Rahab.

Ruben gestured for Radley to resume the chair, but Shifra took off, limping up the hill, tears blurring her vision. She didn't want the men behind her to see the agony on her face.

Welch hustled to her side and had her arm over his shoulder, propelling her forward with his own grimace. Radley slid under her other arm, and the three of them reached the vehicle far faster than was good for Ruben lungs or Shifra's leg.

The men deposited Shifra at the open passenger door of the SUV, and she grabbed the handle above and dragged herself in the rest of the way, jerking on her seatbelt. "Hurry. Can you drive, Ruben?"

All she got from him was a nod as he used the last of his wind to crawl into the driver's seat and buckle up for the pursuit.

She hated to push him, but Rahab's life was the most important thing at the moment, and she knew he would agree. "Lord, please. We need a miracle."

Fortunately, the enemy had wanted Ruben's

Expedition drivable. They had concentrated their bullets on the windshield rather than taking out the tires or radiator.

The Expedition rocked, and she heard Radley's boots on the hood. There was the sound of him using the heavy footwear to rake away as much of the windshield glass as he could. Radley flung the tattered vests and ballistic shield to the ground. Diving in, he slid and rolled himself past her and started rummaging in the back of the vehicle.

Ruben had the SUV started and he stepped on the gas. As they roared away, the airflow flipped the remaining windshield glass off the hood, pelting them as they picked up speed.

Radley reached forward with a riot helmet. Positioning it on Ruben's head, he pulled down the clear, shatter-resistant shield on the helmet to protect Ruben's eyes. Ruben made a one-handed adjustment to the headgear as Radley fastened the chin strap. He handed another to Shifra. Soon, they tore down the road, surrounded by the roar of the wind and the tiny pings of fragmented glass on their plastic face shields.

Shifra peered into the darkness, searching for any sign of the Suburban ahead of them. The sounds all became background noise to the pleading of her heart. *Please help us stop them.*

There you are." Gretchen zeroed in on the

headlights on the display from the drone's bottom camera. The vehicle zipped along the switchback roads that traversed the Ozark hills above Lake Gallant. She watched as the driver expertly slid around each corner. *Let's see if I can help him miss one of those turns.*

Driving the drone toward the moving lights on the road, Gretchen concentrated. This was going to take some fancy flying. The drone wasn't a racing drone, but it should be able to match the vehicle's speed on the winding roads.

She kept the drone high, waiting for the next turn. *Here it comes.* She rotated the drone and swooped in right above the cab of the Suburban. Navigating through the rear camera, she kept the laser aimed and waited as the turn approached, posing one finger over the firing button.

"Now." She punctuated her audible command by pushing the drone forward and down and pushed the laser button. Her eyes flitted between the drone's camera displays. The front display sparkled with light bouncing back from the vehicle's windshield as the dazzler laser poured blinding light into the cab of the SUV. The rear camera showed rapidly approaching trees. Gretchen pulled back the joystick, and the drone rose into the sky, clipping leaves from the top of the trees that she barely missed.

Hovering the drone, she spun it to see what she had accomplished. Even with the night vision, she could barely see the vehicle's headlights through the dust and tire smoke obscuring the scene. It cleared to reveal the SUV resting against a tree at the bend in the road. To her displeasure, the vehicle pulled away from the tree, ripping off bark with the protruding metal from a wrinkled door.

"Oh, snap!" *They'll be wary now. I've lost my surprise advantage.*

Gretchen matched the vehicle's pace again, much slower now. She flew with one hand and zoomed out on her map program with her other. There were plenty of turns between them and Rahab's position. She let the vehicle make the next turn without interference. *Go ahead. Get comfortable again.*

Chapter 34

Welch could feel Shifra's anxiety permeating the cab of the Expedition as much as the air volume that came through the windowless front. She had a right to her fear. Getting her to their vehicle had put them way behind the other SUV. She needed medical attention and he sure wasn't going to leave her behind in her condition.

He was a strategist, never as good in the fast action decisions. He had probably fumbled this one. He should have watched for the other vehicle while Radley helped Shifra.

If something happened to Rahab, he might have saved Shifra physically, but would she endure emotionally? Welch would feel his own failure, but his pain would come mostly from what it would do to Shifra. She had been through so much already in her life.

Would she blame him or herself, or both? Could

their relationship survive that kind of pressure? Welch feared he was about to lose in so many ways.

As he drove, he prayed, *Father, I am a fool. I have probably made a mess of this and have no hope of success without You. I am begging You for an intervention. Slow them down or speed us up.*

Shifra smacked her hand against her side window. "There they are!"

"Where?" Welch couldn't see over the bank on her side where she was looking.

"Below us. The road switches back. They're so close!" Her head swiveled toward the rear to follow the enemy's vehicle as it moved away from them. "There they go."

With a quick glance, Welch saw that Radley had his window down and his rifle aimed. Putting on the brakes would only make him miss for sure. *Help him make the shot, Lord.* Welch tipped the rearview mirror so he could watch the other man.

Radley drew in his weapon, plopped in his seat and refastened his seatbelt. He knew his limitations. Welch let out a frustrated sigh for both of them.

Shifra whimpered. "They're turning again. Another switchback."

With his eyes back on the road ahead, something by the side of the road caught his attention—a large utility pole. He applied the brakes as hard as he dared. Cranking the wheel, he brought the Expedition around to shine his lights at the pole. The trees had been cleared and the ground leveled around the pole then beyond to another pole farther down the hill. Welch had seen such a sight before. Poles marching in a straight line up the sides of mountains, green turf surrounding them like a steep road. This one was going down.

Welch smiled at God. *You never want to do it my way, do You? Okay. A shortcut works.*

Welch engaged the four-wheel-drive. Shifra gasped as he pushed the SUV over the edge. They bounced across the ditch and were careening down a steep slope. The terrain was not as smooth as it appeared. As they barreled down the hill, the rocks and ruts tried to jerk the wheel from his grasp. The road that the enemy vehicle had just traveled loomed in front of them.

Welch had only a moment to deliberate. If he took the road, they would still be far behind the other vehicle. Shifra had last seen the enemy Suburban turning on another switch back. That would put them on a road farther below. The utility right-of-way Welch was on must also intersect with that road. He continued forward, hoping to catch them on the next switchback.

His tires slid on the grassy slope as Welch tried to slow to cross the road. Hitting the ridge of the ditch at teeth jarring speed, the nose of the SUV launched upward. The front tires landed on the edge of the roadway as the rear tires slammed into the ditch and caught traction. The underside scraped hard as the tires pushed and pulled the vehicle onto the road. Bouncing their way across the road, they repeated the process on the far side. The vehicle made hideous sounds at the mistreatment, and Welch prayed it would hold together.

As they jounced down the next rugged expanse, Welch caught sight of headlights. His gamble had been correct. They were set to intersect the vehicle's path…Maybe too fast.

Though perhaps better than failure, a suicide ramming was not the plan. Welch jammed on the brake pedal. They slid, causing the Expedition to fishtail. He eased off, trying to correct. The rear end went one way, then another.

Headlights were flying toward their trajectory. The enemy faced his own decision—stop to avoid a collision or try to make it past. He chose the latter.

Welch fought the steering wheel, trying to get it under control. As they approached the road, he had no choice but to hit the brake again. The Expedition slid and bounced with little reduction in speed. The front rose then came down hard. Welch felt the lurch of a front tire gouging into the dirt. The wheel was jerked from his grip. The rear end came around, the SUV tipped violently, and everything began to spin.

Gretchen had the drone poised above the cab of the vehicle again as they approached a switchback. She flew the drone in front of the windshield, dazzling the driver with laser fire. The vehicle wavered but made the corner. They had learned the game, probably shielding their eyes and watching the edge of the road.

Zooming up high, Gretchen followed the vehicle and considered the problem. She could dazzle them at every corner and slow them to a crawl, but that much laser use would deplete the battery quickly. She would be out of the game, and they would be unhindered for the rest of their trip to Rahab.

If this was a video game, how would she play it? In the digital world, everything followed a pattern. Find the pattern and defeat it. Maybe she could make her own pattern in the real world.

Gretchen locked the auto track feature of the drone on the headlights and turned her attention to the satellite view of her map program. She followed the road as it twisted and turned up and down the mountain sides. *There. That could work.*

Releasing the auto feature, Gretchen took control. At the next switchback, she dazzled the driver and watched the vehicle navigate around the corner toward the passenger's side. In spite of her efforts, they made the turn. *That's right. Watch for the trees at the edge of the road and keep turning to the place where there are no trees.* Gretchen followed them around the corner with the laser, then broke off.

The vehicle climbed higher up the mountain, heading toward the next reversal in the opposite direction. When they got to the next switchback, Gretchen was there again with her now impotent light show. This time she moved lower into the turn with the laser, forcing the driver to search harder for the trees. No trees must mean the road was there, and the laser took the corner with them again.

One more leg higher. The next switch back was the same. The passenger had his head out the window, hand blocking the laser, and found the opening that took them up again, the laser light leading the way around the corner. No trees meant they were following the road.

Gretchen readied herself for the next turn for the vehicle. She came down in front of the driver's view. They knew the drill when she hit them with the laser. She dazzled the driver, moving low toward his side— no help from the passenger this time. The driver should be looking for his opening in the trees, watching the laser make the turn with him.

Gretchen kept moving the drone in a curving motion out into the empty space of the drop off just as if she was following a roadway. The front end of the vehicle went over the ledge that was devoid of trees. The headlights made a sudden drop downward, lighting the way into the abyss. Gretchen switched off the laser and flew away. She didn't want to see the rest. It wasn't a game.

Chapter 35

The world had stopped spinning, but Shifra still wanted to vomit. She was enveloped in a white rough fabric that was receding away—deflating airbags—around and above her. They had undoubtedly saved her life. She straightened the riot helmet she wore and realized that had probably been a factor as well.

Ruben! Her sudden concern for him took away the nausea. She turned toward the driver's side, searching for him. The white fabric blocked her view.

There was a ripping sound. A hand reaching from the back seat, pulling at the fabric while another hand attacked the entrapment with a serrated edge knife. Slicing and tearing, Radley was clearing away the obstruction.

Ruben groaned. She saw his own large hand pulling at the air bags. As Radley sliced and flung the material out of the way, she saw Ruben pushing the steering wheel airbag out of his face. He seemed uninjured. *Thank you, Lord!*

She pushed down the white material in front of her. The roof of the Expedition was crumpled, but she still had plenty of view to see they were sitting in the middle of the road, upright. The Expedition had rolled across the ditch and come back on its wheels on the pavement.

The other SUV was ahead and to the right, half on the road, rear end in the ditch against a tree. The driver must have swerved into the ditch at the last second to avoid a collision with them. A face peeked out the rear door.

Shifra needed to keep them from going after Rahab. She threw open her door and stepped out to go after them. The face jerked back, and the door slammed. Shifra felt a stab from the wound in her leg. What was she doing?

She heard the engine of the other vehicle rev and watched it pull away from the tree and head down the road. Jumping back in her seat and pulling her door shut, she pointed. "They're going again."

Radley slashed away the remainder of the bag hanging from the steering wheel, then dropped into the seat behind Ruben.

Raising his hands as if to get a full view of what was in front of him, Ruben examined the dash. The engine was still running. Grabbing the wheel, his foot came off the brake, where he had apparently kept it without thinking. He mashed on the accelerator and sent them down the road, after their quarry.

The Expedition was full of extra noises. All the windows were gone. The remnants of the airbags Radley had cut and the ones he had to leave flapped violently in the airflow, adding to the mind-numbing din. But they were keeping the other vehicle in sight.

"That was a good move." Radley shouted over the noise. "If they had rushed us, we wouldn't have been ready. Getting out like that with the helmet on was intimidating enough that you spooked them into taking off again instead."

"I don't know what I was thinking. I'm glad it did some good."

Radley climbed into the back as they trailed the enemy SUV around several corners. The off-road shortcut they had taken, including the roll-over, had confused Shifra, but she was getting reoriented to their location. "I think the road where I left Rahab isn't too far. What's the plan?" She yelled to be heard over the wind.

Radley shouted from the cargo area. "I can't find my pack. It must have gone out during the rollover. I had explosives in there that could have come in handy."

He moved back to his seat. "These guys don't seem like the suicide type. They must be planning on taking us all out at the same time. If your drone pilot wasn't able to eliminate the other vehicle, they probably plan on occupying our attention while the other vehicle comes in from behind, putting us in the crossfire. I wouldn't get too close when they stop."

"We can't let them have a chance to hurt Rahab."

Radley was thoughtful. "Your daughter is in a vehicle parked beside the road, right?"

"Yes."

"Which side of the road?"

"The right."

"Is she in the passenger seat or the driver's seat?"

"Passenger. The seat is reclined with her lying down so she can't be seen. They tied her to the seat so she couldn't get away."

"If I was in their place," Radley's voice was emotionless. "I would go by the car she's in and put her between us and them. They won't care if she's hit, but we'll have to be careful how we shoot. It will give them another advantage. We need to be ready for that."

The idea sickened Shifra. "We need to stop them *before* they get to Rahab." Her tone came out sharper than she'd intended.

Ruben spoke without taking his eyes from his intense struggle with the road. "I don't think there's much hope of catching them." He flinched as Radley's rifle barrel poked past his shoulder.

The man yelled, "Welch, I'm going to be shooting close to your ear. Don't wreck us."

Ruben's hands seemed to tighten on the wheel in anticipation. "I'm ready."

Shifra shoved her fingers up the sides of her helmet and tried to cover her ears. The rough vibrating ride caused by the damage to their vehicle was going to make a steady shot impossible. Plus, Radley had nothing to aim at but the black outline of the SUV between the glow of the vehicle's tail lights. *Let him hit something to stop them, please, Lord.*

The gun's deafening explosion was like a physical presence violently expanding to fill the cab. The wind washed it away as quickly as it came, but the ringing in her ears was like a bad aftertaste.

Shifra felt guilty for plugging her ears while Ruben could not. But not protecting them made no sense. She needed to hang onto sense even as difficult as it was at the moment.

Before they could recover, the rifle bellowed again and again.

Focusing on the vehicle in front of them, she tried to assess the damage. The other SUV was too far away in the darkness to see if there were bullet holes in the black metal.

The lights from the other vehicle panned to the right, showing they had come to another switchback. From near the back of the dark hulk, there was the yellow flash of gunfire. Radley had gotten their attention. The wind noise reduced the return fire to distant pops, but she thought she heard a metallic ping on their vehicle.

Ruben slammed on the brakes and let the enemy vanish behind the trees.

Shifra couldn't believe it. "Don't stop! They're too far ahead already!" She was snapping again.

"I'm not getting you shot. We won't do Rahab any good dead, and we won't get there at all if they get our radiator."

Ruben mashed on the accelerator, shot down to the apex of the corner, letting their Expedition drift wide to maintain speed, gaining some of the ground he had lost.

Ruben was only trying to protect her. She knew that. *If I die, I know where I'm going. But Rahab...* "We have to catch them. They'll try to hurt Rahab the moment they get there."

Radley spoke behind her. "Tactically, it doesn't make sense for them to hurt your daughter before they engage us."

Shifra fought to keep her lip from quivering. "I can't depend on that..." *I can only depend on the Lord.* It came to her mind out of habit. It was the right thing to say. It was what had gotten her through before. But— She fought to forget the images that weren't helpful. It wasn't the time for her faith to be wavering.

Ruben cast a look her way, then his eyes were back on the road as he spoke. "We'll do whatever we can to stop them. God is going to help us. We have to trust Him no matter what happens."

He's preparing me for the worst. Please, God, I can't lose her, not knowing where she's...

"Okay, here's the plan." Radley yelled over the noise.

Keeping his eyes ahead, Ruben leaned his head toward where Radley leaned forward from the backseat. "Whatever it is, say it loud. My ears are still ringing."

Radley leaned their way and yelled. "Since the girl in the car is our number one priority, no matter where they stop, we need to come in between them and that car.

Ruben nodded. He glanced at Shifra. "Where are the keys to Rahab's car?"

"In my pocket."

"Good." Ruben sent a stern voice in her direction. "Get to the back. Find something to hang onto, and get ready to bail out the rear door. That will get you as far away from the engagement as possible. Your only job is to get to that car, get it started, and get you and Rahab out of here. Don't look back. If we know you're safe, then we can retreat if we have to. Now get back there and be ready to move."

Shifra heard the words, but her mind was choked by the awful thought that there would be no retreat for the men. It was the only option to save Rahab. The men would be the distraction for her to accomplish it. Ruben was committing his and Radley's life to her escape. He was taking charge, preventing her from having to decide between him and Rahab. She gazed at him in realization that he shared the concern that was outweighing everything else. They didn't know where her daughter stood with God.

For a fleeting moment, he looked away from his driving and met her eyes. She tried to pour all she felt for him into the look she gave. There were no words to communicate it. But his brief expression said he understood and felt the same. They would see each other again in Heaven.

Then his eyes were back on the road. "You better hurry."

Shifra unbuckled. She handed her rifle to Radley, who laid it aside and helped her across the center console. Picking up her gun, again, she moved over as Radley took her place up front.

Making the crawl over the seats to the back was agonizing. Panting from the exertion, she tried to keep her mind clear. Wading through the gear, she stationed herself by the rear hatch.

Radley and Ruben were yelling back and forth, solidifying a plan that took advantage of the few options they had. The wind noise and the pain in her body and heart were drowning out the words. Rahab's soul needed more time. She had to focus on that. She had only one thing to do. God had to do the rest.

Shifra was brought out of her thoughts by the vehicle ahead of them, making a turn she recognized. "That's it! Rahab's down that road!"

Welch had been putting everything into his driving. He had gained ground and made the turn a few moments after the other vehicle.

The Suburban's rear window popped open, and a rifle barrel poked out as they approached Rahab's car. If the ones in the Suburban went by the Mustang, they could get a shot at Rahab from the open glass.

Radley snapped his rifle on the distant target and opened fire, hitting the rear door. The rifle jerked back inside.

The SUV careened past Rahab's car and skidded to a stop. The doors on each side of the Suburban flew open.

Welch moved to the left to continue past the red Mustang as well. "I'm opening the hatch." Nothing. Welch pressed it again. "It's jammed."

Radley leaned left and fired, but he was being jostled and thrown back and forth by Welch's radical driving.

The men did not stop to engage them. Running full out, they fled toward the trees at the right side of the roadway. They were smarter than to be trapped in the vehicle.

Welch skirted the left edge of the road, swinging wide so he could put the Expedition in the gap between the enemy's SUV and the red sports car.

Radley still fought to hold his rifle steady, but he now had a straight shot. "I count seven." He unloaded on the closest man. His rounds were effective. Shifting his sights, Radley fired again. Another went down. He shifted targets, but the others were already using the trees as cover. "Make that five."

Shifra knew the bent frame and twisted rear gate weren't going to open. Slinging her rifle over her shoulder, she threw her injured leg through the vacant rear window. She rolled out, hoping to ride on the bumper until the vehicle came to a stop. Her leg didn't cooperate and slipped off. The force of the drop pulled her weary fingers from the slick metal. She landed on the asphalt, her momentum rolling her body, following the SUV she had just vacated. Her rifle separated from her and skittered to a stop before she did.

Shifra came to rest on her back. Again, she was thankful for the helmet. Her body screamed to be left alone, but her fierce determination won the argument. She rose to a position that resembled standing. Her rifle was lying in the open. It would be suicide to go for it. Shifra headed for the Mustang. Her wounded leg didn't want to move, so she dragged it unwillingly, taking off at a running limp to get the Expedition between her and the gunmen in the trees.

Ruben and Radley had skidded to a stop. They were using the Expedition's open windshield to exchange fire with the men in the trees, trying to keep them pinned down so she could make it out. They both had their doors open, using the framework for cover. She had to hurry because their opponents wouldn't have to move far to get a shot around the SUV.

Shifra closed in on Rehab's car. She had the keys out and pushed the unlock on the fob. A round creased the hood of the Mustang and ricocheted off the frame of the windshield. Another hole appeared on the passenger side of the windshield and spider-webbed across the glass.

"They're making hits on the car." It was Radley yelling at Ruben. He ripped off bursts from his rifle at the trees to keep the men from shooting at the vehicle.

Shifra made it to the Mustang and jerked open the door. Rahab screamed and thrashed at the blanket that covered her.

Crawling in the driver's seat, Shifra tried to sound calm. "Sweetheart, it's Eema. Are you okay?"

"Eema. Oh, thank God. Who's shooting?"

"Just hang on. I'm going to get us out of here."

"Thank you, God. I've been praying since you left me. Thank you, God." A bullet ripped through the roof of the car. Rahab let out another scream.

"Hold on, Tasil."

"Get down, Eema. Don't let them shoot you." The blanket undulated with the activity under it.

"Just keep praying." Shifra jammed the key in the ignition. A bullet smacked into the door frame near her head. Another penetrated the windshield to her right.

Before she could turn the key, another engine roared. Something large came into Shifra's peripheral view. The dented, crushed side of the Expedition crossed in front of the Mustang, lurched over the dirt mounded at the edge of the road, and nosed into the brush. Ruben had angled the vehicle to shield them, keeping the enemy from disabling the little car. He would be exposed. The enemy could shoot through the thin door metal. Shifra could already hear rounds hitting that side of the vehicle.

You have one job. He's making it possible for you to do it. Save Rahab. She turned the key and the Mustang's throaty engine came to life.

The Expedition's door popped open. Radley moved his feet onto the step-side that ran just under the doors of the SUV.

Shifra grabbed the shifter and slammed the Mustang into reverse.

Leaning against the Expedition's door for support, Radley poked his rifle between the door and the frame for maximum cover.

The tires spun, and the sportscar rocketed backwards. Through the Expedition's open door, Shifra caught sight of the interior illuminated by the car's headlights. Ruben's body lay over on the center console. *Ruben, no!*

The steering wheel shimmied in her hand with the vehicle's backward trajectory. Shifra glanced in the rearview mirror to keep herself on the road, but the sight of Ruben fixed her in place like a sword through her middle. The receding SUV became a dark shape peppered by the flash of weapons fire.

Shifra swallowed a sob. Twisting up in the seat to see where she was going caused her leg to protest.

Rahab whimpered under her covering. "Where are we going? Did we get away from the shooting?"

Shifra had no time or heart to give attention to her daughter or her leg. She fought through her misty eyes to keep the sports car going straight while she flew down the road in reverse.

"Hold on." Tears filled Shifra's eyes. She choked on a whisper, almost to herself. "Someone paid a high price to help us. We can't let him down."

She slowed a bit, spun the steering wheel, sending the car sliding around to face the way she wanted to go, and dropped the shifter into drive at the same time. Going forward now, Shifra gave it the gas. Peering through the cracks in the windshield gave her only a fraction of attention to put into the rearview mirror where her hopes and dreams had died.

She left the fight behind, and in moments was sliding around the corner, onto the main road, and out of reach of the men trying to kill them.

Shifra had no sigh of relief. Being safe was not on her mind. She had lost him. If she had just stayed in the fight. Maybe one more gun could have made the difference and he wouldn't be…But if she had stayed, they might all have been killed, including Rahab. Escaping with her daughter had seemed like the right thing to do. She laid her hand on the blanket that covered her baby–grown and wasting her life, oblivious to the battle of good and evil raging around them–but still her baby.

Shifra's foot dropped from the gas pedal and she let the vehicle slow on its own. "Oh, Tasil, what am I going to do?"

Rahab whimpered beside her. "Are we safe now? Please, can you untie me, Eema? I can't take it anymore."

Shifra pulled to the side of the road and ripped off the helmet. The idea that Ruben was gone felt unreal, like a dream. She drifted in a fog as she pulled a tactical knife from the ballistic vest she wore. She considered her faith as she severed the ropes binding her child like a sacrifice to the altar.

Shifra pleaded. *Father, why? I know You don't torment, but this feels like it. Why bring us together? Why bring him back from death just for this— sacrifice?* The analogy she had overlooked awoke in her mind. God was speaking back. The Heavenly

Father had been through this, too.

As Rahab massaged the restraint marks on her body, she took notice of her mother. She stared into Shifra's eyes. "Eema? What's wrong?"

Shifra threw her arms around her daughter, and Rahab didn't even complain.

She swallowed against Shifra's neck. "Thanks for coming back for me, Eema. I'm sorry. I'm sorry to you and I'm sorry to Jesus." The girl began to sob into Shifra's shoulder and Shifra did the same. After some time, Rahab snuggled into Shifra's chest.

Shifra held her child, regained her composure, and spoke. "Tasil, listen. We got away because two men stayed behind and fought so we could make it out. One was very special to me. You won't meet him until Heaven, but I want you to know about him now."

Chapter 36

Welch thanked God he had paid for the extra armor plating in the door panels of the Institute's fleet of Expeditions. He hadn't imagined giving it such a dynamic field test, but he was certainly a satisfied customer.

The upper part of the seat where he had been sitting was ripped and perforated down to the stuffing from all the bullets that whistled through the window. He was surprised at how few he had felt strike the door. The ones that did, however, could have been deadly had they made it through.

"You all right?" Radley called to him in between blazing fire at the four men to their left.

He must be attempting to force our opponents to remain behind cover so they can send fewer rounds in my direction. "I'm unscathed. Thanks to God."

Welch craned his neck to see out the door. "Did Shifra get Rahab out?"

Radley crouched, letting the SUV cover him, and scanned the darkness. "She's gone. I'm trying to keep track of these last four to our left. The fifth one already disappeared down the bank. He'll probably pop up over there at an angle where we don't have cover." Searching the black trees, Radley denoted the direction with his rifle.

Bullets punctured the hood. The four to the left were shooting again. Radley reengaged that direction.

"Then hang on." Welch grabbed the shifter lever and twisted to get his big foot on the brake without sitting up.

An extra volley of rounds spit out of Radley's rifle. Welch twisted his head around to see if he was ready.

The man aimed for another shot. The back of his helmet exploded and his head snapped to his left. Radley pitched sideways, his legs crumpling under him. His rifle hit halfway on the floorboard and flipped out, clattering onto the ground. Radley's upper body landed on the seat as more bullets pounded the metal plating in the door between Radley and the new shooter. His hand groped, grabbing Welch's hair.

At least he's alive. Welch slapped his left hand on top of Radley's and squeezed so the man wouldn't lose his grip.

Jerking the shifter into reverse, Welch contorted to mash on the accelerator in his sideways position. The Expedition lurched over the dirt mound, leveling out when it hit the asphalt. Radley's feet were dragging outside of the vehicle. Ignoring the strain on his scalp, Welch pulled him in further so he wouldn't be caught under the tire.

A renewed barrage of rounds impacted Welch's door.

Boom! The vehicle shuddered, but didn't stop. *Must have hit the corner of the other SUV.*

With his right hand, Welch spun the steering wheel, and the Expedition swung to face the main road. The edge of the roadway rolled by, six feet away, as they continued backwards.

Welch slammed on the brake. The sudden stop shoved them both deeper into the seats.

There was the smell of steaming antifreeze drifting in the open windows. The enemy had gotten the radiator. Being hot from the pursuit, the engine wouldn't run long without coolant.

Welch dropped the shifter into drive. Rounds hit his door. He gave it gas, and the SUV shot forward. Welch steered to what he hoped was the middle of the road. They hadn't gone fifty feet when the vehicle lurched, engine sputtering. Another lurch and it died and rolled to a stop. That was it for the Expedition.

Welch let go of Radley and pried the man's fingers from his shag. "We've got to get out."

The man's grip came loose, and he groped with his hands, letting himself slide onto the pavement.

Retrieving his rifle, Welch assessed the situation. He couldn't let the enemy know their predicament. Without exposing himself, he fired blindly out the window in one direction, then the other.

Using his knee against the steering wheel, he pushed himself over the center console toward the passenger door, dragging his rifle with him. Something cracked under his bulk, but it was the last thing he or the vehicle had to worry about. He poked his head out the open door.

"I can't see." Helmet in lap, Radley sat, back against the vehicle, wiping at his wide-open eyes. Blood covered the back of his head.

Welch wriggled his way out until he crouched, looking at his partner. Radley's wide eyes stared through him. *I've no time to tend to him.*

"Stay put. I must address our adversaries." He brought his rifle up. It didn't have a night scope, but the bright light mounted to the weapon might do well to blind his opponent's own night vision.

Rising, he engaged the light and pulled the trigger at the same time. Sweeping his weapon through each vacant Expedition window, he strafed the length of the trees on the other side of the road. Welch caught glimpses of men, in the process of advancing on them, now turning to retreat to cover. One made it behind the Suburban.

His gun went dry. Welch squatted behind cover as the return fire began. Dropping the empty magazine, he went for another at the same time. He slammed the new mag home and sent the bolt onto a fresh round. Moving to the rear of the vehicle, he swung around the corner, letting bullets and light fly. Ducking, he hustled to the front and engaged the area where the man that had hit Radley had been, but he left the light off. He didn't know if he was fooling anyone, but he hoped to give the impression he wasn't fighting alone.

Panting, Welch dropped in front of Radley and let the enemy take their retaliation out on the Expedition. "Can you see me?"

"Yeah, a little. It's coming back."

Welch sighed in relief. "A blow to the back of the head can cause temporary blindness." Welch checked all his pouches. "That was my last magazine. The one in my gun's about half full." Their priority had been to lay down cover fire for Shifra's escape with Rahab, not to conserve ammo.

Radley patted his own vacant magazine holders. "Where's my rifle?" He removed the magazine harness and let it drop beside him.

Welch gave a regretful look toward where they had been. "Between us and them. Not a favorable prospect right now."

Removing his pistol from its leg pouch was the man's only response to the grim information. "If they get close enough for me to see, I'll use this." Radley gave a weak smile. "Don't worry. I'll only shoot the little ones, so I know it's not you." He took on a puzzled look. "I never make jokes."

Welch gave his shoulder a squeeze and heaved himself up, rifle ready. *Five opponents. Three in the trees to his left, one in the trees to his right, and one behind the Suburban.*

Keeping next to the front door frame, he fired a round to his left, then squeezed the light switch and panned the trees.

A bullet parted the air next to his ear, coming from the right. Welch snapped his barrel toward its source as another round added to the holes in the hood. The shooter was already ducking behind his tree. Welch fired one round to prove his point.

An engine started. *Make that one man now in the Suburban.* A peek showed him the opposing SUV was moving closer to the trees. The other three were going to make a run for the vehicle. Welch dashed to the rear. The one who shot Radley opened fire. He was trying to capture Welch's attention while the others made their move. Welch was at the back corner of the Expedition so the man's rounds couldn't reach him. He prepared for the three to break from the trees where he could get a shot at them.

There was movement in the dark. Welch hit the light. The men were out of the trees, all in the open, running for the Suburban. Welch targeted the first man. Boom, boom, boom, boom. His target dropped. Welch switched to the next runner and poured bullets at him. The man stumbled, fell, tried to rise. Welch fired at the next man, but the last attacker made it to the vehicle.

One backup light lit up on the passenger side of the Suburban. The other side was crumpled from where the Expedition had clipped it when Welch was driving blind.

The man that Welch had been unable to stop appeared at that crumpled corner. Welch pulled back as the new threat sent bullets his way. Every second or so the man fired at the corner. He was trying to keep Welch pinned down. *They're going to use the vehicle as rolling cover until they have a clear shot at us.* He had to stop them.

Welch moved back and stood to where he could poke his rifle through one of the Expedition's empty side windows. Letting loose with a barrage into the back window of the Suburban, Welch hoped to hit the driver. His gun went empty, and he ducked as the man at the corner of the Suburban answered with bullets. The illumination from the back-up lights was still coming. He hadn't hit the driver. The shooter was alternating firing at the places from which Welch had been shooting.

The man in the woods on the other side of them was hammering the front of the Expedition. He was making sure they couldn't move in that direction, either. They were being squeezed between the two attackers. Soon, they would make a nice target for the advancing Suburban.

The shots that had been coming from the woods sounded closer. Welch snatched off the helmet he still wore. He risked peering around at the advancing enemy. There was enough glow from the Suburban's back-up lights to have a shadowy view of the man. Welch drew back and rounds hit where his head had been. He had the man's position fixed in his memory.

That opponent had also left the trees and was closing the distance, sacrificing his cover. He must have been able to tell that Welch was out of ammo. He was in a race with the Suburban to see who could make the kill first.

The attacker had fired a lot of rounds before he left the trees. He might need to reload soon. If Welch could take this man out, or even slow him down, Radley might have a chance against the other with his pistol. Welch had size to his advantage. He realized the impossibility of rushing an armed man at that distance, but with God's help, it could work. *Lord, if you've got another idea, I'm open.*

He had been a good sprinter in his youth. Better than waiting until the man put holes in them where they sat.

There was a pause and Welch heard the man's empty magazine hit the pavement.

Lunging around the Expedition's corner, Welch charged. His adversary wasn't reacting. His eyes must have gone to the fresh magazine he was reaching for—a huge tactical mistake. God was with him so far. Still a lot of distance for an old man's sprint.

The man's night vision headset jerked up. He had spotted Welch. By sheer reaction, he stumbled backwards, fumbling the magazine in his hand. The new mag fell to the asphalt.

Adrenaline poured into Welch. He pumped his huge legs, feeling nothing of his earlier weakness. Would his opponent try to reach for the dropped magazine—another mistake—or take a new one from his vest?

He was still too far. Welch thought he saw the man grin as he slid a new magazine from a pouch, keeping his rifle aimed at Welch with the precision of excellent training.

With twenty feet still to go, Welch heard the man slam the magazine home. His attacker slapped the bolt release, sending a round into the chamber, leaving nothing left but to pull the trigger.

All that came to Welch's mind was, *At least Shifra made it out.*

A zinging, whining sound tickled Welch's ear. His eye caught the impression of a black shape as it slammed into the side of his attacker's head. The man careened sideways and hit the pavement, rifle skittering beside him.

Something else landed a distance away with a plastic clack, bounced twice and began spinning circles on the road. It was a drone, one side too damaged to fly. It had probably been doing forty miles-per-hour on its kamikaze run to take the man out. *Thank you, Gretchen.*

Welch pushed himself the rest of the way, weezing in air. He was feeling it now, but he was still alive and might stay that way if he took advantage of this fresh development.

The drone had stopped spinning and was moving back and forth across the pavement toward Welch. If Gretchen brought the drone here, it meant she must have stopped the other Suburban.

In the dark, the downed man's white skin stood out. Blood oozed from a cut above his temple, resembling molasses in the indirect glow of the back-up lights. The rotors buzzed the drone closer. The downed man's hand came up, and he put it on the pavement like he might try to rise.

Welch shot forward, clamping his arm around the man's neck.

Getting his wits back, the man turned his windpipe into the pocket of Welch's elbow, giving himself room to breathe. His own elbow came flying at Welch.

Tucking his chin, Welch took the blow on his skull instead of his jaw. His thick head still felt stars.

Grabbing Welch's hand, his opponent broke the grip and reached for the rifle. Welch grabbed the man's vest, pulling him back. He felt power in the man's efforts to escape. Spinning around, Welch used his weight to pull the man sideways, twisting his own body to where he was able to kick the gun sliding across the pavement.

Welch braced his feet and drove forward, trying to push the man down. His opponent pivoted. The man had fitness and youth on his side, and Welch was still not fully recovered.

It was enough for the man to gain a reversal and wrap Welch from behind. He had Welch's arms in a full nelson, legs wrapped around his middle, immobilizing him.

The run, the fight, it had been too much. Welch struggled for air.

His eyes fixed on the Expedition. He couldn't see Radley on the other side, but his reluctant partner had nowhere to go. He would be there, sitting, waiting. Even if his eyesight had fully returned, he would be in a bad position. It was rifle against pistol and no cover for Radley.

The drone had made it to Welch and buzzed randomly near his feet. If the cameras were still working, he didn't want Gretchen to see this. Welch kicked at the UAV. His captor, thinking he was trying to get away, tightened his legs on Welch to prevent his movement.

Any second, the man behind the Suburban would have a full view of Radley's position. Welch could do nothing but wait for the sound of the enemy's gun to tell him it was over. Then they would help finish Welch. He had brought the poor man to his doom. *Lord, please take us Home quickly.*

The Suburban moved to where it had a full view of the side of the Expedition. Welch cringed, waiting.

"Where'd they go?" The shooter was talking instead of shooting.

The man holding Welch yelled. "I've got one over here. The other one should be there."

"Well, he's not." The man came around the Expedition, rifle ready. He circled around the front of the vehicle and checked the other side. Then he flashed a light under the SUV.

The man turned his light on Welch and his restrainer. He came forward, and the light dropped enough that Welch could see the sneer on his face. He pressed the barrel of his rifle against Welch's foot. "Where'd he go?"

Pow, Pow. The man crumpled with his rifle into a pile beside the drone.

The blurred movement of something black dropped from about where the man's head had been and vanished at about knee height, like it was tucked into the air. *Those were pistol shots.*

The dead man's flashlight rolled in an arc on the asphalt. It stopped facing the Expedition, illuminating a man hustling around the corner, rifle at ready, also holding a light. "What's going on?"

Must be the one who was driving the Suburban.

"Someone shot Canton. It was close. He's gotta be right here." There was fear in the voice of the one holding Welch. He moved his head, trying to decide which part of Welch to use as cover.

The view of the man in front of them wavered. Welch blinked. *Am I that light-headed?*

The rifle jerked from the new arrival's hands. The weapon hung in the air, while the gun barrel rotated toward him. The man parried the barrel away and managed to re-acquire his grip on the gun.

His eyes were wide, searching the air for something he knew was there, but couldn't find. A ripple went across his body like a video that was misaligned.

His arms twisted and the gun flew and landed a distance away.

He thrashed out, slapping with both hands like a child. The man's image distorted like a bad television picture. One arm straightened, twisted. His hip thrust out, body rotating, feet toward the sky, then slammed hard on the asphalt. Stunned, he rolled onto hands and knees.

Again, the odd distortion.

Swatting at his own shoulder like a snake had landed on it, the man screamed like a girl as he tried to crawl away. "Do something. It's got me. Get it off."

The man holding Welch shuddered.

The wretch in front of them flipped over and ended up facing them in much the same position as Welch. Horror and desperation on his face, he clawed at his own neck. His mouth was open, pleading, but no sound came out. His neck twisted at an odd angle and there was a pop. The man's head dropped. His body flopped over, face down.

The grip on Welch released. His restrainer pushed on him, trying to crab crawl away. Welch pivoted and saw the man scrambling in terror, trying to make it to his rifle.

Welch turned to the body that lay at his feet. He grabbed the gun under it, jerked it out, and turned. He was too late.

Fire and sound spit from the rifle in the man's hand. He was firing past Welch. From the angle, Welch could tell that he was tearing up the area around his comrade's body. Rounds rang off the Expedition.

Welch had to stop the shooter before the man turned the gun on him. His own rifle jumped in his hand, over and over, until the man lay still.

Welch rolled, searching for another adversary in the flashlight's glow. Something flickered nearby, making him jump. He aimed his rifle. It flickered again. A dark shape was there, a body, then it wasn't. Someone was lying on his back near Welch wearing a ski mask. Gone again. A spot on the asphalt began to dim, darkening like a fading afterglow, taking human shape. It was Radley's form, becoming more solid but with details of the roadway stuck on him. The details lost contrast, dimming like a failing lightbulb, fading, fading, gone. Radley was face up, his chest heaving from exertion.

"Radley?"

A hand reached up and peeled back the hood. Radley's face looked ill and exhausted. He stared at Welch. "My eyes are getting better, but I still can't see you very well."

Welch gave a coughing chuckle. "A clear manifestation of the truth that there is good to be found in even the direst of circumstances. You, on the other hand, my surprising friend, look wonderful, and unperforated. I take it this suit is how you got into the Institute?"

Radley nodded, then eased his head back to the pavement and spoke looking to the sky. "The battery that powers it was just about dead, so I quit using it right before I commandeered you and your vehicle. I was worried it would quit on me when I was exposed and I'd be in a worse position. Laying over there with them closing in on us, I realized it really didn't matter anymore. Things couldn't get any worse."

"An accurate assessment. There is no doubt you saved both our lives. Thank you."

Radley lolled his head to face Welch's general direction. "I wasn't sure I was going to pull it off since I couldn't see to shoot."

Welch motioned to the body near him. "I'm glad that didn't inhibit you from preventing this fellow from ending my dancing career."

Radley squinted at the man, then gave up and relaxed again. "Things were getting tense. I put my barrel so close to his head I couldn't miss. The trouble with using a firearm up close with the suit is that floating guns and pistols coming out of nowhere give away the secret.

"It was better for me to go hands on. When that guy almost took his rifle back, I knew I had better get any weapons out of the picture. All the rifle was doing was letting him know where I was. Once I touched him…I know my hand to hand well enough to do it blindfolded."

The man looked pale, even in the dark. "How are you, really?"

Radley massaged his eyes. "I'm worn out. I was happy to let you deal with that last guy. My head's aching." He regarded Welch. "But I'm seeing better by the minute, so I think I'll be all right."

Welch worked his way off the ground. "Sit here while I get the first aid kit out of the Expedition." He scooped up the flashlight. "I'll bandage your head and then get you to the doctors at the Institute."

Radley gave a weak wave of acknowledgement. "On the way back, we need to stop where we rolled the vehicle and find my pack. There's more equipment in there that I need and others don't."

Chapter 37

Gretchen burrowed into Talisa's shoulder and cried. "Help me, God. Help me."

Talisa rubbed her back. "That's right, tell the Lord. But it's over, all right? Look." She pointed to the drone image of Dr. Welch coming back with the first aid kit. "He's okay. Everything's going to be all right."

Gretchen sobbed into her shoulder. "I should have turned it off, but I didn't want to leave Dr. Welch. I thought he might need me. That was the most awful thing I've ever seen. I'll never be the same."

Talisa turned the small woman to face her. "No, you won't. But God knows how to heal you. This will work out. We'll all sit down in the next few days and process this together. Dr. Welch is great at leading peer support sessions. I never wanted to go through something like this again, either, but God knows. Dr. Welch and Shifra had it worse. That must have been her in the car we saw on the other road. I guarantee they'll be here helping the rest of us when they get back."

Gretchen watched Dr. Welch on the monitor, but there were other images nearby that she didn't want to think about, so she went back to Talisa's shoulder. "I'll tell you one thing." She glanced at Talisa. "I'm never watching Modern Hauntings again."

Shifra held Rahab and stroked her head. "You didn't know, Tasil. Yeshua will forgive."

"I'm sorry, Eema. I almost got you killed."

"Don't think about it. You're safe now." Shifra braced herself for the argument she was about to get. "Now I need to leave you." She looked toward the road she had come from. "I know they told me not to go back, but I can't leave the other man who helped us." She worked to keep her composure as she spoke. "He might still be alive. Maybe I can drive in and get him out."

Rahab pulled away. She started to open her mouth, but instead, took on a thoughtful look. She gazed into Shifra's eyes. "I'll go with you."

Shifra hadn't expected that. "You…You can't. There's no reason for you to go. I don't intend to fight them. If they have killed the man, I will turn around and get out again. I am so proud of you for offering…but…you're not ready for anything like that, and it would be dangerous for me to worry about you if you went."

"What about how worried *I'll* be?"

"It is time for you to trust God. No matter what hap…" Shifra's jaw betrayed her with a quiver that brought her to silence.

Rahab took her hand. "I'm sorry." She pulled her eema into a hug.

With her head on Rahab's shoulder, Shifra regained her composure. "He will give us the strength to carry on, no matter what."

Shifra pulled away, got out, went around, and opened the passenger door. "Go hide, Tasil."

A headlight glow caught her eye. She watched as an SUV came off the same road from which they had just escaped. It hesitated, then turned her way. *They saw our tail lights.*

Before they turned, Shifra had evaluated the vehicle's shape. The roof was smooth and undamaged, unlike the SUV they had driven down that road. It was the Suburban. *They must have gotten Radley, too.*

Shifra slammed Rahab's door and ran back to the driver's seat. She shoved the sports car's shifter into drive and the Mustang ate up the road.

Rahab grabbed the dash. "Can we outrun them?"

"They can't match our speed and handling on these roads. They won't catch us."

Rahab glanced her way. "I was praying, but that's good to know."

Shifra nodded.

Chapter 38

R adley watched the Mustang disappear like a sleek animal around the first switchback.

Welch let off on the accelerator. "We'll never catch her, and I don't want to push her to go faster. She'll find out it's us when Jim catches her at the driveway entrance to the house."

Radley ended the call he was on with Jim. "Four of your security were injured, but they'll live. The team has what's left of the strike force secured."

"Thank you, Lord." Welch sounded relieved.

Radley had a new context for the words. "It feels funny for me to say that—to thank Him like that. But I guess I'm supposed to do that, right?"

"The Bible commands us to give thanks. There's nothing we have that we do not owe to God. Tonight, however, I think we have reason to be particularly grateful." Welch scrutinized the man. "The last time I prayed, you said you didn't think you could. Are you reconsidering that?"

"I already did. After you prayed, when I left to run ahead. I made an agreement with God."

Welch glanced at him. "Do you mean you spoke with God?"

Radley looked uncertain. "It was more like thinking, talking to Him in my head. You said Jesus was the only one who saves, so I asked Him to save me. I told God I was all His if He'd show me what's real."

"Did you mean to follow through with that?"

"Of course. I don't want my life to be like it's been."

"Then there's reason for rejoicing. God does not leave such requests unanswered. If you realize your need for God and have truly given yourself to Him, then He will change you. When *you* change, your life will change."

"Did you really pray?" The soft, hopeful voice came from the backseat. Radley whirled around. He started to say her name, but Sarah held her finger to her lips. She leaned forward and scowled at something in front of her.

Glancing back at Welch, he saw the man was dividing his gaze between Radley and the road.

Welch relaxed. "Your friend is back, I take it?"

"Don't answer and it won't be a lie. He won't understand. Act like I'm not here." Sarah's gentle voice took on an urgency. "I'm not sure what's going on but something…" She was looking down like there was something hovering in front of her that Radley couldn't see.

She ignored it and faced him again. "I couldn't bear to watch what was happening, but your pulse and respiration slowed. I knew it must be over and God had kept you alive. Is that a bandage on your head?"

Radley gave a sniff at Sarah's error. He couldn't act like she wasn't there *and* answer her questions. It was time to end this.

He had meant what he told God. He needed to clean out everything. "I have been having hallucinations of a girl I knew. My imagination has always been better than my reality. It's where I lived most of the time…part of my condition. But I always knew the difference before…"

Radley had made the big move. Now he didn't know where to go with it. "I now believe God will forgive me. Will He heal my mind? I want to know what's real."

"Peter, don't do this to yourself. You're not having hallucinations." The concern in Sarah's voice sounded genuine. Again, her eyes darted to the space in front of her.

"Let me think about that for a moment." Welch became intent on his driving.

The image of Sarah filled in the blank time. "I'm not part of your imagination. But I have to be sure. There are things I need to tell you, but part of it is…personal. If you have accepted Jesus, then…But you can't just say it because you don't want me to leave."

Radley was determined not to listen to something that wasn't real. He had asked for forgiveness and

Welch said God would do it. But Sarah had said the same thing. Maybe she was part of his mind that knew the truth all along, and this was his way of communicating with himself. But that sounded like more mental illness.

Welch spoke. "To answer your question about whether God will heal you…There is no 'best practices' manual against which God's behavior can be judged or predicted. He sets the standard, nothing else. With healing, Scripture and life show His variability more than His predictability. Tell me what you are experiencing."

Radley saw Sarah lean forward. "You prayed for forgiveness? Did you really give your life to God, Peter?"

What have I got to lose? The man already knows I'm a hit man. If I'm a delusional hit man, at least I have an excuse. Radley took a breath. "I see her in the back seat, but obviously you don't. And how would she get there? So it has to be in my head. As long as I can remember, I have had vivid images come to my mind, thoughts that seemed like videos playing in my head. I thought this was more of the same. But now it's different."

"What is she doing?"

"Asking me if I really prayed for forgiveness. She's been trying to get me to do it for a long time."

Welch motioned his hand toward Radley. "So now it's happened. You have verified it's true and I believe you. What does she say to that?"

Radley turned in his seat, facing the image of Sarah.

Her eyes looked at him like he was a loved one she had been told was dead and she discovered he was alive. She put her hand over her mouth and sobbed.

Her tears touched him to his core. "Don't cry." Radley let his head drop forward in exasperation. He turned to Welch, then gestured with both hands toward what he was seeing. "She's so real."

Sarah reached toward him and drew it back. "I *am* real. I'm just not really there. But I want you to come to me. I'll tell you how."

"You want me to kill myself?" *Now I know I'm mentally ill.*

Welch pulled to the side of the road. Shutting off the engine, he adjusted to face Radley. "Nothing from God is going to tell you to kill yourself, Radley. What is she saying?"

Sarah gave a desperate glance toward Welch, then gazed directly in Radley's eyes. "Peter, what I am going to tell you will be shocking, maybe unbelievable. I've tried to think of how to tell you this so many times, but..." Sarah's mouth quivered until she got control again. "I didn't want to do it in front of someone else, but maybe it's better. He seems like a good man. It must be God's plan."

Welch gave Radley's arm a shake. "What's the image saying?"

"She's going to tell me something unbelievable. She thinks you're a good man, and it's God's plan that you're here."

Welch glanced into the back seat. "Then let's hear what she has to say, but we'll evaluate it together.

Okay? Demons can look very pretty sometimes."

Radley glanced at the big man. "You believe in that?"

"God says they're real and I've seen too much not to believe Him. They usually keep themselves hidden, but there are exceptions."

Radley looked back at Sarah. She was fiddling with something. Her face was tear streaked with emotion but still very pretty.

She glanced at Welch and then at him. "He's right, Radley. But I'm not a demon. You and I know what demons look like, don't we? My mother and father had *their* demons so long, you could see them in everything they did."

Sarah's chest heaved as if she was preparing. "When you were a child, my father planted an experimental device in your brain. There is nothing wrong with your mind. That device is letting me transmit my image directly into your thoughts. I'm sitting in front of a control console that you don't see. It's like a Zoom call, when you see someone blocking their background, only better. The program processes out everything but the image you want to send. I've never experienced it, but my father said your mind fills in all the pieces and makes it seem real. Like I'm sitting there next to you. By your reaction, it must seem *very* real. I'm sorry I did it this way. I didn't know what else to do."

Welch's hand was on his arm. "Radley, what's she telling you?"

Radley turned toward him. Welch's face told him

his own expression must be showing the confusion he was feeling. Could something like that be true? Was it just more of his delusion? "She says I have something in my brain. That she's…" He turned back and looked at her. *It still doesn't change the fact…* "This can't be real because you're dead."

Squeezing her eyes shut, Sarah hung her head and shook it. She faced him again with the same sorrowful look. "I didn't die in that explosion. I'm alive. I'm sorry I let you believe it for so long."

"They found your body. Your DNA proved it."

Taking on a firm expression, Sarah nodded. "They found *your* body, too. Or what the few that knew about you assumed was your body. I didn't have the luxury of being as anonymous as they kept you. But I had access to my father's database. It was the only place he allowed any genetic record of our family. He knew the power of DNA. His electronic records were the only place for them to get a DNA pattern for comparison. I had been working with those programs for years. It was easy for me to switch my DNA profile with my mother's. It was my mother's charred body they found. You know, we looked a lot alike."

"Athena. Athena is dead?"

Sarah nodded, examining him for a moment. "It's okay, Peter. It's okay to feel relief."

She seemed to know the conflict he had inside.

Sarah wiped her eyes on her sleeve, but continued to squint at him. "You didn't know my parents could spy on you through the unit. That's how they always found you when you ran. I discovered the control room, but I never said anything. I snuck in when I could and watched you. Especially when you went on missions. I always worried you wouldn't come back. I was watching the day you…got the body. When you told me not to go to the lab, I realized what you were planning. I knew *your* way out was *my* way out, too. I'd been thinking about it for a long time."

Blinking her eyes several times, Sarah continued. "I kept my parents busy so you could get everything set up. You added a dead body before the explosion." Sarah was fighting tears. "Then, after you left, I added two live ones by luring my parents to the lab. I convinced them you had discovered what they did to you and were looking for evidence." Sarah's voice broke and she hid her face with her hand. Radley couldn't help but reach for her, only to touch empty air where her weeping shoulders should be.

Welch waved his hand in front of Radley's face. "What's happening?"

Before he could explain, Sarah was talking through her tears. "My father always had me working with him, and my mother managed you and dealt with the contractors that needed their services. It was easy for any interested parties to believe my father and I died in the fire and my mother went into hiding."

Sarah straightened and blinked her eyes clear. With her face still twisted in sorrow, she plastered on a smile of mock lightheartedness. "See, you thought *you* were bad, but I'm the one who killed our parents."

Radley stared at Sarah. He couldn't find words.

Sarah squeezed her eyes shut and gave a quivering

sigh. When she opened them she seemed cleansed, somehow. "My parents abused us. We had twisted childhoods. It's okay to feel glad it's over." She seemed to be speaking to herself as much as him. "I've had to give that to God and let him forgive me and heal me. My church friends helped." She leaned in. "That's what you'll have to do with everything that happened to you—all the things you've done." Tipping her head sideways, she appeared to be getting a different perspective on him. "We're not that different. We have a lot in common."

Welch laid a gentle palm on Radley's shoulder.

Radley held up a hand, showing he needed to listen a little longer.

Sarah gestured around at things Radley couldn't see. "My father had installed a portable unit that could communicate with your device in this motorhome. He hadn't had a chance to use it. He didn't even have tags for it yet. I took it, their stash of money, and the ID for one of my mother's unused aliases, and became someone else. The title to the RV was in the glove box. I had it registered in my new name. It's my home now. I took it and started driving, trying to get as far away as I could."

"You need to tell me what you're seeing and hearing." Welch's face showed his concern. "We agreed to do this together."

Sarah motioned toward Welch. "Tell him, but let him know I'm not the person who did those things. When I finally quit driving, I needed help, so I stopped at a little church. They introduced me to Jesus, and He changed my life. He's everything to me. That's why I had to know you had given your life to Him too. There. Tell him. I'll be quiet."

She looked as if she was checking something in front of her. "Don't take too long. There's something going on with your implant. It works off cellular technology, so connection is usually not a problem, but something is messing up. Since I connected with you this time, you're fuzzy and going in and out. The battery in your unit was made to last a long time, like a pacemaker battery. I knew it was getting to the end of its life. That's why I was pushing you. My time was running out. But your battery shows it's still okay. Something else must be wrong. I'm worried I'm going to lose you. I still need to tell you the most important thing—how to find me." Sarah motioned toward Welch.

Radley took a deep breath. He turned to look in Welch's expectant eyes. The implications sank deeper into him as he passed all the information on to the big man.

When Radley finished, Welch's face displayed inner contemplations. "If you have such a unit inside your skull, the bullet you took to the back of your head might have damaged it."

Sarah reacted. "You've been shot?" Her face moved closer to something beside her. "I can't see you clearly. Are you going to be all right?"

Welch must have observed Radley watching her. "What is she doing now?"

Radley sighed. "She's worried about me because I

was shot."

Welch spoke toward where Radley was gazing. "He will need stitches, but it is a superficial wound. It gave a nasty blow to his head, but I see no signs of lasting effects."

Sarah's face retained its worry lines. "The unit must have been damaged. Your transmission is getting worse. I had better tell you how to find me."

Radley touched the back of his head and winced at the pain.

"Hey, what did you do? Radley, can you see me?" Sarah's voice was loud in his ear, or was it his mind? But her image was no longer distinct. A graininess washed through it. "Radley, are you there? I've lost the video. Can you see me?"

Radley felt desperation. "I can see you, but something's wrong."

Welch addressed the woman that only Radley could see. "Sarah, I know you've taken a big step to trust me, but I want you to take one more chance. If you can do this, it will solve the problems with connection and provide the proof we need on this end. I will say my phone number, and I want you to call it. I'll be able to verify that you're real and put all of us at ease. You know how to block caller ID, I'm sure, so do that, if you want."

Welch gave the number, and the image of Sarah picked up a phone with a shaky hand and began dialing. Her panicked gaze looked through them as if they weren't there.

Radley inspected the image, hoping and fearing at

the same time. What would he say to the real Sarah?

The image of Sarah flickered as she listened to the phone and her face took on a confused look. "Have him give me the number again. I must have misdialed it. I'm hearing you even worse now."

Radley's thoughts stumbled. He realized how much he had been desiring to hear Welch's phone. The panic he was feeling gave way to a realization. It was all too convenient. Just when he was confronting the delusion, she was losing the ability to transmit. *For a while there, I was really believing it. I wanted it so badly. I wanted her to be real.* The idea of Sarah calling became smoke in his mind, disappearing into the rest of the haze that was his reality.

A new notion replaced it. At moments in his life, he had felt as if someone was putting things in his head. Things he was powerless to resist. Maybe the device was real. Maybe his subconscious knew about it all along and Sarah was what his damaged mind had created to tell himself the truth. Radley reached to rub the tickling itch in the back of his neck but felt pain from his wound. At least that was real.

He turned to Welch. "She's asking for the number again, saying she misdialed. I'm afraid even now my mind is trying to hold on to the delusion."

"Peter, don't think that." Sarah's image fluttered in his peripheral. "Give me just a minute to get through."

Radley focused on her. The image wavered again.

Loud and clear, Welch repeated the number, placing his hand on Radley's shoulder again.

Radley sent him a look of appreciation. "It's all

right. If I can get past this, maybe I can get some treatment and move on, with God's help."

The image of the girl looked frustrated, reaching forward as if adjusting something. "Peter, I don't know if I can get through on the phone. I'm going to give you an address to find me." Sarah's pretty face grew fuzzy and dim.

Radley could still detect the panic in her features.

She leaned toward him, longing in her eyes. "I'm in—." The image winked out. Radley realized the strange itching in the back of his neck was subsiding. It faded until it was gone. Was it the creation of a disturbed mind still trying to exist to the end? Maybe the device was imagination as well—a way for him to justify the things he had done.

He gazed at the space that moments earlier had contained someone who had been so much a part of his life. A new concept developed in Radley's thoughts. Was Sarah ever real? Could he trust his memories? Had there ever been a little girl he had grown up with, or had she been a fantasy all along? Was she something his mind had created to help him navigate the horror of his young existence. When he finally escaped, his mind kept her alive the only way it knew how. The fabric of his past was unraveling.

The phone in Welch's hand rang. Radley stiffened.

Welch looked at the screen and patted him. "It's Gretchen." He hit the button and said, "Hello."

Welch spoke with Gretchen, verifying they were all right...the voice faded in the background as Radley was consumed by his thoughts. He considered how powerful the imagination was. *God, I prayed You would show me what's real. Please, You're going to have to help me find my way now that I know.*

Sarah had been the only thing in his life worth remembering. He was a dead man starting over. Empty…except for God. *She always said I could start my life over. I guess You were speaking through her.* What had she told him? It couldn't be about her. *Well, here I am, literally a blank slate. You're all I've got, God. You're going to have to fill it.*

Radley wept.

Welch's hand was on his arm. "Radley, I switched over to a new call that came in." He was still on the phone. "Just a moment. I'll put you on speakerphone. Okay, go ahead."

"Hello, Peter. Sorry I got the number wrong. I'm so nervous. I finally dialed it right."

Radley reeled back from the phone that Welch held. He raised his gaze to Welch's face.

Welch nodded. "It's real, Radley. I hear her too."

Radley stared at the phone. "Sarah?"

"Yes, Peter. It's me."

Radley exhaled a breath that was half laugh. "It's you? You're really alive? I don't know what…" Radley ran out of words.

The voice on the line laughed. "I know. It's funny all that technology I've been using, and this feels more real. I imagined this day, but now I feel like I'm nine years old again."

Radley tried to process. "You're real. This is real." A sob escaped. "I thought I'd lost you. I've known you most of my life, and I thought it was all…I'm sorry…you said nine years old…I feel like I've just been born. I don't remember much from our childhood except you. There wasn't much good to remember."

"Not much." Sarah's voice was tender. "But one thing stands out. We were in my father's lab and somehow we managed to slip away and play together. You took the blame for the shelf of glassware I knocked over. You took my torture for me. And it *was* torture. I hated my father for it, but I loved you." Sarah's voice went up an octave on the last few words. She sniffed. "I have ever since."

Radley looked away from the phone. The idea of a real Sarah had its own pitfalls. "I'm not very good at love. I've never had normal emotions. Lately, I've felt more than I ever remember."

Sarah's voice became intense with compassion. "It's not you. It's the device. My father used it to inhibit the things that got in the way of what they could sell you for. Your empathy, compassion, understanding…your love. You're not a killer, Peter. That's what my parents made you. They made you a machine that spent all your time and energy training to do hits for the highest bidder."

Radley touched the bandage on his head and winced. "It was this device in me, doing that? So, I'm not…I saw a therapist about the condition they said I had. He said all I could do was learn coping mechanisms. It was who I was. But maybe that's not true."

"I've been making adjustments." Sarah was

enthusiastic. "And it's been working. I was scared to change things too quickly because I didn't understand it all. My father didn't leave a lot of notes. I had to learn the system as I went. I didn't know what might happen to you if I did something wrong. But you have been changing."

Radley's face came alive with a bright smile. "That was you. I could feel it." The darkness crept back in. "But now I can feel what I've done. I didn't care before."

Welch touched him on the shoulder. "We're all that way, Radley. Perhaps we don't feel the alteration as keenly as you do right now, but when God's Spirit comes alive inside us, He changes us. We see sin through *His* eyes. When we recognize our sin, we can do something about it. We're all broken. It's what we decide to do inside that brokenness that saves us."

"But now how do I learn to live with those feelings, now that I know?"

"You ask for forgiveness. Have you done that?"

Radley nodded. "But right after that, I had to kill again."

Welch bowed his head and then looked up. "God knows the difference. The awful regret inside is God's way of making sure we do, too. It wasn't your choice. Give it to God. Let Him clean you out and start new."

Radley knew the truth about all the things he had done. "Most of it was my own choice ...and I can never make it right."

"No, you can't." Welch's face spoke of understanding born of experience. "But *He* can. He can do that because Jesus took the punishment for us. Just like you did for Sarah that day. Why did you do that?"

Radley stared into the phone to the girl listening there. "Because I loved her."

There was a sharp inhale on the other end of the line.

"What would you expect from her in return?"

Radley couldn't think of anything. He was happy he had done it. "Nothing."

"Exactly. But what did your act naturally produce in her?"

Radley leaned back in his seat and looked at the ceiling. The heaviness lifted. It all made sense. He had given everything to God, and God had given him everything he needed. Sarah was as real as Jesus, and he knew what he felt for both of them. He breathed out the word, and it filled the air with promise. "Love."

Chapter 39

THE FORMER PLUM ISLAND ANIMAL DISEASE CENTER, PLUM ISLAND, NEW YORK

Roshard's mind was full of issues that needed his attention. He hated subjecting his body to stimulants, but his whirlwind trip to Europe and back had made it necessary. His brain was still in high gear as he left the tunnel tram lobby and made his way to the computer wing of the underground facility. He needed to calm his temper before he addressed Chidlow for not answering his calls.

His meeting with the surviving members of Becker's research team had gone well. Now that the old man was out of the way, they could move forward with planning the release of the new virus. He felt good about being able to get past the team's fear over the rumors that an unknown group was on their trail. But he needed Chidlow to determine if the AI was tracking anything new about someone searching for the team.

His instinct was telling him it had something to do with Welch. He would feel better once Kondo contacted him from Oklahoma telling him the problem was eliminated. He didn't like how long it had been since Kondo last called, but the man was unpredictable.

Kondo must have been able to extract Welch's location from the woman his source led him to. That shouldn't have taken long for someone with his skills. He was probably taking extra precautions in mopping up the team's headquarters because of the risk from the virus. He knew Kondo didn't trust him.

Roshard went through the electronic scans and verifications to enter the wing that housed the AI computer. Using his access badge to enter Chidlow's office, he was miffed to find it empty. He was ready to leave, but a glance out the window stopped him.

The office was positioned to overlook the enormous bay below that housed the rows of interconnected computer cabinets. Psyche's nest, Chidlow called it. The bay was empty. Loose cables were hanging from brackets.

Roshard's phone rang. He answered it immediately. He had made it a habit. It was a waste of time to consider who might be on the other end—quicker to answer it and find out, deal with the issue and move on.

"Hello, Roshard. Do you know who this is?"

"No, I don't. You sound like an old friend, but he

passed away recently. So, who is this?"

"An old friend."

Roshard was ready to snap at the caller, but the empty floor below unnerved him. He couldn't imagine who would sound like the old man. "Forgive me for sounding rude, but I have a matter I need to attend to, so how can I help you?"

"You've done all you can do for me, Roshard. You were like a son to me. Your betrayal hurt."

Roshard rarely felt uneasy, but he did now. "Great impersonation, but the joke's in poor taste and if you work for me, you would know that I don't permit practical jokes. They disrupt the work environment and can damage relationships. You also need to get your facts straight. I don't betray people. That's not my style."

"When you try to kill someone, you should make sure they're dead. You didn't think I still had friends? You haven't made that many real friends, Roshard. I always saw that as a weakness that could bring you down."

"Listen, this has gone far enough. Who is this?"

"After your misuse of the virus, I made sure the genuine stuff was all locked down. What you brought to my house was a fake. But we let everyone think it worked."

The old man chuckled. "Even Rico Kondo was surprised when I contacted him. He's one of those people that's not your friend, Roshard. He works for the highest bidder. I offered him more money to take care of Welch and that woman from New York my way. So instead of going there to seal the place down, he went there with enough people to get the job done right. I'm sure he'll call me any time now to tell me our little problem has been all taken care of."

"Boss, is that really you? I don't know where you got these ideas, but if you really are alive, I couldn't be happier. It will take a little getting used to. It broke my heart when I thought you were dead. It sounds to me like people have been feeding you a lot of false information. Let's get together and talk about it. You owe me that."

Holding his phone to his ear with his shoulder, Roshard headed for the door. He grabbed his private cell phone and tried texting. No signal. Of course they would have blocked cell access into the underground facility. The line the old man called on was probably the only one the system was allowing in. But he was in "try anything" mode.

Schmidt continued while Roshard searched for a way out. "Being dead for a while let me convince some people that we should shut down your program and I'd postpone retirement. They're sending me to Kansas to set up a site near the new facility the USDA will be running. The food supply might be a better way to target our efforts in population maintenance. We won't make the same mistakes you have."

Roshard tried the elevator. No response to his badge. No lights. Where was everyone? He headed toward the stairs.

The old man kept talking as if oblivious to Roshard's efforts. "I do want to thank you for one thing. You have convinced me of the value of this AI computer stuff. I believe, when sufficiently motivated, Mr. Chidlow will direct his efforts toward the proper goals."

Holding the phone in his hand like a baton, Roshard broke into a run. Arriving at the door to the stairway, he already saw there was no light on the card reader. He grabbed the door and jerked it, realizing it was useless. If the facility was locked down, he wasn't getting out.

He also knew the underground floors were rigged with explosives. They would collapse the laboratory into a pile of rubble under the reinforced floor of the dilapidated old building that concealed it. It had been his own idea—just in case they ever needed to hide the evidence.

Roshard took a breath to calm his overstimulated brain. *You need to be negotiating. Talk your way out. You're valuable. Convince him.* "What's my role going to be in all this?"

"Well, Roshard, it's your turn to be dead. That's your role."

Someone else was pounding. The face of Er Koch was looking through one of the door windows at the other end of the hall.

Roshard put the phone back to his ear. "Boss, you don't want to do this. There are other people in here."

"Yeah, we identified a few weak elements that we could eliminate all at the same time."

Roshard should have known sympathy was a bad play. He needed to slow down. *You still have power, even in this situation. Figure out his weaknesses.* "If I die, I have orders for information to be released that will expose all this."

"We took care of your lawyer, and we're willing to take the risk on all the rest. Like I said, Roshard, I don't think you have that many friends. If there is someone, that's the advantage of being dead. They can blame the old me, and I can keep on working with a new identity. I've got nothing to lose. We can deny everything else and we're about to eliminate any evidence. But we're going to do this the old-fashioned way."

Roshard saw the flash as the ceiling came down. The sound was too great for his ears to absorb, so the last sensation he felt in this life was the concussion that slammed him to the floor.

After that, the sensations became much worse.

Chapter 40

THE HOLLENBECK INSTITUTE FOR PEOPLE WITH SPECIAL NEEDS AND SPECIAL ABILITIES, LAKE GALLANT, OKLAHOMA

Welch listened as Talisa made plans for the entire team to attend the upcoming nuptials as he, Talisa, Luke, Shifra, and Gretchen enjoyed an early dinner around the table in the common area. "So after the wedding, they're both coming here, right?"

Welch nodded as he swallowed his potatoes. "Driving here from Montana in Sarah's motorhome will be their honeymoon."

Talisa looked blissful. "Married on their birthdays, I love that. It's sweet that he asked you to come out there and be his best man."

Beside her, Luke shook the piece of steak on the end of his fork at Talisa. "Who else would he ask? As a freelance assassin, you don't make that many lasting relationships."

Talisa swatted him with her napkin. "Stop talking about that. It's like the poor man has had a demon inside him for years. Give him a break."

Luke cringed from her attack, then directed the steak at Welch. "We collect the most interesting people."

Welch used his napkin before he spoke. "Peter *is* an interesting person. I admire that he recognized that he was given a unique way out of his situation. But for those truly suffering from schizoid personality disorder, or any disorder, life can be much more challenging."

Talisa put her hands on Luke's shoulder. "Have they agreed to accept our offer to send them to training to help start a therapy program for the disorder at the Institute?"

Welch returned the napkin to his lap. "They liked the idea. I think they both want some time to adapt to their new life. In Sarah's words, they feel like they need to be on the receiving end for a while before they have much to give. But they want to give back. She quoted the 'freely you have received, freely give' Scripture."

Luke sliced off his next bite. "You don't think we should send a security team to guard this new technology they're bringing with them?"

Welch shook his head. "All we would do is draw attention. They've stayed ahead of the intelligence hounds for a few years. They would shake any team we sent. It's going to be their honeymoon, remember?"

Talisa examined Luke with exasperation. "Ruben, do you think when they remove this thing from Peter, they could put it in my husband? There are a few adjustments I'd like to make."

Teddy snickered. "Yeah, Luke, Mrs. Tee's gonna make you give me all the candy in your office."

Janie gave Teddy's middle a poke. "Hey, oo didn't call her Miss Tee first. 'Oo get'n better."

Luke grinned as he pointed a scolding finger at Teddy, then leaned his head into Talisa's lap and spread his arms. "I'm yours to toy with." He sent her a couple of quick eyebrow raises. "Can we get the RV to go with it? I'll take you away from all this."

Talisa shook her head. "I'm living the best life this side of Heaven. Tell me why I want to leave it?" She gave him a quick kiss. "Get up before you get steak sauce on me."

Righting himself in his chair, Luke displayed a wounded expression. "Well, I'm ready to pack my little bag and run away because you guys didn't let me play. I was hoping to put all these new skills I've been learning into practice, and you didn't even call me when there was a major threat to the Institute."

Welch sighed. He relived the relief of knowing it was over. "Believe it when I say there were many times I wished you were with me. But we didn't know the magnitude of the threat until it was upon us— another reason we know it was a plot hatched in hell. But as always, God has used it for good." He looked at Shiffy, sitting next to him, and placed his hand on her shoulder. "Shiffy tells me Rahab has rededicated her life to Christ. She and Benton have found a Bible-centered church in New York that they plan on attending regularly."

A look of contented gratitude took over Shifra's features as she wrapped both her arms around one of Ruben's. She nodded her affirmation. "God has been good. I owe Peter Radley and this wonderful man my life and the life of my little girl. I can't wait to meet Sarah. I understand completely how they felt—Peter thinking he had lost the person that meant the most to him and Sarah waiting so long for love to come alive in the man she longed for."

All Welch could do was smile. Shifra's hints at her feelings weren't subtle. It seemed a simple matter to her. *Why am I having so much trouble acting on them?*

Gretchen put her hamburger back on her plate and spoke around the bite she had taken. "I can't wait to see this unit of hers. The ability to see and hear what the subject is experiencing is what's got my interest. The microphones inside the ears I can visualize, but the cameras positioned at the back of the eyes must be a new level of miniaturization."

Welch wiped his mouth and dropped the napkin on his plate, glad for a subject he felt adept at wading into. "Indeed. Sarah told us working with it takes some adjustment. She said when she had her conversations with Peter, it was difficult to react correctly. Instead of having a view of his facial reactions, she saw what he was seeing. But that didn't include her own image, because that was in his mind. She would have to look at another monitor to see what she was projecting. I can imagine how confusing that might be, seeing him interacting with something that wasn't there and having to relate that to the other screen which was her own image."

Gretchen's expression showed her mind was running with the idea. "I bet you could meld the images in a 3D virtual reality display. The gaming applications could make us rich." Gretchen saw everyone was looking at her. "I know we're rich already…the Institute I mean…but hey, you got me on board now and I have plans that are going to need financing. The world of super computing is changing rapidly. There's AI, quantum computing, nanotechnology…I'm gonna need upgrades."

Welch sent her an amused yet stern expression. "Before you embrace this brand of neural implant technology too firmly, I want to point out the privacy issues it would create would strictly limit its use. But that is nothing when you consider the implant was designed to insert precise thoughts and impressions into Peter's mind in a subtle way so he would interpret them as his own ideas. He was being programmed in a most diabolical way. I agree with Talisa and Sarah herself. Technology in the wrong hands is demonically inspired."

Shifra patted his hand. "Isn't that what Jesus said? If we're not His children, we are children of the devil. Peter Radley is an extreme living analogy of what we all go through. Without God, we're all slaves to sin. We can't fight it without Him. In their quest to destroy us, the demons start condemning us for the very things they convinced us to do. So, we find ways to block out the guilt and the conviction. If we do that long enough, we become capable of almost anything. Look at what is being normalized in our world today, that, not long ago, most of us couldn't even imagine." She beamed a powerful smile. "But when we find freedom in Jesus, we are finally able to see it all for what it really is."

Welch loved the way she thought. He reached his hand out to her. He was going to ask her to take a walk with him, but his gaze landed on the crutches that leaned against the chair beside her. She staunchly refused the electric wheelchair she had been offered. Said she didn't want to lose her tone.

Everything seemed to be against him. "Would you care to…?" Welch wished he had formed an idea before he opened his mouth. *I'm sixty years old. How can I be so inept at this?*

Shiffy must have seen where his eyes went. "I would love to." She took his hand. "I really enjoy sitting in the arboretum conservatory. I can see the fall leaves through the windows and the green trees inside. It seems the best of everything. And Amelia has made it so French." She turned in her chair and looked toward the door through the archway. "I had Teddy fetch me a regular wheelchair from the clinic this morning. It's over there. Would you push me?"

Even if he had such an inclination, how could any man refuse such a face? "Of course." He hurried to retrieve the chair, and when Shiffy was safely seated, he addressed the group. "Will you all excuse us?"

With a wide smile, Talisa nodded.

Luke grinned and gave him a wink.

Gretchen raised her eyebrows. "You two enjoy yourselves." She eyed them, mischievously biting her lower lip.

Welch pushed Shiffy out by way of the archway, through another room and into a long hallway that ran along what looked like a giant greenhouse. Turning the chair, he backed them through a door into the conservatory constructed of high stone walls full of tall, arched windows and a glass ceiling. Mature trees and plants lined the path that wound through the middle. A fountain at one end fed a small stream that followed the walkway. Occasionally it flowed around trees and plants or widened into tiny ponds filled with various colorful fish.

As Shiffy had promised, the multi-paned windows showed the beauty of the forest outside. Inside was springtime-green and flowers, with a warm, earthy smell. Welch had spent little time in the room. Besides relaxing on his sailboat, his research lab and modest apartment on the other side of the main grounds were all he had needed…before.

Shiffy was quiet. She had learned to read him, seeming to know when he needed to strategize his next move.

Welch leaned on the wheelchair handles. Shiffy's

beautiful hair cascading across her shoulders was pristine splendor next to his hulking hands.

Shiffy had given him a new appreciation of the contrast. It mirrored the rest of their interaction. She seemed so at ease, and he was having difficulty. To be in her presence, to know that she loved him, still caused him to overreact. It was not like him to be nervous. He needed to get back to himself.

They came to a bench and Shifra broke the silence. "Turn me this way and park me here. I would like to sit with you so I can see your face."

Welch complied. As he took a seat, he was determined to take action. What would he say to her if he was not…so deeply in love with her? It was fear that had him. Fear of a different breed and context. Welch did not fear Shiffy's disapproval. She was comfort and simplicity. Her kind heart would accept any offering he presented.

His fear was born from the need for a basic symmetry in all things. She held an enchantment for him that he wished to return. But like a timid creature, the ability fled the more he tried to approach it.

The chaos was over. The Institute's security had been enhanced even further. Welch had called in favors from skilled operatives to make sure the opposition was on the run for the time being. Welch and Shiffy had time for their dream to come true. Since they were both convalescing, they had nothing to occupy their days but conversation. The hours filled themselves with discussions of past missions and past lives. They had poured out their pain to each other over the hardships of the paths they were on. They had cried, comforted, and healed, as much in spirit as in body. Both had found their experience, their thoughts, and their faith so intertwined it could have been shocking had it not been for the faith.

Instead of shock, they experienced confirmation. Shiffy had seen it first, from afar, but Welch now also realized they were meant for each other. What he had mistaken for an unexpected weakness in his defense was his spirit reaching out to the one the Lord had prepared. So many people lost patience or hope waiting for that one of the Lord's choosing. Welch had done neither. He had lost expectation. He had been a sleeping hulk that only Shiffy could awaken.

Welch believed they were both ready to take the next step in the relationship. Perhaps it was sudden, but the connection they had was not measured by time. Then again, they had years together if their connection was not measured by space. Either way, the bond was undeniable.

But there were difficulties that Welch wanted to discuss, and he could not find the right approach. If she were anyone else, he would be direct. "Shiffy, my mind still rebels at the thought of someone with your beauty and charm being linked with someone like myself, so devoid of such attributes."

Shiffy tipped her head with a look that said, 'we've been over all that.'

"However…" Welch inserted the word before she could speak. He smiled the smile of one gazing at a great treasure. "I realize you have enough of those attributes for both of us. Enough, even, to cover someone my size." Welch met Shiffy's smile with a grin. "It is fortunate because my heart will permit no other option than to pursue you."

Shiffy straightened as if she had gotten to the good part of the story.

"But I am in a quandary."

Shiffy's brow wrinkled without losing the gentle smile that graced her. "Ruben, what in the world is the problem?"

"Courtship."

Gazing at him, the wrinkle between Shiffy's eyes shifted to one of confusion.

Welch needed to explain, but how to do it? "I mean, our situation is so…singular. Ruben Welch no longer exists. It will take time, and, I fear, a different location, to create a new identity that will not be associated with the OU professor who disappeared. Until then, I cannot…ask you…out."

Welch spread his open palms in presentation of the difficulty. "I cannot take you to a restaurant or even to a church in the area." He continued to lift his hands, only to lay them open again, as he revisited each element of the conundrum. "Even going for a drive would risk exposure. My appearance is hard to conceal, and…you draw attention wherever you go. It would be impossible for us to slip by unnoticed. I have been pondering over the dilemma for days now. I have even considered shaving my head."

Shiffy recoiled. Placing her hand over her mouth in disapproval, she shook her head. "I'll buy you a large hat."

Welch leaned back, waving his hands as if to erase the idea. Sitting forward again, he moved on to the next issue. "The Institute is lovely, but it would hardly be an appropriate…dating environment. With everyone we know…as kind and well-meaning as they are… I cannot…with the staff and…" He gestured toward the dining room. "You saw what just took place when we go for a simple walk. I cannot ask you to endure such a lack of privacy."

He sat back again and massaged his knuckles. "Leaving here presents even more difficulties. The Institute's private jet is certainly at our disposal but…It would be unseemly for us to leave on an obvious intimate getaway…unmarried." He found himself gesturing again with his hands. "Even if we were to take a chaperone and stay in separate rooms…I mean, if we did such a thing, that is exactly what we would do… Still…"

Welch leaned back and admired her. "I will not expose you to the type of gossip you had to endure in your former life. You are a virtuous lady and will be treated as such. I have considered the matter extensively and I have not devised a way, in this predicament, to court you properly."

Shiffy had placed the tips of her fingers over her mouth. Her eyes did not seem to share his concern. Dropping her hand into her lap, she sat erect and took in a breath. She leaned toward him as she spoke. "Ruben, I love your concern for my virtue. I do. And I understand that a courtship should be done properly to avoid any appearance of impropriety."

She gave him a smile that spoke of admiration. "I have to admit that I hadn't considered everything involved. You're so thoughtful. But in your concern, I believe you have overlooked an obvious solution to the problem surrounding a courtship between us."

Welch was mystified. He had no doubt that she was about to propose something ingenious. "What do you suggest?"

"Since courtship will be difficult, let's skip it."

"Skip it?"

"Yes. Let's not do it." Shiffy did her adorable mannerism of raising her shoulders to cross her arms in front of her waist with a smile and a tilt of her head. "We are older, Ruben. Why waste our time? I am prepared to become Mrs…whomever right now."

Welch scowled at the idea. "You deserve better than that." It wasn't right. He had hopes of wooing Shiffy properly. He gave a halfhearted grin. "Since we met, you have endured nothing but emotional and physical pain. That is not how a lady deserves to be courted. You should have your time for elegance and pampering."

Shiffy released the brakes on her chair.

Welch started to stand.

She stopped him by rolling forward, angling her wounded leg so she could place a hand on his knee. "Ruben Welch, you are truly a chivalrous knight. You've won my heart. You rescued my virtue, guarded my castle, protected my family, and saved my life and the life of my daughter. No pampering could compare with that. Life's not made of providing elegance, life's made of sharing hardship. We've got a head start already. I don't need you to take me out and wine me or dine me or take me to see the world. I've done all that. All I want is you. Let's skip the meal and get to the dessert. Let's get married."

The words touched a part of Welch that he thought had died. He was eighteen again, and God was starting new, showing him his worth, remaking his perceptions through the wonderful woman before him. Without thinking, he let out the elated breath within him and with it came one word. "When?"

Shiffy leaned in close in the manner that had torn down years of defenses the first day they met.

Her eyes twinkled with intrigue. "I worked out all the details with Talisa. You heard how Luke did it. We can outdo him. I found out the Institute has a pastor on staff. I already talked to him." She whispered the words out of her perfect lips. "We can do it…right…now."

"I agree." Welch was in a giddy fog, a dream that he never wanted to wake from. Then it hit him. "I can't be seen in town, and I no longer have a name to put on a marriage license."

Shiffy's eyes went wide like he had slapped her. Then she shook her head like she was ridding herself of a drug's effect. The sparkle was back. Laughing, she pushed herself out of the wheelchair, sending it rolling backward. Hopping on one leg, she pivoted toward Welch, who stood and grabbed her. She threw herself against him so that his best option to protect her was to sit down again with Shiffy on his lap.

Letting out a little squeak of pain at the drop, she moved right into throwing her arms around his neck and pressing her lips against his. She pulled back and fixed him with her beautiful eyes. "We're spies. We'll forge one."

For if a man belongs to Christ, he is a new person. The old life is gone. New life has begun. All this comes from God. He is the One Who brought us to Himself when we hated Him. He did this through Christ. Then He gave us the work of bringing others to Him.

At one time you were strangers to God and your minds were at war with Him. Your thoughts and actions were wrong. But Christ has brought you back to God by His death on the cross. In this way, Christ can bring you to God, holy and pure and without blame. This is for you if you keep the faith.

2 Corinthians 5:17-18 & Colossians 1:19-23a (NLV)

Rebekah and I want to thank you for reading NOT IMMUNE. We pray the story was a blessing. If it was, would you be kind enough to leave us a review? It doesn't have to be long of fancy to help other readers know you liked it. Reviews on Amazon and/or reader sites are so important for authors. Thank you again for spending your time with us. We hope you'll read on and enjoy this

sample of another WyattWove Christian romantic thriller:

Available at Amazon.com: Domestic Enemies: **or through a link at www.WyattWove.com**

DOMESTIC ENEMIES
SELAH AWARD THIRD PLACE WINNER

...and a man's enemies will be the members of his household. Matthew 10:36 (CSB)

Prologue

JULY 3, 1988
Bandar Abbas, Iran

Alireza Hamadani glanced at his watch, his hatred toward the Turk festering. He had hoped to test his bomb at the hotel, but he had to make the flight to Dubai. *If I wait any longer, I'll miss it.* He contemplated what to do. *I can't cancel with this client. It will set the release back at least another week, maybe longer, depending on scheduling.* Large banks didn't like last-minute changes. Neither did the Imam.

"Imam." Alireza used the term out of respect for Islam, but he had seen that the man the rest of the world knew as Ayatollah Khomeini was not infallible as the Imam title was supposed to denote. *The old fool has no respect for the*

scientific community and no concept of the time required to create a masterpiece like this.

Alireza patted the case on his belt to reassure himself. He needed a success, and he needed it soon. Grabbing his bag, he jerked open the door. A dark face made him jump.

Whenever Alireza looked at the Turk, he found himself staring at the scar that crossed his hooked nose and ran down past his mouth. He glanced away as he stepped back so the Turk could enter, but the casual expression on the craggy face angered Alireza.

"This was supposed to happen last night." Alireza clenched his teeth and glared at the floor.

"Yes, it was." The Turk entered the room carrying two identical nylon bags and kicked the door shut with his foot. "You were late."

"Fifteen minutes? You couldn't wait fifteen minutes?" Alireza's eyes connected with dark circles looking at him over the scar, which lifted at the volume in Alireza's voice.

Alireza's gaze retreated to the carpet.

"Sadly, no. Not in this business." The dark man dropped the bags on the other side of him, away from Alireza. "Two Compaq SLT/286 computers. Not scheduled to be released to the public until September. No extra charge for early delivery."

The thump the cases made hitting the floor made Alireza cringe. "Please don't damage them." It was all he could do to restrain his anger. *I doubt he could even operate a computer.*

The Turk smiled. "I hear the Compaq company has a very good warranty." Letting go of the smile, he held out a waiting hand and reminded Alireza, "You were in a hurry, were you not?"

Alireza knew the hazard of asking the taxi driver to get to the airport as fast as he could, but he had no choice. When the cab screeched to a stop in front of the terminal, he was grateful to be the one sliding himself across the seat instead of the inertia. He paid the driver for the abuse and hurried into the building.

Loaded down with the three bags, Alireza glanced at his watch again. No time to test it before boarding. He moved toward the line for the Iran Air counter.

Alireza carried the newly acquired computers and pushed his carryon bag with his foot. After a few minutes, the line stopped moving. Around the heads of the people ahead of him, he could see a man gesticulating in front of a stone-faced official who stood behind the counter. The whispered information made its way down the line, informing Alireza there was an immigration issue. He knew the flight would be delayed.

Wiping sweat from the back of his neck, Alireza used the motion to mask a look around. There was no better place to find out how well his bomb would work. Slipping out of line, he moved to a vacant set of seats in an out-of-the-way part of the terminal where he could still watch the progress of the line.

On each of the seats beside him, Alireza set up one of the portable computers he had obtained from the Turk and turned them on. When Windows 3.1 finished booting on both machines, Alireza took out the disks he had in his case. He inserted one into the computer on his right and ran the program.

Calling up the timer setting, he saw the default of a three-month delay before detonation. He hoped that length would be right for the bomb he would plant at the client's location in Dubai. He wanted the bomb to do the most damage and not be traced back to him.

Looking to the check-in line for Iran Air, Alireza saw there was no movement and some of the customers were sitting on the floor. But that could change any moment. He needed to shorten the time to detonation as low as he dared. He erased the three-month entry and typed in one minute. The default was for his program to keep everything it was doing concealed, but Alireza changed that setting so a countdown timer would be displayed.

Pressing the start button, Alireza drew in a breath. The numbers denoting one minute appeared on the screen and started reducing by seconds…59…58…. Would his bomb work the same with this new breed of portable? Alireza would soon find out.

As the numbers on the screen clicked by, Alireza second guessed himself. He had initially wanted to wait a year before the big detonation, but he had decided on three months to make sure his bomb wasn't discovered before it could go off.

The timer reached 30 seconds.

The earlier version that Alireza had planted in Jerusalem had been found too quickly to have the impact for which he had hoped. *I need things to work this time.*

20 seconds.

Everything was a calculated risk. The longer he waited to detonate, the more widespread the damage—wait too long, and the bomb might be found before it went off.

10…9…8…

He had worked hard to make his bomb undetectable, but he didn't want to be so shortsighted as to underestimate the pace of development of the new virus scanners that were starting to appear... Alireza looked at the timer.

3...2...1.

It was done. The timer went back to one minute and displayed another start button.

To check the files on the computer, Alireza used a separate disk that he had designed to get past the masking features and find the subtle changes his program caused in certain files.

Alireza disliked the word "virus" to describe what he had made. It sounded small and inconsequential. He also did not like that the term had been coined by an American Jew. He preferred to call it his "bomb." This was no ordinary virus. His latest version was invisible and devastating.

Alireza regretted that the Zionists would not be the first to feel the explosion, but it was too risky to go back to Israel. But Dubai, the largest city in the United Arab Emirates, was only a 28-minute flight away. *The spoiled rich Emirates are always flirting with the infidels. They will spread it all over the world.* At the speed Alireza had calculated his new program could reproduce itself, months should be enough. *Let's see what it did in one minute on a portable computer.*

In the minute that had elapsed, his bomb had attached itself to every program. Alireza took another disk containing financial software and loaded it on the computer. His check program verified that the financial disk was immediately infected. He then inserted a game disk and checked it to find the same result.

Alireza was pleased. The new portables were just as vulnerable as the other computers he had tested. "Laptops," as they were being called, were the future of computing, and people would be connecting them to everything.

Even though it altered files on the computer, his program had the traits of what some were calling a "worm." If a computer was attached to a communications port of any kind, including a modem, his creation would silently, aggressively try to contact other computers to link with them and duplicate itself onto the new machine. His bomb attached itself to everything that it touched, and then it waited. The detonation was yet to come.

Alireza switched to the timer window, changed the time to ten seconds and pushed start. At the end of those ten seconds, the timer would simulate what would happen across the world, three months after the bomb's release. As he watched the screen, the time elapsed and the timer reset to five minutes and began counting down again.

Alireza smiled. The bomb had armed itself for the actual detonation. He quickly created a file in the word processor and saved it. Typing rapidly, he created small documents, spreadsheets, batch files—as much as he could in the five minutes he had. He searched for the files and they were all there where he had saved them. Everything looked normal. Then he waited again.

The five-minute timer was the default time he had preprogramed for the detonation on the portable. 3...2...1. The screen went blank.

The beauty of his bomb was that there was no visible explosion. But, once armed, the bomb would surreptitiously begin deleting files. In the version he was going to release in Dubai, the files would vanish one hour after they were created. He had set the five-minute delay for the simulation on the portables to speed up the test.

Alireza searched for the files. The first document he created was gone. Another search a few seconds later showed more of the files were gone. He ran the search program repeatedly, ever more satisfied. Whenever a file reached the five-minute mark, it vanished, its data completely overwritten and irretrievable.

None of the virus scanning software created so far would detect his bomb, and if the computer techs got too aggressive in their effort... From another disk, Alireza loaded a high-level diagnostic and repair tool and ran the program. Though it occurred invisibly, Alireza knew that his bomb was reacting to the deep scan program by replicating itself over and over and each time it was 100% larger. Within seconds, it would fill all available memory.

The computer crashed.

Alireza tried to reboot it, but it would always die at the same point. He tried every method he knew to get it going again, but nothing worked. It was sweet failure.

If the computer had been connected to other computers in any manner, it would have sent the detonate command to them. Whole networks would go down. Alireza also designed the bomb to immediately digitally shred any backup. The backup data would appear normal until it was used to restore the computer. Then the only thing it would do was reload his bomb.

Alireza eyed the check-in line—no movement yet. He switched to the second portable on his left. *I still have time to test the defusing program.*

He inserted a different disk that contained the protection software and let the program load. When it was complete, he put in the disk containing his bomb and ran it. Using the unmasking disk, he searched for evidence of his bomb attached to the programs on the portable computer— nothing. His defusing software had prevented the bomb from loading. It was the same protection program that was being loaded on all of Iran's major computer networks.

Alireza set the computer aside. He would use it to tie into a phone line in some out-of-the-way office or conference room when he got to his client's headquarters in Dubai and make the release there. He glanced across the expanse of the airport lobby. The line was moving.

Approximately fifty miles south

The boom of the deck gun reverberated through the hull of the USS Vincennes, a Ticonderoga-class, Aegis, guided-missile cruiser. The barrel recoiled into the mount housing, and the spent casing ejected onto the deck with a metallic clank.

A young seaman, barely out of high school, pushed his way into the group of crew members gathered on the deck. He had been in the head when all the excitement started. The young man was proud to be part of the fleet of U.S. Navy ships cruising the waters of the Strait of Hormuz, protecting cargo vessels going in and out of the Persian Gulf from both sides of the war between Iran and Iraq. He didn't want to miss a minute. "What's going on?"

The slap of the sea against the ship was overwhelmed by the sound of the next round from the gun. Smoke from the five-inch round barrel followed the faster-than-sight projectile like an old dog after a rabbit but abandoned the chase and dissipated into the hazy atmosphere. The rabbit, a deadly explosive shell, whistled through the air toward its target.

"Boghammers were hassling an oil tanker again." Another seaman, only a couple years older, pointed across the sea toward a group of small Iranian gunboats weaving through the water. "They went too far this time. They fired at our helicopter that was monitoring them."

"They hit it?"

The older crew member shook his head. "Nah, our bird bugged out before they could. But I think the captain's had enough. We're hit'n 'em and so's the Montgomery." The crewman dipped his head toward the other U.S. ship that was also in pursuit of the boghammers.

The young crew member licked his lips and strained to see the action. It was the first time any of them had experienced live combat. He tapped the shoulder of another young man who held binoculars pressed hard against his eyes. "Let me take a look."

The other man glanced at him with a wrinkled forehead, then handed over the binos. "Take a quick look and then I want 'em back."

Through the lens, the first crew member focused on the enemy boats. One of the large shells fired at the boghammars found its mark.

An equally young-sounding voice from the Montgomery came over the radio, "Hey, all stations, I think we just smoked that guy."

The other man grabbed the binoculars with a scowl. "You made me miss it."

The first young man resumed his bare-eyed watch, listening to the rapid overlapping voices around him as some called out details of the engagement and others commented.

Below, in the dark of the Combat Information Center (CIC) of the ship, where the row of computer monitors gave the commanders their view of the action, the mood ran more toward tension than excitement. The skipper of the Vincennes, Captain William Rogers, mulled over the situation. He had taken the plunge and ordered the attack on the Iranian boats. *They're getting bolder. Someone has to put a stop to it. I can't let them take a shot at our bird and get away with it.*

The captain focused on how the Iranians might respond. *We can handle the boghammars. Not much of a threat there, but that P3 is still out there.* Earlier Rogers had his radio man give a warning to one of Iran's long-range surveillance aircraft. The pilot had agreed to keep his distance, but he was still in the area. *He'll have us on his radar. It wouldn't be much for him to call in an airstrike. I'm not going to let this end up like the Stark.*

Rogers remembered how thirty-seven sailors had died when an Iraqi jet hit the USS Stark with two Exocet missiles a year earlier. The Stark's captain was retired under the cloud of not acting to defend his ship. *I'm not going to let my career end that way.*

Alireza sat in the first-class section of the airliner designated as Iran Air 655. Even his anger at the Turk had subsided. He let a smile form and took a minute to let the stress roll off. *The bomb works. That's all that matters.*

Alireza imagined what it would be like to watch an average office setting on the day that his digital bomb *detonated.* Despair and suspicion would run wild through the organization as more and more critical files disappeared. In the banking industry, a customer would deposit money in an account, and one hour later all record of it would be wiped away. People would flood the bank, waving receipts for transactions that could not be verified, demanding their money in cash—far more than the bank would have on hand.

People would be fired, departments reorganized, new security put in place, all on a quest to find who was deleting files. Trust would be gone as the bomb used every weakness and back door to spread itself from computer to computer and organization to organization. Businesses would fail with no knowledge of the program that could hide in the latent memory of every floppy disk and tape drive. Only Iran's technology was protected.

Alireza envisioned the effect on the wealthy westerners and Europeans that presumed to dictate what his country could do right down to denying import of the two portable computers that he now possessed. In less than a year, the world would bow under his electronic jihad, and Iran would hold the keys to power. *The Imam will be pleased. He already likes Failak, and this will secure a place for the boy. We can outlast the old man.*

His thoughts turned to Failak. *One of the portables will make a nice gift.* Alireza would give it to his son on his upcoming sixteenth birthday—after he reformatted it and wiped it clean of any evidence of what he was about to do. *He's earned it.* Alireza knew that he pushed the boy too hard, even with his son's natural aptitude for math and computers.

I need him to be ready, just in case. Not that Alireza took the Imam's veiled threats seriously. He was too important to them. So many intelligent people had left Iran since the revolution. It made Alireza valuable.

Only he and Failak understood the computer code and knew the location of his notes and backups. He needed to maintain his value to the Imam until he passed it on to his son. Someday, Failak would be that "arrow" that his name suggested, piercing retribution even further into the world of their enemies.

Alireza's daydreaming was interrupted by the captain's voice over the speaker. "Our flight has been cleared for departure. Please fastened your seatbelts."

Soon, the plane was under way. As it lifted off, Alireza thought about his next steps. *I'll soon be in Dubai, and I need to be ready.*

Petty Officer Andrew Anderson, the identification supervisor on duty aboard the USS Vincennes, jerked his head to the top of his screen when the dot appeared—a new aircraft contact that the Aegis computer had designated as 4474. The designator then switched to 4130. For a second, he thought he had another plane on the screen, but then he realized that the computer was communicating with another U.S. ship's computer that had already assigned the same aircraft the 4130 number. The computer had settled on using that number to track this particular aircraft and had deleted the 4474 designator—the Aegis was a very smart machine. It was the most sophisticated mix of computer and radar deployed by any military in the world, yet it still couldn't ID the plane. Anderson knew that was up to him.

The aircraft was moving at over 300 knots, so it was something powerful, but beyond that it was just another blip on the radar screen. It had apparently lifted off from Bandar Abbas Airfield. That could mean it was commercial, but the Iranian Air Force also flew out of there. He was fairly sure he remembered that one of the many recent intel warnings the Vincennes had received talked about the Iranians moving F-14 fighters to that field. One thing was certain. The new contact was heading right for them.

The forward five-inch gun on the deck of the Vincennes boomed, and the lights in the CIC flickered off and on as they did each time the gun fired. It irritated Anderson. They were on a battleship, after all. You would think that they would have designed the lighting system to take a little pounding.

Anderson moved his cursor across the screen and onto the dot which represented the new contact. He pressed the button, triggering the IFF (Identification/Friend or Foe) radio frequency squawk that went out from the ship, requesting an identification signal from the plane. Another round from the deck gun caused another flicker of the lights. Anderson made a growling sound in his throat. *Come on. I've got to see what I'm doing.* He waited for the lights to settle so he could verify what the IFF was telling him.

The digital display showed the plane responding on Mode III, a designated commercial frequency. That should mean it was a civilian airliner, not a warbird. The frequency was 6760. As Anderson checked his reference to identify the particular aircraft that used that code, the lights flickered with the next round.

"New bird on the scope," Anderson called out. "It looks like COMAIR. Working on an ID now." He fumbled with the notebook in his hands, turning past the place he needed to be. "Come on." He flipped the pages back the other way. The aircraft identification was crucial. The captain was waiting. Another vibration—another flicker of the lights.

Captain Rogers gritted his teeth in frustration. The last round had jammed the forward gun.

A voice called out. "Captain, topside reports the boghammars are returning fire and heading our way."

Rogers contemplated the risks. The two things the boghammars had in their favor were acceleration and maneuverability. With the forward gun out of commission, even temporarily, the relatively tiny crafts gained a new advantage. He didn't want to underestimate them.

He also had this new radar contact. He could hear the radio operator transmitting on various frequencies, requesting the new contact identify itself and state its intention.

Rogers prioritized. He was waiting for an identification on the aircraft. *The boats are the more immediate threat.* He wanted to be sure he could fully engage them, so he ordered the Vincennes into a high-speed turn. He needed to get it done while the boghammars were still a distance away. "I want rounds in the tray on the rear gun," he snapped, as the ship was swinging around. "We'll show 'em our good side."

Petty Officer Anderson was frantically trying to decipher a copy of the Iranian commercial flight schedule in the dark of the CIC. At least the lights had stopped going out, but he was wishing he had learned how to read the civilian flight schedule prior to that moment. To make matters worse, there were four different time zones used in the Persian Gulf, and Anderson was trying to decide which zone the schedule was based on, but he wasn't sure. He imagined the captain staring in his direction, still waiting. So far, he had not found any flights scheduled for that time.

Anderson routinely pressed the IFF again to verify the contact. A rapid turn of the ship sent his papers and reference binders sliding onto the floor, and he scrambled to retrieve them. As he came back up with the bundle of items, he noticed something new on the IFF. A second frequency was squawking on Mode II—that was definitely a military aircraft. Was it a new bird or the same contact now identifying as military? There was nothing else close.

Anderson slid his chair back up to the console as he deposited the armload of paper and binders onto the workspace. What should he do? The plane looked a lot closer on the screen than it had. Was it speeding up? Speeding up and diving would indicate an attack profile. He was trying to remember how high the plane was before and determine its present altitude, but he decided that he should be identifying this new IFF code.

Anderson tried to calm his mind and focus on what he was trained to do, but none of this fit the training scenarios. The IFF indicator said 1100. Anderson began digging through the pile on the workspace until he found the binder that contained the IFF codes.

Apprehension began to give way to fear. If this was a fighter attacking, Anderson needed to get that information to the captain before it was too late.

He ran his finger down the columns of numbers until he found 1100. As he moved his finger to the column that indicated the aircraft that used those numbers, he was incredulous as he read, "Iranian F-14." He quickly ran his finger back, making sure he was on the right column.

Anderson pressed the transmit button and practically

yelled into his headset. "All stations. I have a possible Mode II on track 4-1-3-1, 1-1-0-0 which breaks as an F-14."

Anderson had everyone's attention. "You got an F-14?" one of the other crew members asked in disbelief.

Anderson was shaking as he searched the radar screen, not really seeing the activity he thought he saw before. The CIC began to crackle with the news.

"Possible Mode II, breaks as an F-14," was repeated throughout the Command Center.

Captain Rogers looked away from his screens to the sound of the voices that were transmitting the ominous announcement. All eyes were on him.

Shifting back to the monitors, Rogers saw the tactical display in front of him had changed. The contact "blip" had been relabeled as an F-14. The title moved with it as the dot advanced, bringing potential destruction with every refresh of the screen. Rogers was not a man who hesitated.

"Radio command," he ordered the operator. "Tell them what we have and request permission to engage the aircraft if it crosses within 20 miles."

In a moment, the radio operator gave the response. "Theater commander concurs. Warn the aircraft first and then fire on it if it continues."

And continue it did. The dot moved, but the crew was fixated on the "F-14" trailing along with it. With every rotation of the radar, it closed in on the circular display now encompassing the Vincennes indicator on the screen—the ominous twenty-mile radius.

The officer standing behind Rogers called out, "Sir, possible Comair." He pointed at the IFF squawk that had changed to the civilian frequency.

What was going on? Rogers considered what it meant. *It might be a warbird masked as a commercial flight.* The missiles that hit the Stark were fired from a retrofitted civilian jet.

The radio operators in the CIC were again calling out warnings to the aircraft, but it was not responding. The lieutenant sitting next to Rogers announced that the aircraft had crossed the twenty-mile boundary.

Rogers inserted his launch key into the slot on the console in front of him but didn't turn it. To fire his deck guns on the boghammars was one thing, but to launch the deadly SM-2 missiles at a plane that was now identifying as "civilian" was beyond frightening. He could feel his hand shaking on the key, and he hoped no one else could see it in the dim light. Moments passed.

Beside him, the lieutenant was poised. "Captain, do you wish to engage the target at twenty miles?"

Rogers deliberated. *Would they really risk an attack like this?* He wondered if the Stark's captain had thought the same thing.

"Captain, do you wish to engage the aircraft?" The Lieutenant's voice made it sound like a plea.

If the contact was an Iranian fighter, it would soon be able to launch its own missile first. Still, Rogers hesitated. "Negative." *What if it's a civilian aircraft? How many people would be on board a jet like that?* He needed more than what he had. Why weren't they answering?

The buzz from the earlier information was still moving through the crew. Inside the command room, someone called out, "Altitude declining!"

Declining? The word was like a slap to Rogers. All

indication was that the plane had just taken off from the Bandar Abbas Airfield. There would be no reason for it to decrease altitude unless it was a fighter diving to attack.

Rogers realized he wasn't breathing and took a deep inhale. It was much louder than he intended. His priority was to his crew. He grabbed onto that thought and his mind used it to push the confusion aside.

Rogers turned the key. He had never done anything so simple and yet so difficult. "Take order on track 4131." Rogers pronounced the fate of the unidentified aircraft that was now within eleven miles. The captain's words set the CIC in motion.

Rogers thought about the possibility of dying. The dot had moved far inside the circles surrounding the Vincennes indicator. It was close enough to fire a missile accurately.

The activity buzzed around Rogers along with the deep metallic thumps and vibrations of the missiles moving into firing position. The missiles launched—first one, then the other.

"Birds away. Rails clear."

When Rogers heard the verification called out, he was both relieved and petrified. The object the missiles were streaking toward had better be an F-14.

Hovering his finger over the hold fire button, Rogers considered the reality of the situation. If he pushed the button, the missiles would self-destruct before they reached the target. The button represented his last chance to stop what he had done. He wanted to push it, but he dared not. The missiles also represented the last chance for him to protect his ship from the potential enemy that was closing on them.

The radio operators were yelling warnings to the plane on all the frequencies they had available to them.

"Come on. Respond, you idiots." Rogers was immersed

in contradicting emotions. Everything else faded into the background. All he knew was fear and resolve crashing against each other like the sea against the hull of the ship.

So many apprehensions were running through Alireza's mind as he stared out the window and watched the water widen below the airliner as it climbed out over the Persian Gulf. He went over what he remembered about the client in Dubai, strategizing about the best place to make the release undetected.

There was a flash of light. The entire plane shuddered, jerking him hard against the seat. His body lurched sideways, following the radical bank of the aircraft. His hands were clamped onto the armrests, gouging deep indents as his face was pulled against the clear plastic window. In milliseconds, he processed changes, more sky, a mass of jagged metal and broken hydraulic hoses sticking into the open air where the wing had been. Thin streams of oil stretched out toward the tail of the plane. He had no time to realize the significance of the sight.

The second missile slammed into the tail of flight 655 ripping it apart with a shock wave so strong it blew the clothes from Alireza's body, tore the seat belt from his waist, and crushed the two computers under his seat. Naked and lifeless, Alireza fell through the hazy Persian Gulf sky, unaware of the triumphant cheer that went up from the young men on the deck of the Vincennes in celebration of a direct hit.

It did not take long for the mood to change on the Vincennes as they began to pick up the traffic on the distress frequency indicating that a civilian jetliner had crashed in the Strait.

Ironically, but certainly to be expected, the Vincennes was the first on the scene of the disaster. The enthusiasm on deck was gone. The young seamen stared in shocked disbelief as the Vincennes slowly moved through the macabre scene of floating bodies and debris. They watched like wide-eyed children, aged in moments. The horror would be the subject of many nightmares to come, both asleep and awake.

The inquiry into what happened would go before the military court, Congress, the United Nations and the media. In the end, it would be ruled a horrible, perhaps preventable, accident by most of the United States. The strange events in the CIC that day would be explained as human error brought on by a combination of lack of training and misinterpretation of data in the stress of the event. "Scenario Fulfillment" the psychologists called it—fear so strong that it caused crewmembers to see what they feared they would see even in the face of conflicting data. The event would eventually fade in the memory of most. But some would not forget.

JULY 7, 1988

Iranians poured through the streets of Tehran like blood in an artery, separate corpuscles, unique but mingled and adhering into a flowing unit where all personality was lost. Failak's right hand was raised above his head as he partially supported his father's coffin. There were so many others assisting in carrying his father's remains that he hardly felt the weight. People moved in from all around just to touch the box, people he did not even know, as if the physical contact would somehow establish a connection with the unknown man inside, entitling them to a share in the outrage.

The coffin he carried was one of many, draped in honor and lifted up on the flow of people. Failak struggled to keep pace, fearing that the simple wooden box would be carried away from him on the throngs of uplifted arms. Only the slow movement of the masses allowed him to stay with it. The noise from the shouts, the wails, the hate-filled chants, was so extreme that it became a feeling as much as a sound. Failak knew he could not escape it even if he wanted. The people were packed so closely around him that he, along with the others, had no choice but to flow gradually down the street wherever the current took them. His body was pressed on all sides by other bodies, but the crowd was connected even more by the emotion than the proximity.

Yet Failak felt detached. Those around him did not know what he knew. Even in his grief, the knowledge lifted him above the crowd, much like his father's coffin. The Imam had honored him, but it must be in private. No one else must know. He was not part of this group, but Failak had no desire to escape the scene. He wanted to hear the crowds pay tribute to the martyrs. He wanted to think of his father that way—to feel something besides the ache inside. He needed somewhere else to channel his feelings. The horror of it was too much to contain. It was easier to blame and to hate. So that is what he did.

Available at Amazon.com: Domestic Enemies: **or through a link at** www.WyattWove.com

Keep reading to learn more about Domestic Enemies

DOMESTIC ENEMIES
SELAH AWARD THIRD PLACE WINNER

Little seeds we sow, and someday they will grow. What if the ill weeds our society wades in today were being planted decades earlier? What if someone had a chance to uproot them?

Whole families are being murdered in middle-class neighborhoods in Colorado Springs. Everyone is looking to Police Lieutenant Darrell Jacobs, one of the only amputees able to return to police work with a mechanical hook, to find the murderer before he kills again.

Bioelectronic genius Callie Williams has followed Darrell's inspirational story and decided he is a gift from God to test her high-tech prosthetic arm. But Darrell, with scars both inside and out, is not the Godly man she believes or remembers him to be. He also comes with enemies—the face that lurks in the lost parts of Darrell's memory and the God Darrell can't forgive. They both want to finish what they started.

Facing clashing elements of faith and yearning, Darrell

and Callie must battle an enemy with an agenda that takes homeland security to a whole new battlefield. When Darrell's inquiry brings the enemy right to his doorstep, he becomes a suspect in Callie's disappearance. With the help of a young man whose high-speed mind is humorously perplexing, Darrell must outwit the FBI to rescue the woman who is changing his world.

Even if he succeeds, his problems are just beginning as he confronts a new kind of terrorist. The intricate mystery leads him to a plot designed to tear the United States apart—a scheme so vast it may be too much for the police, the FBI and Homeland Security combined. There's no way for Darrell to stop it alone, but who do you trust when your enemy is someone you know, and the greatest danger might lie in your own heart? A danger that will leave you with the uneasy realization that locking your doors will be useless.

HEA, standalone, with no cliffhanger.

<u>What readers are saying about DOMESTIC ENEMIES</u>

"Unforgettable, original plot that had me on the edge of my seat. All too real scenarios — I'm still looking over my shoulder…loved the Christian perspective…proves a great story can be written without vulgar language…" ~Amazon Review~

"A great adventure, and a great love story too! And God is in the midst of it all! I highly recommend this book!" ~Amazon Review~

"Domestic Enemies is a great book! It is well-written with lots of action and advanced technology. What I like most about it is that it is similar to what has been going on in America the last few years. It really makes you think. I also

like the Christian perspective and being reminded that God is in control. The book also has some good romance in it." ~Amazon Review~

"The author grabs the reader from the first scene and doesn't let go! Full of action and pathos. When the suspense got too great, I laid down the book only to pick it back up because I had to know what happened! Highly recommended!" ~Amazon Review~

"Domestic Enemies has everything! Action, suspense, humor, and heart. The author...describes technical equipment as if the reader is looking right at it, and makes it easy to follow along. The action scenes were like watching it on the big screen (which by the way, this would make a great movie). For all the intrigue and gritty (but clean) cop lingo, I was pleasantly surprised when the author pulled out his 'sensitivity pen' for the love story hidden inside." ~Jen Jeffrey Billington, author of BREADCRUMBS-Finding True Love's Trail~

"I loved this book. I love it when I find a good read that you just don't want to put it down until the end. Reinforces faith and, through God, all things are possible." ~Amazon Review~

"Overwhelmed by how insightful and timely this book is!!! There are many twists and turns that lead to the final end. Really, folks, so many things spoke to my heart here. I will need to read it again to absorb all the nuances and depth of thinking put into this. It's such a plausible revelation of what is happening in America, even as I write, that I feel stunned. The character Link made me lol several times. I enjoyed meeting him especially. Well done, Sir Wyatt."

~Amazon Review~

"This has a very relevant and frightening premise…and there is some great technology used through the story which I expect is what gives it the science fiction tag." ~Amazon Review~

"Fascinating viewpoint thru classic storytelling… keeps you up late reading, reading, reading!"
~Amazon Review~

Keep reading to see more books available from WyattWove, but first we want to share with you what we are convinced is the most important thing in life.

In our books, as in life,
people have encounters with God.
Some rejecting, some receiving.
Receiving God's forgiveness and
repairing your relationship with Him is the
most important decision you will make
and the most life-changing experience you can have.
It is not about religion; it is about reality.
People ask, "Why doesn't God show Himself
and fix things?"— Well, He did.
He came in a form we could easily understand,
doing things no man could do,
but just like now, most misunderstood Him,
being caught up in their own sin and agendas.
The problem was different than we thought,
the solution different than we expected.
He was called Emmanuel,
which is translated "God with us."
He came under the name, translated in English as Jesus,
which means "the Lord is my salvation."
There is truth,
understood for thousands of years
by those willing to hear. This is it:
without The Savior, you are a slave to sin,
which will destroy you in the end.
There is only one thing you can do about it:
Truly, humbly admit that, like all of us, you are lost and
broken then put your faith in Jesus Christ to save you. If
you mean it, everything will change. His Spirit will come
inside you and give you the desire and the will to follow
the Way Jesus taught.
As you hold on tight to your faith in Christ,
running back to Him every time you fail,
the old you will fade away—

you will become a new person.
You will have the God-given ability to weather everything
this world and the powers of hell can and will throw at
you. You can endure until the end
and spend eternity with God. The Bible has always, and
still does, hold all the answers. Start with these Scriptures
and have a sincere talk with your Heavenly Father.

For no one is put right in God's sight by doing what the Law requires; what the Law does is to make us know that we have sinned. But now God's way of putting people right with Himself has been revealed. It has nothing to do with law, even though the Law of Moses and the prophets gave their witness to it. Romans 3:20-21(GNB)

We are made right with God by placing our faith in Jesus Christ. And this is true for everyone who believes, no matter who we are. For everyone has sinned; we all fall short of God's glorious standard. Romans 3:22-23 (NLT)

They are made right with God by His grace. This is a free gift. They are made right with God by being made free from sin through Jesus Christ. God gave Jesus as a way to forgive people's sins through their faith in Him. God can forgive them because the blood sacrifice of Jesus pays for their sins. God gave Jesus to show that He always does what is right and fair. He was right in the past when He was patient and did not punish people for their sins. And in our own time, He still does what is right. God worked all this out in a way that allows Him to judge people fairly and still make right any person

who has faith in Jesus. Romans 3:24-26 (ERV)

Brothers and sisters, my heart's desire and prayer to God on behalf of the Jewish people is that they would be saved. I can assure you that they are deeply devoted to God, but they are misguided. They don't understand how to receive God's approval. So they try to set up their own way to get it, and they have not accepted God's way for receiving his approval. Christ is the fulfillment of Moses' teachings so that everyone who has faith may receive God's approval...If you declare that Jesus is Lord, and believe that God brought Him back to life, you will be saved. By believing you receive God's approval, and by declaring your faith, you are saved.
Romans 10:3-4 & 9-10 (GW)

So get rid of all immoral behavior and all the wicked things you do. Humbly accept the word that God has placed in you. This word can save you. Do what God's word says. Don't merely listen to it, or you will fool yourselves... However, the person who continues to study God's perfect teachings that make people free and who remains committed to them will be blessed. People like that don't merely listen and forget; they actually do what God's teachings say....If a person thinks that he is religious but can't control his tongue, he is fooling himself. That person's religion is worthless. Pure, unstained religion, according to God our Father, is to take care of orphans and widows when they suffer and to remain uncorrupted by this world.

My friends, what good is it for one of you to say that you have faith if your actions do not prove it? Can that faith save you? Suppose there are brothers or sisters

who need clothes and don't have enough to eat. What good is there in your saying to them, "God bless you! Keep warm and eat well!"—if you don't give them the necessities of life? So it is with faith: if it is alone and includes no actions, then it is dead.
 James 1:21, 22, 25, & 26 & 2:14-17 (GNB)

You believe that there is one God. That's fine! The demons also believe that, and they tremble with fear… You see that a person receives God's approval because of what he does, not only because of what he believes. A body that doesn't breathe is dead. In the same way faith that does nothing is dead.
 James 2:19, 24, & 26 (GW)

If this has led you to make a commitment to God, the Bible says it is important that you tell people about it. We would love to hear about your experience. Please email us at contact@WyattWove.com. We have a free short story to share with you about someone who had the same experience and the difference it made in his life. Like all our writing, it is from an unusual perspective. It might give you a little idea of what to expect.

We have also put together a page on our website to help you in living this new life or in case you have more questions. It is full of what we have learned from our experiences. The page is full of links to other sites that better explain and expand on all types of topics about this walk of following Christ. We invite you to check it out at, https://www.kentwyatt.org/living-the-new-life/.

SEEING BEYOND
Special Heroes | Book One
Selah Award Finalist

Talisa had to believe Teddy's visions were from God because she had seen them save lives. But being involved in the wildest events in Gilead county, along with caring for her sister Janie and Teddy's special needs, was driving Talisa crazy. Or maybe she already took that trip when her father died.

Either way, Teddy's latest vision brought everything too close to home when it corresponded with the woman screaming next door. But there is no woman next door and discovering how the two events connect will force Talisa to revisit the past that haunts her and entangle her in the biggest mysteries in the area.

If there was any way she could do it by herself, she would never get involved with Luke again. He was part of that past. But his bad guy catching methods were unique, and they worked. She had hoped that he, at least, wouldn't interfere with her potential relationship with the handsome psychiatrist next door. Who was she kidding? That was like keeping a kid out of wet cement.

Now, none of that matters. Janie and Teddy are missing, and if the psychiatrist is right, Talisa's world just turned upside down. The man she hoped would heal her might be a killer, the man she trusted like family might be a deceiver, the gift she believed in might be a fake, and the only person who can help her is the one man she can't forgive.

Humor and suspense collide as Talisa discovers how little she knows about the people around her and herself. Can she see beyond it all, to where the truth, true love, and the power of God might finally set her free?

HEA, standalone, with no cliffhanger.

Available at Amazon.com: Seeing Beyond or through a link at www.WyattWove.com

"One of the best books I ever read. The story truly captures the imagination." ~Amazon Review~

"Mystery and surprising turns…I enjoy the romance woven into Wyatt's fiction. I fell in love with the characters and I could easily hear and picture those with special needs as their voices were beautifully brought to life." ~Amazon Review~

"This book has everything!!! I literally couldn't put the book down!…I read it in one day…I was so hooked. It was so well written and had an amazing storyline with mystery, romance, & action. Totally unpredictable! Then the spiritual aspect really blessed me. My heart was touched! I found myself with a big grin at the end. LOVE IT!" ~Amazon Review~

This author creates very likable, unique characters and then gets them into situations you would never anticipate. ~Amazon Review~

Great book and a quick read! The characters—sometimes funny, sometimes quirky, sometimes touchingly vulnerable—bring the story to life. Powerful truths are blended with suspenseful action. Attention grabbing to the final page. I couldn't put it down! ~Amazon Review~

I thought I'd read for a bit before I went to sleep. Ha. I finally put it down reluctantly at 4 am!!…This is a new author to me & I look forward to reading his books. He deals with tough issues like depression, grieving, & gifted adults with tact and understanding. ~Amazon Review~

EARS TO HEAR
Special Heroes | Book Two
Daphne du Maurier Award for Excellence in Mystery/Suspense finalist

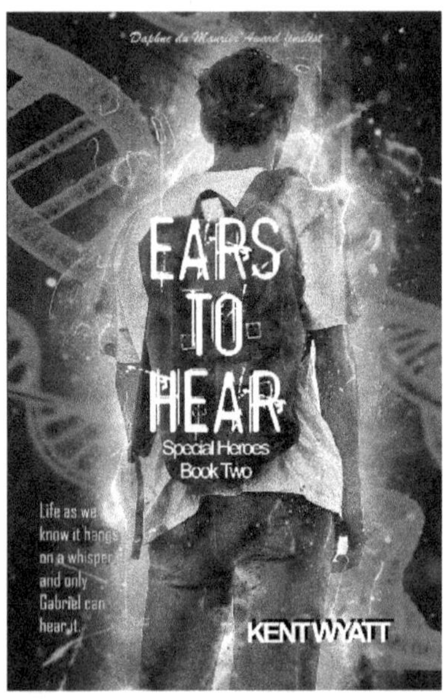

Amelia's brother, Gabriel, hears things - practically everything. His autism gives him savant auditory abilities. He heard the men who were planning to kill them in the park. It could have ended there. But Amelia couldn't leave and let the killers catch the mysterious man who saved them.

In a madcap turn of events, the artisan jam maker finds herself experiencing the life and death struggle of espionage. But things are getting even more intense. The agents want Gabriel and Amelia to help bring down a powerful organization that is using genetic testing in an antisemitic plot. Did God plan Gabriel's gift for such a time as this? They will need God on their side because someone else is in the game, and the other side's plan might equal two wrongs with no right in sight.

The more she discovers, the more Amelia grows to trust and care for the mysterious man. But even his skills might not have prepared him for this type of foe or the bizarre twist the mission takes. As circumstances suck Amelia and Gabe farther into the operation, she realizes what they face threatens the deepest fabric of humanity and will challenge how the team members view life itself.

HEA, standalone, with no cliffhanger.

Available at Amazon: Ears to Hear: Christian Thriller **or through a link at** www.WyattWove.com

"Unpredictable and unique page turner with endearing characters." ~Amazon Review~

"I love a book that goes beyond a good story. This book can change the way you may think...about the ease in which things can be hidden in plain sight. It reminds us to look closer at the things we may do or how we may look at others that are unique and not see the value in who God created them to be. This book speaks of a God whose love can change the heart of any person." ~Amazon Review~

"Author gives insightful and gripping view of autism...Action packed and surprising twists. What an imagination to put all these things the world faces in proper perspective like this. Great read! Enjoy" ~Amazon Review~

"After just the first chapter, I knew it was gonna be a page turner & finished it within a day. Pick up a copy, you won't be disappointed!" ~Amazon Review~

"I LOVED this book!! It kept me on my toes the whole time. I lost myself for hours without realizing it. I found myself praying for the characters! Lol" ~Amazon Review~

More About Kent and Rebekah Wyatt

Kent Wyatt was born and then he died. Wait a minute, I'm getting ahead of myself. (Whew! I'm glad I put that part in because, for a second there, I thought I was dead.) Now that you know the beginning and the ending of my story, let's go a little closer to the middle…

Actually, my novels are "our" novels, produced by the team of Kent and Rebekah Wyatt. My wife, Rebekah, will always be quick to tell you she is not a writer, but she contributes greatly to the finished product of our books. Rebekah (whose official title in the Wyatt Republic is Minister of Household and Finance) is a voracious reader of Christian Fiction. In the Wyatt writing world, she serves as (among other things) editor, researcher, manager, financial planner, contributor to the storyboard, plot, and characterization, and of course the final word on all things romantic. So when you see our characters behaving like ladies and gentlemen instead of blowing snot, passing gas, and belching—thank Rebekah. (Disclaimer: the second half of this sentence was not Rebekah approved.)

Kent and Rebekah's novels have been semi-finalists in the American Christian Fiction Writers Genesis contest, a Finalist for the Daphne du Maurier Award for Excellence in Mystery/Suspense, a Selah finalist, and a Selah third place award winner. Kent and Rebekah are founding members of the NW Arkansas Chapter of American Christian Fiction Writers where they serve on the board.

So how did such a partnership ever get started? I mean, really, a man and a woman, together, they're so different. Whoever came up with such an idea? Oh. Sorry, God. Great idea, by the way. (Disclaimer: the preceding portion of this paragraph was not Rebekah approved). Of course, such an unlikely alliance could only begin in somewhere remote and mysterious—like the flatlands of Northwest Kansas.

I was born there. Rebekah was dropped there, like a tornado drops a rare orchid in the middle of a wheat field. Both our early days were, like most young lives, bizarre in their own ways. Mine full of the mundane misadventures of the son of a firmly-planted, fourth generation farmer, and Rebekah's comprised of the exotic escapades of a traveling evangelist's daughter. When we were in our early teens, we met and fell madly in opposite directions and both skinned our knees. For the few months that her family stayed at our farm, we rode horses and performed magic shows together, but then Rebekah's family was off to the next ministry opportunity.

Over the years, we both strayed from God's plan in our own ways and then were thrown together again in our late twenties. In a few months, we were married. God has rescued us from our own imprudence, grown us in our understanding of His plan, and bound us together for His purpose. We love Him greatly because He has saved us exceedingly. Our prayer is that through our stories we might introduce others to THE ONE who longs to do the same for them.

To understand how this whole writing thing began, there is one thing you need to know about Rebekah: She is a faithful helpmate to her husband and selflessly supports his dream far better than he deserves.

There are two things that you need to know about me: I was born a writer, but I became a cop.

As a child on the lonely plains of Kansas, I always enjoyed reading and telling stories to the other kids. When I was thirteen years old, I read *R is for Rocket* by Ray Bradbury, and I decided I wanted to write stories like that, ones that haunted you and made you think. John Boy Walton became my hero, and I was going to change the world with my pen. Over the years, I learned that I wasn't Ray Bradbury, but God had given me a writing voice of my own, and He could use that if I would let Him. The only problem was I didn't have enough life experience so…

When I was seventeen years old, a car almost ran my mother and me off the road. With my terrified mama holding onto the dash beside me, I pursued the other vehicle in my 1973 Mercury Montego and forced it to pull over. It was the town drunk doing what he did best. He came at me. I knocked him down, picked him up by his belt, and threw him in the back seat of his car to sleep it off. My mother decided that I should be a police officer. She knew that writing nonsense was never going to get me anywhere.

In 1983 she saw an ad in the paper saying a small town nearby was looking for a police officer. She convinced me to apply. I got the job and spent over thirty years following that path. But all the time I was being a cop, the bite I received from the writing bug became infected and grew septic. I fed the fever over the years with short stories, award-winning poetry and a humorous newsletter that I put out for a growing email list.

Another life-changing event was when I read *This Present Darkness* by Frank Peretti. It helped get me back on track with my faith and introduced me to Christian Fiction. Everything C. S. Lewis also helped form me.

I had found the direction God wanted me to go with my writing. Foolish fans encouraged me by saying that they loved my newsletters and re-read them when they wanted a good laugh. Many even said I should write a book.

With my work in law enforcement and my family to raise, I could never commit to writing full time. So I satisfied myself with learning the craft and producing short works. After 32 years, I ended my law enforcement career. I still have many friends walking the thin blue line, and I have a deep love for the profession. But God seemed to be telling me it was time to fulfill my other destiny. Now, with God's help, maybe my writing can change the world after all. Where are my old reruns of The Waltons? Look out, Ray Bradbury, something Wyatt this way comes.

You can find Kent and Rebekah on the web at the following links: Hashtags: #AuthorKentWyatt,

#SpecialHeroes

Website:
https://www.WyattWove.com (free gifts/more info)
Amazon:
https://www.amazon.com/Kent-Wyatt/e/B07GSHF65Q
Facebook: https://www.facebook.com/kentwyatt.org
Twitter:
https://twitter.com/authorkentwyatt
Pinterest:
https://www.pinterest.com/AuthorKentWyatt/
Goodreads:
https://www.goodreads.com/user/show/36911883-author-kent-wyatt
LinkedIn:
https://www.linkedin.com/in/kent-wyatt-b162b014a/
Instagram:
https://www.instagram.com/authorkentwyatt/
YouTube:
https://www.youtube.com/channel/UCW_AzksI3It_PSJQFt4oo4w